THE MATCH FAKER

A FAKE-DATING, ENEMIES-TO-LOVERS ROMCOM...

OLIVIA SPRING

HARTLEY PUBLISHING

First Edition: March 2024

Copyright © 2024 by Olivia Spring

All rights reserved.

No part of this book may be reproduced in any form or by any electronic or mechanical means, including information storage and retrieval systems, without written permission from the author.

This is a work of fiction. All characters and happenings in this publication are fictitious and any resemblance to real persons living or dead, locales or events is purely coincidental.

www.oliviaspring.com

Follow Olivia on Facebook/Twitter/Instagram: @ospringauthor

TikTok: www.tiktok.com/@oliviaspringauthor

1

MIA

'How's your love life, Mia?' Aunty Doreen appeared in front of me, eyes wide.

My sister's extravagant tenth wedding anniversary party had only started an hour ago and I already wanted to leave.

Although I knew this annoying question always came up at family events, I still hadn't worked out the perfect response.

I could either tell the truth and confess that my love life was as vibrant as a corpse and end up being pitied like I had an incurable disease.

Or I could lie, say I was madly in love and enjoy the validation that came when people heard you'd been 'saved' from being single.

But I was rubbish at lying, so I decided to change the subject instead.

'Aunty Doreen!' I gripped the stem of my champagne flute tighter to calm my racing heartbeat. 'What time are they cutting the cake?'

My eyes flicked to the long tables dressed with white-and-gold linen which matched the decor of the grand hall my sister Alice had hired in central London. Must've cost her a fortune.

Silver platters of fancy canapés were elegantly laid out alongside the elaborate three-tier anniversary cake that was still intact. Dammit.

'Not sure.' Aunty Doreen shrugged, adjusting the pearl necklace resting on her brown patterned dress. 'It's still early.'

'I'll go and check.'

'Wait!' She blocked my path. The DJ turned up a popular Beyoncé song. Wouldn't be surprised if my aunt had requested that he play 'All By Myself' by Celine Dion next. 'You didn't answer my question. So? Are you dating? I heard what happened with your last boyfriend. Terrible thing.'

My stomach twisted. *Terrible* was an understatement, but the less I thought about what my scumbag ex had done to me, the better.

'Strange that you didn't see that coming'—she pursed her lips—'but it's been ages. You must be seeing someone else by now!'

I glanced at Alice on the dance floor, wondering if she could save me from what I knew was about to become a full-blown interrogation. Alice was dressed in a white silk gown, her long wavy hair extensions flowing behind her as she gazed lovingly into her husband's eyes.

My sister's brown skin was the same tone as mine, but whilst I had an oily T-zone that always made me look too shiny in photos, Alice's complexion was flawless. Just like her make-up tonight.

I smoothed down the front of my blue knee-length dress and fiddled with my thick, dark hair, which I'd styled into an updo.

Alice wouldn't have to deal with awkward questions like this. Despite being two years younger than me, she always landed on her feet. Perfect house, perfect job and perfect husband. I was glad one of us was doing well.

My aunt twiddled her thumbs impatiently. She wanted an answer and wasn't going to leave until I gave her one.

'I've been focused on my business, so haven't had a chance to date.'

There. Done. Stock answer remembered and successfully delivered.

Time to move on and speak about the weather, the Kardashians, global warming or house prices.

Anything except my love life.

Please.

My cousin's two little boys sprinted across the hall, and as one of them almost slipped on the shiny tiled floor, my heart jumped in my mouth. They were playing dangerously close to the DJ's laptop. I was about to suggest they be careful, but didn't want to spoil their fun. The DJ waved his finger at them, so hopefully they'd move somewhere safer.

'Oh yes! Your escorting business!'

'My *what*?' I replied, my eyebrows almost hitting the ceiling.

'Don't worry!' she shouted over the music. 'Your secret's safe with me. If you want to help sad, desperate men, why shouldn't you?'

'But I—' Before I had a chance to set her straight, she cut me off.

'Your aunt Mary said you'd been corrupted by the devil and needed Jesus, but isn't prostitution one of the oldest professions in the world? At least that'll never get replaced by technology!'

My cheeks heated. It was no surprise they'd been talking about me. This family had more gossips than a tabloid newspaper.

'I don't employ escorts. I run a professional matchmaking agency. I help people find love.'

'So there's no escorts or prostitutes?' She raised her voice. I was glad the music was loud so no one else could hear her question.

'No.' I shook my head.

'But that doesn't make sense.'

'What?'

'I said that doesn't make sense!' she repeated.

'Why?' I frowned, wishing I'd plucked three glasses of champagne from the waiter's tray instead of one.

Just as my aunt opened her mouth to reply, my cousin's sons crashed into the DJ. His laptop plummeted to the floor and the music stopped.

'If you run a *professional matchmaking agency*,' she yelled, somehow not realising the hall was now deathly silent, 'then *why* are you still single?'

Mic. Drop.

Everyone's eyes spun so fast in my direction I was surprised they didn't get whiplash.

The heat of a hundred gazes burned into me. My pulse raced.

It was bad enough that Aunty Doreen wanted an update on my love life, but now, *everyone* in the hall was staring, waiting for an answer too.

Most singletons could just shrug their shoulders or complain about how rubbish the men were on dating apps. But when you were supposed to be a matchmaking expert, that wasn't going to fly.

It was like a plumber having a broken toilet. Or a dance instructor with two left feet.

'Oh, y'know.' I forced a smile, wishing the ground would swallow me up. 'It's like the builder who's so busy fixing other people's homes, he never has time to do his own.' I laughed awkwardly, sweat pooling under my armpits.

'*Awww.*' She patted me on the head like a wounded puppy. 'Hopefully, you'll find someone before you get left on the scrap heap. How old are you now? Twenty-nine?'

I glared at the DJ to see if he was any closer to putting the music back on, but like the entire hall, he was too busy eavesdropping on my car crash conversation.

People had even moved closer to get a front-row view of me dying of embarrassment. Any minute now someone would start handing out popcorn.

'Thirty-two,' I murmured, swallowing the lump in my throat.

'Oh...' She winced. Groans from sympathetic spectators echoed behind me. 'Better get a move on!'

'I... excuse me.' I hurried through the crowd, trying to ignore everyone's sad stares. The DJ chose that moment to play the next track.

As Akon's 'Lonely' boomed around the hall, I sighed. If he had to play a song about flying solo, I'd prefer Beyoncé's 'Single Ladies'. At least that was empowering.

'You okay?' Mum asked as I passed her near the exit. Dad's arm was wrapped around her waist and my stomach twisted as I saw pity written across their faces. I supposed it was to be expected.

When I'd arrived, the first thing Mum asked wasn't how I was, but whether I'd brought a date.

After saying I hadn't and seeing the disappointment in her eyes, I'd headed to the toilets. Which was exactly where I was going right now.

'Course!' I straightened my shoulders. 'I'm fine.'

When I got to the toilets, an elderly woman I didn't recognise was struggling to open the door and hold on to her walking stick.

'Let me get that.' I held it open so she could walk through.

As tempting as it was to hide in the cubicle, there was only one free and I wasn't going to jump in front of an old lady. She reminded me of my grandma. God, I missed her so much.

My eyes started watering.

Come on, Mia. Woman up.

I didn't know why I was so upset. Mum and Aunty Doreen weren't the first to question why I was single and they wouldn't be the last.

I should be used to their comments by now, but it still hurt.

Some people, like my best friend, Trudy, were happy to be single, but I believed in love. How could I not? As my aunt reminded me, it was my job.

In a few months my parents would be celebrating forty years of being happily married. My maternal grandparents had been married for sixty-two years and it would've been longer if they were still alive.

And all of my friends were loved up. I'd made sure of it.

I'd literally found the perfect match for everyone I knew.

So why was I having such a hard time finding my own Mr Right?

2

LIAM

'Let's get out of here.' The tall blonde with the pink minidress grabbed my hand and led me out the door.

We were leaving a private party at one of LA's most exclusive venues. We'd only been speaking for half an hour, but from the way she'd kept stroking my biceps, I wasn't surprised she'd invited me back to her place.

She opened the limo door, slid onto the back seat, then pulled me inside.

I wasn't really in the mood for sex, but I hated these industry parties, so this was a good excuse to escape. I'd done enough schmoozing for one night.

The only reason I'd come was because Geena, my agent, had told me Henry Kane would be here. She said it'd be good to butter him up some more before we signed the contract and I was officially announced as the lead in a brand-new action franchise.

My chest tightened.

This deal meant I'd be committed to three movies and tied to the studio for years. But like Geena reminded me, I was lucky. Loads of actors would kill for a role like this, so I was grateful. It'd be good for me.

Anyway, Henry hadn't turned up, so tonight was a waste of time. I was on my way to the bathroom when this woman, whose name I couldn't remember, approached me. We got talking and now here I was, on my way to her place to bang.

From the corner of my eye I saw her staring. I shifted uncomfortably in my seat. Sometimes I seriously questioned how I got myself into these situations.

'Sally,' I said, relieved that I'd remembered her name, 'maybe this isn't a good idea…'

'It's *Sunrise*.'

Of course it was. This was Hollywood, where the more *unique* the name, the better.

'*Sunrise*, I…'

'Shhh!' She pressed her manicured finger on my lips. It tasted weird. Like rotting fish. Whatever it was, I didn't like it. I gently moved her hand away. 'You're wrong. This is awesome!'

Before I had a chance to argue, she planted her inflated lips on mine.

Yep. Definitely a bad idea. A slobbering bloodhound produced less saliva.

I pulled away and winced as I wiped the back of my hand over my mouth.

'Listen, I'm really tired'—I dragged my fingers through my short dark hair—'so if you could just get your driver to pull over, I'll get out.'

I didn't know where the hell we were, and roaming the streets wasn't ideal because someone might recognise me, but I just wasn't feeling this.

'We're almost here,' she snapped.

The car stopped and the driver opened the door.

Whoa. Nice place.

I'd seen my fair share of fancy houses, but this was next-level. With grand white pillars, it looked like the mansion from *The Fresh Prince of Bel-Air*.

At least I knew she wasn't a gold digger who wanted to sleep with me to get ahead.

'Come on.' She ushered me out of the car with one hand whilst tapping away on her mobile with the other.

Once we were inside, she led me up the wide marble staircase. I wondered what business she was in. No offence, but from the limited conversation we'd had, she didn't strike me as a tech mogul or successful producer. Then again, I shouldn't make assumptions.

'What was it you said you did?' I asked.

'I'm an actress,' she beamed and I tried to mask my frown.

To afford a place like this, she'd have to be pretty successful, so I should've heard of her.

I was tempted to ask her surname, but reminded myself it was irrelevant. I wasn't looking for a relationship, so what did it matter? As long as she didn't screw me over with some sordid kiss-and-tell or start asking if I could get her a role in my next film, it was all good.

She opened the bedroom door. The decor was dated. There was a grand four-poster bed with gold floral bedsheets, which didn't fit her personality, but like I'd said, not important.

This was a one-time thing. Once I'd taken care of business in the bedroom, I'd be on my way and would never have to see her again. She knew that was the deal, right?

'Before we... y'know this is just sex? A one-off, okay?'

Sunrise pushed me on the bed.

'Take off your clothes!' she demanded.

'Maybe we shouldn't...' I was about to suggest a rain check when she straddled me.

'Come on, don't be shy.' She reached for my belt buckle.

Shit.

Right now my dick was limper than a wet lettuce leaf. If I didn't get hard, fast, she'd think I couldn't get it up, which could lead to some bad press if she ran her mouth.

Or she'd think I wasn't into her, which was the truth, but I didn't want to make her feel bad or hurt her feelings.

There was only one solution. I'd got myself into this situation, so I had to get myself out of it. Even though I didn't want to sleep with her, I had to give her what she wanted. At least then she'd be happy.

My mind drifted to *her*. The woman from my past who I still thought about a lot more than I should.

It'd been years since I'd seen her, but I still remembered her smile. Her scent. The way she'd looked in my T-shirt that night, especially when she bent over and I got a flash of her bare arse...

Bingo.

Thinking about her always worked.

It's showtime.

I rolled Sunrise off me and onto her back, then straddled her. The quicker I got this over and done with, the better.

'Oh God, *yes!*' she moaned dramatically, pulling up her dress, then tugging at my zip. 'I love a man who takes control!' She yanked down my trousers and boxers and my dick sprang free. 'Holy shit! I knew you'd be big, but fuck! I better cancel Pilates tomorrow. After you put that magic stick in me, I won't be able to walk right! Can you move to the left a little?'

'What?' I paused. 'Why?'

Something wasn't right.

My gut was telling me to get the hell out of here.

Just as I was about to leave, I heard heavy footsteps.

'What the fuck's going on?' the deep voice boomed.

I spun around and my jaw dropped.

No. Fucking. Way.

It was Henry Kane. What the hell was he doing here? Please don't tell me I was about to screw his wife. I jumped off the bed.

'*You?*' he roared. 'What have you done to my sweet baby girl?'

'Hi, Daddy!' She grinned.

'*Girl?*' I glared at Sunrise. 'How old are you?' She'd told me she was twenty-eight.

'She's twenty-fucking-five!'

'Oh, thank God.' I blew out a breath.

'I know all about your reputation! I know where *that* has been!' He pointed a shaking hand in between my legs. 'How dare you put your dirty dick anywhere near my daughter!'

'I didn't know!'

'Daddy, you should've seen us together! You said we wouldn't have the right chemistry, but I'm so hot for him right now and look at his boner!! Don't worry. I filmed it so you could see.'

She did *what*?

Sunrise picked up her phone and showed us the screen. Fuck. It was a live feed of this bedroom.

Then before I had a chance to grab it, she pointed the phone at me and started taking pictures.

'What the hell's wrong with you?' I shouted, realising my dick was still hanging out and quickly pulling up my boxers and trousers.

This was a fucking nightmare.

'Baby, I already told you. You're not going to be in the movie. And neither is *he*.' His head swivelled to face me. 'The deal's off. You're out.'

'Hold on!' I zipped myself up and walked towards him. I couldn't lose this deal. Geena would kill me. 'We had an agreement! I didn't know she was your daughter. C'mon, please! It was an innocent mistake.'

'Innocent? The only person in this room who's innocent is my sweet baby, who you've defiled with your monster dick!'

'But we didn't even—'

'Get the fuck out of my bedroom and my fucking house!'

Wait, what? This was *his* bedroom?

Now the decor and size of this mansion made sense. Sunrise must've called her dad and told him to come here.

She wanted us to be caught. She planned it all.

Shit.

'This isn't my fault!'

'Save your lame excuses. You're done, Stone! No one takes advantage of my little girl and gets away with it!'

I opened my mouth to argue, then closed it again.

Telling him that we didn't have sex wouldn't matter at this point. The damage was already done.

Henry's face was redder than a ripe tomato. He looked like he was seconds away from punching me, and the last thing I wanted to do was retaliate and knock him out.

So I left, knowing that although it wasn't my fault, losing the movie deal was only the beginning.

You didn't need to be a psychic to know there'd be serious consequences from tonight.

And there wasn't a damn thing I could do to stop them.

3

MIA

Two weeks later

The sound of my high heels on the shiny white tiled floors echoed around me as I walked towards the reception of my office building.

'Morning, George.' I smiled.

'Morning, Mia. Got some post for you.' He picked up a pile of letters and passed them over the glossy black reception desk.

'Thanks! Have a good day.'

As I headed towards the lift and pressed the button to the third floor, I took in my surroundings. I loved this building. Everything was immaculate.

It was built a few years ago and because a lot of people were used to working from home, they'd struggled to get businesses to fill it. That meant I'd secured an amazing introductory deal on the rent for the first two years. There was no way I could've afforded it otherwise.

Although my deal was ending soon, I'd been a good

tenant, so hopefully the landlord would take that into account when he set the new rate.

The doors slid open and I stepped inside, taking in the views of the River Thames and Tower Bridge in the distance through the glass walls.

Whenever clients came for meetings, they always gushed about the views. It created a good first impression and made them think the business was doing well. I was glad they didn't know the truth.

I exited the lift and walked along the corridor to my office. The light was on, which meant my best friend, Trudy, was already here.

The strong aroma of coffee hit me as soon as I opened the door. The medium-sized office had wooden floors, two large glass desks and a vibrant red lips-shaped sofa, which was another talking point for clients.

Photos of happy couples I'd matched adorned the walls of my side of the office. Looking at them always made me smile.

'You bought coffee!' I said as I pulled out my chair.

'Yep! I needed it. I look like death warmed up this morning.'

She totally did not. Trudy's chocolate-coloured bob still had those cool natural waves that would take anyone else ages to recreate and although her white skin was a little paler than usual, her brown eyes still sparkled. Plus, Trudy was a fan of colourful patterns and clothes. So that bright red, yellow and orange blouse she was wearing made her look very much alive.

'You're chatting rubbish! You're glowing!'

'Thanks, babes. The power of caffeine should never be underestimated! I thought you might need a decent coffee too. I don't know how you can drink that crap.' She grimaced, pointing to the jar on top of the mini fridge opposite my desk.

I'd swapped my fancy coffee shop lattes for supermarket-brand instant coffee and Trudy was right. It didn't compare.

'I know it tastes awful, but it's cheap. I can't justify paying almost five pounds a day for a coffee. That's over a hundred pounds a month!'

This week, as well as going through my finances, I definitely needed to focus on marketing to attract more clients.

'Drinking proper coffee is a gift to myself. And to you. You wouldn't want to share an office with me if I wasn't fully caffeinated first. I don't mind getting them if you're short. I know business has been a bit slow…'

'Thanks, but it's okay.' I dropped the post on my desk, then sat down. 'I'll be fine.' I wasn't sure I would, but was trying to stay positive.

Trudy was an agent who represented actors—mostly working in theatre. We'd been friends since we were eleven. We both attended the same school, but it wasn't until we were around eighteen and went to university together that we became really close.

Since then we'd been bona fide besties. Trudy had started her business a year before me, and when I'd mentioned I needed an office, she'd offered to share so we could split the rent.

My phone pinged and I glanced at the message preview on the screen.

Mum

Will you be bringing someone to our anniversary

party? I need to know how much food to make and how many bottles of white rum to ask Uncle Eggbert to bring back from Jamaica for the punch.

I shoved the phone across my desk and groaned.

'What's up?'

'Mum wants to know if I'm bringing "someone" to my parents' anniversary party, which is months away! Reckons she needs to know how much food to make and how many bottles of rum to ship from Jamaica.'

'Doesn't she always make enough food to feed the five thousand?' Trudy sipped her coffee.

'Yep. She always sends us home with a pile of leftovers too.'

My parents were from Jamaica and no party was complete without a spread of traditional dishes and a potent rum punch. But she didn't need my uncle to bring anything over. Everything she needed was right here in London.

'You reckon she's fishing?'

'Definitely. She just wants to know if I've found a man yet. My single status is tarnishing the family's flawless relationship record. No doubt Aunty Doreen will hunt me down again at the party to ask why I'm still alone too.'

I opened the first envelope on the stack of post. As I caught sight of the rent invoice, I sighed.

I knew there'd be an increase, but I wasn't expecting it to be *that* much. According to this letter, in three months, my rent would double. With my current income, there was no way I could afford to stay here.

Rental rates in London were all ridiculously high. The

offices in my budget were all run-down and in dodgy areas.

It was hard enough getting a new business off the ground, and my competitors' offices were fancier than mine, so I needed a decent-looking place to reassure clients that I was on the same level.

My stomach churned. I doubted Trudy would be happy about the increase either, so I'd have to cover all the rent myself.

I ripped open the next envelope. Another bill. I knew most people went paperless. It was better for the planet. But after what had happened before when my ex switched everything online, I made sure all my bills came in the post. It was safer that way.

'Don't worry. I'll be there this time. But if Aunty Doreen asks why you're not coupled up, just tell her you're getting too much cock to settle down with one man! That'll shut her up!' Trudy cackled.

'I'm not, though...' I couldn't remember the last time I'd had sex.

'She doesn't know that!'

'We both know I'm no good at lying. And I'm not doing a great job of running this business either. Maybe I should pack it all in. Go back to banking. Or find another job with a steady salary.'

'No! You were miserable doing that. We both agreed that when we were thirty, we'd follow our dreams. Give it time. You're a brilliant matchmaker! Your match rate is amazing and you've got two more weddings coming up in the next six months: weddings that *you* made happen by bringing your clients together. You're a legend!'

'You're my best friend, so you would say that.'

'But it's true! Remember when I asked you to set up my mate Helen? She'd been single for years. Then that customer came in the bank one day and you just knew he'd be perfect for her. How, I have no idea, but they're still together five years later because of *you*! So like I said: *legend*.'

'Thanks. But unfortunately, being *a legend* doesn't pay the bills.' If I didn't get some more paying clients soon, the choice would be taken out of my hands.

When I'd first started the company almost two years ago, I'd known I needed to build a pool of clients, so I hadn't charged for joining. And I'd budgeted for that. After all, I couldn't match people if I didn't have anyone to match them with.

I'd had savings and the money my grandma had left me when she passed. I'd calculated everything carefully, and I would've been fine. But then my ex screwed me over. And now not only did I have nothing left, I couldn't even get a loan. I was in danger of losing everything. Including my business.

'Something will come up soon.'

'I hope so.' I opened the red envelope that was next on the pile. At least this looked like junk mail rather than a bill.

When I saw what it was, my eyes bulged.

'What's up?' Trudy asked.

'This can't be right?' My brows knitted together as I scanned the text. 'It's a letter confirming they've received my entry for the Matchmaker of the Year category for the Happily Ever After Awards and are putting me through to the first round of interviews. But I didn't enter.'

'That's great! They obviously heard how brilliant you are!'

'*Trudy?*' My eyes narrowed. 'Did *you* enter me for this?'

'Wh-why'd you say that?' she stuttered, typing frantically.

'I can see the reflection of your screen in the window. You haven't even turned your computer on, so stop pretending to type!'

'Okay!' She threw her hands in the air. 'It was me! I kept asking you to enter, the deadline was looming and I didn't want you to miss out.'

Trudy's heart was in a good place but... shit. Every part of my business would be under the spotlight. Including my matchmaking methods.

Naturally all clients completed an extensive questionnaire, asking what they wanted in an ideal partner, their hobbies, relationship goals, etc.—all the standard stuff. And I always interviewed them face to face.

But whilst some of my peers used fancy algorithms or the latest technology to determine the perfect match, I used my gut. When I met someone, I just *knew*. I got a feel for the kind of person they'd be right for. My granny was the same and said it was a gift I got from her. It wasn't scientific, but it worked.

Like Trudy said, my track record was good. I'd matched ten couples in my friendship group, and last year three couples I'd paired after starting the agency got married. Shame I didn't have the same success for myself.

'What's the problem? The prize is worth over fifty grand! When you win, your money worries will be over.'

That was true. The winners got a cash prize plus a

double-page spread in *Happily Ever After*—one of the most influential women's magazines in the UK. A feature in there was guaranteed to lead to success.

After last year's article had come out, the winner's business had exploded. Now she had a team of matchmakers and a shiny new office and was even featured as an expert on breakfast TV.

'Thanks for the vote of confidence, but I've got more chance of finding a unicorn in my back garden.'

'But you don't have a garden?'

'Exactly! I'll have to withdraw my application.'

'Why?'

'You didn't read the entry form.' I'd studied it meticulously several times. I'd been tempted to enter, then realised I couldn't. 'They study your match rate and ask for client case studies. That part's fine. But they like to know personal stuff too.'

'And?'

'Personal stuff like my *own* love life. I've been single for well over a year and my only long-term relationship ended in disaster. How can I put myself forward for the Matchmaker of the Year award when I can't even find my own Mr Right?'

Some clients even told me they preferred to work with a matchmaker who was in a relationship. Knowing I'd found my own perfect partner was proof that I had the skills to help them find theirs.

Thankfully others were open-minded and realised that my marital status or relationship history didn't impact my ability to do my job for others, but in my line of work, it was a hindrance rather than a help.

'That's so narrow-minded! A person's success

shouldn't be defined by whether or not they have a partner!'

'I agree. But it is what it is. No one would say that's how it works publicly, but everyone knows it's an unwritten rule.'

Every single past winner was coupled up. And every magazine profile of the winner included a prominent romantic photo of them with their partner and focused on their love story.

I went over to my filing cabinet and pulled out the old issues of the magazine, then flicked to the profiles.

'There.' I dropped two copies on Trudy's desk. 'Look at the question in bold: "Did being a matchmaker help you find true love?" and the same question worded differently in the previous year's winners' issue: "Did being in a relationship make you a better matchmaker?"'

The magazine, which was part of Dite Global Media, the same company that ran and funded the awards, valued relationships and marriage. It was called *Happily Ever After* for a reason.

'Well, I think it's bollocks! But you need the money, so just play along and pretend you're coupled up for an interview. Simple!'

'I wish it was, but these awards have a quick turnaround. If I go through with the entry, they'd want to interview me soon.'

'What, like tomorrow?'

'It says here that the first round of interviews start'—I skimmed the letter for the key dates section—'next week!'

'That's fine! So we have seven days to find you a boyfriend!'

'If it was that easy, I wouldn't be single. And I'd be out of a job.' I sighed.

'He doesn't have to be real. Just hire someone.'

My mouth dropped. She couldn't be serious.

'Did they put brandy in your coffee? I can't *hire* a fake boyfriend for the interview! What if they check my social media and don't see photos of us together? They'd know I was lying.' I was never one for splashing loads of photos with my ex online, but I'd had a few. Until I'd deleted every trace of him.

'So post photos of your fake boyfriend.'

'And he'd have to come to the ceremony. It's the beginning of August and the ceremony isn't until October. Only a professional escort would agree to commit for two months. A real single person would want to keep their options open in case they met someone. Which is another reason why they wouldn't want their photo all over Instagram.'

'So hire an escort for the interview, a few dates and the ceremony.'

'Too risky. Knowing my luck, someone would recognise him. Plus I can't afford to hire someone. I need to save money, not spend it!'

'Think of the return you'd get on your investment when you win.'

'*If.*'

'Find someone to do it for free! Let me see if I have any single friends you haven't met…' She scrolled through her phone.

I knew Trudy was trying to be helpful, but the last two guys I'd dated since my break-up were people she'd set me up with.

Both were actors she'd just met. And both were disasters. I hated to stereotype, but dating actors definitely wasn't for me.

It wasn't that I didn't meet men. Part of my job involved attending business networking events, and if I met someone I thought could be a good fit for one of my clients, I'd ask if they were single, give them my card and find out if they'd be interested in signing up to my agency.

Somehow approaching them knowing it was for business was less awkward than if I was trying to chat them up to go on a date with me.

'Sorry.' Trudy groaned. 'Can't find anyone.'

Didn't surprise me. When I'd started the agency, I'd contacted every single person my friends and family knew.

But even with a list of men on my books, I'd never ask them to get involved in something like this. It'd make me sound desperate and unprofessional. Could you imagine?

Yeah, hi. It's Mia. I know I'm supposed to be an expert at helping people find love, but I can't find myself a real boyfriend, so I wondered if you'd mind lying through your teeth and pretending to be my boyfriend for a couple of months so I can win a competition to save my business?

No way. Just thinking about it made me cringe.

'Even if I met a handsome stranger tomorrow and convinced him to be my fake boyfriend, it wouldn't work. The judges would see straight through it. We'd need chemistry and to know each other inside out. That's impossible to do in a week.'

'*Nothing's* impossible.'

'And it's dishonest. I'm a professional matchmaker. I can't *lie* about finding love. Let's face it. I'm screwed.'

'Aunty Doreen really messed with your head. You know what you need? Well, apart from a fake boyfriend.'

'What?'

'A night out with your bestie. One of my actors is in a new play tonight. Come. It'll cheer you up. I might even buy you a cocktail afterwards.'

This evening I'd planned to curl up in front of the TV. But imagine if I found a new client at this show? I might even meet someone with a whole circle of single friends eager to be matched up. If I convinced them all to join my agency, my troubles would be over.

'Okay!' I nodded, excitement flooding my stomach. 'You're on.'

4

LIAM

My phone rang.
I sat on the rock-hard sofa and glared at the screen. It was Geena.

Ever since those photos Sunrise posted had gone viral, I only answered calls from the few people I could trust. Geena was one of them.

'Just checking on you,' she said in her thick New York accent.

'Thanks. Just arrived at the house.' I nestled my phone between my neck and shoulder.

I'd spent the past two weeks holed up in my LA mansion, waiting for shit to die down. But a man could only stare at the same four walls for so long. So when a friend had said I could lay low at his place in Notting Hill whilst he was in Australia, I'd jumped on the first plane to London.

'Anyone recognise you?'

'Don't think so. Harry and Meghan landed just before me, so the paps were more interested in them.'

'Good. You're still set to start shooting *Grudge Match* in October, and I've spoken to Flavio and he still wants to go ahead with the underwear shoot. Reckons the whole world seeing your dick could be good for sales. Shame the other producers I was in talks with don't feel the same…'

'Fuck's sake.' I shook my head. 'She shouldn't have been allowed to post those damn photos.'

My legal team had ordered Sunrise to take them down, along with the grainy video, but the damage had already been done.

'I know it sucks, but Henry Kane is powerful. And no one wants to go against him by working with you right now. The only reason you're still doing *Grudge Match* is because the producer and Henry already hate each other. But for everyone else, right now your name is mud. You're lucky Henry isn't influential in the fashion and beauty industries—otherwise your endorsements would be screwed. You need to stay out of trouble.'

'Trouble?' Sarcasm dripped from my voice. 'I'm *always* on my best behaviour.' Humour was the only way I could get through this shitstorm.

'Maybe it's not those serious drama roles you keep asking me to put you forward for that I should find. You'd be better suited to comedy. That's the funniest thing I've heard all day!'

'I can definitely do those roles, Geena.' My smile dropped. 'I'm ready.'

'Honey, you know I love you, right?'

'Yeah…'

'But like I keep saying, you need to stay in your lane. Action films are what you do. It's what you're good at. If you want to be considered for the serious stuff later down the line, you've gotta stop screwing around and keep your dick in your pants!'

'I do what any thirty-two-year-old single man in LA does. Go out and have fun. It's not a crime. Like *I* keep telling *you*, I didn't know she was Henry's daughter! Life's for living, right? What's the point of working hard to earn all this money if I can't let my hair down once in a while?'

Okay, I admit. I'd chosen the wrong person to 'have fun' with, but we all made mistakes.

'Letting your hair down once in a while would be fine. It's carelessly letting your *pants* down that isn't. If you didn't change your women more often than your underwear, maybe you'd get taken more seriously.'

'How do you know how often I change my underwear?' I joked. From the loud sigh that echoed down the phone, she didn't find it funny.

I knew she was right, though. Producers of serious dramas wouldn't want to hire me if they thought I was gonna be part of another scandal. I'd be taking the focus away from what really mattered.

'Did you see the article plastered all over the internet?'

'You told me not to go online.'

'Fair. Well, there's another kiss-and-tell on you. This one isn't about Sunrise. It's someone else.'

'Fucking tabloids! I only have to breathe next to a woman and they run a story about us dating.'

'So you *weren't* getting cosy with a redhead two weeks before the Sunrise scandal hit?'

I paused. *Oh yeah...*

'There are photos?'

'There's *always* photos.'

I googled *Liam Stone with redhead*. Within seconds a

string of pictures of the two of us in a compromising position popped up.

I blew out a breath. I'd been acting for years and this wasn't the first kiss-and-tell that'd come out about me, but it didn't make it any less frustrating.

A friend of a friend had introduced us and when she'd suggested we check out a new bar and said it'd be private, stupidly I'd believed her. At least there were no photos of us screwing.

'Shit.'

'As bad as it is for your career, she gave your ego a good stroking. Said you went all night and were hung like a horse. So that story along with the photos Sunrise leaked would explain why I had a call earlier asking if you'd be interested in the lead role for a new *adult* film called *Rock Hard*. Apparently, it's like *Die Hard*, but with less clothes.'

'You're joking, right?'

'Nope.'

My jaw clenched. Those damn photos were gonna haunt me forever.

Don't get me wrong. I knew I'd got to where I was because of how I looked. People reminded me of that every day. Without that shirtless jeans commercial I'd modelled in almost a decade ago, I'd never have got scouted for my first movie.

My appearance was my 'brand' (God, I hated that word), which was why I worked so hard every damn day to stay in shape.

Being known for being 'hot' was one thing. But having my dick plastered over the internet and getting calls about it from my parents and every Tom, Dick (no pun intended) and Harry was another.

When I worked my arse off in drama class years ago, if I'd known that the biggest story about me would focus on the size of my cock instead of my acting abilities, I would've thought twice about continuing.

I dreamt of getting my teeth into gritty roles or maybe even a feel-good, wholesome drama. And now not only was I trapped on a conveyor belt, churning out one predictable action movie after another, I was attracting offers to star in pornos?

But Geena was right. I just needed to stay out of trouble. This story would blow over eventually, right?

Except despite our efforts to stop it, those pictures were still online, so that wasn't completely true, but *whatever*.

'London always feels like home. It's where I'm most grounded. I'll keep my nose clean.'

Maybe I could even use this time to work on my…

No. That project would never see the light of day. It was a stupid idea.

Like Geena said, I was an action star. I should stay in my lane. If I just focused on staying in shape for the underwear, fragrance and other shoots I had coming up and my next role, everything would be fine.

'Good. But we've gotta find a way to fix your image, Stone. You can't keep out of the public eye forever. We want people to forget about what happened, sure. But we can't afford for them to forget about *you*. Or worse, assume you're holed up in your mansion with a bunch of hookers. Somehow we gotta make sure you're seen in public, but without being seen as a man whore. I'm gonna speak to Annalise and see what ideas she has, okay?'

'Okay.' I gritted my teeth. Annalise was my publicist.

She'd better not suggest some BS like setting me up with some wannabe actress like she tried to do before. People would see right through that fake relationship shit.

Luckily last time one of my hook-ups had threatened to post sex pics, my legal team made her see sense before she took it further, so I didn't have to go down that road.

'Until then, don't forget, even though the story has died down, you're still on thin ice. I've promised the *Grudge Match* executives you'll be on your best behaviour. But mess up again and you're out.'

'Got it. I'll be a good boy.'

'Where have I heard that before?' Geena scoffed.

'Promise. No women. No more trashy stories. For the next couple of months, I'll be more celibate than a monk.'

A loud cough and splutter echoed down the phone.

'You okay?'

'Yeah. Just processing what you said about being more celibate than a monk. You're really on fire with the jokes today!'

'Who says it's a joke?' I said, convincing no one.

'You might want to duck, honey.'

'Why?' I looked up to the ceiling and frowned.

'To avoid all the pigs that are flying! Talk soon.'

5

MIA

The audience jumped to their feet and applause rippled through the air.

When Trudy had told me that the play was about a man who was burnt out, I'd thought it'd be depressing. But it was better than I'd expected.

'Did you like it?' Trudy faced me.

'Yeah, it was really good. Thanks for inviting me.'

'Pleasure! Fancy going backstage? Don't think I didn't see you eyeing up the stage manager I introduced you to earlier. Let's find out if he's single and wants to be your temporary leading man.' Trudy winked.

'I told you, I'm withdrawing my application!'

In the end, I was so busy that I didn't get a chance to email the awards organisers.

Running the agency was always full on. I was responsible for everything. As well as the actual matchmaking, I had to meet new clients, answer the phone, handle enquiries from existing clients, log feedback after their dates, do admin and marketing, network to try and find new members... the list felt endless.

It was hard work. But whenever I got a phone call from a client telling me they'd had the best date of their life or had just got engaged, it was so rewarding. There was no other buzz like it.

Yes. Having some extra cash to pay the bills and hire an assistant to ease my workload or securing a feature in *Happily Ever After* magazine was what I desperately needed. But I had to pull out of the awards, so I didn't know why Trudy was still talking about the stupid fake boyfriend idea.

She was right, though. I *was* checking out that guy. Wouldn't hurt to find out his marital status, just in case. Not because of the awards. Just out of curiosity. And who knows? If he didn't fancy me, maybe he'd be interested in signing up to my agency.

Trudy led me through a door close to the stage. Once the security checked our names off the list, we disappeared through a corridor and into the backstage area.

The cast were chatting away to various guests. I couldn't see the stage manager yet, but hopefully I'd find him later.

'I just need to speak to Chester.' Trudy handed me a glass of wine she'd swiped from a table which also had some nibbles. 'Will you be okay mingling?'

'Course!' I said. It'd give me a chance to hand out more cards.

As Trudy disappeared to speak to her client, I scanned the room.

Just as I was about to take a spoonful of peanuts, I froze.

Oh. My. God.

Can't be?

My eyes widened and my lips parted.

I drank him in, starting from his short, dark hair, smooth tanned skin, full lips, then his broad shoulders and sculpted chest, moving down to his…

'Mia?' A deep, gravelly voice snapped me out of my thoughts and I diverted my gaze from between his legs back up to his face.

'L-Liam?'

Our eyes locked and my traitorous stomach flipped.

He strode across the room and my heart thudded. As Liam got closer, his rich woody scent hit me and I bit my lip. If there was an aftershave called Eau de Hot Man, it'd smell like him.

'Well, well, well.' His eyes raked over me from head to toe, then back again. 'Mamma Mia is all grown up!'

And just like that, the warm bubbly feelings in my stomach evaporated.

Hearing those two words, Mamma Mia, took me right back to school, when he used to call me that. He knew how much I hated it. I'd told him several times. Any normal person would take that on board and stop. But not Liam Stone. It only made him use it more.

Arsehole.

'Clearly you haven't!' I barked. 'You're just as annoying as ever.'

'Ooof. Harsh!' He gripped his chest and I warned my eyes not to look at the outline of his pecs in that fitted navy-blue jumper. The whole world had seen that chest anyway. Whenever one of his dumb action films came out, it was splashed over billboards *everywhere*. I was surprised he was wearing clothes tonight. I'd started to think he was allergic to them.

'Accurate,' I spat back, trying to ignore his dazzling smile. His teeth were perfectly straight and white. He'd definitely had them done. They weren't like that before. I supposed it was to be expected now he was a Hollywood star.

'OMG! Lee!' Trudy barged forward and threw her arms around him.

I definitely wasn't bothered that Trudy got to press herself against his hard body and smell his delicious scent up close.

Yeah, he was good-looking, but only on the outside. His cockiness made everything about him ugly.

'Hey, Trudes! Long time!'

'Too long!' She pulled back. 'I don't think I've seen you in the flesh since you left school and pissed off to Spain! You look great! All that LA sunshine is agreeing with you.'

'*Gee, thanks*,' he said in a fake American accent. I rolled my eyes. Why was she complimenting him? He already knew he was hot. Now his ego would be bigger than five continents.

'What are you doing in London and at this show? Do you know Chester?'

'I don't start shooting again for a couple of months, so decided to chill in London for a bit. I was at a loose end tonight, and when I saw this advertised, I thought I'd check it out.'

'I thought nightclubs were more your style,' I muttered, thinking of the countless times I'd seen photos of him snogging women in them.

'I like to switch things up now and again—you know, it's fun. Oops! Sorry, I just used a word you wouldn't understand.'

'What?' I frowned.

'*Fun*. Have you heard of it? It's what people do to loosen up and enjoy themselves. You should try it sometime.' He smirked and I shot daggers at him. If looks could kill he'd be six feet under by now.

'Oooh! You're here for a couple of months, you say?' Trudy raised her eyebrow.

'More or less. I've got some shoots coming up here and in Paris, so makes sense to be based in London rather than trekking back and forth from LA. I'll see how it goes.'

'Did you hear that, Mia? Liam is here for *two months…*'

'Yeah? So?' I shrugged. He could stay here for two years for all I cared. We weren't friends anymore. He'd seen to that when we were seventeen.

Oh no.

She wouldn't.

'So I was thinking…'

'Trudy!' I warned.

'Maybe we should meet up,' she continued. 'For a drink. The three of us. Y'know, and have a catch-up. It'd be just like old times.'

'I'm sure he's too busy hanging out with his celebrity friends to mix with the likes of us,' I jumped in, turning my dagger stare to Trudy.

'I'd like that! It's been ages.' Liam's eyes met mine. My stomach did that involuntary flipping thing again. That sandwich I ate before I got here must've been dodgy.

Yes, Liam was handsome. Yes, he could be charming. Yes, annoyingly I was currently picturing that billboard image that was plastered opposite the station I used every day with him in a white vest, his huge muscles bulging as he held his weapon. And by weapon I mean his gun, not the one in his pants, which if the stories were true was licensed to thrill.

But we wouldn't get on. He'd been cocky before he was famous, so his ability to annoy me now was going to be monumental.

No, thanks. Hard pass.

'Here's my card.' Trudy thrust it into his hand. 'Message me and we'll set something up. Better still, Mia, where's your card? Give one to Liam.'

My stomach dropped.

'I-I just gave the last one out. To a man. With long hair, who was a… dog. No, *he* wasn't a dog, he was a dog *walker*. And he just broke up with his… wife. No, it was his girlfriend. He was upset. Really sad and…'

I was a terrible liar and Liam's smirk told me he knew it too.

'When did we all get so formal?' Trudy jumped in to rescue me. 'We don't need business cards. We can just WhatsApp.'

Liam started typing on his phone and Trudy's mobile pinged.

'Now you have my number,' Liam said.

'Cool. Let's set something up this week.'

'Great, nice seeing you.' He directed his gaze at Trudy. 'See you later, Mamma Mia.' He grinned as he strode off.

'Ugh.' I ground my teeth. 'He hasn't changed.'

'You're joking, right? He's sex on legs! You need to

get your eyes checked. And your pulse. You'd have to be dead to not let him affect you.'

'You'd have to not have a brain or any self-respect to fall for his charms. That man's had more women than I've had hot dinners and you know how much I love my food. If I were you, I'd get yourself checked at the sexual health clinic tomorrow. You never know what you might've caught.'

If you looked up the definition of man whore in the dictionary, there'd be a jumbo-sized photo of Liam Stone.

'I only hugged him! You can't catch STDs from hugs.'

'Normally I'd agree, but who knows what germs he has!'

'Exaggerating much?' Trudy took my hand. 'Come on. Let's go and get those cocktails. I have an idea I'd like to run by you.'

'It better not involve anything to do with a certain arrogant action film star whose name begins with L.'

'Leonardo DiCaprio? Nope. As far as I know he's not arrogant and doesn't consider himself an action film star, so I guarantee it has absolutely nothing to do with him!' she laughed.

I'd happily chat about Leonardo.

Liam, on the other hand, was a no.

So why did I get the feeling that my best friend had other ideas?

6

LIAM

Mia Bailey.
   Damn.

I took another gulp of my scotch and shook my head. Of all the people I could've bumped into backstage at an obscure theatre show, she was the last person on earth I would've thought of seeing.

How long had it been? Fifteen years? But she hadn't changed.

Still wore her hair tied up in that tight bun.

Still had that giant judgemental pole stuck up her fine arse.

And still annoyingly attractive.

But I still wasn't going there…

Not that she'd ever be interested anyway.

Once upon a time, I thought we might have something. We lived on the same street, went to the same school. We were even in the same class.

Despite the fact that Mia always got good grades and I

was seen as the class clown, somehow back then it didn't matter.

We used to hang out together every day after school. But when we were sixteen, things changed. Mia went cold. She started avoiding me and hanging out with that dickhead boyfriend of hers, Boris, and we grew apart. With all the shit that was going on at home, the timing wasn't great.

And when Mum took me away to live in Spain, Mia didn't even bother to come and say goodbye. Or reply to my messages.

If anyone should be pissed off, it was me. Yet she acted like I was a piece of trash the cat dragged in.

I ground my jaw as I scanned the room. Looked like she'd left. *Good.*

To think that when I'd seen her, I'd thought about going in for a hug and letting bygones be bygones. But after she'd sneered, I'd seen sense.

Trudy was chill, just like she'd always been at school. She was happy to share her number and meet up, but Mia made it clear she'd rather suck a leper's dick than sit with me. What was her problem?

Whatever.

My phone chimed. I pulled it out of my pocket, then groaned when I saw who'd messaged me.

The Sperm Donor

Can you send me some money, son? Kids need new computers.

Arsehole. The Sperm Donor was my dad. Giving Mum his sperm was the only thing he'd contributed to my life. And these days, he only ever contacted me when he wanted something.

Actually, that wasn't true. When those pictures Sunrise posted went viral, he'd messaged to congratulate me.

Nice to see you take after your dad in the dick department, he'd said. *Ladies love a big cock. You're welcome, son.*

What kind of a father said shit like that to his child? But he wasn't a father. That was why he'd always be known as *The Sperm Donor*.

And boy did he love to spread his seed. I'd lost count of how many children he had. Several were conceived whilst he was still married to Mum. And now he wanted *me* to pay for their fucking computers? *Plural?* He could go to hell. I shoved my phone back in my pocket.

A brunette at the bar who I recognised as one of the actresses in the play made eye contact. She smiled, twirling her hair around her finger. I raised my glass at her and smiled back.

Just at that moment, Mia walked past swinging those perfect hips and pouting her full lips. The lips I used to dream about when I was a dumb, horny teenager. And maybe a few times since. I knew better now, though.

Mia's eyes narrowed. She looked between me and the woman at the bar, then shook her head like a disappointed parent.

See? Exactly what I was saying. Mia hadn't changed.

Since when was smiling at another woman a crime?

And what the hell did it have to do with her anyway?

I knocked back my drink and walked past Mia and straight over to the lady at the bar.

So what if she thought I was some low-life man whore?

If I wanted to have fun, no one, especially not some stuck-up ex friend I hadn't seen for years, was going to stop me.

7
MIA

As I squeezed into the Tube carriage and spotted an aftershave advert, I groaned and muttered under my breath.

Liam bloody Stone.

The man was everywhere. It was bad enough that I'd seen him last night, now I'd have to stare at his face for the entire journey to work.

Ever since I'd bumped into Liam, I couldn't stop thinking about him.

No. Not like that.

I was a grown woman, not the silly lovesick girl that used to go gaga over those sparkling brown eyes, long lashes, annoying dimples and crooked smile. Those days were long gone.

Yeah, there was a time when we used to hang out together after school that I thought something *might* be brewing between us. But those delusions were quickly crushed when Liam started dating Natalie Davies. Then

Angela Peters, swiftly followed by Simone Wokoma, Annabel Elliot…

The list of Liam's conquests was endless. The saying that a leopard didn't change its spots was definitely true.

So, no. I wasn't thinking about him in a romantic way. It was just weird to see him again in the flesh after so long. Now he was a big star, I expected him to hang out at fancy parties. Not small theatre productions.

I'd got used to seeing him on billboards and the big screen. Not that I'd watched his films. Romcoms were more my style. Okay, maybe I'd seen one or two things he'd been in, but only out of curiosity or because there was nothing else on.

And I'd have to live on Mars to avoid the constant stream of tabloid stories. I didn't seek them out. They were just *there*.

But, *whatever*. So what if I'd seen him? I was already over it. I wasn't giving Liam another thought.

I stepped into the office and saw Trudy tapping away on her keyboard with one hand and holding a cup of coffee with the other.

'Morning!' she chirped.

'Thanks for the coffee.' I glanced at the cup on my desk. Whilst Trudy seemed full of energy, I was still recovering from last night's cocktails.

Thankfully after cocktail number three, Trudy had given up talking about Liam.

'What time did you leave last night?' I switched on my computer.

'After midnight!'

'Did you go home alone?'

'Yep. Wasn't in the mood for any extracurricular activities!' she laughed.

Since Trudy's divorce three years ago, she'd been a free spirit, insisting she never wanted to get tied down with a relationship ever again. She was the complete opposite to me. Despite my messy break-up with Boris, I still wanted to meet someone.

'What's your diary looking like for tomorrow night?' Trudy said.

'I've got a hot date… with my sofa!' I added. 'These days my social calendar is emptier than a ghost town.'

'Glad to hear it!' She rubbed her hands together.

'Hold on a minute…' My eyes narrowed. Trudy was looking far too pleased with herself. 'What are you up to? Please tell me you're asking if I'm free because you want me to come and see another one of your plays.'

'I could tell you it didn't have anything to do with a certain old school friend of ours, but then I'd be lying…'

'Trudy!' I blew out a breath. 'I told you, I'm not interested!'

'Don't be such a spoilsport! Can't you see Liam's the answer to your prayers?'

'More like my nightmares!' I scoffed.

'Listen. You need a fake boyfriend for two months. He's going to be here in London for roughly the same amount of time. It's perfect!'

'It really isn't. There's so many reasons it'd never work.'

'Such as?' She rested her finger on her chin.

'Where do I start?' I blew out a breath. 'First up, he's a big Hollywood star. And don't you read the papers?'

'Who reads *the papers* these days?'

'You know what I mean! Okay, let me rephrase: don't you read the news *on your phone*? He's with a different celebrity, influencer or model every night, so no one's going to believe that he's suddenly in a committed relationship with *me*. Secondly, I can't stand him and the feeling is mutual, so he's never going to want to help me out. Thirdly... anyway, it just wouldn't work. It's not even worth trying to explain why. It's *obvious*.'

'Oh how you underestimate me.' She rolled her eyes. 'I've thought about it. Firstly the press haven't seen him for weeks, so for all they know he could've been dating you. Second, you could be seen as the woman who finally tamed the playboy. The magazine and judges will lap that shit up. It's a great story. And third, even though you two have your issues, you wouldn't be the only person to gain something from this.'

'What do you mean?'

'Well, I *do* read the news and like you said he's always in the gossip magazines with different women. It's screwing with his reputation. Didn't you see those dick pics online?'

'No! I refused to look.' It seemed wrong somehow.

'I seriously think he should change his nickname to Big Will! Y'know, because Liam is from the name William and he's got a big *willy*, get it?'

'Why are we talking about Liam's dick?' I sighed.

'Because a little industry birdy told me that it was a woman called Sunrise Kane who posted those pics, after a night of passion with Liam.'

'And?'

'And Sunrise is the daughter of that huge Hollywood producer Henry Kane. And he was *not* happy about Liam putting his cock-a-doodle-doo inside his precious princess's vajayjay!'

'Vajayjay? Seriously? Sounds like a *Strictly Come Dancing* routine!'

'You're missing the point! Rumour has it that Liam was supposed to star in Henry Kane's new action film franchise. But when Kane caught Liam sticking his giant oar in his daughter's fandango, he pulled out. Oops. Wrong choice of words, given the context. Let me rephrase: Kane dropped him. And now with pics of his fuckpole and all these stories about him bedding different women all over the internet, Liam's rep is in the crapper. He needs some good PR.'

'Liam's been screwing around for years. It doesn't seem to have hurt his reputation so far.'

'I dunno. I know we haven't spoken for ages, but I doubt he wants to do those roles forever. Remember, before he went to Spain, I was in his drama class. He took it *really* seriously. Action films helped him break into Hollywood, but at some point he's going to want to try something different.'

'Why? Just because he was at the show last night?'

'Call it *agent's intuition…*'

'Anyway, what's that got to do with me?'

'You need a fake boyfriend to help you win this competition and he needs to show the world that he's not just a horny, soon-to-be-washed-up action star who doesn't know how to keep it in his pants. It's mutually beneficial. He helps you and you help him.'

'It'd never work.' I shook my head. 'Anyway, that only covers objection number one and part of point number two. You're forgetting the bit about the fact that we can't stand each other. He was a dick when he pissed off to Spain and he's even a bigger dick now.'

'Even though it was wrong for that woman to post those pics, I'm not gonna lie, I wouldn't mind having a ride on his big dick!' Trudy cackled.

'Gross!' I started peeling the banana I'd brought in for breakfast, then swiftly dropped it on my plate. Putting the tip in my mouth whilst talking about Liam's penis made me lose my appetite.

'I'm sure you could get over this whole *hate* thing. You two used to be good friends, so I'm sure you could be again. The prize is worth fifty grand, Mia! After what Boris did, your options are limited. Don't think I don't know the office rent's increasing soon. This is a lifeline. That money could change your fortunes.'

She was right. It'd really help with bills and the exposure I'd get from the magazine profile would be priceless. If I didn't get a serious influx of new clients or an investment soon, the business would go under and I wouldn't be able to pay the rent on my flat.

But this was Liam Stone.

And even if I thought it was a good idea, which for the record, I definitely did not, there were deeper issues at stake.

I'd always prided myself on being authentic, so lying went against who I was. Plus I was rubbish at it, so the judges would see straight through whatever stories we cooked up.

And it was too risky. If anyone found out, it'd ruin my reputation. What kind of matchmaker hired a boyfriend? I was a match*maker*, not a match *faker*. My whole business would be a sham.

If I had to lose my company, I'd rather keep my integrity.

Granny would be so ashamed. She'd left me some of her savings to help me start the agency because she believed in me, so failing would be bad enough. I couldn't let her down by being branded as a liar too.

No.

Trudy was trying to help and I loved her for it, but pretending to be in a relationship with Liam Stone was not the answer.

I'd think of another solution.

What exactly? Right now, I had no idea.

8

LIAM

'Nice job, man.' I finished stretching and glanced in the mirror.

I was at home, working out in the room my friend had converted into a gym. It wasn't as kitted out as mine in LA, but that was to be expected, considering staying in shape was part of my job.

'Thanks,' Nate replied. 'But it's you that put in the effort. That's why I always liked training you. You were never afraid of hard work.'

Nate had trained me years ago when he also lived in LA and I was new to the industry. We'd always got on well. Not only was he one of the best in the business, but like me, he'd grown up in South London and we had a lot in common. So when he left the States, we'd kept in touch.

Although rehearsals and filming wouldn't start for a couple of months, I had to stay in shape for them and the photoshoots I had coming up. That was why I'd asked Nate to train me whilst I was here.

I wasn't stupid. Even before the whole Sunrise shitstorm, I knew I was on borrowed time. There were newer, hotter actors coming on the scene all the time, so I had to play to my strengths.

As my parents and what felt like the whole world loved to remind me, it wasn't my acting skills that pulled in the roles and endorsement deals for everything from underwear to health supplements, sportswear and cars. It was my shell. No one cared what I said or thought, as long as I looked 'hot'.

What was it that Geena told me? "Men want to be you and women want to bed you."

Whenever an unflattering photo came out, Mum or Dad would call warning me that if I didn't take care of my looks, my career would suffer.

Don't get me wrong. I wasn't complaining (okay, maybe a little). Superficial or not, this face and body had helped me buy a mansion and multiple cars and paid off my mum's mortgage. Dad's too. Not that he deserved it. I'd done well out of it. But I knew all this wouldn't last forever.

'Appreciate you saying that. You done for the day?' I picked up a towel and wiped the sweat from my face and the back of my neck.

'Yep.' Nate pulled a T-shirt over his head, being careful not to mess up his short curly hair. He'd always taken pride in his appearance.

As well as being ripped, like you'd expect from a personal trainer at the top of his game, his beard was always immaculate, like every hair on his light brown skin had been meticulously cut, then brushed into place.

'Wanna grab a drink?' After having a couple of glasses of scotch last night, I couldn't have any more alcohol, but that didn't stop Nate from having his favourite rum and Coke. 'It'd need to be here, though, because...'

'I get it. I can stay for one, but then I gotta get home to my lady.'

Poor guy.

His fiancée, Melody, had probably given him a curfew and if he wasn't home by a certain time, he'd get an earful. I didn't need that kind of stress. The single life suited me just fine.

Although I didn't want the ball and chain that came with having a woman, I could do with having some friends in London.

After moving to Spain, I'd lost contact with a lot of people. And when Mum had forced me (she'd say *encouraged*) to do modelling, I'd started moving in different circles. Then came the film audition offer in Hollywood and since my career had taken off, I hadn't come back here often.

It was hard to make new friends. I never knew if they were genuine or just interested in money and fame.

So, yeah. This was gonna be a very lonely couple of months. Especially if I kept my promise not to sleep around.

Walking away from that actress at the theatre last night wasn't difficult, but who knew how long my willpower would last?

'One drink: got it.' I threw the towel in the laundry basket. 'Can you gimme five while I grab a quick shower?'

'Sure. It'll give me time to text Mel and let her know I'll be a bit late.'

Wow. Nate was well and truly under his woman's thumb. That'd never be me. I liked my freedom too much.

I'd hoped Nate and I could hang out whilst I was here, but sounded like he preferred to spend his evenings at home with his pipe and slippers.

Just as I came out of the shower, my phone rang.

'Hey.' I wrapped the towel around my waist and put Geena on loudspeaker.

'I've spoken to Annalise and she's come up with two options.'

'Oh.' I'd hoped she was calling with news on a role.

'We can either say you've been staying in a sex addiction clinic, getting treatment…'

'Hell no!'

'Or we could set you up with Kandi Beaumont.'

'That young actress?'

'You know her?'

'Yeah. Saw her coming out the bathroom at a party a few months ago—off her head on coke. The public might think she's sweet right now, but she's a train wreck waiting to happen. And if we pretended to date and that got out, people would think I take drugs too.'

'Shit, I hear you. I'll speak to Annalise again and get back to you.'

I hung up and shook my head. Was that really the best they could come up with? Pairing me up with Kandi fucking Beaumont or making me out to be a sex addict?

This was worse than I thought.

Fucking Sunrise. More like *Sunset*. If things went on like this, my acting career would be over. And I still didn't know why she'd even released the photo. Revenge? Just for shits and giggles? Well, I wasn't laughing.

Whatever the reason, the damage had been done.

Before shit had hit the fan, I'd worked hard and played hard. Now, not only had my work dried up, my social life was non-existent too.

I was about to leave the bathroom when my phone pinged. It was a message from Trudy.

As I read her text, my eyes widened.

Interesting.

Maybe I wouldn't be at a loose end after all…

9

MIA

'Hi, is that Mia?'

'Speaking,' I replied, grabbing the notepad on my desk.

'This is Joss. You set my friend Carly up with Horace and she recommended you.'

'Oh, hi! I love Carly, and Horace is such a sweetheart. How are they?'

'They're great—madly in love and that's what I want. I'm tired of the apps.' She huffed. 'At first they were fun. Now swiping is so frustrating! You match with someone, but then they want to keep messaging like a bloody pen pal and never meet. Or you meet and it's a disaster. Or you like them, but never hear from them again. I get so fed up that I delete the apps, but then end up downloading them again and going through the same crappy cycle. Finding love shouldn't be this hard!'

'I understand.' I found myself nodding, even though I knew she couldn't see me. 'That's why I'm here. I do all the hard work to find you the perfect partner so you don't have to sift through the apps.'

'That's exactly what I need. So how does it all work?'

'I send you a form, which you complete and send back to me. Then we meet for a chat, so I can get to know you, find out what you're looking for and see whether I can help.'

As much as I needed the money, I couldn't take on everyone. If I got the slightest whiff of someone being sexist, misogynistic, racist, violent or abusive, that was an automatic hard no. I'd rather go broke than knowingly set someone up with a partner who was toxic and could affect a client's mental or physical health.

And people looking for hook-ups, sugar daddies or seventy-year-old men searching for hot eighteen-year-old playthings weren't for me. No judgement. If that floated their boat, that was fine. But my members wanted long-term, committed, monogamous relationships.

'Okay.'

'Then if we both want to go ahead, once you've signed the terms, provided photo ID and paid the fees, I arrange for a professional photo to be taken and prepare your profile to approve, then I start searching for a match.'

Checking their identity was essential. I'd heard too many stories of catfishing to take the risk. Same for photos.

Some apps were like the Wild West. Anyone could post a random photo from the internet and you had no way of knowing whether it was real until you met them in person.

That was why I always sent Penny, a freelance professional photographer, to take a photo of new members in their natural setting. That helped make sure everyone's photos were up-to-date and representative of how they looked *now*. Not twenty years ago.

It also avoided members having to see those annoying photos of men flexing their biceps in the bathroom mirror, posing in front of flashy cars they didn't really own, or holding a cute baby that wasn't theirs.

'And how do you find a match?'

'Because I interview everyone personally, when I meet you, I often get a feel for who could be a good fit, but I also take into account their age, location, hobbies and what they want for their future.'

That last point was important. I knew what it was like to waste years with someone, only to find you want different things. If one person wanted marriage and kids and the other didn't, how much you had in common on paper meant nothing. The chances of it going the distance were slim. Shame I hadn't realised this sooner in my own relationship.

'And then?'

'Once I find a match, I recommend you meet as soon as possible to do a chemistry check. You can have lots in common, but the only way to know if there's a connection is to see each other—in person.'

'Okay. If you send me a link to the form and your fees, I'll take a look.'

'Great!' I took down her details. 'Thanks for calling, and give my regards to Carly and Horace.'

After we said our goodbyes, I whizzed an email straight off to her and crossed my fingers.

'Recommendation?' Trudy asked.

'Yep!' Most of my clients came from word of mouth.

That had kept me going for this long. But it wasn't enough.

I reached for the envelope I was about to open before Joss called. As I scanned the letter, I gasped. 'Shit!'

'What's up?' Trudy frowned.

'My landlord's increasing the rent for my flat by three hundred pounds a month! Where the hell am I supposed to get that kind of money from?'

'So sorry, M.'

'And the council tax and business rates are going up soon. With the office rent increase too, it's just all too much!' I buried my head in my hands.

An email notification sounded. I reluctantly looked up at my computer, then clicked into my inbox.

It was a newsletter from the Happily Ever After Awards organisers. There was a list of all the different categories. They all related to love, romance and having a happy relationship including Wedding Planner of the Year, Sex Therapist of the Year, Steamy Romance Author of the Year and even Sex Toy of the Year.

I'd devoured every single book from last year's winning author, and I may have ordered the Waterfall Turbo 3000 vibrator that won Sex Toy of the Year too. And I wasn't the only one. These awards were so influential.

My gaze flicked to the Matchmaker of the Year category and prize package that was highlighted in bold.

Winning that cash and all that publicity could literally change my life.

Beneath it was a photo of one of my competitors, Gillian Madely, flashing her stupid smile and saying how confident she was about winning the Matchmaker of the Year award *again*.

'Aaaarghhh!' I screamed.

'Whoa! If things are really that bad, I can try and help?'

'Thanks, but it's not just that crazy bill. I really need to make a go of this business, Trude. I'm good at what I do.'

'Well, you've entered, so you're already in with a chance. Now it's up to you to do the rest…'

'Yeah. I just…' I sighed. I knew what I had to do.

As much as I disagreed with the way they seemed to discriminate against single candidates (obviously they'd never admit it, because it'd land them in hot water, but everyone knew it was an unspoken rule), the bottom line was that to increase my chances of getting any further, I needed a boyfriend. And with the interviews starting next week, I needed one fast.

I had to be realistic. Given my luck with men in the past year and a half, the chances of me finding one within the next week were non-existent.

It wasn't ethical for me to date my own clients, so I had to rely on fate or new recommendations from friends. Since I'd broken up with Boris, I'd dated two men.

The first was Silas. When we had sex on the third date, it was a disaster: zero chemistry or coordination. Somehow we just couldn't get the rhythm right and it was super awkward.

Me being nervous couldn't have helped. I'd dated Boris since I was seventeen and he was the only guy I'd ever slept with. So having sex with someone else was a big deal, but I knew I needed to get back on the horse.

Knowing Boris had cheated probably affected me too. I

was plagued with self-doubt about whether I was good enough in bed and if that was the reason he'd strayed. I wasn't surprised when Silas didn't call again.

A couple of months later I dated Marlon. The sex was better (still not great, though), but it didn't matter because I knew it couldn't last. He loved himself more than I loved chocolate and I loved chocolate a *lot*.

Our conversations were always about him and his job (a small role in a daytime TV soap). He was so into himself that when we were walking along the River Thames and a girl came up to ask if he'd mind taking a photo, he automatically assumed she wanted a selfie with him.

'Of course!' He'd beamed. 'Anything for my fans!'

'Selfie?' She'd frowned. 'No, I just want a photo in front of Tower Bridge!'

I'd burst out laughing. I couldn't help it. We ended things soon after.

So yeah, my dating experiences hadn't been great, but if I was to stand a chance of winning this competition, I knew I only had one option.

Just thinking about it made me sick. But it had to be done.

'I know you're nervous,' Trudy said softly, 'but just give it a try. Meet Liam. See what he says. If he says no, at least you'll know you tried. But imagine if he said yes and you won the whole damn thing!'

'Okay.' I pictured myself on stage at the awards ceremony, clutching the trophy and most importantly that big fat cheque. 'Message him.' I blew out an exasperated breath. I couldn't believe I was really doing this. 'Set up something in the next few days if he's free. We don't have much time.'

'Already done!' Trudy smiled.

'What?'

'We're meeting him tomorrow at eight.'

Oh God.

'But how did you even know I'd agree?'

'Because I know you. And I know you need this.'

She wasn't wrong. So why did I feel like I was going to regret this?

10

LIAM

I was on my way to a private members' club in Soho to meet Trudy.

And her annoying friend.

When Trudy texted, she'd said they had a 'proposition' for me.

I had no idea what that meant, but I was intrigued. I was pretty sure it wasn't anything to do with money. That wasn't Trudy's style. Or Mia's.

And because *she* was coming, I knew it definitely wasn't anything sexual. If it was anyone else, the first thought that popped into my head would've been *threesome*. But that was just because I was horny.

Whatever the reason, I was glad to get out of the house. Even if it meant I'd have to sit at the same table as Ice Queen Mia.

After stepping through the doors and handing over my jacket, I headed up to the lounge, sat on the velvet armchair and ordered a sparkling water with lemon. I wished I could drink alcohol, but I had a shoot next week, so had to watch what I ate and drank.

A few minutes later, I heard someone call my name. When I looked I saw Trudy.

And *Mamma Mia*.

As much as I didn't like her, I couldn't deny she was pretty. Mia was wearing a fitted light blue dress which looked like it had been sewn onto her skin. It accentuated every curve. Her generous breasts, those hips and…

'Someone likes what they see,' Trudy teased.

Shit.

'Trudy.' I stood up and kissed her gently on both cheeks, deliberately ignoring the fact that she'd just caught me checking out her best friend. Correction: I wasn't checking Mia out, I was just looking at her… *dress*. I liked the fit. I had no interest in the body that was wearing it.

'Mia.' I nodded to acknowledge her before sitting back down. There was no way I'd attempt to give her a cheek kiss. The way she was scowling, she'd ask the waiter to bring her some bleach and a scourer to scrub her face afterwards.

'You get in okay?' I turned to Trudy.

'Yeah, fine. Thanks for agreeing to meet.'

'Can I get you both a drink?'

'I'll have a vodka tonic and Mia will have red wine. Rioja, right?' Trudy checked with Mia, who confirmed with a nod.

Once I ordered, we sat in silence. Mia's gaze dropped to the floor.

Well, this was awkward.

'So, you said you had a *proposition*?' I raised my eyebrow.

'Yeah, so… we okay to talk here?' Trudy asked.

'Sure.' I scanned the lounge. There were a couple of guys in tailored suits in the far corner, but they were well out of earshot. This place was safe. The club's reputation depended on it.

'I'll cut to the chase.' Trudy paused. 'Mia needs your help.'

Mia's head shot up and her eyes widened.

'Tell me more…' I sat up straighter.

'So…'

'It's okay,' Mia jumped in, her face tight. 'I can tell him.' She shuffled uncomfortably in her seat.

'I'm listening…' I could tell she hated having to ask me for something and I admit, I kind of enjoyed watching Little Miss Perfect squirm.

'I've been entered for a competition: the Happily Ever After Awards. And you kind of need a partner to stand a chance of winning and so…' Mia paused and Trudy nodded, encouraging her to continue. 'So, I wondered if you could help.' She blew out a breath.

'I don't follow.' I frowned. 'You're looking for a business partner? Someone to invest in your company?'

'No.' Mia fiddled with the hem of her dress. My eyes dropped to her smooth, toned legs and I quickly moved my gaze back to her face. 'Not a business partner. A… *personal* one. A… boyfriend,' she whispered.

'Wait, *what*?' My eyebrows almost hit my hairline. 'You want *me* to be your boyfriend?'

'Yes,' she murmured.

'Sorry, what was that? I didn't quite hear you.' The corner of my mouth twitched.

'I said *yes*.'

'I *knew* you liked me!' I joked. I wasn't Mia's type.

'I *don't*!' she said through gritted teeth, fighting to keep her voice low. 'This would just be… pretend. For the competition.'

'So let me get this straight: you're a matchmaker, as in you charge people money to find them the perfect match, and you're asking *me* to be your fake boyfriend, because *you*, the professional, *expert* matchmaker, can't find someone to date? This is comedy gold!'

I let out a low chuckle. I couldn't help it. After the way she'd ignored me towards the end of our friendship, I would've paid good money to see her knocked off her perfect perch.

And to think I'd considered whether they'd wanted a threesome. Seeing Mia squirm was a hundred times more satisfying than any orgasm.

'I'm leaving.' Mia grabbed her jacket and turned to Trudy. 'Told you he was a dick.'

'Don't start obsessing over my manhood just yet, sweetheart. I'm trying to turn over a new leaf by not putting out on the first date, but if you play your cards right, I might make an exception.' I grinned.

'Ugh!' Mia grimaced. 'I'd rather lick vomit off a dirty pavement than go anywhere near your communal cock. You're such an arrogant twat!'

'Is that any way to talk to the man you want to save your bacon? If you want me to help you out, you'll need to be a bit nicer.'

'But it's not just *you* who'll be doing the favour,' Trudy said calmly. Relief washed over Mia's face and she sat back down.

'Meaning?' I cocked my head to the side.

'Mia can help *you* too. Face it, Liam. Your reputation's in the toilet. You want to move away from the clichéd action films, right? But no one's taking you seriously because you keep falling out of nightclubs with different women. And you just fucked one of the most powerful men in Hollywood's daughter, who posted pics of your love stick all over the internet…'

I froze. How the hell did she know about all that?

Okay, the whole world knew about the nightclubs and women, but how did she know *Sunrise* was behind the photos, or that I wanted to try different roles? That wasn't public knowledge.

'Go on.' I swallowed hard and readjusted myself in the seat, trying to keep my cool.

'So I'm saying it can't hurt you to be seen to be in a serious relationship for a change. Having a beautiful British businesswoman on your arm for a couple of months could do *you* some good.'

'I appreciate you thinking of me, but I'm not exactly short of offers. If I wanted a fake girlfriend, there's a million other women I could choose. If I was desperate enough to hire a fake girlfriend, I'd pick someone who actually liked me.'

Geena had called again earlier to say she and Annalise had another prospect to set me up with that they thought would be a much better fit and would get back to me soon with more info. Just the thought of it made me want to vomit.

'You reckon?' Trudy said calmly. 'If you picked someone who liked you, they'd end up falling in love or getting clingy, and let's face it, you're not a relationship kind of guy. That would get messy. And when you ended things, chances are they wouldn't take it well. Imagine the headlines when they went to the press and dished the dirt on your arrangement?'

'That's what NDAs are for,' I said quickly. If Annalise set me up with an actress, surely she and my legal team would sort that shit out.

'They can only cover so much. There's other ways you could get screwed over and you know it. With Mia, you know you can trust her. She'd have just as much to lose as you have.'

'And the fact that we can't stand each other is a bonus,' Mia added. 'I can categorically say that there's *zero* chance of me ever liking you. It'd be business. Pure and simple. We date whilst you're in London. Then once the competition's over, we'd break up and you'd go back to LA. We can say the distance put a strain on our relationship or some crap like that.'

I took a second to mull it over. On the surface it was a terrible idea. It meant being tied to Mia for two long months. A prison stretch sounded more appealing. But they'd made some good points.

As much as Mia didn't like me, I knew I could trust her. Probably more than some actress I didn't know.

Being seen with Mia might not be such a bad thing. Despite her judgemental personality, she was smart and sensible. A world away from the women I normally dated, which *could* be beneficial. The fact that she was attractive didn't hurt.

And if I was supposed to be with her, I'd definitely need to keep my dick in my pants. Dating different women was one thing. But a cheater? No way. Given my family history, being unfaithful, even in a fake relationship, was something I'd never do.

Plus it'd stop Geena and Annalise setting me up with whatever disgraced or wannabe actress they were in talks with.

Hmmm.

'I'll think about it.' I picked up my drink, downed it in one, then stood up. 'Gotta run, but feel free to stay and put your drinks on my tab. I'll be in touch.'

Whilst Trudy smiled, Mia's eyes bored into me.

But I didn't care.

As I strolled out of the lounge, a smile touched my lips.

I'd told them I'd think about it, but I'd already made up my mind.

11

MIA

I tossed my door keys down on the hallway table, yanked off my heels and shook off my jacket.

The audacity of that man.

Who the hell did he think he was?

When he started sniggering about the fact I couldn't find myself a boyfriend, I wanted to wipe that smug smile off his face with a metal sponge.

Aaarrggh.

He'd really pushed my buttons. That was why, even if he'd agreed, this fake-dating farce would never work. To convince people we were together, we'd need chemistry. They'd expect to see attraction. Not two people scowling like they were plotting how to murder each other.

Speaking of looking at each other, why was he staring when I arrived? Trudy said he was eyeing me up, but I wasn't Liam's type.

The women he was always papped with were the kind you saw in magazines or on the catwalk. They didn't have a big bottom, thick thighs and average-sized boobs like I did.

Anyway, I shouldn't care what Liam thought of me. After tonight's debacle and how quickly he wanted to leave, that'd be the last time I saw him. Well, face to face. No doubt I'd be tormented with pictures of his naked chest on billboards and buses for years to come.

Annoyingly, he was in great shape.

Whenever his latest advertising campaign came out and I was subjected to looking at his eight-pack (not that I'd counted), I was convinced the photos had been heavily airbrushed.

But the way that jumper clung to his biceps whenever he picked up his drink this evening and the glimpse of his toned stomach that I saw when he stretched told me they hadn't had to retouch his photos at all.

Not that it was important. He could be the most athletic-looking man in the universe and it wouldn't make up for his personality.

"I'll think about it."

Arsehole.

If anyone had something to think about it was *me*. Like how I was going to get myself out of this mess.

∼

It was now Friday. Exactly a week away from the first competition interview. When Susie, the lady from the awards, called to set the date, she'd explained that they'd come to my office to see my set-up and ask about my clients. No doubt they'd slip in a question about my relationship status too.

Soon after that they'd schedule the second interview at home, which, again, I was sure they'd want to do with my *partner* there.

I didn't know why I hadn't withdrawn my application when it was obvious I couldn't take it all the way.

Part of me, the stubborn side, still wanted to enter. Like Trudy said, my relationship status shouldn't have any bearing on my ability to do my job.

Wasn't it better for me to be single than in a toxic relationship? They were basically saying I was only worthy of recognition and success if I was part of a couple.

Granted, the nature of my business meant relationships and love were obviously important. But surely I was a stronger candidate than Gillian.

Just like when I met people and knew they were meant to be together, every time I saw Gillian, I got the feeling she wasn't as angelic as she seemed.

I hated to say it because I believed women should support other women (given how hostile she was to me, I didn't think she shared that sentiment), but I'd always thought she'd seemed overly friendly with some of her male staff.

Then at a conference earlier this year, I'd seen her coming out of a toilet cubicle with her younger male personal assistant, both adjusting their clothes. And I'm pretty sure they weren't in there checking her diary.

Whatever she chose to do was her business, but she was married with two children, and if I was going to be judged because I was single, it didn't seem fair not to question her values as a married person too.

To me, having a cheater as a winner was much worse than having a singleton like me.

Anyway, even if one day the unofficial rules were changed, the only way I'd have a sniff of getting to the finals this year was if I found a partner.

Trudy and I had been through our contacts again and drawn blanks.

My ability to matchmake was a blessing, but when you were searching your friendship groups for a prospective fake boyfriend, it was a curse. I'd paired up so many of our friends that there were no singles left.

'M.' Trudy called my nickname, snapping me out of my thoughts.

'Hmmm?'

'What you doing?'

'Just looking through my client list to see who else to contact for the case study videos I need to submit for the competition.'

'I bet that'll be a walk in the park! Your clients love you!'

'Two have already agreed, so I just need one more. If only the face-to-face interviews were so straightforward.'

'When you see this, it'll make things a whole lot easier.' A wide grin spread across her face.

She got up, clutching her phone, then thrust the screen in front of me.

It was a text.

From Liam. I scanned it quickly.

Liam

I'm in.

Holy shit.

12

MIA

Although it was a cool Monday evening, as I stepped out from the Tube station, beads of sweat trickled down my back.

Must be because the carriage was hot. I definitely wasn't nervous. I was only meeting Liam. I wasn't one of those women that swooned over him or thought he was some kind of sex god. He was just the guy I grew up with from the age of seven until he moved to Spain at seventeen. No big deal.

Yeah, we were meeting alone at his place in Notting Hill to discuss the *terms* of our fake-dating agreement, but he had as much to gain or lose from this as I did. If he thought I was going to kiss his feet because I was so grateful, he'd better think again.

I took out my phone and pulled up directions. According to the map, it wasn't too far to walk from the station, so I must be close.

My ankle twisted. I shouldn't have worn these heels. Or these bloody knickers.

After crouching behind a car and checking the coast was clear, I discreetly pulled the flimsy piece of fabric out of my bum where it was wedged.

I hadn't got round to doing the washing over the weekend because I'd been at the office working all day on Saturday and most of Sunday too. So it was either these lacy panties that Boris had bought me that weren't really my normal style (or size) or the ones I'd had for at least a decade with multiple holes that I hadn't got round to throwing out. I'd thought these would be the better option, but now I was having second thoughts.

Even though it was mild, I'd worn a hat too. My hair needed washing, but again, I hadn't had time.

Although I generally wore my hair straight, my natural hair was thick and curly, so even though I got a keratin blow-dry, it always took me a couple of hours to wash, condition, and dry it, then smooth it out with irons and style it. Especially because my keratin appointment was long overdue. So today I'd thrown it up into a bun and hidden it under a hat.

I took in the sight of the colourful houses and expensive cars lining the streets. After walking for a few minutes, I eventually found the road. Wow. *How the other half lived.*

It was a white two-storey double-fronted house with a garden and black iron-gated entrance.

Even if I lived to a hundred, I'd never be able to afford a place half the size of this. It was funny how two people could grow up on the same street, but one went on to live in a fancy house in an area like this and the other ended up being me, struggling to make ends meet in a one-bedroom flat.

After finding the house, I rang the buzzer. Several seconds later, I heard the latch on the gate go. I walked through towards the door, pushed it gently and stepped inside.

'Hello?' I called out. It was boiling in here. I quickly took off my jacket and silk scarf. Even though it was still supposed to be summer, the British weather was temperamental, so you had to be prepared for all seasons.

I took off my hat too. I'd rather sit in front of Liam with a bad hair day than with sweat pouring down my face.

'In here. The room on the right.'

A normal person would've greeted me at the door, but then I remembered I was dealing with Liam.

When I got to the room, Liam was sprawled out on a white leather sofa, scrolling through his phone.

'Drink?' he asked.

'Yes. Please,' I said, trying to focus. Liam was wearing grey tracksuit bottoms (aka the sexy grey *sweatpants* I loved reading about in American romance novels). He'd paired it with a white vest top and his arms were huge. I swallowed hard.

'You wanna tell me what you'd like to drink or are you just gonna keep staring at my arms?' Liam smirked.

My eyes widened. Shit.

'I wasn't looking at your... I was just...' I tried to think of an excuse, but my mind went blank.

'So?' He smiled. 'What's the verdict?'

'I mean, they're...'

Lie. Tell him you don't care about his arms. That they're average. Or just okay. Or shrug.

Whatever you do, do NOT tell him that they look great.

'Um, you have... your arms are pretty impressive.'

Gah!

If I couldn't even lie about something simple like this, how the hell was I supposed to lie about him being my boyfriend? I'd barely been here two minutes and this was already a disaster.

'Good to know.' The corner of his mouth twitched. 'But when I asked for your verdict, I meant what you wanted to drink.'

Ground, swallow me up.

Now the arsehole would think I liked him.

'Um, water. Please.' If I couldn't even hold it together when I was stone-cold sober, God knows what crap would fall out of my mouth after drinking something stronger.

'Still? Sparkling?'

'Still.'

He got up and strode across the room. Even though he was metres away, his woody scent hit me. And I hated how much I liked it.

I reached into my bag to look busy. There was no way I'd give him the satisfaction of seeing me staring at his firm arse. I mean, his firm *arms*. I definitely didn't look at his bum at all when he walked past.

'Here.' He handed me the glass, then sat down. 'So, what's the plan?'

Plan. I liked that word. *That* I could deal with. I pulled out my pad and found the page where I'd made some notes.

'Well, as I mentioned when we met, I've been entered for the Matchmaker of the Year competition at the Happily Ever After Awards…'

'I have to ask,' Liam interrupted. 'This whole matchmaking *thing*: don't you feel bad? For selling a false dream?'

'What do you mean?'

'Perpetuating the myth that people will find one person and live *happily ever after*.' He rolled his eyes.

'It's not a myth!' Anger bubbled in my veins.

Matchmaking had been around for centuries. It'd been proven to work. Time and time again.

Although she hadn't done it professionally, my maternal grandmother, Eleanor, had been famous for her skills. She'd probably matched hundreds of couples in her lifetime. Including my parents. And I was lucky enough to inherit her gift.

She'd always told me to look out for that 'sparkle'. It wasn't something you could touch. It was the magic you felt and saw when two people who were meant to be came together.

Granny E., as I called her, was one of the few people in my family who hadn't been fooled by Boris's charms. She'd said she never saw that sparkle between us. Of course, at the time, I was in denial. I should've listened.

Before she died, three years ago, Boris and I were going through a rough patch. He was being a dick about my plans to set up the agency. She told me I'd make a success of it and not to worry about Boris because one day, the right man would come back to me.

I remember thinking that didn't make any sense, because it was just a blip between me and Boris. We'd get back on track once the business was up and running. I was wrong. Granny E. was too because I hadn't made a success of the business and I was still as single as a Pringle. Hence why I was stuck here, having to listen to bloody Liam talk shit about my job.

'Look at the statistics. Most marriages end in divorce. *Fact*. As a child that was trapped in the middle of my parents' war, I know that *forever* stuff is BS.'

'It's not! My parents are still together!' I snapped.

'But are they really happy, though? Most so-called 'perfect couples' just stay together to keep up appearances or avoid an expensive divorce because they weren't smart enough to get a prenup. Or they stay for convenience because they can't be arsed to start again.'

'Pessimistic, much? My parents *are* happy. You know *nothing* about their marriage!'

'And you probably don't know the full story either.'

I took a deep breath, ignoring what he'd said. Whether he believed in love, marriage or relationships was irrelevant. He just needed to pretend he did. He was an actor. He could do this in his sleep.

'As I was saying, I've been entered for the Happily Ever After Awards…'

Liam snorted.

'Look, if you're just going to make fun of me, let's just forget it!'

'Sorry. Go on. I'm listening.'

'And although they don't explicitly state it in the rules, candidates stand a better chance if they're in a relationship. And I'm… not. But I *am* good at my job, so I don't want to be held back just because I don't have a partner.'

'So you need me to put on the performance of my life by pretending that we're together.'

'Basically.' He could've left out the *performance of my*

life bit, but I supposed I would be doing the same. Just being in the same room as Liam and not wanting to scream was a big enough ask as it was, so he wasn't wrong to say that we'd both need to pull out all the stops to be convincing.

'And when's the finals for this competition?'

'October.'

'Could be worse. They could've held it on the most commercialised bullshit day of the year.'

'What?'

'Valentine's Day.'

'I think you meant to say the most *romantic* day of the year.'

'No. I meant what I said: it's a bullshit day.'

'I'm going to need you to show a bit more enthusiasm for romantic things in front of the judges. And when we go out.'

'Yeah, so about that...' He rubbed his chin. 'How many times do you think we'd actually need to be seen out together?'

'As little as possible,' I replied quickly. 'They'll want to interview us together at home in the next couple of weeks, then there's the ceremony.'

'As little as possible sounds good. We could go somewhere public for the first date. So we could be photographed together, do the interview, go out one more time after that to make it look legit, then lay low until your awards ceremony and that's it.' He sipped his water.

'*Photographed* together?' My eyes widened. 'Like, *papped*?'

'Exactly.'

Obviously I knew that Liam would want some way of declaring he was in a serious relationship, but my brain had conveniently neglected to think about the implications.

Me. Getting papped.

Me. With my photo splashed all over the gossip magazines.

Having people picking apart the way I look and questioning what Liam was doing with someone like *me*.

Fuck.

Maybe this wasn't worth it after all. I liked a quiet life. Work, then home to read or watch Netflix. I preferred to watch the action taking place rather than being part of it.

My heart thundered against my chest.

'Isn't there a way to announce it without it being so, erm, *public*?'

'Sure. I'll just get my publicist to send out a press release declaring that I'm in a serious relationship and the media will be happy with that.'

'Oh, thank God!' My shoulders relaxed. 'That'd be great. For a minute there I thought…' When I saw Liam grinning, I paused. '*Oh*. You're joking.'

'Of course I'm joking! Did you really think it'd be that easy?'

'I… just wishful thinking, that's all.'

'You sure you wanna do this? The paps thing is real. Sometimes it can get pretty ugly. I'm used to it, but still hate it. You're better off finding someone out of the public eye.'

If only.

I'd exhausted all of my options.

'Believe me, if I thought I had another viable option, I'd take it.'

I'd rather have anyone else be my fake boyfriend than

Liam. I *really* didn't want to get papped. But I was stuck with him, so I had to deal with it.

Once we'd agreed on an official start date, I'd go to the salon and get everything done: hair, nails, waxing... It was an expense I could do without, but at least I'd look half-decent on our first public fake date.

I hated getting my picture taken, but maybe Trudy could give me some tips on how to pose so they'd get my good angle (if I even had one).

But yeah, with some careful prep, maybe being photographed would be slightly less awful. I'd call the salon tomorrow and get something set up.

'So four dates in total,' I confirmed.

It would've been nice to add in some other events I had in the diary that I didn't want to go to alone. Having a date for my parents' fortieth anniversary would be cool so I didn't have to face my family and the barrage of questions. But that was after the awards ceremony. Plus my parents knew Liam, so I wasn't sure how well we'd be able to lie to them in person.

No. I needed to spend as little time with Liam as possible.

'Okay. Just four dates.' He nodded. 'What's the exact date of the ceremony?'

I checked my diary, then told him.

'That might be tricky. I'm due back in LA in October. I'll try and move some stuff around. If I stay for the awards, I'll have to fly back straight afterwards, say the next morning. That gonna be okay?'

'Fine.' Didn't bother me. Once the ceremony was over, it wouldn't matter as much. It was the lead-up to the finals that was most important.

'Good.'

'Maybe we can have the first date at the beginning of next week?'

That would give me time to plan things carefully. I could prepare a questionnaire that he could complete and I'd do the same.

'Whatever. At least by that point it'll be about a month since I'd been seen out with a woman, which will be good for my rep.'

'Fine. Then after that date, we can start revising, so you're prepared for the interview.'

'Revising?' He grimaced.

'We need to know everything about each other. In case they ask in the interview. And we'll need to agree on a story of how we met.'

'That's easy. You kissed my arse,' he laughed.

'I did not! I always hated the way you told that story.'

'But it's true!'

'Is not! I think what you meant to say was that I had the unfortunate task of playing the back end of a donkey in a school play when we were seven and you were at the front and our coordination wasn't always great, so my mouth *may* have *accidentally* skimmed your bum once!'

'It was more than once.' He grinned.

The teacher said we should practise and when we discovered we lived on the same street, we started hanging out after school. Then after the play, whenever his parents were working late, Liam used to stay at my house and we became good friends all the way up until we were sixteen, which was when we started drifting apart. Then a year later, he upped and left.

'Whatever. Anyway, I didn't mean how we met as

kids, I meant how we met like *now. Recently*. Like, how did we start dating?'

'Unless you've had a personality transplant since I last saw you, you're a shitty liar. So we should just stick to the facts: we bumped into each other backstage at a play and sparks flew.'

'The meeting backstage thing is true, but the sparks thing isn't,' I clarified.

'I'm hurt!' He clutched his chest and smiled. It was annoying when he did that. It showed his dimples and they weren't horrible.

'Let me guess: you'd prefer me to make up some bull about me realising the reason I went off the rails in LA was because I was missing *someone to love*. So I flew to London, decided to use a matchmaking agency called Soulmate Connections. I had a match that was ninety-nine point nine per cent compatible and when I went to meet the lucky lady, I discovered it was you: the girl I'd loved and lost when I was seventeen…'

'That's actually not a bad idea…' I went off into my own little world.

If people heard that someone as high-profile as Liam found a match using my company, sign-ups would rocket. And there'd be the added bonus of showing that I was good at my job.

Plus, that story was so romantic. People would lap it up. Especially my family. No idea why, but my parents had always had a soft spot for Liam.

'It's a terrible idea!' Liam shook his head. 'Too many opportunities for mistakes. That kind of shit would end up getting us in trouble.'

'Yeah.' Annoyingly, he was right. And as cool as it sounded, it was unethical to date clients.

'Like I said, stick to the facts: we met backstage, got talking about old times, and the rest is history.'

'Sounds kind of boring, though.' I knew it was better to stick to the truth, but I couldn't help but feel like if I was going to go through all this, the story should be a bit more romantic. Something to make the judges swoon.

'KISS,' Liam said.

'What?' My jaw dropped. 'No! I will *not* kiss you!'

'You really haven't changed.' Liam laughed. 'I wasn't *asking* for a kiss. I said KISS as in the acronym for *keep it simple, stupid.*'

Oh.

'Anyway, how did you know the name of my company?'

'Google.'

'You *googled* me?' My jaw dropped.

'Like you've never googled me.' He rolled his eyes.

'We also need to agree on when and how to end our fake-tionship,' I said quickly to avoid answering the question. I may have googled Liam once or a few dozen times over the years.

'Will five minutes after your awards ceremony be too soon?' He smirked.

'Look, I don't want to be paired up with you any longer than necessary either. But we have to make this seem realistic. If I'm lucky enough to win, the last thing I need straight after the ceremony is people gossiping about my relationship ending again. Maybe we could hold off for about a month? Then we can say that even though we were great together, the long-distance thing made it difficult?'

'Could do.'

'And obviously, we need rules. So we both need to be single until this ends. If a photo of you with another woman came out before the interview or ceremony, it'd be a disaster.'

'Fine,' Liam huffed. 'Why do you want to win this competition so badly anyway?'

'I need… let's just say the prize would be helpful.'

'How much is it?'

'It's worth fifty thousand. Twenty cash and thirty grand's worth of publicity.'

'Fifty grand? Maybe we can just come to an arrangement. I don't normally like to lend people money. It can get messy. But it'd be easier for me to give you a loan than go through this charade. I'll get my lawyer to—'

'It's not just about the money. It's… I want to be taken seriously. It'd be nice to get that recognition and publicity to help grow my business. These awards are huge and the magazine is super prestigious—it's the equivalent of being featured in *Vogue*. It's a bit like you wanting to win an Oscar.'

'Okay. I get it.'

'I think that's the most important parts covered.' I rubbed my eyes. It'd been a long day. And I wasn't sure if the mascara I'd worn today agreed with me. 'So'—I started writing on my notepad—'four dates, to include first date, interview, one other date and the ceremony. We met backstage at a play. Two months of fake dating and we both agree to break up one month after the awards, citing long-distance relationship struggles. Okay?'

'Okay.'

After rewriting the agreement onto another sheet of paper, I thrust it in front of Liam with a pen.

'What's this?'

'Our contract. So there's no confusion. Sign at the bottom.'

'Whatever happened to good old-fashioned trust?'

'Trust?' I scoffed. I trusted Boris and look what he did to me. My stomach twisted. 'I prefer to have things in writing.'

'Fine.' He took the pen, scrawled his signature at the bottom of both sheets, then handed them back to me. I did the same, gave him back his copy, then stuffed mine in the sleeve of my mobile phone case.

Done.

'And of course, no one can know about this.'

'Trust me. The last thing I'd want is for someone to know I have a fake girlfriend. It wouldn't be good for my street cred.'

'Who said you have any?' I laughed.

'Give me your phone.'

'Why?'

'If I'm gonna be your fake boyfriend, you'll need my number. We can't keep going through Trudy.'

I sighed, unlocked my phone and gave it to him.

He tapped away on the screen, smiled, then handed it back to me.

My phone chimed. It was a message from…

My Hot Boyfriend

'What the hell?'

'What?' He smirked. 'Is that not accurate?'

'It's time for me to go.' I rubbed my eyes again. 'I'll give you and your ego the space you need.' I left the room.

'Bye, honey!' he called out in a fake, saccharine voice.

After pulling my hat on, I decided against it and yanked it off. It was only a short walk to the Tube and now it was getting dark, I shouldn't need it.

'I'll be in touch,' I replied, slipping on my shoes and jacket before opening the door, then closing it behind it behind me.

I was about to walk towards the gate when I felt the stupid knickers wedged in my bum again. Best to pull them out now before I set off.

Just as I reached behind my arse, I heard the front door open.

'You forgot this.' I turned to see Liam clutching my scarf. Suddenly a huge flash of light blinded me.

'Shit!' Liam shouted. 'Take your hand out your arse and get inside. Quick!'

'Why?' I dropped my hand, then raced back through the door.

'Congratulations, Mia.' Liam sighed. 'You've just been papped.'

13

LIAM

A sharp ringtone vibrated in my ears.
What time was it?
I lifted the duvet, picked my phone off the bedside table, then groaned as I answered the call.

'What happened to being on your best behaviour and keeping your dick in your pants?' Geena snapped.

They'd published the photos.

Fuck.

'It's not how it looks.' I sat up, dragging my hand down my face.

'It looks like a woman is leaving your place fixing her dress because you've just screwed.'

'Come on! You know that photos aren't always what they seem.'

'No, *you* come on! Of course *I* know that. But I also know *you*. Are you seriously telling me the two of you were sipping cocoa and playing tiddlywinks?'

'She's... an old friend. And I swear—I didn't lay a finger on her.'

'Honey, I've been your agent since day one and you and I both know you don't need to use your fingers to get yourself in trouble.'

She wasn't wrong...

With the way Mia's dress clung to her curves, I'd be lying if I said the thought of using my mouth on her didn't cross my mind. Only for a second, though, before I saw sense.

Even though Mia admitted she liked my arms, like I said before, *never gonna happen*.

'Okay, let me rephrase: I didn't lay a finger on her and I didn't use my mouth or dick anywhere either. I *swear*. We were just *talking*.'

There was silence.

This was good. When Geena was silent for more than a few seconds, I knew she was thinking. I could literally hear the cogs in her brain turning.

'For some reason, I believe you. At least this one looks more sophisticated than your normal type. Well, apart from having her hand halfway up her butt... Annalise is pissed. You were supposed to be laying low while we find someone to set you up with. It might take a bit longer than planned, especially now.'

'Tell Annalise there's no need. It's early days, but I think this thing with Mia could go somewhere.'

I had to stop myself from laughing. The idea was crazy, but I'd already agreed and fake-dating Mia was better than the options Geena and Annalise would offer.

'Seriously, Stone. I'm not in the mood for your jokes. We'll let you know when the actress's agent gets back to us. Until then, keep your shit together.'

'Any news on that Netflix drama series?' I asked, ignoring her comment.

'Not yet, but I'm sure being in the headlines again like this won't help. For the hundredth time, stay out of trouble!'

'Will do.'

Geena hung up.

Now it was my turn to think.

If Geena knew about the arrangement with Mia, maybe she'd understand and even support it. Appearing to be in a real relationship with someone outside of the industry who I'd known since I was a kid was more believable. I reckoned it could help me land different roles.

I knew Mia said we shouldn't tell anyone, but Geena was my agent and Annalise was my publicist. Surely they should both know what Mia and I were up to? They could help *control the narrative. Get in front of the story* and all those other fancy phrases they used when dealing with this kind of shit. Basically advise us how to make it work out for the best. And shut the whole actress set-up idea down for good.

Hmmm.

Then again, if either of them got wind of this, they'd call me a fool for agreeing to do it without consulting them or my legal team in the first place.

And maybe they'd be right.

I knew I shouldn't have said yes. But as much as I liked winding Mia up, I'd always had this unexplainable thing about wanting to protect her. No, that was the wrong word. Mia had always been strong and independent, so she didn't need anyone to *protect* her. Maybe 'look out for' was a better way of putting it.

She'd always been too trusting. And people took advantage. Like Boris. That guy was a dick.

I remembered he used to always get Mia to do his homework or buy him things. I was surprised it took her so long to dump him.

Ironically, given her profession, if Boris was anything to go by, Mia didn't seem to have good judgement when it came to choosing men. So if I didn't agree to this, she'd find some other idiot and they'd let her down. Ruin her and her business.

And even though we'd fallen out, hadn't spoken for years and I shouldn't care, for some dumb reason, I did. Like Trudy said, Mia and I could trust each other.

The phone rang again and I groaned. I really wasn't in the mood, but I had to answer—otherwise she'd just keep calling.

'Hey, Mum.'

'Seriously, Liam? Another woman? The apple doesn't fall far from the tree.'

'What's that supposed to mean?'

'You're just like your father. When are you going to stop all this womanising?'

'How can you compare me to *him*?' I ground my jaw. 'Dad was married. I'm not, so I can do what I want.'

'Not when everyone in town is still talking about the fact that my son's penis is all over the internet you can't. I thought you'd gone to London to lay low? You've only been there five minutes and you're already screwing around. And what happened to this big action film franchise you told me about?'

'That's not happening anymore,' I sighed.

'For God's sake! Your looks won't last forever. You

need to bring in the cash whilst you can. To safeguard your future. See if your agent can get you some more endorsement deals.'

'I don't want any more deals. I want to do different things.'

'Not this nonsense again. God gave you that face and body for a reason. When you get to my age, you'll regret not making the most of your looks. I wasted all my good years on your father and for what?'

'I've gotta go. Can we speak another time?'

'Don't forget to send the money for my appointment.'

'What appointment?'

'My facial refresh! I told you. Do you even listen to me?'

By *facial refresh*, I guessed she meant another facelift. Mum was obsessed with trying to freeze time. She was convinced that the only way to keep her boyfriend, Alejandro, from straying was to have different treatments to look younger.

She'd had so much done already. If you asked me, she didn't need to. But who was I to tell her what she should or shouldn't do with her body or face. I was just the cash machine she used to fund it all.

'Send the details and I'll take care of it.' I couldn't say no. She was my mum and I felt bad about what Dad had put her through.

'Good. And stop shagging around! Bye, son.'

'Bye, Mum.' I hung up and put my head in my hands.

Jesus. Did she really believe I was like him? My chest tightened.

Anyway, I didn't have time to worry about that shit. I had to think about Mia.

I wondered if she'd seen the pictures. I needed to warn her. After dialling her number and putting it on loudspeaker, I swung my legs out of the bed. The phone rang out. Either she was busy or she'd seen the photos and was avoiding me.

As tempted as I was to look online to see how bad it was, I decided against it.

I'd like to think that now they'd got a photo, the paps would leave us alone. But I knew from experience that this was only the beginning.

14

MIA

As embarrassing moments go, I'd had a few. But they paled in comparison to seeing a photo of me trying to pull my knickers out of my arse splashed all over the internet. What a way to introduce myself to the world and my new 'relationship'.

If the bottom picking wasn't enough, my mascara smudges made me look like a deranged panda and my hair... God. Because I'd taken off my hat, my bun was lopsided and messy. And not in the sexy, undone way models wore their hair on the catwalk. Mine was more dishevelled than chic.

Everything about that photo had *just fucked* vibes.

After Liam had pulled me inside, he'd tried to calm me down, but I'd been adamant that I needed to get out of there. Luckily there was a gate at the end of the garden that I was able to slip out of and I got the Tube home.

He'd offered to get me a cab, but he was already doing me a favour. I didn't want any more charity.

When I woke up I hoped this had all been a nightmare. No such luck.

'Good morning, M.' The corner of Trudy's mouth twitched. 'Or should I call you Liam's new *mystery lady*?'

'Don't!' I groaned.

'So I see operation FBF has started with a bang!'

'FBF?'

'Fake Boyfriend! Did his publicist call the paps? I was surprised at the pics. I thought you'd get them to take a more flattering photo. *Oh… I get it.* You wanted it to look like you'd genuinely been caught out. *Smart.*'

'What? No! We didn't arrange it. At least I don't think so…' No. Liam and I weren't friends anymore, but he wouldn't want to humiliate me.

'Why were you picking your bum?'

'It was those awful knickers Boris bought. They were wedged up my bum and I was trying to pull them out! I didn't know I was going to get papped. And I forgot to put on mascara at home yesterday, so I used an old one I found here and it didn't agree with me. Hence the panda eyes.'

'Ohhhh. Well… don't worry. Today's news is tomorrow's chip paper.'

'But the story's *online* too!'

'Nothing you can do about it now. Just make a note to adjust your underwear *inside* the house from now on. And anyway, there's no shame in it. There's not a woman on this planet who can't relate to their mascara running or having an involuntary wedgie. And look on the bright side.'

'There's a *bright* side?' My eyes widened. 'The only bright side would be if the entire internet disappeared.'

'Course! Now the world knows you and Liam are an

item. The first seed of your relationship has been sown. And you're one step closer to winning Matchmaker of the Year!'

True. The photo wasn't planned. But it did hint that we were together, which was exactly what I needed.

Plus, seeing as we were focusing on the positives, at least people weren't ripping me or my appearance to shreds. They put my sorry state down to us having a good time in the sheets. It could've been worse.

But this was a warning. I needed to be on high alert at all times. Who knew when the next pap might strike? We had to be better prepared.

It was only a matter of time before they started asking questions. And I didn't know anything about my 'boyfriend' apart from the fact that he was a promiscuous actor who made mediocre action films and liked to take his shirt off at every opportunity to make money.

People would want to know not just how we'd met, but what I saw in him. Of course, as much as I disliked him, you'd have to be blind not to see he was hot, so they'd assume it was his looks.

Thanks to those photos, they'd also think we'd already slept together. But there'd need to be more to it than just sex.

Ugh. I shouldn't even be thinking of Liam and us having sex. It made me want to take a shower. Not a cold one to cool my libido down. I needed to wash away those dirty thoughts. I'd *never* sleep with someone like him.

Anyway, for this relationship to look real, we'd need some common ground. Shared history was a good start, but we had to do better.

I picked up my phone to send Liam an emergency

message, then sighed. I'd had two missed calls from him already.

I really needed to change his name in my contacts. 'My Hot Boyfriend' was so lame.

Me
Saw the photos. We need to meet. ASAP!

He came online. After a few seconds he started typing.

My Hot Boyfriend
Yeah. I can do tomorrow night. But I should come to yours.

No way.

At school, I'd had a bright future ahead of me. I wasn't the smartest. I didn't get top marks and excel at everything like my sister, but I did okay.

Teachers thought Liam was the class clown and would never amount to anything. He'd had the last laugh, though. Liam was the school's most successful student. Ever. And now they didn't shut up about it.

Liam knowing my business was in trouble and my love life was crap was bad enough. I didn't want him to see the shithole I was living in too.

Me
No. Too many nosey neighbours. Can you come to my office instead? You can come through the back door.
My Hot Boyfriend
Wow. So soon? Shouldn't we at least kiss first?
Me
What?

My Hot Boyfriend

You said I could come through the back door. That has another meaning…

Me

Oh my God. Seriously?

My Hot Boyfriend

It was a joke!

My Hot Boyfriend

Sorry, I forgot. You wouldn't understand that kind of joke because with that stick up your arse, there's no room for anything else!

Me

I do NOT have a stick up my arse!

My Hot Boyfriend

Sure, sure.

My Hot Boyfriend

I can come around seven. Sorry, let me rephrase: I can ARRIVE at your office around seven. Send me your address.

Me

Fine.

After sending it over, I logged off, steam coming out of my ears. Even texting Liam was annoying.

We'd barely been fake-dating for twenty-four hours and he was already winding me up. Surviving the next two months together was going to be torture.

15

LIAM

I pulled my baseball cap down and slid through the back door. Of Mia's office building. Didn't know why I'd made that joke before. Thinking about Mia in that way was just... wrong. I had no interest in sliding into any of her entrances. Fake-dating her was already way too messy.

Mia stood at the entrance in another fitted dress which clung to every one of her curves. My gaze dropped to the ground. I didn't want her to catch me staring again and get the wrong idea.

'This way.' She signalled.

'After you.' I stepped behind her.

As she climbed the stairs, I swallowed hard. I knew I wasn't supposed to be looking at her like that, but you'd have to be blind not to notice how good her arse looked in that dress. Did she work out? It looked firm. So did her calves. Her black stilettos accentuated them perfectly.

And her scent. I'd noticed it when she came to my place last night and when I went downstairs this morning it still lingered in the air.

It was floral, but not in that old-fashioned way. It was like a bouquet of sweet, freshly cut flowers that you just wanted to inhale.

Not that I was thinking about burying my head in her neck to sniff her. There was nothing wrong with a man appreciating a woman's perfume. It didn't have to mean anything.

Mia opened the door to a sleek office. My eyes were drawn to the red sofa which was shaped like a pair of lips, and somehow my gaze drifted straight to Mia's. She'd always had a pretty mouth.

'Hey, you!' Trudy said, stopping my thoughts from wandering down a very slippery slope. 'Welcome to our office!'

'Hey, how's it going?'

'Good! Don't worry, I'm just leaving. Got a play tonight.'

'What you going to see?'

'*Forgiving Salma.*'

'I heard about that. It's in Soho, right?'

'Yeah! How did you know?' She got up from her desk.

'I love the theatre.'

'I can get you tickets if you like?'

'That'd be great.'

'Excellent! Text me or let your *girlfriend* know and I'll sort it.' Trudy smirked. 'Right, I'll leave you lovebirds to it!' She closed the door.

'You wanted to talk?' I walked to Mia's desk.

She sat behind it, legs crossed and arms folded. Mia looked powerful. Like a woman in control. If it was anyone else, I would've said it was hot.

The women I slept with usually had a pretty face and

good body, but not a lot going on in the brain department. That was fine, though. I wasn't looking for anything serious. My days as an action star were numbered, so I didn't want to spend them tied down with a wife and kids.

But if I ever dated someone properly, I'd like a strong woman who knew her own mind and didn't take any shit.

Someone with their own career and goals. Not someone who was dependent on me and agreed with everything I said.

Mum had fucking worshipped Dad. She'd cooked, cleaned and done every damn thing for him and it still wasn't enough. As much as I hated being pulled away from London, I was glad she'd finally had the strength to leave.

'That's right,' she replied. 'We need to get to know each other better.'

'Oh yeah?' I smirked, wheeling Trudy's chair in front of Mia's desk and sitting opposite her. 'What d'you have in mind…'

'Get your mind out of the gutter. There's more to life than sex!'

'Is that so?' I arched a brow and Mia sighed. 'So if you don't like to swing from the chandeliers, what do you do for fun?'

Mia froze. From the way her eyes had widened, you'd think I'd asked her to multiply nine million by seven, then divide it by twenty-three.

'It's not a trick question. Tell me some of your hobbies.'

'Well, I… I like reading.'

'Okay, just like when we were kids.'

'Yeah and watching TV and films.'

'Action by any chance?' My mouth twitched.

'No. Definitely *not* action.'

'So you've never seen any of my films?' I teased. Mia started playing with the paper clips on her desk like they'd suddenly become interesting.

'Maybe one or two,' she murmured. 'Anyway, what about you?'

'Me? Apparently sex is my only hobby. That's what you think, isn't it?'

'Can you blame me?'

'Actually, I can. We grew up together. You should know me better.'

'That was years ago. We're adults now. People change.'

'Sure'—I paused—'but in many ways they stay the same. That's why this "let's get to know each other better" interview thing is kind of pointless.'

'Trust *you* not to take things seriously. This is important! People are going to start asking what we see in each other. Why we're together. And if we don't study each other's personalities, they'll know we're lying!'

This was *so* Mia. What I'd said was true. Although we'd matured, I bet we hadn't changed much. Physically, yeah. Mia was cute when we were teenagers, but she'd blossomed now, in *every* way. But her personality seemed the same. She was still serious. Still obsessed with doing everything by the book.

'That's not how you get to know someone. You do that by spending time with them. We did a lot of that, so I know you better than you think.'

'You don't know anything about me anymore.' She folded her arms.

'You still terrified of spiders?'

'Well, yeah. But most people are. Except you.'

'Yep. And are you still afraid of wooden lollipop sticks?'

'Ugh!' She shuddered. '*Don't!* Just the thought of them makes me cringe...' She shivered again. 'I know it's irrational, it's just... the thought of touching or licking them makes me shiver. You know, like when people—'

'Drag their nails down a blackboard,' I finished her sentence.

'*Exactly!*'

'And is your favourite ice cream flavour still tutti-frutti?'

'How did you...?' Her jaw fell open. I tapped the side of my head.

'You still a fan of games, like Guess Who, Connect 4 or Jenga?'

'Oh my God! I haven't played those in years!' she laughed and her face lit up. It was a nice change to see her smile. All she'd done since we met up again was scowl like she was plotting different ways to murder me as slowly and painfully as possible. 'I always used to beat you at Connect 4.'

'*Always* is too much to say. Occasionally is more accurate.'

'Dream on! And remember when my parents took us to Brighton and we played Hangman in the car and you cried because you kept losing?'

'I was ten years old!'

'Such a bad loser!' she laughed again and the corners of her eyes crinkled. She'd always had pretty eyes. For a devil.

'You're evil! How can you find such joy from laughing at my pain?'

'Because it's funny! You were always so competitive.'

'So you *do* remember something about me from back in the day.' I leant forward, propping an elbow on her desk.

'Yeah, I remember.' Her smile dropped. 'Too much…'

I was tempted to ask what she was thinking, but didn't want to get heavy. I liked the Mia from a minute ago. The one who smiled. Like she used to. Before things went to shit between us.

'To answer your earlier question, I like reading. Mostly non-fiction, but I don't mind the occasional thriller.' There was something else I loved, but I'd stopped. I hadn't shared details of that project with anyone and I wasn't gonna tell Mia. She'd laugh. 'I enjoy cooking and baking too.'

'Baking? Come on! Action hero Liam Stone does not *bake*!'

'I do! Not so much these days because I have to watch what I eat, but I enjoy doing it when I can. Who used to help your mum in the kitchen when she was baking for family parties and school fairs? It wasn't *you*.'

'Oh yeah! I forgot about that.'

'Like I said, I'm pretty much into the same things now as I was then.'

More or less.

There was a time I was kind of into Mia. But not anymore.

'Okay.' She held her hands up in surrender. 'You've made your point. Maybe we do know each other a bit more than I thought.'

'Wanna know how we can get to know each other even better?'

'Liam! You're obsessed!' She rolled her eyes.

'What?' I frowned. 'No! I wasn't thinking about that! Sounds like *you're* the one who's obsessed! Been a long time, has it?' I couldn't resist. It was like she had 'please wind me up' stamped on her forehead.

'What were you thinking, then?' She raised her eyebrow, deliberately ignoring my question.

'We've just started a relationship, so we need to go out. Properly. So what do you say, Mamma Mia? Wanna go on a date?'

16

MIA

'Please don't call me that!' I snapped, annoyed at the stupid nickname. 'You know I hate it.'

'It's cute! So? Shall we go on a proper date on Friday night? Don't leave me hanging, sweetheart.' He clutched his chest, causing my gaze to fall there.

I'd tried (and failed) not to look at his body all evening. His burgundy jumper clung to his defined pecs and I could see the outline of every muscle. Not to mention his toned shoulders and firm arms. I had to get a grip.

I couldn't believe that he'd remembered all those things about me.

My fear of spiders was something anyone could guess. But remembering how much I disliked lolly sticks and my favourite ice cream flavour? I would've thought that had evaporated from his mind years ago.

Of course there was a lot I remembered about him. Like how ticklish he was. Not under his armpits or his feet like a lot of people, but along his ribcage.

And how when he ate a pizza he pushed the edges of the slice together—almost folding it in half before he took a bite.

Yep. All that still lived rent-free in my head. So did the time he promised to be my date for the school dance but then went with Natalie instead. And when he moved to Spain without bothering to say goodbye.

'That's a stupid question. You know I'll go on a date with you. We already agreed to that in our contract. Actually, let me clarify—I'll go on a *fake* date. Obviously if this was real, there's no way I'd accept.'

'If this was for real, you wouldn't be able to resist my charms.' He smiled, flashing his annoyingly cute dimples, then licking his lips.

I watched in a trance as his tongue moved across his mouth for a few seconds before coming to my senses.

'I'd rather stick pins in my eyes than spend time with you voluntarily. This is just part of the deal. Nothing more. It's just business.'

'If you say so, sweetheart.'

'And stop calling me sweetheart! My name is Mia. Not Mamma Mia, not sweetheart, just Mia.'

'Everyone knows people in relationships use terms of affection. So you'd better learn to suck it up.'

'I think we're done for the day.' I rubbed my temples. This man was insufferable. 'Message me the details for our *date*. And try and think of somewhere pretty. I have the first interview for the competition on Friday afternoon, so I'll probably be stressed. And if I have to suffer a whole evening of your company too, I need a nice view to distract me.'

'You mean my gorgeous face isn't enough?' He smirked.

'Oh my God.' I blew out a frustrated breath.

'Leave it to me. I know exactly where to take you.'

17

MIA

'Do you think it'll take much longer?' I glanced at my watch nervously as the beautician applied what felt like the third layer of blusher on my cheeks whilst the hairdresser stood behind me tugged on my hair.

This time, I was leaving nothing to chance. If I was going to be papped on my date with Liam tonight, I needed to look good. That was why as soon as I'd got to the office yesterday morning, I'd rung my favourite salon to book a hair and make-up appointment.

Unfortunately, because it was Friday, they were fully booked. So were the next three salons I tried, but thankfully, I'd found one online that was able to squeeze me in and said that they could manage Afro hair.

At first I was grateful, but with every minute that passed, my stomach sank a little more.

Because my hair and make-up were being done at the same time, they'd faced me away from the mirror so I couldn't see what was being done. And that worried me.

The hairdresser had been backcombing my hair for

what felt like forever and had emptied at least one can of hairspray on my head.

At first when the make-up artist suggested she apply some false lashes, I was excited. I'd always wanted to try them, but chickened out. She was a professional, though, so she knew what she was doing, right?

But now the lashes had been applied, my lids felt heavy, like they were carrying two big wings. I had a very bad feeling about this...

I turned my thoughts to the first competition interview I'd had earlier this afternoon. It had gone okay. Especially considering I'd spent the morning feeling low after following up with Joss, the potential new client who'd called last week. She'd decided not to sign up, which was a blow.

But I'd put on my game face for the brief interview with Susie. A colleague was supposed to join her, but cancelled at the last minute.

Susie was impressed with the office, which was a good start. She'd looked over the client sign-up form and asked me a few questions about the case studies I'd submitted last week, my matchmaking methodology, what I thought my unique selling points were as an agency and stuff like that. And of course, she asked me if I was in a relationship.

Luckily, I was able to say yes, and before she got a chance to probe any further, her phone rang. She said she had to go but would call soon to arrange the home interview.

And that was that. At least another phase of the interview was complete. I should feel relieved, but as the hairdresser sprayed another layer of lacquer over my hair, my shoulders tensed.

'Almost done!' she chirped.

'Can I have a look?' I tried to turn to face the mirror.

'Not yet!' The make-up artist forced the chair back. 'You'll ruin the surprise! You're looking a-mazing, hon!'

I glanced at my watch again. It was seven fifteen. Liam was picking me up at eight. It'd take at least twenty minutes to get back to the office and I still had to get dressed.

'Sorry, but I've got to go.' I'd been sitting in this chair for two hours and my bum was aching. 'I'm sure everything's fine as it is.'

'You're done!' The make-up artist waved her brush dramatically.

'Now for the big reveal!' The hairdresser spun my chair round to face the mirror. '*Ta-da!* What do you think?'

Oh. Dear. God.

My eyes flew from their sockets.

They'd given me a beehive. But not the sexy kind. This one was so high you could fit an elephant's arse in it.

And as for my face, imagine a child stole their mum's make-up bag and decided to use every item. Three times over.

Instead of the smoky eyes I'd asked for, she'd given me two black eyes (worse than the panda eyes I'd been papped with).

The fake lashes looked like I had spider legs hanging from my lids (and I hated spiders), the bright red lip liner was wonky and the blusher hadn't been blended properly.

And don't get me started about the foundation. Instead of matching the red tones of my brown skin, it was at least a shade too light and looked grey and streaky.

'It's er... very'—*awful, horrendous, an absolute shit-*

show—'*unique…*' I jumped up from my chair. I wasn't lying. It really was unique. I'd never seen anyone look this bad. 'The foundation shade is too light,' I blurted out.

'That was the darkest shade they do.'

'Maybe you should try a different brand? Like Fenty Beauty, MAC, Lancôme or…' Or literally anyone. Most decent brands recognised that they needed to cater for a wider range of skin tones.

The women looked at me like I'd just suggested they lick dog shit from my big toe. I could see I wasn't going to get anywhere.

'How much do I owe you?' I grabbed my jacket.

'Normally we'd charge two hundred, but for you, we'll do it for one fifty. And if you do a TikTok video saying how much you love it, next time we'll give you a bigger discount!' She grinned.

One hundred and fifty pounds to be made to look like this? It was daylight robbery. But I didn't have time to argue. After handing over my debit card, I left, walking as quickly as I could back to the office.

As I turned down my street, I looked at my watch again. Ten to eight. There was no way I'd be able to scrape all this crap off my face by then.

Liam would already be on his way, but maybe he could take a detour to give me some extra time. I pulled out my phone to text him.

Me
So sorry, but I'm running late.

. . .

My office building was now in sight. I hoped Trudy was still there. Making myself look half-decent was going to be a two-woman job.

My Hot Boyfriend
I'm already here.

Shit. Hopefully I could slip inside before he saw me.

But just as I approached the building, the car door of a black Mercedes swung open and Liam stepped out.

My eyes widened. Not just from the shock that he was here, metres away from me, but also because, wow. He looked so... *good*.

His hair was freshly cut, his square jaw looked smoother than a baby's bottom and he was dressed in smart trousers and a crisp white shirt with the top buttons undone. I swallowed hard.

'Mia?' He frowned. 'Is that *you*?'

At that moment I remembered I was wearing about twenty-five layers of ugly make-up and my hair so big my head might not fit through the door.

Seeing anyone right now was embarrassing, but standing in front of the guy that was voted Sexiest Man Alive *twice* was next-level mortification. Dancing naked along Oxford Street would be less humiliating.

'Don't say a word!' I warned. 'I need time to scrape this off and...'

'It's okay,' he said softly. 'Take all the time you need. I'll let the restaurant know we've been held up.'

Oh. I knew I'd warned him not to say a word, but the way I looked right now was ripe for teasing. I thought he'd start making stupid jokes, but he actually seemed understanding.

'Thanks. I'll message you when I'm ready.'

He nodded, then got back in the car.

After slipping through the door, I headed upstairs. Trudy had left, so I went to the bathroom. The bright glare of the overhead lights made everything look worse. I grabbed a stack of paper towels, ran them under the tap and started scrubbing.

Water alone wasn't going to be enough to get this warpaint off and the strong hand soap would probably irritate my skin, and I was already worried about the cheap make-up they'd used.

To rescue my hair, I'd need to wash it, which would take hours.

Just as I contemplated slumping on the floor, my phone rang.

'I'm sorry!' I said to Liam. 'I'm going as quick as I can, but…'

'I wasn't rushing you. I'm at the back door with supplies. Come down.'

He hung up.

Supplies?

My stomach churned. Although I'd scraped off the lipstick, the eye make-up, blusher and foundation weren't budging, so I didn't want to give him another opportunity to see me looking like crap. But I had no choice.

Reluctantly I went to the door. Liam was clutching a large bag.

'I wasn't sure what to get, so I brought a selection.'

'A selection of what?'

'If you let me in, I'll show you.'

When we got to my office, he tipped the bag's contents on the sofa.

My jaw dropped. There were face wipes, cleansers, cotton wool pads, coconut oil, a facecloth and a load of other stuff.

'The shop assistant said these were the best brands. Oh, and the face wipes are biodegradable, so they won't pollute the sea.'

I went to open my mouth, then closed it again. Liam had bought a load of products to help me remove my make-up because he knew I hated it.

That was so... kind.

'Th-thank you.'

'No big deal. I got the feeling that wasn't the look you'd asked for...'

Still lost for words, I opened the creamy cleansing lotion and smeared it over my face before wiping it away with several tissues.

'It's coming off well.' Liam's gaze met mine and my stomach flipped.

'Y-yeah,' I stuttered. 'One layer down. A hundred more to go!'

Liam didn't laugh. I shifted in the sofa. I knew how to deal with jokey Liam or annoying Liam, but *nice* Liam? That threw me off guard.

'The cleansers will remove the make-up, but you'll need something else for the lashes. Unless you wanted to keep them?'

'No way!' Loads of women wore fake lashes and they looked nice and natural. These didn't. 'I can't wait to get these spider legs off.'

'Where are your toilets?' He grabbed the bowl, coconut oil and spoon.

'Down the hallway on the left.'

A few minutes later he returned with a bowl of water.

'Close your eyes,' he commanded.

I did as I was told. The sofa shifted. Liam had moved closer. His rich scent filled my lungs.

My heart stalled, then raced. I hadn't been this close to Liam since... since maybe never and it was freaking me out.

I tried to keep calm, but when he swiped the damp cotton pad over my eyes, it became impossible.

'That okay?' he said softly.

I nodded. I couldn't talk right now. I couldn't even think straight.

'On the way back from the shop, I called a make-up artist friend and she said to use hot water, soap and coconut oil to loosen the glue, then hopefully the lashes will fall off.'

I attempted to speak again, but still couldn't. There was something so calming about the heat of his palms resting against my cheek. The soothing sensation of the warm pad sliding across my lids and his hot minty breath tickling my skin when he spoke.

As I thought about how close he was to me, my pulse raced. This felt so intimate.

'There,' he said. 'No more lashes. You can open your eyes now.'

I didn't want to. I wasn't sure how they'd react to seeing Liam's perfect face right in front of me.

'You okay?' I heard the concern in his voice. I had to

open my eyes. If I just remembered I was here with annoying Liam, I'd be fine.

Except right now, he was being anything but annoying.

I opened my eyes slowly and a flurry of tingles raced through my body.

How was it possible for someone to be so attractive? His big brown eyes sparkled and his lashes... God, it was so unfair. If I had lashes like that I wouldn't have even considered getting fake ones.

His lips were parted and for a second I wondered how it would feel to have them pressed against mine.

'You good?' He frowned, pulling back.

'Y-yeah, I was just...' He'd have to be blind not to notice me staring, so I had to address it before he thought I liked him. 'I was just thinking how unfair it is that you have such long eyelashes.'

'Don't tell anyone, but these are extensions.' He fluttered his lids.

'Really? They look so natural!'

'I'm joking!' he chuckled.

'Oh!' I slapped his arm gently. God, it was even firmer than it looked.

'Mum used to say the same—that long lashes were wasted on me.'

'She's right. You're already too pretty for your own good.'

Oops, that slipped out. My cheeks heated.

'So you think I'm pretty?' He fluttered his lashes again.

'Um, well, you do modelling and stuff, so... I... I better check my face.' I jumped up from the sofa, then picked up a handful of products.

Once I was in the bathroom, I let out a deep sigh. As if I hadn't embarrassed myself enough already today, I had to blurt out the fact that I thought Liam was hot. Well, I didn't use that word exactly, but close enough.

I squeezed my eyes shut, not wanting to look in the mirror. But I couldn't hide forever, so I opened them slowly, ready to assess the damage.

Oh.

Ginormous beehive aside, I looked *much* better. All of the eye make-up had gone. There was just a smidge of foundation on my jaw.

I grabbed the washcloth and swiped it off. This cleanser was good.

'All gone!' I declared triumphantly as I returned to the office.

'Cool. Feel better now?'

'Much. Thanks again.' I sat back on the sofa.

'It was nothing.' He waved his hand dismissively. 'What made you... you know, get that done?'

My throat went dry. This was awkward.

'I... I wanted to look nice. I didn't want to get papped again looking like shit.'

'What? You never look shit. In all the years I've known you, you've always looked'—he paused, his eyes meeting mine—'good.'

Liam Stone thought I looked *good*? That was a revelation.

'*Come on.*' I rolled my eyes. 'Even with my awful thick black glasses?' For a couple of years in my teens I used to wear glasses and I hated them because they were so ugly. But it was all my mum and dad could afford.

'Even with your *adorable* black glasses.'

Liam held my gaze.

'Oh,' was the only word I could muster.

I was still trying to process what he'd said. Had he liked me back then? Before, I would've said that was a hard no. But now, now I was questioning everything I thought I knew about him.

'So.' He broke the silence. 'Rain check on dinner?'

'Okay.'

My heart sank. Surprisingly, the last hour or however long it'd been with Liam hadn't been horrible.

Plus I hated that he'd got dressed up and I'd wasted his time.

Maybe a rain check was for the best. I was tired, so wouldn't be great company, and I wasn't even sure if my dress would fit over my head.

'You free Monday night?'

'Yeah,' I said a little too quickly.

'Great.' Liam stood up to leave. 'It's a date.'

18

LIAM

I rubbed my eyes. I hadn't slept well since Friday night. I couldn't stop thinking about Mia.

Not in a sexual way. Yeah, she was pretty, but like I'd said from the start, I was never gonna go there. I just felt bad, that was all.

Ever since we'd agreed to this fake-dating thing, I hadn't given enough thought to the impact this could have on her.

Sure, I'd warned her about the paps, but I hadn't been explicit about the toll it could take on you mentally if you weren't fully prepared.

I was used to the scrutiny, and most of the time I didn't give a fuck what they said.

They didn't really comment negatively on my appearance. When they objectified me, I just took it in my stride. But the press weren't so kind to the women I was papped with. They always had something to say about their clothes, hair and make-up. And when you weren't used to that scrutiny, it could screw with your self-esteem. So seeing Mia's face covered in make-up and her hair like that worried me.

Mia was naturally beautiful. Whenever she wore make-up, it was subtle and sophisticated. Nothing like the heavy layers on her face when I came to meet her. She was normally confident, but when she couldn't look me in the eye, I knew she was embarrassed and that I needed to help. So I got those supplies.

It was only when I was paying that it occurred to me that I might get recognised. But Mia needed me and that was all that mattered. And the look of relief on her face when she saw the products proved it was worth the risk.

For once, we didn't argue, and seeing that softer side of her took me back to the good times we'd spent together as kids.

There was something about that moment when I removed those fake lashes. Sitting there, our faces just inches apart, with her bare skin, listening to the sound of her breathing and inhaling her beautiful scent was so calming.

When my gaze dropped to her full lips, for a second I wondered how they'd feel against my mouth. Were they as soft as I'd always imagined?

I'd quickly pushed those stupid thoughts away and was glad when her eyes opened so we could go back to being normal around each other.

Hearing her confirm that she'd got her hair and make-up done because she was worried about looking nice for the paps cracked my heart. That was when I realised that although I'd weirdly been looking forward to dinner with her, it wasn't a good idea. She needed to go home.

I'd planned to take her to a swanky restaurant in

Mayfair where the probability of being photographed was high. Although it would've served me well to be seen with someone sophisticated like her for a second time, Mia wasn't ready for another experience with the paps. I needed to protect her.

So tonight I was taking her somewhere more low-key that was away from the spotlight. But first, I had to check she was sure she could handle the shit that came with being with me. It wasn't too late for her to back out.

'We're here,' Phil, my driver, announced. Mia had asked me to meet at her office again. I pulled out my phone.

Me
I'm downstairs. You ready or do you need more time?
Tutti-Frutti
I'm ready. Coming down now.

My lips curved into a smile as I looked at the name I'd used for her. I was tempted to put her as Mamma Mia, but I knew how much she hated that nickname, so I chose her favourite ice cream instead.

Minutes later, the back door opened and...

Wow.

I lowered the window to get a better look before she saw me.

Tonight, her make-up was natural. Much more her. Her hair was styled into an elegant updo, with a few loose tendrils falling around her face.

She was wearing a fire-engine-red knee-length dress and, as always, looked elegant. Most of the women I dated always had their cleavage on show. No judgement from me. How they dressed was their choice. But Mia never seemed to wear anything low-cut. Yet she still looked sexy. Maybe it was the mystery of wondering what was underneath.

Wait. Why was I even thinking about Mia naked?

'Hi,' she said as she got closer.

I jumped out of the car and held the door open for her.

'Oh…' She frowned. 'Thanks. But you didn't have to…' She slid onto the black leather seat and I got in next to her.

'This is a date. It's something that I always try and do.'

'Right. Course.'

Mia might think this was a joke to me, but when it came to work, I took that shit seriously. I was a professional. Mia had asked me to play a role, and so I was gonna give it my all.

By the time I returned to LA in October, the world would believe we were madly in love. Only me, Mia and Trudy would know that it was fake.

'You look pretty.' I turned to face her as Phil set off.

'Thanks. Is that part of your dating spiel too?' she whispered.

'No. It's the truth.'

Her eyes widened, then she started fidgeting with her handbag. Something told me she wasn't used to getting compliments.

'So.' Mia broke the silence. 'How was your day?'

'Busy. I had an early start with my PT, then calls with my agent and the shoot people all day.'

'You have a personal trainer?'

'Yeah, Nate. I've known him for years and he's helping to get me in shape for my next movie.'

'Right... so if you're not preparing for a film, do you just look like an average guy, with a beer gut and moobs?'

'Not really. Even if I'm not filming, there's always some kind of shoot or something that demands I take my top off.'

Some days I thought about how freeing it'd be not to have to worry about what I ate, but this was how my life was, so I didn't have a choice.

'Admit it! You love the attention. Women wanting to jump you, men wishing they could be you.'

'What can I say?' I shrugged my shoulders. 'There are worse ways to earn a living.'

That was what I told myself every day. Maybe one day I'd believe it.

'And you?' I deflected the focus onto her. 'Do you enjoy your job?'

'I love it!' Her face brightened. 'Well, the matchmaking part. The business side of things, not so much.'

'When I heard you'd left banking, I was surprised.'

'How did you hear?'

'Oh, you know. On the grapevine.'

Otherwise known as Google. She used to work in a local bank. But she didn't need to know I'd regularly looked her up over the years.

'At least you didn't hear that I was running a brothel.'

'What?' My eyes bulged.

As Mia filled me in on how her relatives gossiped about her job, I caught myself smiling.

This was how it used to be. Her chatting about something crazy her family had said and us finding it funny. Her brown eyes sparkling, her face animated. This was the Mia I always liked. Not the version that avoided me.

'I know people can change, but to go from a goody-two-shoes to a madam would be a stretch, even for you.'

'I'm not a goody-two-shoes!'

'You were...'

'Okay. Maybe.'

'So what made you get into it, then?'

'Running a brothel?' Her mouth turned into a smile. I wished she did that more often. As much as I enjoyed sparring with her, I liked smiley Mia a lot more. 'I always loved how my gran set people up.'

'Granny E., right? How is she?'

'She passed a few years ago.'

'Shit. Sorry to hear that,' I said softly. Mia swallowed hard. 'She was a really lovely woman.'

'She was. And she really liked you too. Whenever she made her coconut drops, she'd always give me a batch to give to you.'

'I remember. They were delicious!'

Those Jamaican coconut drops were one of my favourite snacks. They were pieces of fresh coconut chopped into pieces, then covered in a kind of ginger and brown sugar syrup.

'Yeah. Makes me hungry just thinking about them! So yeah, she was the inspiration. I started matching friends at uni. At first it was the obvious stuff, like, *Oh, you like Alicia Keys, you should meet Sylvester. He's a big fan of her too*. But then I got braver. So if I overheard someone talking about something I knew my single friends were interested in, or say I saw someone playing tennis in the park that I thought looked nice, I'd ask them if they were single, show them a photo of my friend who was crazy about Wimbledon and see if they were interested.'

'Wow. That's kinda weird and cool at the same time.'

'Yeah!' she laughed. 'I got some strange looks and comments, but most people were fine when you explained. And because it wasn't for me, somehow that made it easier.'

'And I guess it worked?'

'It did! And once I'd done it for a few friends, people started asking me to help them out.'

'Is that what led to you starting the agency?'

'Kind of. I did it on and off for a while and always thought about doing it professionally. Trudy and I always said we'd follow our dreams by the time we were thirty. But it wasn't until I heard about Sarah, a friend of a friend who had a disastrous experience with a matchmaker, that I gave it serious thought.'

'What happened to her?' I leant forward. This was actually interesting.

'Well, first she set her up with a guy in his seventies, when she'd asked to date someone of a similar age. She was thirty-five and recently divorced. Then the matchmaker said she'd found someone who Sarah would be perfect for. It was her ex-husband. The one she'd just divorced!'

'No way!' I laughed.

'Yes, way! So I thought I must be able to do better than that. I offered to find her someone for free, and when I did, she said I should set up my own agency. I'd wanted to for ages, so I decided to go for it! I love the idea of bringing two people together. It's the most rewarding feeling.'

'Good for you. I'm glad you followed your dreams.' What I'd said the first time she came over to my place was wrong. Although I didn't believe in marriage, I was genuinely happy she was doing something she loved.

'Like you did.'

'We're here, sir,' Phil announced via the intercom.

'Great, thanks.' I undid my seat belt, grateful that now I could avoid responding to Mia's last comment.

'Where are we?' Mia glued her face to the window. 'Wait. No way!'

I stepped out to open the door for her again.

'Mademoiselle.' I held out my hand.

A jolt of something shot through me. Her palms were soft and her hands seemed tiny wrapped in mine, but it felt surprisingly nice.

'But this is... Chung's?'

'Yeah. You still like Chinese, right?'

'Course, but I didn't think you'd bring me *here*.'

'Sorry.' My face fell. 'If you want, we can go somewhere else?'

'No way! I'm just surprised, that's all. It's perfect!'

Fake date or not, hearing those words fall from Mia's lips was a relief.

The date had started well.

We'd survived a whole journey without strangling each other.

Now I hoped we could survive the rest of the night...

19

MIA

As Liam placed his hand on my lower back and guided me to the restaurant door, my heart thundered against my chest.

I'd sent an emergency message to my brain to calm the hell down, but clearly my body hadn't got the memo. When Liam had taken my hand to get out of the car, that same feeling had raced through me.

His palm was big and warm and it felt so comforting. It'd been ages since a man had touched me.

But then I remembered. This was a *fake* date. Liam was just playing a part. He said so himself. Hopefully I'd get used to pretending soon too.

'Mr Stone,' the waiter greeted him. 'Welcome. Madame.' He nodded in acknowledgement. 'Please. Follow me.'

The man led us through to a large room. It was empty except for a single candlelit table in the centre.

'I can take it from here.' Liam nodded.

'Very well. We will start bringing the food shortly.'

Liam stepped forward and pulled the chair out, then gestured for me to sit down.

'You're really going all out on the whole chivalry thing.' I raised an eyebrow.

'Standard date behaviour.' He shrugged.

I had to admit: I kind of liked it. Opening the car door, pulling out the chair. I knew in this day and age, equality was important, but there was something romantic about it.

And I could slap myself for thinking it, but I also liked when Liam called me pretty. Even if it was pretend. When he'd said it, a weird tingly sensation raced through me.

This time, I'd done my own hair and make-up. Even though I'd had to apply my eyeliner twice because my hands wouldn't stop trembling, I was happy with how it turned out. I knew what suited me and made me comfortable. I'd much rather be photographed being a hundred per cent myself rather than looking like a cheap imitation of someone else.

'Are they bringing the menu?' I liked to look at it as soon as possible because it took me ages to figure out what to choose.

'No. I've already ordered.'

'You've... wait, what?'

'You heard.' He folded his arms.

'That's taking the chivalry thing too far. I can choose my own food.'

'Really?' He raised his eyebrow. 'This restaurant closes at eleven and it's already close to nine. No offence, but if we waited for you to choose, the kitchen would be closed.'

'That's...' Shit. He was right. 'But how will you know what I like?'

'Salt and pepper prawns? Vegetable spring rolls? Satay chicken?'

Dammit.

How did he remember these things? We'd had Chinese takeaway a few times as teenagers, but that was years ago.

'I *suppose* that's okay…' I said, not wanting to admit he was spot on.

He'd been right about a lot. Like his decision to bring me here.

Back in the day when this restaurant first opened, it was the talk of the town. I'd always wanted to go. Liam and I had even spoken about saving up enough money to take me, so I'd hoped we could go after the school dance. But of course that had never happened.

'So did you ever end up coming here?' Liam asked.

'No, but I always wanted to.'

'Why didn't you come with your ex?'

'Boris wasn't really very adventurous when it came to food.'

Our relationship wasn't that exciting. We moved in together when we were twenty-four and quickly settled into a routine. When I left uni I got a customer services job at a local bank and Boris went into sales. After work we'd come home, have dinner, watch TV and go to bed.

Boris always went to the pub with his friends on Fridays and Saturdays and would rather watch football with them than go on a romantic evening out with me. If I wasn't at home reading or watching TV, I'd meet up with Trudy or go to my parents'. It was scary how easy it was to get stuck in a rut and how one year just merged into the next.

'I never understood what you saw in him.' Liam shook his head.

I'd asked myself the same question so many times.

'I thought he was… nice.' That was true. To a degree.

I'd thought it was because I loved him. But really it was the familiarity and safeness I believed the relationship gave me. That sense of belonging.

At the time I didn't think it was a bad relationship, per se. I'd reasoned that it could've been a lot worse. Boris wasn't violent or physically abusive. I'd believed he was faithful and we got along okay. I just thought that it was natural for things to go a bit stale after you'd been with someone for a while.

I knew from the single friends that I'd eventually paired up how hard it was to find a partner. I listened to their stories of the failed dates. And I told myself I was lucky to have found love so young and that I didn't have to go through what they did.

When I decided to start my own business, I was disappointed that Boris wasn't supportive, but I let that slide. With all the extra work that was coming my way, the last thing I needed was extra stress. I thought it was better to have the stability of a long-term relationship. I believed it'd impress clients too. Little did I know that Boris's actions would force my hand. There was no way I could stay after what he did to me.

'Are we talking about the same Boris? The one I remembered used you.' Liam was right again. 'Why did you break up?'

'I'd rather not talk about it.' I swallowed the lump in my throat.

'Fair enough.'

'And you? Did you ever have a proper girlfriend?' I quickly deflected the question onto him.

'What do you mean by *proper*?'

'A girlfriend that lasted more than one night...' I raised my eyebrow.

'So you don't want to talk about your relationships but you want me to talk about mine?'

'I was just... making conversation.'

'Food will be here in a minute.' He rested his elbows on the table, then fixed his gaze on me. I was glad he'd changed the subject, but why was he staring?

'Do I have something on my face?' I dabbed the napkin around my mouth self-consciously.

'No.' He didn't look away. I reached into my handbag and pulled out my powder compact. I must have lipstick on my teeth.

'You're *staring*,' I whispered.

'I'm not staring, I'm looking into your *beautiful* eyes.'

'What?' I blinked quickly. 'Why?'

'Because we're on a date... and like I just said, the food will be here soon, which means so will the waiters...'

'Oh... oh, yeah. Got it.' I nodded absentmindedly. 'Sorry.'

God, I was rubbish at this. I should be getting into character too. I needed to smile a bit more. Then I'd look happy. I started grinning and tilting my head to the left and then to the right.

'What's wrong?' Liam's face creased.

'Nothing,' I said, my cheeks beginning to tremble, 'I'm smiling because I'm *so* happy to be on a date with my *hot boyfriend*.'

'You don't look like you're smiling. You look

deranged. Maybe take it down a notch. And what's up with your neck? Did you pull a muscle?'

'No! I'm trying to look playful,' I murmured. 'Like how flirty women move their head seductively and then play with their hair.' I tugged a tendril from my updo and wrapped it around my finger. 'Ouch!' I'd pulled too tightly.

'This is explaining a *lot*,' Liam sighed.

'What?'

'Now I understand why you didn't want to take GCSE drama... And if this is how you flirt, it kinda explains why you've been single for a while.' He smirked.

'Arsehole,' I mouthed, shooting daggers with my eyes.

'*Now, now*,' he whispered, the corner of his mouth twitching. 'Play nice. Remember, you're supposed to be crazy about me.'

There was a knock at the door and we quickly sat up straighter. Liam reached over and put his hand on top of mine.

Whoa.

A bolt of electricity shot through me.

My eyes bulged and I remembered I had to compose myself.

He's touching my hand because he's acting. Like I should be doing right now.

'I'm *so* glad we reconnected after all these years, sweetheart.' Liam looked into my eyes and his gaze was so deep it was like he was staring into my soul. Someone give this guy an Oscar.

Now it was my turn to say something.

Lights, camera, action!

'Me too, honey pie.' I grinned, then remembered what

he'd said about taking it down a notch, so tried to reduce my expression to a simple smile.

This acting thing was harder than it looked. And it was weird holding eye contact for so long. I was tempted to look away, but had to keep up the pretence, so I followed his lead and stared deep into his eyes.

He had really nice eyes. They were dark brown, like rich, creamy chocolate buttons, but they also sparkled like someone had sprinkled them with diamonds.

And his lashes. Like I'd said the other day, they were unbelievably long and curled up at the tips like he'd used one of those painful-looking eyelash curlers. It was so unfair.

His eyebrows were pretty amazing too. Thick, but naturally defined. They framed his face perfectly and I bet he'd never even had to suffer getting them plucked, waxed or threaded.

Actually, looking into Liam's eyes wasn't as hard as I'd first thought. Maybe it was because I'd compared them to chocolate buttons.

Yeah. In future, whenever I needed to do this faking stuff, if I just imagined Liam was covered in chocolate, it'd be easy to pretend I liked him.

A vision of melted chocolate drizzled over Liam's bare chest, along his muscular arms and all over his body flashed into my mind.

'Sorry to interrupt.' The waiter stood at the table, clutching plates.

I was glad he'd spoken. I didn't like where my train of thought was going. I should not be imagining Liam naked or covered in chocolate.

Get it together, girl. Time to perform.

'Oh!' My hand flew to my chest dramatically. 'I didn't even see you come in! I was too busy gazing into my *boyfriend's* amazing eyes.'

The waiter chuckled and laid the plates down on the table.

Yes! He was convinced. My acting skills weren't so terrible after all.

It felt weird saying the word *boyfriend* out loud. It'd been so long. For a second, I felt a flutter of happiness, then reminded myself again that it wasn't real. I was just as single now as I was two weeks ago.

'I will leave you to it.' He smiled and quickly left the room.

'*Honey pie*?' Liam raised his eyebrow.

'What? You said that people give their partners terms of affection. There's nothing wrong with honey pie! Everyone loves honey and everyone loves pie. It's a compliment.'

'If you say so.' He yanked his hand away from mine and I instantly felt the drop in temperature. His palm was so nice and warm. But now the waiter had left, there was no need for him to keep up the pretence. I tore my gaze away from his face. He'd dropped the act, so I should too.

Wow. I took in the sight of the food in front of us. There was a lot. But one dish in particular stood out.

'You ordered salad for me?' I frowned.

'It's for me, not you. But you can have some if you want.'

'And you said you hadn't changed. The Liam I used to know would never come to a Chinese restaurant and eat *salad*!'

'I have a shoot coming up, so I have to watch what I eat.'

'So all the good stuff's for me?'

'Yep. I don't get to look like this by eating fried food.' He gestured to his chest.

'You really think a lot of yourself, don't you?' I shook my head.

'It's my job.'

'What, to be arrogant?'

'I'm not arrogant. I'm *confident*. I play a ripped action hero, so it's my job to look good. Is it working?'

My eyes bulged, then dropped to my plate. It was obvious he looked good. It didn't have to mean anything.

'I suppose you're not completely hideous,' I said, keeping my tone neutral. I wasn't giving him the satisfaction of boosting his ego.

'I'll take that as a compliment.'

'Take it however you want.'

'Actually, you've given me multiple compliments tonight. Maybe you're not so bad at this faking stuff after all. Then again, you dated Boris for years, so I'm sure you got pretty used to doing that...' He laughed.

Right again. Boris hadn't exactly rocked my world in the bedroom. But after thirteen years, that was normal, right? Those mind-blowing orgasms in the films were fake. Actors did a million takes to make it look like they were having the time of their lives. But it didn't happen in real life.

'We're not talking about him, remember?'

'My bad. How are the prawns?'

I'd been so busy thinking, I hadn't even eaten yet.

'Oh God!' I groaned with pleasure as I took the first bite of the salt and pepper prawns. 'These are *so* good!'

Liam's face lit up like a firework and my stomach flipped. Right in that moment I was catapulted back to when we were kids. When he used to wait for me after school and we'd walk home together. Or when I'd ring his doorbell and he saw I was on his doorstep. He'd always had a great smile.

It wasn't just the fact that he had amazing teeth— perfectly straight and even and white (but not that fake white that was so bright you needed sunglasses, just natural looking). It was also those damn dimples.

Wasn't it enough that he had that great body, those eyes, that mouth, and that panty-melting smile? Why did he have to have cute dimples too? It was as if there was some kind of *order one great feature, get a dozen free* deal on when he was being created.

His dad was good-looking and his mum used to do modelling, so it made sense that he'd inherited their hot genes.

'Glad you like them.'

As Liam ate his salad and grilled chicken, I polished off the rest of the prawns. He had the willpower of a saint. I didn't know how he managed to smell the gorgeous aroma of chilli, pepper and salt and not be tempted.

In between eating, we chatted easily, with Liam filling me in on his mum, who still lived in Spain, and me talking about my family.

When the waiters had returned with the mains, Liam put on a show again. This time he'd stroked my hand and my brain scrambled. Before I knew it, we'd finished eating and Liam had asked for the bill.

'Shall we split it?' I asked. Fake dating was my idea, so I wish I could've paid for everything.

'No.' He shook his head. 'I've got this.'

I was about to protest but he shot me a look that said not to bother.

'Thank you,' I said as the waiter approached.

'My pleasure, sweetheart. You know how much I love to treat you.'

The waiter smiled, lapping up Liam's performance.

Once he'd paid, Liam walked over and pulled out my chair. My traitorous stomach flipped again. Couldn't believe I kept getting jelly legs because a man moved a piece of furniture I was capable of moving myself.

Just as my stomach recovered, Liam placed his hand on my lower back, guiding me out of the room, through the restaurant and onto the street.

My pulse raced. I tried to calm it down, but I could feel Liam's gaze burning into me. I made the mistake of looking up at him by my side. Our eyes locked and it sent my pulse through the roof.

'Did you like it?'

'Y-yeah,' I stuttered. It would be much easier if I looked away. But I couldn't. And anyway it was rude not to look at a person when you were speaking to them, right? 'The food was great…'

We stopped outside the restaurant and Liam scanned the street.

'Phil should be here. I asked him to wait outside.'

Just as I was thinking about where I should ask Phil to drop me off and whether to get the train or the bus home, Liam leant forward.

What the…

I froze as his mouth came closer to my face and just as I thought he was aiming for my lips, he moved to my ear.

'Don't freak out,' he whispered, 'but the couple by the window are taking photos of us, so I need you to smile, then laugh like I said something funny.'

I knew women were renowned for our ability to multi-task, but Liam clearly thought I was a magician. All my brain power was currently being used trying to ignore the fact that he was so close to me. I didn't have any bandwidth left to do anything else.

Liam's warm breath tickled my neck and his scent was intoxicating. It was woody like always, but it was mixed with the fresh lemon from his water.

'Any time now would be good,' he whispered again. 'And I just spotted a pap across the road, so put your hand on my chest and look into my eyes like you think I'm amazing.'

My hand. On Liam's chest?

Sure, sure, sure!

No problem.

A fake laugh and a fake touch-up of his chest coming right up!

The fact that he'd asked me to do all of that and expected me to be totally casual about it was funny in itself.

Channelling my inner actress, I threw my head back, laughing, then as Liam moved his head away and stood in front of me, I lifted my hand, ready to touch him.

I can do this. It's just a chest. I used to touch Boris's chest. Okay, that was different to touching a muscular torso like this, but still. No big deal.

After raising my palm, I quickly placed it on his firm pecs.

Holy hell.

Liam's chest was even firmer than it looked. It was like touching a brick wall. Well, if a brick wall was warm and comforting. His heart raced. He must be nervous about being photographed too. Which reminded me. There was something else I was supposed to be doing.

Liam leant forward.

'Good, now when I pull away, I need you to look at me like you want to take me home and fuck me.'

Whoa.

If my pulse was racing before, Liam's words had just set my veins on fire. I swallowed hard.

'O-okay,' I said, stroking his chest.

Liam pulled back slowly, then brushed his thumb gently across my cheek.

Doing as instructed, I looked up at him. His chocolate-brown eyes were molten. I'd underestimated him. His acting skills were off the charts, because he actually looked like he wanted me.

I bit my lip.

His thumb traced my jaw, then my chin.

We stood there, frozen. My hand trailing along his chest, our eyes locked. Desire flooded my veins as I replayed the words he'd just said:

I want you to look at me like you want to take me home and fuck me.

If I was going to be convincing, it would be better if I allowed myself to think about it. Just for a second. To get myself into character.

I imagined Liam opening the door for me to get into

the car. He'd look at me like I was a banquet of forbidden food he couldn't wait to devour.

He'd pull me into him, press his lips onto mine and kiss me passionately.

But because he was so highly sexed, he wouldn't wait for us to get home. So he'd suggest we do it in the car. I'd be hesitant at first, because I'd never done anything so risqué, but when I felt his hardness pressed against me, I wouldn't be able to hold back.

I'd push Liam down on the back seat. After asking if it was okay, I'd unbuckle his belt, pull down his trousers and...

'Mia?'

Liam would want me so badly he'd be calling out my name.

'Mia!'

'Sorry...' I was so deep into the fantasy of me doing unspeakable things with Liam that I'd completely zoned out.

'Phil's here.' He moved, causing my hand to fall from his chest. 'You did great, though. I was hoping that coming somewhere low-key like this, we'd avoid the paps, but everyone has a phone, so it's kind of impossible. But I think you'll be much happier with the photo this time. Come on.' He rested his hand on my back as he led me to the car. 'Let's get you home.'

Liam had said I'd be happier with the photo, but right now I couldn't think about that. My mind was too busy trying to work out how my thoughts had taken an unauthorised detour with Liam down Sex Dream Street.

That wasn't supposed to happen.

There was a big 'No Entry' sign that said so.

When he said, 'Let's get you home,' he meant dropping me off, not to have sex. Those words were just to help me act in front of the camera.

We were *fake*-dating. With a heavy emphasis on the fake.

And the sooner my stupid brain understood that, the better.

20

LIAM

As Mia slid onto the back seat, her dress moved above her knee. I tried to look away, but couldn't resist stealing another glance of her smooth skin. What the hell was wrong with me?

I knew she'd look good tonight, but that red dress was fire. *Damn*.

When I said she looked pretty, I meant it. But the way my cock reacted wasn't right. This was a *fake* date. Dick twitching was not allowed.

I thought I'd got my shit under control. But when I took her hand to help her out of the car I realised I was in trouble. Her palm wrapped in mine felt kinda *nice*. Like when you've been out in the cold, you get home and wrap yourself in a warm blanket.

What the fuck? That sounded so damn cheesy.

Liking that feeling wasn't good, so I'd let her hand go and decided to rest my palm on her back instead to guide her inside the restaurant.

That wasn't much better, though. My hand almost

slipped down to her butt. And don't even get me started on how good it looked in that dress.

Putting my hand on hers at the table seemed to surprise her. The fact that I liked it was a shock to me too. It felt too comfortable, which was why, as soon as the waiters left, I pulled away. This was a job. I was playing a role. Pure and simple. There couldn't be any blurred lines.

Easier said than done, though.

Seeing the fried food and not being able to eat it was torture. But it didn't compare to the temptation of watching Mia devour those prawns.

When she squeezed her eyes shut and groaned with appreciation, I imagined how she'd sound if she experienced a *different* kind of pleasure.

Telling her to look at me like she wanted to take me home and fuck me was asking for trouble. I knew Mia loved chocolate, so I could've said, "Look at me like I'm a giant brownie." But I said what I said because it was what I was thinking.

Could you blame me? Like I said, she looked hot.

In my defence, she was stroking my chest. And even though I'd asked her to, she was looking at me like... like she *did* want me.

I'd always remembered her being terrible at acting in drama class, and she wasn't a good liar. But tonight, she was acing pretending to like me.

But this was Mia. And knowing how much she hated me, that couldn't be true. All these crazy thoughts had no business being in my head.

'You can just drop me at the station. I'll get the train home.' Mia stared out the window.

'No way.' I shook my head. 'I always make sure my date gets back safely.'

'I'll be fine!'

'Maybe. But it's late and I'm already a bad sleeper, so I don't need to be up all night, worrying about whether you made it home or not.'

'Awww.' A mischievous grin spread across her face. 'Would you really worry about me?'

'Of course, sweetheart.' I stroked her cheek, then drew my hand back. The privacy screen was up, so I didn't have to put on a show. 'You're my girlfriend. I'm not letting you get the train when I can take you, okay?'

'Okay,' she sighed. I pressed the intercom button.

'Phil, I'd like to drop Mia home first, please.'

'Yes, boss. What's the address?'

After Mia told him where she lived, she shuffled in her seat. She seemed uncomfortable.

'You okay?' I whispered.

'Yeah,' she murmured.

There was a long pause. She wasn't okay, but it didn't feel like it was my place to probe her.

Bad word choice. The sooner I dropped Mia home and pushed these thoughts out of my head, the better.

'It's just…' She paused. 'The place I'm renting. It's temporary. It's…'

'Doesn't matter,' I said quickly. 'No judgement. Okay?' She nodded.

As we pulled up outside her block of flats, I admit, I could understand why she was apprehensive bringing me here.

The streets were covered with litter, there were a group of rowdy teenagers loitering, holding beer cans, and the downstairs window of the ground floor flat was boarded up like it'd been smashed.

Was this place even safe for her to stay in? I ground my jaw. I knew it wasn't my business, but I didn't like the thought of her staying here.

Never in a million years would I have pictured Mia living somewhere like this. Not because I was judging her. We were both from the same working-class background.

It was strange because Mia was always so careful with money, so I was surprised she was renting. Having a mortgage was more her style.

She was also a clean freak. She'd be the type to have plastic covering her sofas to stop them getting dirty. I'd always imagined her living somewhere immaculate, so to be living here, things needed to be pretty bad.

And I wondered why, if she needed money, she didn't get a bank loan.

Something told me there was more to her story than she was letting on, but it was Mia's business, not mine.

'Thanks for tonight.' She unbuckled her seat belt, avoiding my gaze.

As she went to open the car door, I grabbed her arm.

'Wait. Let me walk you up to your flat.'

'No,' she jumped in. 'Thanks, but it's better if you don't. This car already stands out. Someone might recognise you and we'll be drawing the wrong kind of attention. Like I said, I'll be fine.'

'Okay, but text me as soon as you're inside.'

'Will do.' She looked up, her gaze finally meeting mine. I couldn't put my finger on what was behind her eyes. Maybe vulnerability? Like she was apprehensive about me seeing what her life was really like.

This building was worlds apart from the polished office that she rented and the immaculate image she presented. But to me it didn't matter. I knew who she really was. I wished she remembered that.

'Well.' She paused. 'Goodnight.'

'Goodnight,' I replied, wondering what to do next. Normally, it was clear. Once I went home with a woman, the night was only headed in one direction: straight to Sexville. But what did you do at the end of a fake date?

We'd discussed how long this would last, the number of dates, and agreed not to see other people, but not talked about moments like this. Like whether we'd pretend to kiss or what level of physical contact was allowed.

We hadn't even discussed sex. That was because as far as I was concerned, it was implied that it was never going to happen. But for some reason, now it felt like something that we might need to address…

'So, I'm going now,' Mia said.

For a second, I wondered if she was thinking the same. Whether she was waiting for me to kiss her.

Did I *want* to kiss her?

It wasn't the worst idea. Better that we had our first kiss now instead of in front of the cameras. Less pressure.

I leant forward an inch. Then two more.

Mia's lips parted and her eyes widened.

All it would take was one move for my mouth to be on hers.

The loud rumble of a car alarm pierced the air, snapping me out of my thoughts. I yanked my head back.

WTF.

Was I seriously considering kissing Mia? On the lips?

I needed my head tested.

'Get inside safely.' I leant forward again, this time pecking her softly on the cheek and trying not to inhale her sweet floral scent.

'I-I will,' she stuttered before opening the car door.

After waving to Phil, she walked up the pathway to her building, pushed the front door open, then waved again.

She'd barely left the car a minute ago, so why was I already wondering when I would see her again?

21

MIA

'No need to ask how your first date went!' Trudy grinned as I stepped into the office. 'Those snaps of you guys last night were smoking! Did you go back to his place and fuck like horny teenagers? Is that why you're late?'

'No!' I sat down. 'It was...' I lowered my voice. 'It wasn't real.'

My stomach jolted. I'd be lying if I didn't admit that there were moments where it felt like I wasn't acting. And I enjoyed 'performing' more than I should, but they were just moments.

Anyway, I was only human. Who wouldn't get hot under the collar (or in my case, a little damp in the knickers) after stroking Liam's chest?

'Yeah, right!' She grabbed her phone and breezed over to my desk. '*This*'—she zoomed in on the photo on her screen—'does not look fake. Look at your face! Look at his! You're practically snogging! Everything about that photo screams *I want to take you home and rip your clothes off!*'

Liam predicted I'd be happier with these pictures and he was right.

My dress looked nice. It fitted me well. The lighting in front of the restaurant was surprisingly flattering. Our pose looked authentic. Liam was gazing into my eyes like he thought I was amazing and, yeah, I seemed totally smitten. His acting advice had worked like a dream.

The press had printed my name too. No idea how they'd found out, but I guessed it was easier once they had a clearer photo of me.

'The reason it looks so real is because that's what Liam said to me just before the picture was taken.'

'Come again?' Trudy gasped. 'Liam told you he wanted to take you home and rip your clothes off? You lucky cow!'

'No! He told me to look at him like I'—I felt awkward repeating it—'wanted to take him home and... and *fuck* him.'

'Oh my God! You two are *so* gonna get it on!'

'Never going to happen!' I scoffed. 'Like I said before, it's not real.'

'*Sure, sure.*' Trudy smirked. '*Whatever you say.* You've only been on three dates and already you're looking at each other like *that*. Imagine what you'll be like after two months!'

'We've been on *one* date, not three! And I told you, I won't fall for him. He's a man whore who lives thousands of miles away.'

'That may have been your first proper public date, but the

first time you went to his house was a date. And when he caressed your face, oops, sorry, took off your make-up, that was too. Every time you meet up, it brings you closer together. The sparks are gonna fly, babes! You mark my words!'

My phone rang and I was grateful for the interruption. Trying to explain to Trudy that she was deluded was exhausting.

On the plus side, she was the only other person who knew the truth. And if she was convinced we were crazy about each other, that meant the rest of the world would believe it too.

'Hi, Mum,' I answered.

'Sweetheart! I saw the photos! Why didn't you tell me you'd reconnected with sweet little Liam? The phone's been ringing all morning! I told your father you'd find someone soon. We were all so worried after Boris broke your heart.'

'I know, Mum.' I swallowed hard. My parents were shocked when I told them what he did. He didn't visit my parents' house often, but when he did, he'd bring Mum flowers or chocolates (whatever was cheapest at the supermarket). Not because he cared. It was all for show.

'But look at you now! Dating your childhood sweetheart! We're so happy for you!'

Oh crap. I supposed I should be grateful that the family had only seen the photos from last night and not the earlier Bumgate snaps.

It was awkward. Lying to the judges and people I didn't know was one thing, but my parents knew Liam, so not telling them the truth was different.

Actually, was it really so bad? People lied all the time to get ahead. It was no different to *tweaking* your CV. My competitors did worse. This was a good lie. It wasn't impersonating a surgeon, just pretending to like someone.

Plus, Mum sounded happy that I wasn't going to end up like a lonely cat lady (I hated that stereotype). If I fessed up now, she'd be disappointed. And I wasn't like Alice. I hadn't done much lately to make her proud.

Thinking that made me wince. Was being photographed with a man really how my worth and achievements were measured?

Anyway, back to focusing on the positive. Everyone was convinced Liam and I were an item. This was *good*. If Mum had seen the photos, that meant that the industry (and hopefully the competition organisers) may have seen them too. The plan was working.

But as much as I didn't want to burst Mum's happy bubble, I had to manage her expectations.

'It's still very early days… remember, he lives in LA, so who knows how long this can last?'

Yes. That was good. I was setting things up for the future.

When this fake-tionship ended, I'd refer back to this conversation and quote the *long distance putting a strain on the relationship* spiel that Liam and I had agreed on.

'You two are made for each other. You always were. This is fate!'

'Mum, we were just friends back then, not…' I caught myself.

Despite the fact that it wasn't true, saying we were childhood sweethearts would actually make our story sound more convincing.

Note to mention that in the interview.

My stomach twisted. This all seemed so manipulative.

So contrived. Doh. That was the point. I couldn't help feeling a bit guilty, though.

'Yeah, you're right,' I added. 'It *must* be fate. What are the chances of us bumping into each other after all of these years?'

'Exactly!' Excitement bubbled in her voice. 'So how did it all happen? Tell me everything!'

'Um, I'd love to, but maybe another time? I've just got to the office and I've got loads on.'

And even though Liam said to stick to the truth, I haven't rehearsed the story of how we met properly yet.

'Course, darling! Your father's calling me back to bed anyway... *stop*! Chris! Our daughter's on the phone. Behave yourself!'

Mum giggled like a schoolgirl and I winced at the thought of what my parents were getting up to. It was nice that they were still in love. If only I could find my perfect match like they had. And my grandparents and Alice.

'And that's my cue to leave...!'

'Hold on. Can you two come for lunch on Sunday? It'd be lovely to see Liam again.'

I should've known Mum would suggest this. I might've got away with faking it in front of the cameras, but I couldn't pull it off in front of my parents.

'Sounds nice, but...' *Think, think, think.* 'I've got to do the housework.'

I slapped my forehead. I *did* need to do the housework, but *come on*. I could've come up with a better excuse than that.

'Forget about the chores!'

A light bulb went off. I'd be better at lying if I made it about Liam.

'Liam has to… work.' *Yes. Good save.*

'On a Sunday?'

'He's a big star! *Busy, busy, busy!*' My voice went up ten octaves.

'Oh, I understand. Well, tell him I said hello and that when he gets time, we'd love to see him again.' Phew.

'Will do.' My shoulders relaxed. 'Speak soon.'

'Bye, darling,' Mum said.

I hung up and blew out a breath. Hopefully she wouldn't ask us to come round again, but knowing Mum, I wouldn't get off the hook that easily.

'So, is she convinced?' Trudy asked.

'Yep.'

'Excellent! And don't feel guilty. People lie all the time,' Trudy added, reading my mind. 'Especially in the bedroom. I did it last night with some dude I hooked up with: '*Course I came, honey! You're the best lover I ever had!*' Trudy threw her head back laughing.

'You hooked up last night? Where did you meet?'

Just as Trudy was about to spill, the phone rang. 'Hold that thought! Good morning, Soulmate Connections, how may I help you?'

'May I speak with Mia Bailey?'

'Who may I say is calling?' I replied in my best telephone voice.

'It's Susie from the Happily Ever After Awards.'

'Susie! Hi! This is Mia speaking.'

'Hi! Lovely to meet you last week.'

'Same here!'

'Are you free next Monday for the home interview?'

'Should be fine. Let me just check my schedule…' I rustled some paper to make it sound like I was flicking through my diary. Then I remembered that most people used the calendar on their phone and felt stupid. 'I have a couple of openings. What time did you have in mind?'

'Does six thirty work?'

'Perfect!'

'And will your, erm, partner be there?'

'My partner?' I asked before remembering I had one. It was going to take time to get used to it.

The fact that she'd asked about my partner confirmed what I'd always suspected: they preferred entrants to be in a relationship and used the home interview to unofficially check we'd be a good fit for the magazine feature.

It also meant she'd seen the article.

'We heard you're dating Liam Stone. You're a very lucky lady!'

'Yes, I am,' I said as calmly as I could. 'I'm sure he'd love to be there. I'd just need to check his diary.'

'We can change the time to suit him or come at the weekend?'

She seemed more interested in meeting Liam than interviewing me. That had to work in my favour, though, right? Having a high-profile 'boyfriend' on top of my matchmaking record hopefully meant I had a good chance.

'I'll ask him and get back to you ASAP.'

'Great! We really feel it's beneficial to conduct these interviews with the nominee's partner present, so we can get a feel for your relationship and values. A great matchmaker isn't just someone who brings other people together. They know how to build a strong relationship within their own lives too. After all, you wouldn't trust a plumber to fix your sink if he had a leaking tap in his own house!' She laughed loudly.

I disagreed. You could still be a great matchmaker and be single. But the objective wasn't to be besties with Susie. It was to win the competition.

'I understand,' I said diplomatically. 'Leave it with me.'

'Great! Look forward to hearing from you.'

'Speak soon.' I hung up.

I blew out a breath. If they wanted to meet next Monday, I needed to check Liam was free, then double down on the preparation.

There was no going back now.

We needed to ace this interview.

My future depended on it.

22

LIAM

'Congrats!' Geena chirped. 'You've been papped with the same woman twice!'

'Very funny,' I groaned as I sat on the shitty sofa.

'At least this time she didn't have her hand up her butt and you looked respectable. Well, you looked like you were ready to take her to bed, but what's the deal with this Mia chick? Annalise needs to know if she's gonna have to deal with another kiss-and-tell while she's trying to negotiate this set-up for you. Being seen with another woman isn't helping.'

'No. I told you: she's an old friend. I trust her. We have'—I almost said we had an agreement. Then I reminded myself that I wasn't going to tell Geena or Annalise anything about our fake relationship—'a connection.'

'Is that what you're calling sex these days?'

'We haven't slept together.'

'You're joking, right? When I saw that photo, I expected a follow-up story to drop with you two banging on the sidewalk. You two do *not* look like people who are not about to get busy.'

'So anyway, I don't need Annalise to set me up with anyone. Mia and I... we're... *together*.'

Silence.

'For real?'

'Like I said, we're dating. This isn't a one-night thing. It's more serious than that.' At least all of that was true.

'Well, shit!' Geena laughed. 'Never thought I'd see the day! Okay, honey. I'll speak to Annalise.'

'Any news on that role?'

'I told you: I'll let you know. How's training going?'

'Good. I'm ready for the shoot.'

'Great. Don't fuck this up.'

I ended the call.

At least she was convinced that me and Mia were together. Like I'd predicted, the photos had come out well. We looked like we had serious chemistry. And I knew Geena wouldn't be the only one to notice I'd been seen with Mia more than once.

For anyone else, that wouldn't be a big deal. But me being spotted with the same woman twice was verging on serious relationship status. I wouldn't be surprised if the tabloids started talking about wedding bells.

That meant that I was good at my job. I knew how to make the audience believe I was the character I was playing. As for things going any further, hell no.

I admit: I'd had a few weak moments around Mia yesterday, but I had it under control. I was keeping out of trouble, just like Geena told me.

One date down. Only three more to go.

How hard could it be?

23

MIA

As I sat back on the bus, a wide grin spread across my face. Today had been great.

The date for the Happily Ever After Awards home interview was confirmed. Liam was leaving for a fragrance shoot and meetings in Paris on Thursday morning, but said he'd be back by Monday afternoon.

My phone had blown up with texts and messages from friends and family saying that I was a 'dark horse' and gushing about how happy they were that Liam and I were together.

Even Aunty Doreen had called to offer her congratulations. Anyone would think I'd invented a cure for a serious disease.

Still, I wasn't complaining. As sad as it was to admit it, I was happy. *Relieved*. Not just that the plan was working, but also because I felt accepted. I'd even got a few excited calls from people in the industry.

The press had been surprisingly nice. The articles had complimented my outfit. That was two articles in a row that'd been positive, so I'd worried over nothing. Journalists weren't so bad after all.

And maybe I might get a decent new client or two off the back of this exposure, which wouldn't hurt. I needed all the business I could get.

A message notification sounded. It was Alice in our family group chat. I thought maybe she'd messaged about me and Liam being 'together', but when I looked, it was a photo of her and Jack on a beach in Bali.

Alice

Can you believe this was taken two years ago! Such wonderful memories!

Mum and Dad had replied with gushing comments. I supposed if I was madly in love like her, maybe I'd be wrapped up in my own life too.

Alice was lucky to have found her perfect partner. When she'd first brought Jack to meet us not long after she started university, I was surprised they'd hit it off because I never would've put them two together. He was quiet, reserved and into heavy stuff like politics and watching historical documentaries, whereas Alice was more outgoing and into fashion and parties. But I supposed in their case opposites did attract.

They got married when they were twenty. Some people said they were too young, but they proved the haters wrong. Alice was lucky that Jack was ready to commit so quickly. I was with Boris for more than a decade and he always put it off.

First he suggested we wait until we lived together. Then he said it made sense to do it after we bought our own place. After that it was "don't you want to wait until we can really afford your dream wedding?"

He used to make me feel guilty by saying, "You keep talking about marriage... am I not enough for you as I am? I'm starting to think you care more about being able to show off a diamond ring than about us just being happy together." Which of course wasn't true.

Oh, and then there was the time he said, "My parents got married, then divorced eight years later. Mum's been with her partner for twenty years since then and they're not married—which would you prefer?"

Arsehole.

Anyway, he'd done me a favour. I was better off without him. One day I'd find someone who shared my values just like Alice had.

After typing out a quick reply to say what a lovely photo it was, I pressed the bell to get off at the next stop. The bus pulled over and I stepped outside. The temperature had plummeted. I pulled my scarf tighter around my neck and headed towards my street.

My thoughts drifted to Liam and when he'd dropped me home. Given the choice, I'd never have let him see where I lived, but he was insistent that he wanted to make sure I got home safely, which was sweet.

God knows what he must've thought.

I wasn't here by choice. I used to live in a nice house in Clapham with a mortgage I shared with Boris. But one morning, I'd received a call from the bank that sent my whole world crashing down.

They'd told me that multiple mortgage payments had been missed. I said there must be a mistake. Boris was taking care of the finances. I'd always managed them—

after all, I used to work in a bank. But when he saw how busy I was trying to run my new business, he'd offered to take over.

At the time I was grateful that he was finally showing an interest and being supportive.

Little did I know that he was using the money that was meant for bills to invest in some crazy get-rich-quick scheme. Later I discovered he'd also used it to pay for hotels and expensive gifts for different women.

To avoid me seeing the statements and getting caught, he always intercepted the post and moved everything online, using his own password.

I was so focused on my agency, I hadn't kept track. And the rare times I did remember to ask to see statements, he'd get jumpy and ask if it was because I didn't trust him. Then I'd feel bad, try to convince him that I did, then say not to worry about showing me. *So stupid.*

I didn't find out that I was right to have doubts until it was too late.

Once he'd maxed out his own credit cards, he'd started to use mine. By the time the bank called, he'd run up so much debt that we had to sell the house to cover it, and even then, the perfect credit rating I'd worked so hard to build was ruined. Which meant I couldn't get another mortgage, loan or credit card.

I'd tried to speak to the bank, but it was my fault. I shouldn't have shared the PIN for my credit cards. I should've been more insistent about checking the statements. I shouldn't have trusted him. But I did. And now I had to suffer the consequences.

That was why I had to rent a flat in this crummy area. And why now, I always paid every bill as soon as I received it and insisted on getting hard copies of everything and triple-checking that everything had been paid.

It would take years to repair the damage Boris had done. Not just financially, but also emotionally. Knowing that I wasn't enough for him, so he went elsewhere, multiple times, didn't exactly help my self-esteem.

But it wouldn't be forever. There was a good man out there for me. My *soulmate*. I had to believe that. Otherwise I couldn't do my job.

Now the plan was working, I had to do whatever I could to win. This competition could change everything. With that prize money, I could get my business off the ground properly and start building my credit rating back up. Then hopefully in a few years, I could find somewhere half-decent to live.

As I turned the corner and walked towards my building, my eyes flew from their sockets. Half a dozen photographers were outside.

I ducked behind a van. Two men walked towards it, then stopped.

'Dwayne, d'you know which flat a chick called Mia lives at? The posh-looking one.'

'Who wants to know?' said a deep voice. Sounded like the boy who lived at the other end of my floor.

'Dem paps. Said they'd pay.'

'How much?'

'Dunno. Lemme ask.'

Their footsteps faded. This wasn't good. Yeah, I could hold my handbag up to my face to avoid being photographed. But what worried me was that they wanted to know which flat I lived in.

What if they got inside the building? It wasn't difficult.

The lock on the front door didn't work properly. They could wait outside my door or worse.

I fished my phone from my bag and called Liam.

'Hey,' he answered after a few rings. 'What's up?'

'I'm trying not to freak out, but there are some photographers camped outside my building and they're asking my neighbours what flat I live in. They're offering them money and I... I don't know what to do.'

'Shit. You hiding somewhere?'

'Yeah. Behind a van. Across the road.'

'Okay. You can't stay there. I'll send a car right now. Is there a shop or somewhere you can go and wait?'

'I could go to the train station. That's not too far.'

'Good. Text me the details and I'll send someone.'

'Where will they take me? Trudy's at a show, so I can't go to hers. I could go to my parents', but I don't want to bring this to their house.'

'Come to mine.'

'What? Thanks, but you live miles away, so it'll take ages to get back here later.'

'You won't be going back there. It's not safe. We can argue about this later. Get to the station and send the location before they spot you. Okay?'

'Okay.' My heart thudded.

Although I agreed that the most important thing was to get away from here, there was no way I'd be staying at Liam's. Once the photographers realised they wouldn't get a photo of Liam or us together, they'd go home.

I peeked around the van. More photographers had arrived. I had to leave before it got worse.

After unwrapping my scarf from my neck, I draped it over my head, hoping that it'd serve as a better disguise. I checked the coast was clear, then raced across the street. Several minutes later, I arrived at the station and sent Liam my location.

It wasn't long before my phone vibrated. I answered the call.

'Car's outside. It's a black Mercedes. I'll text you the number plate. I'm on my way home now, so I'll see you there.' Liam hung up.

I spotted the car and the number plate matched, so I headed outside.

'Mia?' The driver got out.

'That's me.'

'Come.' He opened the car door. 'Let's get you home safely.'

He'd said he was taking me *home*. Except he wasn't.

I was going to Liam's and he wanted me to stay there.

Overnight.

During our date, I'd struggled to keep my cool around him for a couple of hours. But at least I knew I could go home and compose myself.

But tonight we'd be sleeping under the same roof and that was a *whole* different ball game.

24

LIAM

When I opened the car door and saw Mia's face, my heart bloomed.

Then I saw the fear in her eyes and my chest tightened.

The photos of us last night were a success. But they'd also fanned the flames. Now the press wanted more.

I shouldn't have put Mia in this position. I should've known that once they'd got her name, it was only a matter of time before they found out where she lived and tracked her down. I should've warned her.

My first instinct was to take her in my arms and tell her everything would be okay, but we didn't have that kind of relationship anymore.

'You okay?' I asked. She nodded. 'We'll drive the rest of the way in my car.' I opened the door wider and held my hand out for her.

The heat from her palm instantly set my blood on fire. Her hand was just as soft as I remembered and I loved how it felt.

Phil drove us a few streets away to the house, where, unsurprisingly, there were a load of photographers.

'When you get out, try to look straight ahead instead of at the cameras, okay?' I said. Mia nodded again.

Once we were safely inside, my shoulders loosened.

'That was… intense.' She exhaled loudly.

'If this is too much for you…'

'It is a lot, but I'll be fine. I've just got to get used to it, that's all. I'll change the times I leave work and get home.'

'Your office seems secure, but your flat doesn't. You can't go back there. Not for at least a couple of weeks, until this calms down.'

'I can't just leave home! All my stuff is there.'

'We'll get you new stuff.'

'But—'

'*Mia*,' I said firmly. 'What security do you have there?'

'Well, nothing. The main door doesn't always close, but… I thought about it and I overreacted. There must be rules about paps trespassing.'

'If the public are responding well to photos of us, they'll be sold for a lot, so the paps will do whatever it takes to get them. It's safer to stay here. There's cameras and an alarm system, and if it gets bad we can hire security.'

'But where will I sleep?'

'There's four bedrooms. Well, technically two, because one's been converted to a gym and another into an office, but there's a spare room my friend uses for storage. You can stay there.'

'I don't know…' Mia chewed her lip and I could hear the wheels turning in her brain as she weighed up the options.

For me it was simple. The most important thing was keeping her safe.

'Okay,' she said softly. 'This was my idea, so for this to work, we have to go all in. And it'd screw up your reputation if I turned out to be just another one-night stand. I can't leave you high and dry now.'

A warm sensation flooded my veins. She was actually worried about affecting my reputation? That was kinda sweet. Most women I'd dated didn't care. Some barely waited until the next morning to sell their story.

'You're sure? You know that once the press find out you're staying here, they'll be more interested in us.'

'I guessed that. It's okay. I'm ready. Well, I'm not, but I will be. I'll need something else to wear, though. Otherwise tomorrow's headline will be "Liam's new girlfriend seen wearing the same clothes two days in a row!"' she laughed. Mia was always so serious, so seeing her smile, especially after the night she'd had sent a jolt of happiness to my chest.

'Wouldn't put it past them.'

'I could ask Trudy to stop by my place later and pick something up. I don't want to put you out.'

'Don't worry. I'll make a call and get some clothes delivered first thing. I've got an early start for a shoot, so I'm gonna hit the sack soon, but let me get you set up in the spare room. Pretty sure I saw an airbed in there. First, I'll give you a tour.' I led her through to the lounge. 'So you know this is the living room. Dining room is next door, but I don't really use it much.'

I wasn't a fan of a lot of the furniture in this place. It didn't have any personality. The white leather sofa probably cost a bomb, but it was uncomfortable as hell. Like sitting on a concrete park bench.

The huge grey marble dining table could seat about twelve people, so sitting here alone would feel lonely. I preferred to eat in the kitchen.

I led Mia through. There was a massive white marble island in the centre, which stood out against the sleek black leather stools, kitchen cabinets and double-door American-style fridge-freezer.

'Nice kitchen!' Mia gushed. 'Do you use it much? Looks spotless.'

'Yeah, I love cooking. It's relaxing.'

'Wish I could say the same!' She smiled again. Two smiles in one evening? I wondered if I could do something else to make it three.

'Have you eaten?' I asked.

'No, I was going to make something when I got home.'

'There's some chicken cacciatore in the fridge that I made for lunch. It's like a chicken stew with peppers and mushrooms in tomato sauce. You can warm that up if you want.'

'Are you sure?'

'Mia.' I fixed my gaze on her. 'I wouldn't offer if I wasn't. Let me take you to the bedroom.' Her eyes bulged. 'The *spare* bedroom,' I added.

The clarification wasn't just for her. It was a reminder for my dick, which had jerked at the mention of the word *bedroom*. I didn't know how I was gonna survive this whole abstinence thing. Especially with Mia here.

Since I lost my virginity at fifteen, I didn't think I'd gone more than a few weeks without sex, so this was a new experience.

'Y-yeah,' Mia stuttered. 'Of course. Okay.'

Was she thinking about sex too? She'd broken up with Boris a while ago, but had she dated since? I doubted Mia did hook-ups. She'd always been a hearts and flowers kind of girl.

Unlike me, Mia grew up in a traditional family. Her parents had been together for ages. So even when we were teenagers she'd talked about getting married and having kids. I definitely wasn't interested in that shit.

I led her up the stairs.

'This is the office.' I stepped aside. She poked her head through the door, then followed me to the next room. 'And here's the gym. My PT, Nate, comes here most days to train me.'

We walked down the hall, where I pointed out the main bathroom.

'It's—wow. Amazing!' Mia said, taking in the sight of the waterfall shower and brilliant white roll-top claw-foot bath. We moved down the hallway and I stopped at the doorway of the master bedroom. 'So this is… your room?'

'Yep. This is where the magic happens…' I teased.

'Remember the rules.' Mia glared.

'I'm winding you up.' I stood next to the king-sized bed, which had a midnight-blue velvet-upholstered headboard which matched the walls. The floor-to-ceiling wardrobes and bedside tables had a walnut finish that complemented the wooden flooring. 'I use the en suite, so the main bathroom is all yours. Let's go to your room.'

'Okay,' Mia replied as we walked to the bedroom directly opposite, which was much smaller than mine.

'Sorry it's a tip. This is how my friend left it.' I pushed some boxes to the back wall.

'It's fine. I can sort it out. You're already helping me and it's late.'

'I just need to find the airbed.'

Mia helped me go through the boxes. 'Found it!' she called out.

'Great. The pump should be inside.'

'I'll find it after I've had dinner.'

'Okay. I'll get you some bedsheets. What else do you need?'

'A towel, shower gel…'

'Should all be in the bathroom. Back in a sec.'

When I returned, Mia had already made space for the bed.

'I'm gonna sleep now.' I handed her the sheets. 'What time do you need to be at the office?'

'Eight-thirty-ish.'

'I'll get Phil to take you. Just in case. The clothes will be here before I leave, so I'll put them outside your door.'

'What time are you going?'

'Five.'

'Wow. You better get some sleep.'

'If you need anything, just shout.'

'I'll be fine. And, Liam…'

'Yeah.' I turned back.

'Thanks.' She smiled.

Three smiles in one night.

To anyone else it might not seem like a big deal. But given how tense things had been between the two of us, to me it was a big win.

25

MIA

The microwave pinged. After taking out the steaming-hot plate, I sat at the island and picked up a knife and fork.

This kitchen was a world away from my tiny one. It was almost as big as my entire flat.

To think that tonight I thought I'd be sitting in front of the TV. I had no idea I'd end up being hounded by the paps and staying at Liam's house.

That reminded me. I should message Trudy.

Me

Paps were outside my flat, so Liam sent a car and I'm staying at his (IN THE SPARE ROOM) tonight. See you in the morning xx

I slid a forkful of food into my mouth.

Oh. My. God.

I squeezed my eyes shut and groaned with pleasure.

Liam made this?

The chicken melted on my tongue, the tomatoes were deliciously sweet and it had just the right amount of seasoning.

Liam was already blessed with good genes and now he had to be an amazing cook as well? *Save some talents for the rest of the world.*

I devoured dinner at lightning speed, then crept up the stairs so I wouldn't wake Liam and went to the bathroom. A pile of towels and a selection of fancy toiletries were neatly laid out. I popped open the lid of what looked like a very expensive bottle of shower gel and inhaled.

Mmm. It smelt like Liam. Woody, fresh and delicious.

He'd been really sweet tonight. Sending a car, checking I still wanted to go through with this and suggesting I stay here.

Of course, it would've been a million times easier if I could've found a fake boyfriend who wasn't famous. But this was what I'd signed up for, so I had to accept the good and the bad. And it was only for a little while. Hopefully they'd get bored soon and move on. Or maybe we'd argue and I'd end up leaving anyway.

I was also concerned about where I would sleep. At first I'd thought he'd use it as an excuse to get me to share his bed. But that ridiculous idea lasted for a millisecond. Liam didn't see me like that.

Pretty sure he'd said last night at dinner that Nina Rose, one of Hollywood's most beautiful actresses, was starring in his next film. If he'd be snogging her every day on set, he'd never be interested in someone like me.

Not that *I* was interested in *him*. Why was I even thinking about this?

Once I'd showered, I crept into the spare room. My

phone sounded and I quickly switched it to silent and closed the door. It was almost midnight. Trudy had texted.

Trudy

OMG. OMG. OMG!! This is SO exciting! Can't you just accidentally fall into Liam's bed?

Me

Why?

Trudy

So you can find out if the rumours that he's hung like a horse are true. Please! Do it for meeeee!

Full disclosure. I may have wondered once or twice whether they'd stuffed something down his boxer shorts in those underwear ads he starred in because that bulge looked too big to be real. But there was no way I was telling Trudy that. Or letting my eyes drop to his crotch.

Me

No! I have my own room and my own bed, and that's exactly where I'll be staying. Anyway, I thought you looked at those photos online?

Trudy

Spoilsport! The photos could have been altered. Seeing his man meat in the flesh will give me proper confirmation!

Trudy

You must be the only woman on earth who doesn't want to jump Liam Stone's bones.

Trudy

There's no way I'd be able to sleep knowing that sex god was in the next room.

Me

I'll sleep just fine. On my own. Anyway. I need to sort out this airbed.

Trudy

Can't believe you're choosing to sleep on a poxy airbed when you could be sleeping on top of Liam.

I added a row of eye roll emojis before wishing her goodnight.

After resting my phone on one of the boxes, I pulled out the airbed pump, plugged it in and connected it to the mattress. Then I realised that I didn't have anything to wear to bed. I should've asked Liam for a T-shirt.

Normally I wrapped my hair in a silk headscarf too, but I'd have to do without that tonight.

The bed began inflating, but minutes later, a weird sound filled the air. The pump had stopped. The bed was barely a couple of inches off the ground. I looked for the power button and switched it off, then on again. Still nothing.

I tried the same thing with the plug on the wall. No joy.

After trying several more times, I gave up. I'd just have to sleep on the flat mattress. I threw the bedsheets Liam had left in the room over the top, wrapped the duvet around my naked body, then moved another box away from the bed to create more space.

Just as I was about to turn off the light and lie down, a huge hairy spider ran out and headed towards the mattress.

OMG.

I screamed so loudly my eardrums almost burst. My heart raced and my body froze.

Before I had time to work out my next move, the bedroom door flew open and Liam burst in.

'What happened! What's wrong?' He squinted.

'There's... there's a sp-spider!' I shouted, scanning the floor. 'It was about to go on the mattress!'

'Wait...' He frowned, then rubbed his eyes. '*That's* why you screamed like someone was about to murder you? Because of a *spider*?'

'Yes! You know I hate them!' I trembled, my heart still racing as I imagined its long hairy legs on my bare skin.

'How big was it?'

'It was huge!'

'Bigger than you?'

'Of course not! But it was, like, the size of my hand. Maybe bigger!'

A smile tugged on Liam's lips. This wasn't funny. Arachnophobia was a thing. Lots of people were afraid of spiders.

Once I read about a woman who came home from work and saw a spider. She was so terrified, she ran outside and locked herself in the car until her husband arrived because she was too scared to stay inside alone.

'Okay.' He nodded. 'That *does* sound scary. Where did you see it?'

'There.' I pointed.

Liam stepped forward. I hadn't noticed before because I was so terrified, but he was topless, with a towel wrapped around his waist.

His back was broad and beautifully sculpted, and Jesus, his arms were so defined it looked like they'd been carved from marble.

He bent down to take a look at the side of the bed and

his towel lowered a little so I had the briefest flash of his arse. My pulse raced as I found myself wishing that it'd fall to the floor so I could have a proper look.

What was wrong with me? I was supposed to be focusing on finding where that spider went, not eyeing up Liam's bottom.

'I can't see it. Can you?'

'No. It could be anywhere! What if it crawls over me in the middle of the night?' I fanned my face with my hand to try and cool myself down.

This duvet was making me hot, but I couldn't unwrap it. I was completely naked underneath. I was grateful that in my shock it hadn't dropped. If Liam had walked in on me naked, forget the spider getting me—I would've died of shame.

'I'm gonna lift up the mattress and have a look, okay?'

I nodded. Liam shook off the sheets, then tipped the mattress on its side. He bent down to study the dark wooden floor beneath it. There was no sign of it anywhere. Shit.

'I'm sleeping on the sofa,' I said. 'I can't stay in here knowing it's roaming around, ready to jump on me. I know it sounds stupid. Like you said, I'm a million times bigger than it is, but… I just can't.'

'I get it. I was only teasing before. Everyone has things that they're afraid of. Fear isn't always rational. Why didn't you inflate the mattress?'

'The pump stopped working.'

'Unless it's inflated, that's just as bad as sleeping on the floor. And forget about the sofa. That thing isn't even comfortable to sit on.' Liam rubbed his hand across his jaw. 'Take my bed.'

'What?' My eyes bulged. 'No way. I already feel guilty about disrupting your sleep when you've got an early start. I can't take your bed too.'

'Unless…'

'What are you thinking?'

'Forget it.' He shook his head.

'Tell me!'

Liam paused. His eyes met mine, then darted away again.

'We could *share* my bed…'

I swallowed what felt like a block of concrete lodged in my throat.

Share a bed.

With Liam.

Sleep with his body just inches away from mine.

'That's not a good idea.' I shook my head.

'Why? Worried you won't be able to keep your hands off me?' He smirked.

'No! I wouldn't touch you if you were the last man on earth!'

'So then there's nothing to worry about.'

'But… how do I know that you'll…'

'That I'll what? Behave myself? For starters, I'm fucking exhausted. It's after midnight and I have to be up by four thirty. So even if I found you irresistible, I wouldn't have the energy. Trust me.'

I glared at Liam, trying to assess whether I could. Then I reminded myself for the second time tonight that he had zero interest in me. My cheeks heated with embarrassment.

Of course I'd be safe. He dated models and actresses. Liam wouldn't even touch me if I was covered in honey. I could sleep naked with 'seduce me' written in bold letters across my boobs and he wouldn't bat an eyelid. I needed to get over myself.

'Okay,' I murmured. 'Out of curiosity, why do you sleep with a towel around you? Are you worried about wetting the bed?' I grinned.

'Very funny!' He rolled his eyes. 'I sleep naked and when I heard you scream, I thought the paps had broken in to get a picture and I didn't want to run in here and end up getting my dick photographed again, so I grabbed the nearest thing I could find, which was this towel.'

'So you'll be in your bed... *naked*?' I bit my lip and squeezed my thighs together, trying not to think about Liam lying next to me in the buff.

'No... I'll put on boxers. Just for you.'

Liam's eyes flicked to mine and he held my gaze. Him wearing underwear was the most appropriate thing to do. But although I tried to suppress it, thoughts of his body pressed against mine flooded into my head.

'That would be'—*a shame, disappointing*—'a good idea,' I said, trying to keep my voice level. 'Speaking of clothes, do you have anything I could wear? I'm... I don't have anything on under this duvet.'

Liam's Adam's apple bobbed and his eyes darkened.

'You're *naked*?'

I nodded.

We stared at each other in silence, the air between us crackling with electricity.

Liam was stood a few feet away from me, his solid chest glistening, with just a towel around his waist. And here I was with only this duvet. If either of us moved too quickly, both items could easily fall to the floor. Then we'd be face to face in our birthday suits.

And as much as I hated to admit it, I'd be lying if I said I didn't want to see what was underneath that towel.

'I-I...' Liam broke the silence, his eyes dropping to the floor. 'I'll find something for you. Give me two minutes.' He quickly left the room.

Was he...?

I shook my head. For a second, I wondered whether hearing that I was naked underneath this duvet turned him on, but that was ridiculous.

The poor guy had to get up in four hours, so he probably wanted to cut the chit-chat so he could get to bed.

Bed.

It hit me again that I was about to share a bed with Liam: the man that millions of people around the world fantasised about.

If you'd asked me a week ago if I'd consider it, I would've shivered with disgust.

And only minutes ago I'd said I wouldn't touch him if he was the last man on earth.

So why was my body now tingling with anticipation?

26

LIAM

I was in deep shit.

Suggesting that Mia share my bed was a mistake. But what could I do? I couldn't let her sleep in the room when she was so afraid.

Mum had the same phobia. Once she'd climbed on the dining table and almost broken it because there was a spider on the floor. Just because insects didn't bother me, that didn't mean I thought Mia's fear wasn't real.

Sleeping on that sofa was a punishment I'd only inflict on my worst enemy. Although there was tension between us, I didn't hate her.

I should. And for years I'd told myself that I did. Even right up to a couple of weeks ago I'd wanted to believe I still hated Mia. But the more time we spent together, the more it felt like no time had passed. It was starting to feel like the days when things were good between us all over again.

And that was exactly why I had to leave the room.

When Mia said she was naked under that duvet, I started getting hard. It was like I was a damn teenager.

There was no way I could stand in front of her with a boner, so I bolted. I needed a few minutes to sort myself out. But a few minutes had already passed and the *situation* still wasn't under control.

Even though it was only her smooth shoulders that were exposed, she still looked so damn sexy. Maybe it was because I knew that with just one tug of that duvet she'd be naked.

This was bad.

Very, very bad.

I strode over to my wardrobe and took out some boxers. Shit. All of them were fitted. I couldn't hide a hard-on in these.

'Can I come in?' Mia knocked the door.

'One sec.' I grabbed a pair of boxers, quickly put them on underneath my towel, then slid under the duvet. 'Come in.'

Mia stepped inside looking like a fucking goddess. My dick jerked again. At least I was under the covers. I'd promised I'd be on my best behaviour and I needed to honour that. Mia had already made it clear that she wasn't interested, so I didn't want to make her feel uncomfortable.

What I'd said was true, though. I *was* exhausted. So even if she was interested (dream on), I wouldn't seduce her. After all these years, if anything was to ever happen, I need to make it a night she wouldn't forget.

If Mia ever gave me the chance, I'd give it to her so good that every man that came after me would be a disappointment.

But why the hell was I even thinking about this?

'Do you have something I can wear?' she said, avoiding eye contact.

'Shit, sorry.' I dragged my mind out of the gutter. 'I was supposed to get you something. Just take anything.' I pointed to the wardrobe.

'Okay.' She walked over, tightening the duvet around her. *What a damn shame.* 'Where do you keep your T-shirts?'

'Top rail, on the right.'

Mia walked over and reached up, clutching the duvet with one hand and rifling through the T-shirts with the other.

The thought of her wearing my clothes and the fabric brushing against her bare skin, made my dick harden again. This was out of control. If I'd known she'd be here tonight, I would've got myself off before she came. I mean, before she *came upstairs*. But everything was so unexpected.

Mia went on tiptoe as she tried reaching for a white T-shirt. She attempted to pull it down with one hand, but when it didn't budge, Mia reached up with the other to try and yank it free from the hanger. But she must've forgotten she also needed to hold on to the duvet, so it dropped to the floor, leaving her standing there.

Butt naked.

Sweet. Jesus.

Her back was fucking exquisite. As for her arse, it was what wet dreams were made of. My cock agreed. If I didn't look away right now, I was in danger of coming in my boxers.

'Shit!' She bent down to pick up the duvet.

Holy. Fucking. Guacamole.

Mia's arse when she was standing upright was already beautiful, but seeing it in the air as she bent over was... I had no words.

I should help her, but I couldn't let her see me like this. The semi I'd had when I was in the spare room was nothing compared to the wood in my pants right now. There was no way she'd agree to sleep in my bed if she saw what was between my legs, and I couldn't blame her.

'Oh my God!' She wrapped the duvet around her. 'I'm so embarrassed.'

'You've got nothing to be embarrassed about. I... sorry I didn't mean to look and I hope you don't think I'm a creep for saying this, but, Mia, your body's fucking amazing.'

'Oh... thanks,' she murmured. 'I-I don't think I'm tall enough to reach the T-shirt. The rail's too high. Could you help?'

'Why don't you take one of my shirts instead? They're on the lower rail to the left.'

'Okay.' She shuffled over, gripping the duvet like her life depended on it. 'I've got one. Can you turn the light off?'

'Sure.' The room went dark. I heard the hanger being plucked from the rail and the sound of the wardrobe doors closing.

'I'm getting in bed now.'

'Okay. I'll face the other way.' I whipped my body around. 'You can put your duvet in the middle, between us. So you don't have to worry about me touching you. Not like *that*,' I added quickly. 'I mean our bodies touching. By accident. When we're sleeping. Like if we move around.'

I couldn't even string a damn sentence together. The

image of Mia's naked body was ingrained in my brain. Again.

Although I'd always been too chickenshit to admit it, I'd always liked Mia. Even when I went to Spain, I still thought about her. Didn't matter who I dated, she was always in the back of my mind. Sometimes at the front too.

That shitty night that I'd ended up with Sunrise and couldn't get it up, it was Mia that I thought about. I'd pictured the first time I'd seen her bare arse.

I must've been sixteen. One night Mum and Dad were arguing, so I'd gone over to her parents'. Her mum answered the door and sent me upstairs to find Mia.

It was a hot summer's evening and when I went to her room, she was just wearing a T-shirt and nothing else.

But it wasn't any T-shirt. It was mine. I couldn't even remember how she got it, but that wasn't important.

Seeing her in my T-shirt set something off inside of me. The whole time I was there I couldn't stop thinking about what was underneath. My eyes were drawn to her bare thighs. And the temptation to reach over and kiss her or touch her was insane.

Then when Mia bent over to pick up something on the floor and the T-shirt rode up, exposing her naked arse, I nearly lost my damn mind.

That vision had been ingrained on my brain ever since.

Whenever I was with a woman and wasn't really into it, all I had to do was press play on that mental movie of Mia's beautiful butt and I'd be good to go.

But now, I didn't have to rely on past memories. Now Mia was here in my bed. Wearing my shirt. With nothing on underneath. I'd managed to control myself that night, but I didn't know if I'd have the same willpower.

I desperately wanted Mia to put that duvet between us.

I *needed* her to.

Ever since we'd met up again, I'd told myself that it was just a crush I'd had when I was a kid and that things were different now.

I was an adult. I wasn't interested. I'd never go there.

But I was starting to realise that wasn't true. And even if my mind wanted to tell me that it was, my dick was telling a very different story.

Given the chance, if Mia said the word, whether I had a shoot in a few hours or not, I'd climb on top and bury myself so deep inside her that she'd forget her own name.

Even though I was so tired my eyes burned and my head hurt, I'd use every last drop of energy I had to rock her world.

'No,' she said softly. 'It's okay. I'm sure we'll be fine.'

I wished I shared her confidence.

'Goodnight.'

'Goodnight,' I replied, knowing that sleeping so close to her and keeping my hands (and my dick) to myself was going to be anything but *good*.

27

MIA

'So let me get this straight.' Trudy's hand was suspended mid-air and her eyes widened as I relayed the mortifying story of what happened last night. 'You flashed Liam? In his bedroom?'

'Yes! No! You make it sound like it was deliberate. I was trying to reach the T-shirt and the duvet dropped and I wasn't wearing anything underneath because I didn't have any clean clothes, so he saw my arse.'

'That's hilarious!' Trudy snorted.

'It wasn't! It was embarrassing!' I winced.

If he'd got the T-shirt out of his wardrobe like he'd agreed, it wouldn't have happened. He knew I couldn't reach, but just watched me struggle.

I wanted to call him an arsehole, but after all he'd done to help me, that wouldn't be true. He could've teased me and said to sleep on the floor, but instead he'd tried to find the spider. And when he couldn't, he'd offered me his bed.

That wasn't arsehole behaviour. Those were the actions of a caring man. But I couldn't say that out loud, because then I'd be admitting that I liked him a lot more than I thought.

'I don't know why you're so embarrassed. He only saw your backside. It's not like he saw your boobs or your flaps! What happened next?' Trudy leant forward like she was watching a film on the edge of her seat.

'I picked the duvet off the floor, obviously! And then…'

'He pulled you onto the bed and made sweet, sweet love to you!'

'No! I said I was embarrassed and he said… that I shouldn't be because'—I lowered my voice—'he thought my body was… *amazing*.'

'I *knew* it!' Trudy jumped up with excitement, drops of coffee spilling on her desk. 'I bloody knew he liked you! Didn't I always say that at school?'

'I don't remember.'

'Liar! He likes you! Liam bloody Stone fancies the pants off you!'

'Just because he complimented my body, it doesn't mean anything.' I rolled my eyes.

'That's crap and you know it! So come on! What happened next?'

'I put on one of his shirts, because that was easier to reach, then we went to bed.'

'As in, you *shagged*?'

'Get your mind out of the gutter! I told you! That's never going to happen. I got in bed, with the shirt on. He said I could put the duvet between us if I was worried we might accidentally touch each other whilst we were sleeping. *Don't…*' I warned, anticipating that she was about to make a comment about the 'touch each other' thing. 'And that was it. We went to sleep. I was so tired I didn't even hear him leave at four in the morning. Next thing I knew, my alarm was going off. Like he'd promised, there were clothes, shoes and underwear waiting for me. I got dressed and his driver brought me here. End of story.'

That was the truth. More or less…

I may have left out the part where I couldn't sleep for ages, because I was freaking out about Liam's half-naked body being inches away from me.

As I lay there, a video recording I didn't know I had stored in my brain played on repeat.

First it showed Liam standing topless in the spare bedroom. Then the imaginary camera zoomed in on his pecs, his abs, that flimsy towel and what lay underneath. Next, this erotic imaginary film focused on how sexy Liam had looked when I'd come into the bedroom.

His arm was casually resting behind his head, which accentuated his biceps. His hair was wavy, like he'd just run his hand through it.

Then those words he'd said played on loop. Every time I pictured him saying he thought my body was amazing, a bolt of lightning shot straight to my core.

Liam Stone. The man with a body that women craved and men envied had said *my* body looked good. How was I supposed to think straight or sleep after hearing that?

I'd lain next to him for hours, those visions replaying over and over, fantasising about what it would be like if he whipped the duvet off, climbed on top and buried himself inside me.

I hadn't had sex for ages and was used to going without. But never had I wanted it more than in that moment.

There was no point denying it. I wanted Liam.

I was such a cliché, so I wasn't going to tell Trudy that. Especially after how much I'd said I hated his guts. No way.

Admitting to wanting to jump Liam's bones was more embarrassing than flashing him my arse last night. And that was saying something.

This was a big problem. If I was staying at home, I could keep these feelings under control. I wouldn't have to see Liam in person until the interview. That would probably only last half an hour. An hour tops. I'd be able to hold it together for that long. Especially as he'd be fully clothed.

But now that we were living under the same roof, even if it was only for a week or two, things would be a lot harder.

Yeah, I could try to avoid him, but our paths would cross at some point. And Liam didn't even have to be in the same room to send my hormones wild.

The whole house smelt of his addictive masculine scent. This morning when I woke up, I caught myself sniffing his pillow.

Yep. Like I said. This was *bad*.

And him arranging for those clothes to be sent for me did nothing to calm my desire either.

Last night, I'd worried how he'd know what would fit me without taking my measurements. I should've known not to doubt him. Every single item fitted me perfectly. The gorgeous red underwear set, the designer structured dresses, the high heels: it was like everything was made for me.

When I saw that he'd ordered a silk scarf for my hair

too, I'd gasped. How did he know I needed that? The man was some kind of mind reader.

Liam looked hot. He smelt amazing. He was a phenomenal cook. He was kind and understanding about my phobia. He'd offered me his bed. He complimented me. And he bought me a shitload of gorgeous clothes and accessories. *Come on.* Show me a human being who wouldn't develop feelings for a man like that, and I'd show them a hundred unicorns.

I was fighting a losing battle.

'Well, you might not have done the deed last night, but it's only a matter of time.' Trudy grinned. 'You two locked away alone in his house, sheltering from the paparazzi, sharing a bed. Before long, you'll be sharing bodily fluids too!'

'Whatever.' I couldn't admit that as crude as it sounded, I wished it was true.

'It's nature, sweetie. You can't fight it. And why would you want to? It's been about a year since you had any action, right? If you're not careful, your vag will close up!' she cackled.

'Not funny!' I didn't need a reminder that it'd been a while.

'That's why you two getting busy would be perfect. I say this with love, but you might screw up that interview by blurting out something you shouldn't. But if you two are shagging for real, you'll be more relaxed because all you'll need to do is tell the truth: that you two are crazy about each other.'

Trudy was right. About me saying something I shouldn't. Not the other bit.

'We're going to rehearse what to say beforehand. So it won't be like thinking of a lie on the spot.'

'Really?' She raised her eyebrow. 'And how will you rehearse the answers when you don't know the questions?'

Valid point...

'The questions will probably be standard stuff, like how we met, what we like about each other, that kind of thing.'

'And what about the physical stuff? You gonna rehearse that too?'

'They're not going to ask us to shag in front of them so they can check our chemistry.'

'Obviously not! I meant how will you show other forms of intimacy and convince them? And how are you going to kiss?'

Kiss?

My body froze.

'They won't expect a snogging session,' I scoffed, my heart racing. 'That'd be crass. Lots of couples aren't into public displays of affection. We'll just be one of those. We'll sit close to each other and maybe we'll touch hands. Or he could stroke my cheek or something.' A thrill raced through me as I remembered how good it had felt when Liam did that outside the restaurant. 'We'll be fine.'

'I think it's worth you doing a dry run, just in case. At some point, if you really want to convince people you're together, you're going to have to lock lips. And you don't want it to be a mess. The kiss needs to look smooth and natural like you've done it a zillion times before. And that'll only come with practice. You should try it when you're in bed together again tonight.'

'We won't be sleeping in the same bed again. I'm

buying a new airbed with a working pump at lunchtime. Then I can sleep on it in the living room. They'll be no more bed sharing and *definitely* no kissing.'

Staying at Liam's house to avoid the paps was one thing, but playing tonsil hockey was a different story.

I'd barely survived the night sleeping in the same bed as him. If his mouth touched mine, I'd never recover.

We might be forced to live under the same four walls, but from now on, I was staying as far away from Liam's body and lips as possible.

28

LIAM

I shrugged off my coat and took off my shoes. It was good to be home. I'd had a long day and was so shattered, I could sleep right here in the hallway.

After hauling myself to the living room, I collapsed on the sofa. I hated this damn sofa.

Which was exactly why Mia had ended up in my bed last night. And why I was so tired. I'd be surprised if I slept for more than a couple of hours.

It was impossible to focus on sleep when I knew she was beside me. I kept picturing the moment when the duvet had dropped. The curve of her arse, how much I'd wanted to grab hold of those butt cheeks…

When I woke up, I'd turned on the bedside lamp. Seeing Mia lying there wearing my shirt took my breath away. She looked so fucking beautiful.

Watching the way her chest rose and fell as she slept was so calming. At least she hadn't been up all night having dirty thoughts like me.

Even after I'd dragged myself to the shower, then to

the shoot, I still couldn't stop thinking about her. Fuck knows how I was going to survive sleeping in the same bed with her again tonight.

I'd thought about getting a new bed, but the paps were still hanging around. So if they found out what was being delivered or the bed company leaked a story, that could spark unwanted headlines. Sounded paranoid, but this shit had happened to me before, so I was speaking from experience.

Best-case scenario, they'd think Mia and I were having so much sex we'd broken the original bed. Worse case, they'd start a load of 'trouble in paradise' stories saying that we'd fallen out already and I was staying in the spare room.

It'd make no difference whether the stories were true. Perception was everything. It was easier to just share a bed. It wouldn't be for long. I could handle it.

Hopefully.

I heard the key in the door. I'd left one for Mia this morning so she could come and go freely.

'Hey.' She stood at the doorway. Damn. I knew that dress would suit her.

Whilst she was eating dinner last night, I'd picked out some stuff online that I thought would be a good fit and emailed my London stylist. I'd had to guess Mia's measurements. It wasn't difficult. Growing up, Mum had dragged me along to enough clothes shops, and yeah, I'll admit, dating more than a few women of all shapes and sizes helped.

And the fact that I'd caught more than a few glances of Mia's body didn't hurt.

'Been shopping?' I gestured to the large bag she was

holding.

'I bought an airbed. So I wouldn't have to disturb you tonight.'

My stomach sank. I knew it'd be sensible not to spend another night together, but I liked having her in my bed.

'You didn't disturb me... it'd be better to stay in my bed. The cleaner's coming tomorrow morning and it's hard to know who to trust. If she sees you sleeping in the spare room she might leak something to the press.'

'Oh. I see what you mean. I hadn't thought about that.'

'Welcome to my world!' I paused. 'So, you okay with that? We slept in the same bed last night and survived, so we can do it again, right?' I didn't know if I was trying to convince Mia or myself.

'Yeah. At least I have clean clothes, so there won't be any incidents like yesterday.' Her gaze dropped to the floor. She must still be embarrassed. I meant what I'd said when it happened. Mia had nothing to be embarrassed about. If she was mine, I'd be happy if she chose to walk around naked all day. 'Thanks again for everything.'

When I'd checked my phone this morning, there were three gushing messages from her about how grateful she was for the clothes. And now she was thanking me again. Most of the women I'd bought stuff for in the past barely grunted their appreciation.

'You're welcome.' I stood up.

'How did you know I'd need the silk scarf?'

'You used to put one on before bed. Can't remember why, but you said it was important.'

'Wow.' Mia's eyes widened. 'Your memory is scarily good. You're right. I always wear one to protect my hair whilst I'm sleeping. I used to relax it, so the hairdresser recommended that I wrap it before bed, which is basically brushing my hair round in a circle, then covering it with the scarf to keep it smooth.'

'Relax?'

'Relaxing is chemical hair straightening. Now I get a keratin blow-dry treatment instead.'

'Cool.' I nodded. 'Well, whatever you do, it looks good.'

Damn straight. Mia could shave off one side of her head or wear her hair in a rainbow-coloured Mohawk and still look great.

'Thanks!'

I caught myself staring and knew if I stood here any longer drinking her in, I'd get myself in trouble. Time to get out of here.

'I should… go.'

Mia was still at the doorway. As I got closer, she shifted to the right, just as I did. We both then moved to the left.

'Sorry.' She smiled, sending a bolt of electricity to my chest. 'Let me get out of your way.'

'I was just gonna make dinner.'

'You've been up since crazy o'clock! If anyone should make dinner it's me. Then again, you don't want to be ill tomorrow, so maybe I better not! I can go to the supermarket and buy pizza or something.'

'Can't.' I winced as I breezed past her, inhaling her sweet scent. 'Gotta watch what I eat. I'll make a turkey salad. Won't take long.'

'Life without pizza must be hard.' She followed me into the kitchen, then pulled out a stool at the island.

'You have no idea.' I loved pizza. And fried chicken,

fries and ice cream. Sometimes I wished I could just eat whatever I liked instead of always having to worry about how I looked. But if I wanted to keep these sponsorship deals and pay the bills, I had to stay in shape.

'At least you're a brilliant cook. That chicken stew was delicious.'

'Thanks.'

After washing my hands, I took the bag of salad and fresh turkey fillet from the fridge, then poured some olive oil into the frying pan.

'So how was your day?' Mia asked.

'It was okay. I did a shoot, then came back later this afternoon for a phone meeting.'

'What kind of meeting?' She rested on her elbows and leant forward like she was genuinely interested.

'With the intimacy coordinator for my next film.'

'Intimacy coordinator?'

'Yeah, they help out with the sex scenes to make sure we're comfortable. Before we start filming they like to find out our boundaries.'

'Oh! I thought you just got on set and just started going at it!'

'No.' I tossed the meat into the pan, then sprinkled on some herbs. 'Everything's coordinated. Before we start shooting, we know where we're going to touch and what we're going to do. Since the whole #McToo movement, the studios realised just how important it is.'

'That's good. Must be weird getting naked and rubbing up against a stranger.'

'We're never completely naked.'

'But sometimes you see their bits on screen!'

'Nah. We have a Hibue or Shibue, which is a strapless

thong that sticks to our pelvis so there's no direct contact. And a lot of the time, when you see a man's dick on screen, it's not real. It's a prosthetic cock. Same for the woman. They can wear a merkin, which is like a pubic wig. There's never really any proper dick and pussy touching.'

'Wow. I thought it was all real! But what about kissing? Don't tell me you wear fake lips!' she giggled and the sweet sound warmed my chest.

'No,' I chuckled, flipping the turkey in the pan. 'Our lips are real, but the kisses are obviously fake. It's not as enjoyable as it looks.'

'Trudy was talking about us kissing earlier,' Mia blurted out.

'Us? Kissing?' My eyes widened.

'Er, yeah.' She fiddled with the hem of her dress, avoiding my gaze. 'She said we should… practise. That at some point, people will expect us to kiss. Like at the interview.' Mia shrugged. 'Stupid, really.'

'Maybe we *should* practise.'

What the hell?

I really should think before I speak. I blame the tiredness. Kissing Mia was worse than letting her sleep in my bed. It was just asking for trouble.

'Oh.' She paused. 'I-I didn't think you'd agree.'

I didn't. This was my horny dick talking. But now I'd said it, I couldn't take it back.

'Last time we were papped, we looked like we were kissing. So when we're next in public, to be convincing, we might need to do it for real. And if our first time is in front of a load of photographers, it might look awkward.'

'Good point.' She looked up. 'Maybe we should've

discussed this at the beginning. Like you do with your intimacy coordinator person.'

'Exactly. It's good to know our boundaries.'

'We need to think about whether we use tongues or not.' Her eyes dropped to my mouth. 'Or we could just peck on the lips?'

'A peck won't show them that we're madly in lust, though. Maybe tongues are more convincing. Unless that'll be too much for you?' I didn't want to make her uncomfortable.

'No, no.' She nodded. 'We can... tongues are fine.'

'And what about touch?' I pinned my gaze on her. 'Where are your boundaries?'

Mia's eyes bulged.

'You want to know where you can *touch* me? When we kiss?'

'Mmm-hmm.' I walked to the fridge and opened the door, hoping that the cold air would cool down my cock, which was thickening at lightning speed. Thinking about where Mia would let me touch her was too much.

'Anywhere, I suppose... I mean, that you think would be normal and, y'know, *convincing* if we were dating for real. Because, y'know, that's the important thing.' She swallowed. 'We need to be convincing.'

'Okay.' I tried to control my excitement. My dick was happy to hear that Mia had given me free rein to touch her anywhere. 'This is why it's good to practise, so that if my hands wander somewhere that's *convincing*, and you don't feel comfortable, you can tell me to stop.'

I took out the tomatoes and walked back to the island, hoping she wouldn't notice the growth in my pants.

'Exactly.' Her eyes flicked to mine. I held her gaze, my mind racing at a million miles an hour.

Where would I touch her first? There were too many places I'd dreamed about. Her arse, her tits, between her legs...

Sweet Jesus.

Being given an all-access pass to Mia's body was like being offered a lifetime pass to an all-you-can-eat gelato buffet.

But if I started devouring her, would I be able to stop?

'So...' Mia broke the silence. 'When should we practise?'

'Now?' The word flew out of my mouth before I could stop it. 'Just to get it out the way,' I added, hoping I sounded less eager.

'True. Best to just get it over and done with. Then we won't have to do it again. Until we have to perform in front of the cameras.'

'Yeah.' My heart pounded against my ribcage. Why the hell was I nervous? I'd kissed lots of different women on and off set. No big deal.

'Should I brush my teeth first?' she asked.

'You're fine. I hope I am too. If you want, I can have a mint?'

'No, it's okay.'

We stood there in silence.

This was nuts. It was just a kiss. Nothing to be nervous about.

I counted to twenty in my head, picturing a group of politicians discussing some boring shit, to try and calm down my erection, then pulled my T-shirt lower, hoping to disguise it.

'Come here,' I growled. She walked over nervously. I stepped towards her. Mia's eyes widened as she tilted her head upwards. 'So I'm gonna kiss you now. You sure you're okay with this?'

She nodded.

'Mia, I need to hear you say it.'

'Yes,' she said softly. 'Kiss me, please.'

'So, if I was gonna kiss you, first I'd look into your eyes and maybe stroke your cheek or tuck those cute strands of hair behind your ear…'

As I pinned my gaze on her, Mia's breath hitched and my dick twitched. I lifted my hand to her face, brushing my thumb over her cheek before slowly touching her hair, just like I'd said I would.

'Then I'd move my face closer to yours…'

'Mmm-hmm,' she said softly. 'Very convincing.'

'And then…'

My mouth crushed onto hers and Mia let out a low moan.

She parted her lips and I wasted no time sliding my tongue inside.

Jesus Christ.

She tasted like sweet berries and my hungry mouth moved over hers like I was sampling my favourite meal.

I slid my arm around her waist, pulling her into me, and as her perfect tits pressed against my chest, a husky groan flew from the back of my throat.

Fuck.

Her lips.

Her taste.

I knew kissing Mia would be good, but this was off the scale.

This was *everything*.

She thrust her hand in my hair, her nails grazing my scalp, and it felt so damn good.

Her hands trailed down my back, then she grabbed my arse, causing my rock-hard cock to poke her belly.

Holy shit.

Mia was actually enjoying this.

So was I.

Way too much.

I knew where this was going. In a few seconds, my hands would be up her dress. Then I'd lift Mia onto this kitchen island and fuck her.

And if that happened, there'd be no going back.

I had to stop this before things got out of control.

Reluctantly, I pulled away.

Mia opened her eyes, her lips still parted.

'Th-that was...' she panted. 'That was, um, I think we'd convince them if we did that. That was pretend, right?'

'If I was kissing you for real, sweetheart,' I growled, 'you wouldn't be able to stand or see straight right now.'

Mia swallowed hard.

The fact that I wanted to kiss her was very real. But as much as I'd enjoyed it, that was just a warm-up. A taster.

I meant what I said. If Mia was mine, I wouldn't just kiss her. I'd devour her.

And judging by the look of desire on her face, that was exactly what she wanted me to do.

29

MIA

'I should...' I stepped back, wracking my brain for something to say to excuse myself from this situation. I needed a minute to gather my thoughts.

Scrap that. Even if I had a week, I wouldn't be able to compose myself after *that* kiss.

Liam's words played on repeat in my mind:

'If I was kissing you for real, sweetheart, you wouldn't be able to stand or see straight right now.'

And the thing was, I believed him. That kiss was... *everything*.

It had ended a few minutes ago and my body was still tingling. And my knickers were soaked.

If that was pretend, imagine how my body would react to the real thing.

And that was a problem. Because even though I knew a real kiss with Liam would ruin me, I was desperate to have him. *Properly*.

As Liam held my gaze, every inch of my body lit up like a fireworks display.

'I should... use the bathroom,' I said, my breath still ragged.

'Okay. Dinner will be ready in ten.'

I walked out of the kitchen as quickly as my legs would carry me.

This was my fault. If I hadn't mentioned that Trudy suggested we should practise kissing, I'd never have felt his soft lips, touched his firm arse or felt his hard dick pressed against me.

I started climbing the stairs, then paused midway.

Hold on.

Liam had said it was pretend. But he was hard. *Very* hard. Which meant he must have enjoyed our kiss, more than just a little bit.

Was Trudy right? Did Liam really like me?

No. I continued up the stairs. That was just a natural biological reaction. If he liked me, he wouldn't have stopped. I mean, this was *Liam the man whore* we were talking about. He'd never pass up the opportunity for a quick shag. And it was pretty obvious from the way I'd pulled him into me that I wouldn't have turned him down.

There was no point denying it. That kiss may have started as practice, but by the end of it, I would've spread myself open for him in a heartbeat.

I'd wanted Liam last night. But right now, I *craved* him. And I didn't know what to do about it.

We'd be sleeping in the same bed together again tonight. I could make a move, but if he rejected me, it'd make everything so awkward. Especially with the interview coming up.

Everything needed to go smoothly. I couldn't jeopardise my chances. Otherwise all of this would've been for nothing.

I had to keep these illicit thoughts out of my head.

In just five days, the interview would be over and I'd be a step closer to winning the prize money.

∽

The day was finally here. In eight hours, Susie would be at Liam's house and the interview would finally be underway.

Things had been a bit awkward at dinner last Wednesday night when we'd first kissed. It'd improved when I'd suggested we should get our stories straight about how we'd rekindled our 'long-lost love' after Liam had returned to London.

After about half an hour, I could see that Liam could barely keep his eyes open, so suggested he go to sleep and said I'd clear up the kitchen.

When I'd crept up to bed, he was fast asleep and when I woke up the following morning, he'd gone to Paris.

The cleaner gave me a knowing grin when I'd emerged from the bedroom, so it was a smart move for me to sleep in his bed. I'd hidden the air mattress in his wardrobe. I'd return it to the shop when I got time.

Although Liam was away, we'd messaged every day. Multiple times. He'd send me funny memes and check I was okay in the house alone and I'd ask how the shoot was going and to send photos. He'd sent pics of the French food, which looked nice, but I would've preferred photos of him. Anything to help me relive that panty-melting kiss.

Liam was coming back later this afternoon, though, so

we'd have to sleep in the same bed again. And I wasn't going to lie. If his dick *accidentally* slipped inside me, I wouldn't be sorry about it.

'All set for tonight?' Trudy asked, popping some grapes in her mouth.

'I think so.' I logged out of my emails and faced her. 'We did a mini rehearsal last week.'

'Good idea! And did this rehearsal include a kiss by any chance?' She raised her eyebrow.

My cheeks heated. Without even opening my mouth, I'd already given the game away, so it was pointless trying to deny it.

'Maybe…' A massive smile spread across my face.

'You kissed Liam last week and you didn't tell me?'

'You were away on tour with your actors. I didn't want to disturb you!' It'd been hard, believe me. The first thing I wanted to do after that kiss was call her.

'I would've found time! This is *big*! Seriously, I should play the lottery! The way I can predict the future is astonishing!' she cackled. 'So, I'm guessing from the way you're grinning like a Cheshire cat that it was good?'

'I'm screwed.' I blew out an exasperated breath. After holding in my feelings for days and not being able to tell anyone, they were eating me up inside. 'It was more than *good*! He said it was just fake, but his dick told a different story.'

'Oh my God! You turned Liam's dick to *stone*! See what I did there?'

'Not funny!' It was a little bit. 'I hate to admit it, but… I like him.'

I dropped my head in my hands, then spilled my guts,

confessing all the things that'd happened between us that I'd deliberately left out before.

'Hon, don't sweat it. What you're feeling is normal. Especially given how long you've had a dick drought! I'd be more worried if you kissed Liam and *didn't* feel anything. But this is good. You couldn't have timed it better.'

'Huh?'

'Right now, don't suppress your feelings. Lean into them. Act on everything. At least for tonight. So the more you're into him, the better you'll do at the interview because it'll be the truth.'

'Hmmm.' I nodded. 'That's not a bad idea. But my emotions aren't a tap. If I turn them on tonight and don't hold back, I'm not sure how easy it'll be to switch them off again tomorrow.'

'Worry about tomorrow, tomorrow. Today you are Mia Bailey, sex goddess and girlfriend of the world's hottest movie star. You two are madly in love. You can't get enough of each other. *That* should be your mantra for tonight. Repeat it over and over again and start to believe it.'

'Okay.' I nodded, sitting up straighter in my chair. 'It's on.'

30

MIA

I glanced in the tall mirror in Liam's bedroom and admired the emerald-green dress and skyscraper heels he'd got me.

After leaving the office early, I'd come home and done my hair and make-up whilst rehearsing my responses to potential questions. I'd also tried repeating Trudy's mantra over and over, hoping it would stick.

I peeked out of the bedroom window, anxious to see whether Liam had arrived. At least the paps weren't milling around anymore. They must've got bored or followed Liam to Paris. When I'd gone back to my flat last night to get some stuff, it was clear there too.

A few minutes later, I heard the front door slam.

'I'm back!' Liam shouted.

'Hi!' I called out. 'How was the shoot?' Whenever I messaged to ask, he promised to tell me about it in person.

Liam entered the bedroom, clutching a black leather suitcase. He looked tired, but still gorgeous.

'Forget about the shoot... wow.' He raked his eyes

over me slowly, drinking me in from head to toe. 'You look… incredible. That dress really suits you.'

'Thanks.' I stepped forward, then pressed my lips onto his. Liam froze and I quickly pulled away. 'Sorry!' I winced. I was so focused on getting into the boyfriend/girlfriend zone, I hadn't considered whether he'd be okay with a kiss. 'I should've asked you first.'

'Don't apologise. I just wasn't expecting it, that's all.'

'I'm trying to get into character. I thought if I acted like I was into you, then I'd be more natural in the interview. It was a… spontaneous rehearsal.'

'Makes sense. Want to do it again?'

My stomach flipped. That was like asking a kid if they liked ice cream.

Sign. Me. Up.

'Great idea!'

I barely had a chance to catch my breath before Liam crushed his lips on mine. I parted my mouth and he slid his tongue inside.

'Oh God,' I groaned. 'Don't stop.'

Liam pushed me against the wall and I ran my hands down his arse, then lifted my leg up and wrapped it around his body.

I squeezed my eyes shut. There was nothing fake about the goosebumps that had erupted over every inch of my skin.

'Fuck,' Liam growled, trailing kisses along my neck and down my chest before hitching my dress up around my waist.

Just as he reached for my knickers, the doorbell rang.

'Shit!' I lowered my leg. 'That must be Susie. She's early.'

'I need to shower. You okay to let her in?'

'Course. But be quick.'

'I usually like to take my time, but I'll do my best...' He smirked, then walked to the en suite.

My legs turned to jelly. I'd love nothing more than Liam to *take his time*... in bed with me.

Once I'd composed myself, I raced downstairs and opened the door. Susie was standing there with a tall, stern-looking man with dark hair and thick black-rimmed glasses.

'Hi! Welcome!' I gestured for them to come in.

'Hello. Nice lipstick...' She smiled as she stepped inside.

'Thanks! Thought I'd try a new shade.' It was the same daring red I'd worn for my date with Liam. I liked the confidence boost it gave me.

'What a lovely home.' Susie scanned the surroundings as they followed me through to the lounge.

'Thanks,' I repeated. I was so grateful I was able to invite them here. If they saw where I was really living, there was no way they'd put me through to the finals. 'It's Liam's. Sort of—well, it's his fr—'

'And will Mr Stone be joining us this evening?' the guy interrupted, saving me from babbling on about it being Liam's friend's house and not his.

'Yes! We were just in the bedroom—I mean, not like *that*... he just got back from a shoot in Paris, so he's having a shower. In the bathroom, that's in the bedroom. You know. The en suite.'

Oh God.

So much for keeping my answers short.

Susie and the man glared at me like I was crazy. I

didn't blame them. Maybe that glass of wine I'd had earlier to 'relax me' wasn't a good idea. Speaking of wine...

'Can I get you a drink? Wine, water, juice?'

'A glass of white wine would be lovely!' Susie chirped.

'Mineral water for me. Room temperature. With a slice of lemon.'

'Coming right up!'

I darted out of the room. As I passed the mirror, I gasped. My lipstick was smeared around my mouth, chin and cheeks.

Oh... So when Susie complimented my lipstick, she was really saying *I know what you've just been up to.* And then I said we'd just been in the bedroom. How embarrassing.

Then again, this was good. It proved we were a bona fide couple doing normal boyfriend and girlfriend things. It was fine.

After wiping away the lipstick smudges, I prepared the drinks, then returned to the living room.

'Sorry, I didn't catch your name,' I said to the man as I handed him his water.

'Mr Morgan.' Wow. So formal.

'Very nice to meet you, *Mr Morgan*.'

'Will Mr Stone be much longer?' He glared at his watch. 'My wife and children are expecting me home for dinner.'

'I'm sure he'll be down any minute.' Beads of sweat trickled down my back. They hadn't even been here five minutes. And they'd arrived ten minutes early, so it wasn't as if we were late.

Just as I was about to suggest I'd go and find Liam, I

heard him walking down the stairs.

'Hi!' He strutted into the room looking like a sexy hero from a romance novel and my heart flipped. 'Sorry, sweetheart.' Liam bent down and planted a soft kiss on my lips, causing my ovaries to explode. His hair was still damp and he smelt of shower gel and Eau de Hot Man. 'Sorry for keeping you waiting.' He walked towards Susie and held out his hand. 'I'm Liam.'

It was sweet that he introduced himself, but I was pretty sure there wasn't a person on the planet who didn't know who he was.

'So lovely to meet you!' Susie gushed, fluttering her eyelashes. 'This is Mr Morgan, one of the senior competition judges.'

Liam stretched out his hand to her colleague, who shook it without muttering a word.

'I see you've both got drinks.'

'Shall I get you something, honey?' I asked.

'Water would be great, baby.'

Normally I hated when people, especially men, called me *sweetheart* or *baby*, but for some reason, hearing it from Liam tonight made my insides light up.

As well as getting the water, I used the opportunity to quickly reapply my lipstick. I needed all the confidence I could get if I was going to pull this interview off.

When I returned to the room, Liam was complimenting Mr Morgan on his glasses, but it did nothing to crack his stony expression.

'Shall we get started?' Mr Morgan sighed as I returned to the sofa.

'Of course!' I squeezed up closer to Liam. He rested his hand on mine. The heat from his palm caused a spark of electricity to race through me. It was so intense I almost jumped out of my skin, but luckily I caught myself just in time and remembered that Liam was supposed to be my hot boyfriend and we touched all the time.

'How long exactly have you two been together?' Mr Morgan, aka Mr Grumpy asked.

'Our romantic relationship is in the early stages, but we've known each other for over twenty years,' I said calmly. I knew that question was coming, so it felt good to get one prepared answer out of the way.

'Hmm. So how long?'

Why couldn't he just accept my perfectly crafted answer and leave it at that? I didn't like this guy.

'Since the end of July,' I murmured, knowing it didn't sound great. But at least I'd practised enough to deliver the line successfully.

Technically it'd only been two and a bit weeks since Liam had messaged to confirm he'd fake-date me, but it was almost September, so that made it sound like it was longer.

Liam and I had worked out the dates to make sure it was after the Sunrise scandal, which was around mid-July. No one had seen him for weeks after that, so technically he could've been with me.

'So barely two months?' He raised his eyebrows, clearly unimpressed.

'That's what's so incredible,' Liam added. 'On paper that might not sound like a long time, but when you meet *the one*, time is irrelevant. I'm sure being in the business you're in, you've met people that fall in love quickly and the feelings they experience in a couple of months are more intense than what some people experience in a lifetime. And when you consider our history and how close we were, it's a powerful combination.'

Liam weaved his fingers into mine and squeezed. That one gesture made me melt like hot ice cream. It was telling me *I've got you, Mia*. And in that moment, I was so grateful that he was here.

'It's true. I find with my clients that often the older they are, the faster things happen. They've got a clearer idea of what they want.'

Grumpy Guts scribbled something on his notepad and Susie nodded.

We were only a few minutes in and I already knew that this interview was going to be tougher than I'd feared. I thought it'd be enough to have a boyfriend, but the fact that we hadn't been dating for very long felt almost as 'bad' as not having one at all.

'How did you meet?' Susie asked.

'We were best friends at school.'

'And I always had a crush on her,' Liam added.

I almost blurted out *really?* but then remembered he was acting. He said it so convincingly, I almost believed him.

'I was pretty into him too…' No acting required for that answer. It was true. I looked at him and smiled. *Jesus*. He was so bloody handsome.

'But when my mum took me to live in Spain, we lost contact. I never stopped thinking about her, though.' Liam reached up and stroked my cheek.

Someone give the guy an Oscar. Trudy was right. Hiring an actor to be my fake boyfriend was genius. I couldn't imagine anyone else putting on a performance as good as this.

I wanted to say that I'd never stopped thinking about him too, but considering I'd been in a long-term relationship for all of my adult life, that would've sounded bad.

'So why didn't you get in touch?' Grumpy Grump spat.

'I knew Mia was in a relationship, so I had to respect that. I thought that if we were really meant to be, like I'd always believed, fate would bring us together again. And I was right.'

'Awww,' Susie swooned. 'That's so romantic.'

'Now you can understand why I'm crazy about him!' I leant forward and pecked him on the lips.

God, what did he use to make his lips so soft? And how long would be appropriate to wait before kissing him again?

'I must say I'm quite surprised by your *relationship*.' Mr Grumpy said the word 'relationship' like he wasn't convinced. Shit. 'Forgive me, Mr Stone, but you do have a certain *reputation* with the ladies.'

My nostrils flared. Liam's past was none of his business. I reminded myself to keep my cool, then held my breath, waiting for the response.

'I'm aware,' Liam said calmly. 'You shouldn't believe everything you read, Mr Morgan. I'm no saint, but when you're a young guy who came from humble beginnings in South East London, who's catapulted into the bright lights of LA, it's hard not to be affected.'

'I can imagine.' Susie nodded sympathetically.

'My fortunes changed very quickly. All of a sudden I was earning a lot of money, my face was splashed over billboards and I had women flocking around me. I'm not complaining. I was living the dream. I don't know many people who wouldn't go off the rails. But that's in the past. Thanks to Mia, I've turned over a new leaf.'

That was actually a great answer. If you're single and women are offering themselves on a silver platter, there's no reason to turn them down.

'Humph.' Unsurprisingly, Mr Morgan wasn't impressed.

'What do you love most about Liam?' Susie asked.

'Where do I start?' I turned to face him, resisting the temptation to press my lips against his again. 'He's kind and so tuned in to my needs.'

Susie raised an eyebrow. Clearly she thought I meant sexually. I had a feeling he'd be great in the sack and hoped I'd get the chance to find out.

'In what way?'

'He always tries to make me comfortable. He listens and remembers the important little details that most people would forget. When he's around, I feel safe. He makes me feel seen.'

'Awww. And, Liam? What do you love about Mia?'

'She's caring, smart, sexy and brilliant at her job. Did you know that thanks to Mia, almost all of her friends are either married or happily coupled up? And in less than two years, her agency has already had more than a dozen engagements and marriages? That's like one every other month. That's fucking phenomenal. Excuse my French. She does this job because she wants to make people happy. If there were more Mias in the world, it'd be a better place.'

Liam Stone: Marry Me.

A million butterflies floated in my chest. That was one of the nicest things I'd ever heard anyone say about me.

'That's lovely. And, Mia, what do you think is the secret to a happy relationship?'

'Mutual respect and understanding. And love.'

'Anything to add, Liam?'

'Communication. And… great sex.' He smirked.

Mr Grumpy Grump's head shot up from his notepad and my eyes bulged.

Everything was going so well.

'Come on, guys. We all know it's true. It's a basic need. Great sex isn't just carnal. It's about intimacy. Having that connection. And it makes us happy. And happiness is important in a relationship, am I right?'

The room fell silent.

'That's an important point,' Susie said.

'I agree,' I added. 'There are many reasons relationships break down: infidelity, money…' My voice trailed off as I thought about my ex. 'The pressures of family life, but sexual incompatibility can be a factor too.'

'We have everything we need.' Mr Grumpy Grump put his notepad in his briefcase and stood up. What would it take for this guy to crack a smile?

They didn't even ask the question about whether being in a relationship made me a better matchmaker, and I had a brilliant answer ready for that. Maybe they saved that for the actual magazine profile interview. If his lack of enthusiasm was anything to go by, I wouldn't get the chance to find out.

'Thanks for your time.' Susie got up. 'We have your paperwork and client testimonials, so we'll go through everything next week, then we'll be in touch soon about the finals.'

'If she makes it that far,' Mr Grumpy Grump added.

Arsehole.

'You'd be crazy not to put her through.' Liam shot Mr Morgan a look, then followed it up with a saccharine-sweet smile.

'He's my biggest supporter!' I loved that Liam had my back. 'Thanks again for coming.' I followed them to the front door.

'Great to meet you,' Liam said as we waved them off.

After shutting the door, I exhaled deeply, returned to the living room and collapsed on the awful sofa.

'I'm so glad that's over!'

'You did great. Don't be put off by Mr Dicky Dick.'

'Ha! I'd nicknamed him Mr Grumpy Grump! It wouldn't have hurt the man to crack one smile!'

'Forget about him. We should celebrate.' Liam took my hand and led me to the kitchen. My pulse raced. I loved the sensation of his palm wrapped in mine. I loved him touching me full stop. 'I know this was a big deal for you. And now it's done.'

He plucked a bottle of champagne from the fridge, placed it on the island, then grabbed two glasses.

'I'd better open this.' He released his palm and I instantly missed the skin-to-skin contact.

After popping the cork and pouring it into the glasses, he handed a flute to me and raised his glass.

'Here's to you winning this competition!'

'Cheers.' I clinked his glass. 'And thanks for your help,' I said, trying not to think about how much I wanted to kiss him to show my appreciation. I took a large gulp of champagne, then leant against the island.

'It was nothing.' He waved his hand dismissively.

'It wasn't *nothing*! You were amazing. You put on the

performance of a lifetime. Everything you said, you know, about having a crush and what you liked about me, was brilliant. You were so convincing.'

Liam let out a little laugh and stepped forward.

'The reason it was so convincing, Mia, is because it was all true.'

'Ha!' I laughed. 'Good one!'

'I mean it.' He took another step forward. He was so close I felt his sweet breath tickling me when he spoke.

'What?' I frowned. 'No, you don't. You told me. The other day. When we were practising our kiss. You told me that was fake.'

'I didn't say it was fake.' He plucked the glass from my hand and moved it to the far end of the counter next to his. 'I said that if I was kissing you for real, you wouldn't be able to see or stand straight. And that was true. I was holding back. I wasn't kissing you how I really wanted to.' His face inched closer.

'H-how did you want to kiss me?' I swallowed hard.

'Like this.' He closed the gap between us and slammed his lips onto mine.

My legs trembled. Shit. He was right. He'd only been kissing me for a few seconds and the intensity of his lips was so much, I wasn't sure how long I could support my body weight.

I gripped the edge of the island to steady myself. Liam's hungry mouth moved against mine, teasing my lips open before sliding his tongue inside. As it flicked against mine, every atom in my body came alive.

This was the best kiss I'd had, bar none.

It was frenzied and delicious.

And I wanted more.

31

MIA

I wrapped my arms around Liam's back, pulling him into me. His hard length pressed against my stomach, and not for the first time, I wondered how amazing it'd feel if he buried it inside me.

But we shouldn't.

This was just supposed to be fake. Now the interview was done, I only really needed Liam to come to the finals with me. *If* I made it through.

There was no one watching us now. No cameras, no judges. And…

Ohhhh…

Liam's mouth trailed across my cheek and down to my neck. *Holy shit.* My knees buckled again as he nuzzled into my neck.

'Mia, I want you so fucking much right now,' he growled. 'Get up on that island.'

'Wh-what?' I asked, still savouring the feel of his hot lips on my skin.

'You heard. I want you to sit that fine arse on the edge

of this island. But pull up your dress first. Or take it off. It's up to you.'

I did as he asked. Or should I say *demanded*. Normally I hated being told what to do—especially by a man—but Liam's commands turned me on.

After pulling my dress up around my waist, I attempted to jump up on the island. Two unsexy attempts later, Liam scooped me into his arms, lifted me up and pulled me to the edge.

'How was the kiss?' he asked, desire burning in his eyes.

'It was… amazing. You have a very talented mouth.'

'Good. Want to know what else I can do with it?'

I nodded, my throat dry with anticipation.

'Is that a yes?' He paused. 'I need to be sure.'

'It's definitely a yes.'

'Good. I'm gonna take off your panties now.'

My eyes widened. Was I really going to let Liam Stone fuck me?

'Wait.' I paused. 'Maybe we shouldn't do this.' My vagina weeped, wondering what the hell I was thinking. 'I mean, I really want to. Like a *lot*.'

'Then why not?'

'Because this is supposed to be pretend…'

Because if sex with you is anywhere near as good as the way you kiss, I'll never recover.

'And?'

'And… we're not even supposed to like each other.'

'*That's* what you're concerned about? I wouldn't worry about whether I like you, sweetheart.' He smirked. 'Because if you give me the green light, I'm gonna fuck you so hard, it'll feel like I don't.'

My breath caught in my throat and my legs flopped open. My mind had lost control of my body and desire had taken over.

Screw being sensible. Screw thinking about the consequences. Liam Stone, the guy I'd secretly fantasised about for years, was stood here, offering to end my sex drought and give me what was sure to be the best sex of my life. I'd be a fool to pass it up.

'Okay,' I said breathlessly, red-hot need pulsing through my veins. 'Do it. Fuck me like you hate me.'

A smile spread across his mouth.

'Mia Bailey, talking dirty. Damn.' He licked his lips. 'Don't worry, baby. I'll get to that. I told you earlier, I like to take my time. So first I wanna taste you. I haven't eaten all evening and I know *exactly* what I want to feast on.'

Liam stepped forward, his hands trailing up my thighs, then reached between my legs. I threw my head back and moaned. After going so long without, the sensation of his hands touching me there was enough to make me explode.

'Oh God… fuck.'

'You're so wet. I love it. Lift up that arse,' he commanded. I hoisted myself up and watched as he pulled my red lace knickers to my knees, then leant forward and dragged them down to my ankles with his teeth.

Wow. That was the hottest thing I'd ever seen.

Once he'd removed them from my ankles, he dropped to his knees.

'Spread your legs. I need to see that beautiful pussy.'

'Is that… enough?' I opened them a little, feeling self-conscious.

'No. Wider. I wanna devour you.'

This time, I spread myself open without hesitation. Hearing his dirty talk made me putty in his hands.

'That's it.' He came closer. 'Good girl.'

Liam buried his head between my legs and licked me like I was his favourite ice cream. Long, soft strokes of his tongue travelled down from my clit to my opening, then back up to my sensitive nub.

Every time his mouth touched me, a bolt of electricity shot up my spine.

'Oh my God!' I cried out, gripping his hair.

As he circled me, my body sparked, like there were fireworks in my veins rather than blood.

So this was what it felt like to have a real man. I wasn't even sure I was still on this earth. I hadn't even come yet and I already felt like I was in heaven.

I looked down. The sight of Liam's head between my legs was incredible. When I'd read about all those heroes in romance books calling grown women a *good girl*, I'd thought it was demeaning. But there was nothing demeaning about seeing his head buried between my thighs as he did everything he could to give me pleasure.

I pushed his face deeper into me. He could call me *good girl* all night if he made me feel like this.

Just when I thought I'd reached the height of pleasure, Liam slid two long, delicious fingers into me. I gasped, my hips shooting up from the cold marble island. I tried to close my legs. The sensations were almost too much. Liam lifted his head.

'I'm in the middle of fucking you with my tongue. Spread those legs for me, sweetheart.'

As my legs flopped open again, he continued dipping his fingers in and out of me whilst circling my clit.

'I can't,' I cried out. 'I'm going to…'

'That's it, baby.' He continued pumping his fingers whilst lapping at me with his tongue.

'Oh God, oh God, oh, oh, ohhhhhh God!!'

My orgasm ripped through me like an explosion. I felt it from my scalp right down to my toes.

Holy crap. Normally it took a lot of stimulation, usually from my vibrator, for me to even come close. But Liam rocks up with his talented mouth and makes me come faster than a bolt of lightning.

Liam lifted his head from between my legs, a satisfied grin across his face. And that wasn't the only thing on his face.

'Good for you?' He licked his lips.

'Good?' I panted, still trying to catch my breath. 'That was… incredible.' I didn't care if that made his ego swell to the size of five continents. He deserved the praise.

'Glad to be of service.'

'Should I… get down?' I wouldn't mind staying here longer to recover.

'Get down?' His eyebrows knitted together. 'You think we're done?'

'I thought you might be tired?'

'That was just a warm-up. The appetiser. You said you wanted me to fuck you. Have you changed your mind?'

'No. I did. I still do.'

'Good.'

'Shall we go to the bedroom?'

'Too far. Unless you object, I'm gonna do you right here.'

I swallowed hard. I'd never done it in the kitchen before. It always seemed so… unsanitary.

Liam lifted his T-shirt over his head, exposing his bare chest, and a fresh wave of tingles raced through me.

Next he undid his jeans, then pulled them down, slowly. As I took in the sight of his hard-on straining against his boxers, I almost wept.

The man was a god.

What was I just saying about him screwing me on a kitchen counter? Right now, Liam could offer to fuck me in a sewer and I'd agree.

Anything to have him inside of me.

He peeled down his boxers. As his cock sprang free, my jaw crashed to the floor.

The rumours were true.

Liam Stone was hung like a horse.

It was long *and* thick.

I'd be lying if I said I wasn't terrified about the damage that might do to my insides. But desire told logic to fuck off.

He scooped his jeans off the floor, pulled out his wallet, then a condom.

'So?' He stepped forward. 'Do you want this? Or should I put it away?'

'No.' I ran my hand from the base of his smooth dick all the way to the tip, which was already leaking pre-cum. 'Put it inside me.'

32

LIAM

I licked my lips, savouring the taste of Mia's juices.

I'd dreamt about burying my head between her legs for years, so I was surprised I hadn't come already. I'd got pretty close, though.

When she told me to fuck her, I almost exploded in my boxers. And now she just told me to put my cock inside her, it was game over.

I wasn't gonna waste any more time.

After ripping open the condom wrapper and rolling it down my hard length, I stepped forward.

'Last chance to back out.' I lined my cock up at her entrance. 'It's been a while for me and according to you, I'm supposed to hate you, so I can't promise I'll be gentle. You sure you can take it?'

'I'm a big girl. Just hurry up,' she commanded.

What the lady wants, the lady gets.

I pulled Mia to the edge of the counter, then drove my cock into her.

Mia cried out and I paused.

'You good?' I asked.

'I just… please, just fuck me.'

'Yes, ma'am!'

I ploughed into Mia, feeding every inch of my thickness inside her, over and over. She was so fucking wet and I loved it.

'Oh God!' she cried out, squeezing her eyes shut. 'More.'

After gripping her hips tighter, I drove into her, harder, faster.

'Take off your dress.'

'Can't,' she panted, scraping her nails down my back.

'I wanna suck on your beautiful tits whilst I fuck you, so either take it off or I will.'

'Don't stop!'

'I won't. I can do more than one thing at a time.'

Mia's eyes rolled back into her head as I continued thrusting into her. Looked like I'd need to do it myself. I removed one of my hands from her hips and reached for the scissors in the knife block on the counter.

'Hold still.' I dialled down the rhythm a little as I cut into the top of the dress.

'What the…! You just cut the dress!'

'I'm aware. Can't fuck you properly when you're still wearing it.' I stopped pumping. Now I could finish the job myself. Using both hands, I ripped the dress in two.

The fabric fell on the counter, leaving Mia in just her bra.

Her mouth fell open and just as she went to speak, I drove into her again, harder this time.

'God, Liam. Fuck!' Mia cried out.

I reached forward, slid one hand around her back and undid the clasp. Using my teeth, I pulled the bra beneath her breasts.

'So fucking beautiful.' I took in the sight of her perfect tits. I placed my left hand on her arse to pull her further into me, then cupped one of her breasts in my other hand before taking her hard nipple in my mouth and sucking.

Damn. I knew I'd said before that I was going to fuck her like I hated her, but there was nothing to hate right now. My cock was buried deep inside her and the way she was tightening around me was what fantasies were made of.

˙If I could keep my head nuzzled in her chest for the rest of my life, I'd die a happy man.

After a long, hard suck of her left nipple, I moved over to the right, taking it between my teeth and stroking and flicking the tip with my tongue. Mia let out a long, slow groan, bucking against me.

She was close and I knew I wouldn't be able to hold on for much longer either. It was time to pick up the pace.

I lifted my head from her boobs, gripped her butt, then slid my other hand between her legs and started stroking her clit as I powered into her.

'Oh, Jesus!' she screamed. 'I'm not going to… I can't, I-I…'

Mia grabbed my arse, digging her nails into my skin as she pulled me into her and moved her hips in time with mine, her beautiful tits bouncing with every thrust.

I was in awe of this woman. I squeezed my eyes shut. If I looked at her gorgeous body for another second I was gonna bust my load, and there was no way I was gonna come before she did.

As I flicked my thumb over her clit, driving my cock harder and faster into her, Mia's body quivered and she clenched around me.

'Ohhhh, yes, yes, yesssssss!' she cried out so loud the whole street must've heard, but I wasn't complaining.

Mia slumped back on the counter, like her orgasm had sucked every last drop of energy from her body. *Good.* Now she was satisfied, it was my turn to finish.

I lasted a few more pumps before my own orgasm ripped through me.

'Fuuucckkk…' I grunted before a feral sound flew from my mouth.

My knees buckled and I quickly moved my hands from Mia's waist and gripped the counter to steady myself.

Jesus. I knew sex with Mia would be good, but I wasn't expecting *that*. I'd never come so hard in my life.

My breathing was ragged and my legs were weak. I didn't want to pull out. I wanted to stay inside her for as long as possible.

I leant forward, resting my head on her stomach. I felt her heart hammering above my head and her chest rising and falling.

'That was…'

I looked up and saw her watching me through hooded eyes.

'Yeah,' I replied.

'How did you… how are you so… *good*?'

'Practise.' I shrugged my shoulders.

One of the benefits of being eternally single was that you learnt a lot about how to please a woman. And seeing as women were only interested in my body anyway, I had to make sure I lived up to their expectations.

'Well, you're welcome to practise on me anytime.' She smiled.

I quickly lifted my head from her stomach.

'I'm gonna pull out now, okay? Stay there, and I'll get you a towel.'

Mia sat up, reached for the fabric that used to be her dress, then covered herself.

'It's okay.' She slid down from the counter, avoiding my gaze. 'I'm going to have a shower.'

She seemed embarrassed, or maybe hurt? A second ago she was praising my performance and now it was like a switch had been flicked.

Oh.

Got it. It was because she'd said I could practise on her and I hadn't replied.

The truth was, I needed time to process this. I didn't normally stick around for post-sex conversation and never did repeats. It was easier that way. But this was different. Not just because the sex was amazing, but because it was Mia. She wasn't some random stranger. She was… someone I didn't want to hurt.

'Okay. I'm gonna shower too.'

Mia headed for the door

'Wait.' I grabbed her arm and pulled her into me, pressing my lips on to hers.

If this was just going to be a one-night thing, tonight needed to count.

As Mia's breasts pressed against my chest, my dick twitched. I lifted her up and she wrapped her legs around my waist, then gripped my hair.

'If we both need a shower,' I whispered in her ear, 'we should do it together. Help save water.'

'Sounds good,' she said softly.

As I carried Mia up to the bathroom, I knew we wouldn't just be washing in the shower.

We were about to get dirty all over again.

33

MIA

As daylight flooded the room, I slowly opened my eyes. Liam's side of the bed was empty.

It was kind of a relief. I needed time alone to gather my thoughts. Then again, even if I had a century to think, it wouldn't change the fact that I was royally screwed. Literally and metaphorically.

My vagina felt like I'd been impaled on a baseball bat, but in the best possible way.

Sex with Liam last night was out of this world. It wasn't even in the same universe.

I'd heard the rumours, but usually when people said something was amazing and I tried it, I was disappointed. But last night, *that* was... *wow*.

Liam going down on me.

Liam fucking me on the kitchen counter.

Then in the shower.

Jesus Christ.

Just like I'd hoped, the man had given me the best sex of my life.

And that was why I knew I was screwed.

Because this couldn't go anywhere. Liam wasn't into relationships. He didn't even live in this country. This was supposed to be fake. And yet, I'd never felt more connected to anyone in my life.

I tossed the duvet off, sat at the edge of the bed, then groaned. I really wished I didn't like him.

After showering and getting dressed, I headed to the kitchen to grab a banana. I was starving, but didn't have time to eat anything more substantial. Thanks to our third 'workout' in the early hours of this morning, I'd slept through my alarm, so I was already late.

As I stepped into the kitchen, I gasped.

On the island was a pretty pink flower in a glass vase with a note.

Morning!

Sorry I had to leave without saying goodbye, but you were sleeping so peacefully.

Just in case you don't have time to make breakfast, I made you this fruit salad and fresh orange juice.

Will text later xx

Wow. No man had ever made me breakfast. That was so sweet. He'd even put the fruit salad in a container so I could take it to work, which was really thoughtful. My heart melted like ice cream over hot apple pie.

Speaking of apple pie, I'd just realised that Liam had placed the container and flower in the exact spot that I'd sat on the island last night.

A flashback of Liam fucking me popped into my brain and my body tingled. I should give the island a good wipe.

I didn't know if his cleaner was coming today, and even if she was, leaving her to do it didn't seem right.

My phone chimed. When I saw it was Liam, my stomach flipped. There were several messages from Trudy from last night too.

I quickly opened her texts first just to check she was okay. She'd messaged to ask how the interview went. Once I'd fired off a reply to say I'd fill her in at the office, I clicked on to Liam's message.

My Hot Boyfriend

Just checking you're awake! I know you don't like to be late.

Me

Just in the kitchen. Thanks so much for breakfast!

My Hot Boyfriend

Welcome.

My Hot Boyfriend

BTW, don't worry. I cleaned the island/counter with disinfectant.

He added a winky face and I burst out laughing. We may not have been in contact for years, but he knew me so well.

Me

Thanks! Was just about to hunt down the bleach!

My Hot Boyfriend

Knew it!

Better go.

Me

Okay. Have a great day! xx

My Hot Boyfriend

You too! xx

. . .

I floated to work. With the paps leaving us alone, I was able to make my own way to the office.

Even when I had to squeeze onto a packed Tube and my head got stuffed under someone's smelly armpit, it didn't bother me like it usually would.

'Morning!' I chirped as I stepped into the office. 'Beautiful day, isn't it?'

Trudy glanced outside, taking in the dark skies and rain lashing against the window, and frowned.

'Er, no. It's pissing down with rain. *Ohhh…* you're being sarcastic!'

'I wasn't, actually. It is a *beautiful* day!' I smiled and my chest bloomed. I couldn't remember the last time I'd felt this happy.

'So, tell me! How was the interview? Did you nail it?'

'I wouldn't say I *nailed it*, exactly, but it went okay.'

I filled her in on everything, including the annoying Mr Morgan and the fact that I'd hopefully hear whether I'd reached the finals soon.

'And how was Liam?'

'Yeah, great!' A memory of his head between my legs flashed into my mind and my whole body sparked. Oh crap. Trudy was talking about the interview, not his talented mouth, hands and dick. 'He put on a brilliant performance.'

He definitely did…

'Glad it went well. When you didn't reply to my texts, I got worried.'

'Sorry. I was… busy…'

'After the interview? Doing what?'

I quickly walked to the filing cabinets at the far end of

the office, which considering how sore I was from last night wasn't easy.

Facing the wall, I pretended to rifle through some files. I had the feeling Trudy was going to start asking questions. If she took one look at my face, she'd know something happened and start saying *I told you so*.

'Just... stuff.'

I really wished that I could lie off the top of my head.

'You okay? What's wrong with your leg? You're walking funny.'

Trudy was like one of those police dogs. She could smell if something wasn't right.

'Nothing!' I squeaked.

'I know when you're lying. Look at me.'

I turned around slowly, realising I was only postponing the inevitable.

Trudy's brows knitted together. Her eyes narrowed, then she gasped.

'Oh my God!' She jumped out of her seat. 'Something happened with Liam last night, didn't it?!'

'Yeah...' I returned to my desk. 'We had sex.'

'*Knew* it!' She ran over and threw her arms around me. 'Didn't I say that you'd get together?' She squeezed me so hard I could hardly breathe.

'We're not *together*... we just... it just... happened.'

'*Yeah, sure*. He was lying there naked and you accidentally fell on his dick! Why didn't you tell me sooner?' She perched on the edge of my desk. 'You should've called me last night to give me a blow-by-blow account, pardon the pun. Then again, I bet you were busy blowing Liam like a trumpet!' Trudy threw her head back, laughing. 'I know I would've!'

'Oh God.' I shook my head. 'There was no time to call. After we finished in the kitchen, we moved to the shower…'

Trudy's eyes flew so far from their sockets, they probably landed on the moon.

'Wait, *what*? *You* had *sex* in the kitchen? Where? On the floor? Against the fridge? No! Don't tell me you had kitchen counter sex?' I nodded, a smile touching my lips. Trudy's jaw dropped. 'Classic! Who the hell are you and what have you done with my best friend?'

'I know.' A huge grin spread across my face. I was trying to play it cool, but I'd never been cool in my life, so no point attempting to start now.

As annoying as it was that Trudy had predicted this, I had to admit it was pretty amazing. Exciting things like last night never happened to me.

'I thought you'd be worried about it being unhygienic and getting your happy juices everywhere!' Trudy belly laughed.

'I'm sorry, what did you just call it? *Happy juices*?'

'What?' She shrugged. 'Is that not an accurate description?'

'Anyway'—I waved my hand in the air—'normally, I would've been worried, but I was too busy focusing on Liam's head between my legs…' I smirked.

'Wait! He fucked you *and* went down on you? Holy shit! You are officially the luckiest woman alive! And?'

'And what?'

'What do you mean, *and what*? I need *details*! How was it? How big is he? Are the rumours true? Did he go all night? And wait… I was so busy trying to process the whole kitchen counter sex thing, I completely forgot that you mentioned you did it in the *shower* too! Tell me *everything*!!'

By the time I'd finished filling Trudy in on how Liam had made me come twice when he'd pinned me against the shower wall and one more time this morning, her jaw was several hundred metres below the earth.

'I'm bloody speechless. You literally went from nun to sex freak in one night! No wonder you're walking funny. I'm so happy for you, babes.' She threw her arms around me. 'You deserve this. And despite his reputation, Liam's a good guy.'

'Yeah. He even made me breakfast this morning.'

'The man's a keeper. Just like I told you from the beginning. Clearly *I* should become a matchmaker! When you two are walking down the aisle, don't forget to give me a shout-out at the altar. Let everyone know that your best mate brought you two lovebirds together!'

'We're not *together*!' I rolled my eyes. 'Last night was just a one-off.'

'Five big Os doesn't sound like a one-off to me!'

'I mean, it was just one night. It won't happen again. I'm sure of that.'

Liam had pretty much confirmed it. When I'd stupidly blurted out that I'd be happy for him to 'practise' on me as much as he wanted, I saw the flash of horror on his face. He clearly didn't want me to get the wrong idea. The shower shag and this morning was just a final hurrah. Or to ease his guilt. I wasn't complaining. I knew not to expect anything more from him.

'If you two don't bang again, I'll give you a million pounds.'

'You don't have a million pounds.'

'Exactly. And I won't need it either, because I'm right. You'll see.'

The office line rang. *Saved by the bell.*

'Good morning, Soulmate Connections, how may I help you?'

'Yeah, hi. Can I speak to the woman who runs the agency? The one who's dating Liam Stone.'

'Erm.' I paused, worried that it was a pap or journalist. 'Who may I say is calling?'

'Chardonnay.'

'Hello, *Chardonnay*, this is Mia speaking. I run the agency.'

'Cool. So can you set me up, then? I'm looking for a rich boyfriend. Well, preferably a rich *husband*. Someone like Liam. I don't want some old, bald, fat guy. He needs to be fit. And loaded.'

'I see.' I paused, thinking how best to handle this. I'd hoped being with Liam would bring in some new business, but this wasn't the kind of client I wanted to work with. The fact that she'd mentioned that he needed to have a lot of money three times in less than thirty seconds told me she was looking for a sugar daddy, not true love. 'If you're interested in becoming a client, I can email you a link with the questionnaire I ask all new clients to complete. It also includes the fees and payment terms.'

'What? I have to *pay*?' Chardonnay gasped. 'But Tinder's free!'

'Yes, I'm aware of that.' I took a deep breath. 'But this isn't a dating app. My company is a professional matchmaking service, so you pay a fee which covers the time I spend searching for the perfect love match for you. It's a bespoke service.'

'I'm not going to *pay* to meet someone! I'm sure there's a Tinder for celebs. I bet that's free. Can't you just tell me how to get onto that?'

'I believe the app you're referring to is called Raya. By all means, if you feel that may be better suited to your needs, feel free to apply.'

'Yeah. I'll do that. Cheers! And if you need someone to take Liam off your hands, I'm up for it. I'm open to the three of us having fun together too, if you fancy spicing things up a bit?'

OMG. Seriously? That was the first time I'd been offered a threesome by a potential client.

'Thanks for your call, Chardonnay. Good luck.'

She hung up.

'Did you just turn down a client?' Trudy frowned. She'd returned to her desk and was demolishing a blueberry muffin.

'Not really. She was looking for a rich, fit celebrity boyfriend and was horrified that I charged for my services.'

'Oh... got it. But doesn't Raya charge too? And don't they have thousands of people on their waiting list?'

'Mm-hmm.' I nodded, then sighed.

This was the challenge I was up against. People were always sceptical about paying for a matchmaker when they thought it was easier and cheaper to use the apps.

'Don't worry. When you win this competition, you'll have loads of serious clients knocking down your door.'

'Here's hoping.'

The message notification ping sounded on my phone. As I glanced down at the screen and saw who it was from, a warm feeling flooded my chest.

I thought back to when he'd first put his number in my phone and how annoyed I was when I saw that he'd put it under **My Hot Boyfriend.** It seemed ridiculous back then, but now, the description felt... true.

'Is that loverboy?' Trudy smiled.

'Why do you say that?'

'Because you've got a smile the size of Asia on your face.'

'Yeah, it's Liam.' I grinned.

My Hot Boyfriend

What are you doing tonight?

My Hot Boyfriend

I have tickets to see *The Lion King*. You've probably seen it already, but let me know if you want to come.

Was it bad that when I saw the last few words of what he'd written, my mind went straight to the gutter?

Me

I'd love to come...

My Hot Boyfriend

Are you talking about the show or something else?

Me

What else could I be talking about?

My Hot Boyfriend

Hmmm... you know exactly what I'm talking about.

My Hot Boyfriend

I'll send a car for you at 6.30, okay?

Me

I can just get the train to Charing Cross and walk from there. It'll be quicker.

My Hot Boyfriend

The car will be there at 6.30. See you later xx

'Come on, then, spill!' Trudy said. 'Now your smile is the size of *two* continents!'

'We're going out tonight. To the theatre.'

'So another date, eh? Fake boyfriend, my arse. Like I said earlier, there's no way you two won't be shagging again tonight.'

This time, I didn't protest.

If Liam wanted to take me to bed, the shower or the kitchen counter or ravish me on any other piece of furniture, there was no way I was turning him down.

34

LIAM

I fixed the collar of my shirt for what felt like the tenth time. I should've just gone with the jumper. We were only going to the theatre, not a meeting.

Why was I so nervous? I didn't like to stare in the mirror too much. It was dangerous. Too easy for my mind to stray and start worrying about whether what Dad had said the last time he'd bothered to message was true: that I wasn't looking as good as I used to.

That was why I needed to stay in shape. Right now, my underwear and fragrance campaigns paid the bills. Without them, I'd be screwed. My face and body had got me to where I was today. But like Mum had warned me, it wouldn't last forever. I had to get my career back on track, ASAP.

My phone buzzed. Phil was downstairs. There was no time to change now. I'd have to stick with the shirt. Hopefully Mia would like it.

Jesus. It was like I was thirteen, going on my first date. I reminded myself that this was fake.

But nothing about last night felt pretend. It was incredible.

Normally, when I slept with a woman, once we'd both got what we needed, I couldn't wait to leave. But given the chance, I would've devoured Mia over and over, until I took my last breath. The connection was unreal.

I knew I should've stopped when we'd finished in the kitchen, but I couldn't help myself. One taste of her and I wanted more.

I'd hoped that after our session in the shower, I'd be satisfied, but nope. Seeing the droplets of water running down her beautiful tits, then between her thighs, hearing her scream my name as I pinned her against the wall and made her come... those images along with the ones from the kitchen and our quickie this morning played on repeat in my mind all day.

We were treading on dangerous ground. This couldn't go anywhere. And tonight I'd have to remind her of that. Make sure we were both on the same page. The last thing I wanted to do was hurt her.

Thinking about it, inviting her tonight wasn't the best idea. But when I was offered two tickets, Mia was the first person that came into my mind.

'Hey, Phil.' I smiled as he opened the car door and I slid onto the back seat.

Mia was right. Taking the Tube would've been quicker. But it was rush hour and these days it wasn't easy for me to walk around without someone recognising me.

Things had been calmer with the paps, which was a relief. But everyone had mobile phones, so it only took seconds before photos made their way onto social media. The car was a better option.

Getting to Mia's office took longer than expected, so by the time I called to let her know we were downstairs, it was almost 6.45.

As I saw her walking towards the car, my heart jumped into my throat. She was a vision.

Mia was wearing the fitted orange structured dress I'd ordered and black heels. My dick twitched. I'd always thought she looked hot as hell in those formal dresses and imagined what lay beneath. But now I knew exactly how she looked naked. Now I'd felt her soft skin. Now I'd tasted her and I'd buried myself inside her, everything was different.

Phil opened the door and Mia got in.

'Oh!' Her eyes widened. 'When you said you'd send a car, I thought I'd be on my own.' Mia put on her seat belt and Phil pulled out into the traffic.

'I finished early, so I thought I'd come with you.'

Mia bit her lip.

'I'd really like you to *come* with me,' she teased.

Before I could stop myself, I crushed my lips on hers. As her mouth parted, I slid my tongue inside, flicking it gently against Mia's.

Her hands dipped beneath my jacket and she ran her palms over my chest.

'Fuck.' I pulled away. I'd just finished telling myself this wasn't a good idea, then thirty seconds later I end up kissing her. I needed to get a grip. Fast. 'You're addictive, you know that?'

'I'll take that as a compliment.' She smiled, which only made the situation in my pants worse.

'Mia, in case it wasn't obvious, I like you, but…'

'I get it.' She pressed her finger over my lips and I had to fight the urge to slide it into my mouth.

She said she understood, but I wanted to make sure. The privacy screen was up and Phil had been vetted, so I felt able to speak freely.

'I... last night was... incredible. But I'm just not the relationship type. They never last, so it's better not to go down that road. And it's complicated. I live in LA and—'

'Like I said,' Mia jumped in, 'I get it. I know you don't want anything serious. Last night was... fun. Nothing's changed. We can just stick to what we agreed before.'

'It's for the best.' I nodded. 'We shouldn't let anything happen again.'

'Absolutely,' Mia agreed.

I scooted back over to my side of the car. Mia fidgeted with her handbag whilst I stared out the window. The traffic was thick and we were at a standstill, which meant I could enjoy looking at Tower Bridge. As I glanced at the iconic towers and the waves of the River Thames dancing underneath it, I smiled.

It was funny. Even though the river's dirty greeny-brown water couldn't compare to the clear blue sea and pretty beaches in LA, somehow even after all these years, London still felt like home.

My gaze flicked back to Mia, who was now fiddling with the hem of her dress, giving me a glimpse of her thigh. Another flashback of my head buried between her legs jumped into my brain. I pushed it out again.

We sat in silence with just the sound of car horns piercing the air.

'So, have you ever seen *The Lion King* at the theatre?' I said.

Mia faced me and I swallowed hard. She really was beautiful. Her eyes sparkled, her lips were so full and soft. I wondered how they'd feel wrapped around my…

For fuck's sake. This was getting ridiculous.

'Nope.'

'What?' My eyebrows shot up to my hairline. 'You haven't lived!'

'Why? How many times have you seen it?'

'I probably watched the film a hundred times when I was a kid and I've seen the show in London a few times and on Broadway. I know the story so well that I could probably recite everything word for word by now.'

'Your memory's pretty impressive.'

'Thanks. It's part of the job. Need to be able to remember my lines.'

'Speaking of lines, you seem to like the theatre a lot, so how come you haven't done any plays?'

Good question.

'Gotta stay in my lane!' I laughed, avoiding Mia's eyes. 'Liam Stone is an action hero. He doesn't fit on the stage.'

'Sorry, but did you just refer to yourself in the third person?'

'Yep.' I tugged at a cuticle poking out from my thumbnail.

'Why?'

I cracked the window a little. It suddenly felt hot in here. Mia's gaze burned into my skin. She was waiting for an answer.

'Because…' I paused. I didn't know if I really wanted to go into this now. 'Because, sometimes it's how I feel. I feel like Liam Stone isn't really me. He's a character that I play.'

'Do you enjoy what you do?'

Another good question. I shuffled in my seat. I wasn't used to talking about my real feelings.

When people asked questions, it was usually during a press junket when I did back-to-back media interviews talking about a role in my latest movie. My answers were rehearsed and based on what my publicist told me to say, not my own opinion.

Opinions were dangerous. If I said what I really thought, I'd end up saying the wrong thing. Most people could just shrug it off and forget about it. But in my business, saying the wrong thing resulted in a bad headline splashed across the media and dissected in detail all over the internet.

I knew this wasn't a press interview. It was Mia. The person I used to be so comfortable with. I could tell her the truth. I was sure she'd understand. Then again, telling her how I really felt about my job might sound insensitive, given her financial situation.

Nah. Better to just stick to the script. It was safer that way.

'I'm lucky. Thousands of actors would give their right arm to be in my shoes, so I can't complain.'

That was true.

'I didn't ask about other actors, though. I asked about *you*.'

Damn. I should've known Mia was too smart to have fallen for that stock response. I blew out a breath, psyching myself up to speak my truth.

'I love the theatre. That's what I started doing at drama

school. I loved the buzz of doing a live performance. The adrenaline rush. I always dreamt of trying other things too, like a serious drama or even comedy. And I'd love to do screenwriting or try producing, but'—I shrugged—'it's not how people see me, so I just have to keep doing what I do best: running around with my shirt off, shooting people and blowing up buildings in front of the camera.'

My chest tightened. I wasn't looking forward to my next film. It'd be the same old, same old. Creating a film that was completely forgettable.

Sure, that still had value. People needed escapism and entertainment. But for once, I'd love to do something that pushed me out of my comfort zone. Something that really made a difference.

'There's nothing wrong with wanting to try new things and to challenge yourself. It doesn't mean you're ungrateful. Maybe you should try reinventing yourself. You know, like Matthew McConaughey.'

'Maybe,' I said. If only it was that simple.

'I was sad when he stopped doing romcoms, but I get that sometimes people want to change direction. I was terrified about leaving my job to set up the agency. And, yeah, it hasn't quite worked out how I'd hoped *yet*, but I'm still much happier than I was. You can control your destiny. You are Liam bloody Stone! Don't let anyone tell you that you can't do something. If you set your mind to it, you can achieve whatever you want!'

My chest did some weird fluttery thing. I was so used to being told that I should stick to what I was good at: looking pretty, making another film in the same genre and being happy with what I had. So it was strange to hear someone support my dream to try something different.

'I… thanks.' I squeezed Mia's hand. The softness of her skin made my body light up. I didn't want to pull away, but I had to. It felt too good.

'Boss,' Phil's voice sounded on the intercom.

'What's up?'

'Traffic's really thick. I've checked for different routes, but everywhere's gridlocked. We won't make it on time.'

'We're not far from Waterloo.' Mia pressed her face against the window. 'Let's just get the Tube. It's literally two stops to Charing Cross, then it'll take about ten minutes to walk there.'

'But…'

'I know you're worried about being mobbed by thousands of adoring fans, but this is the London Underground we're talking about. People don't even make eye contact. Everyone will be too busy reading the *Evening Standard* or scrolling through their phones to even notice you.'

'Maybe…'

From what I remembered about travelling on London public transport, people preferred to reread the same boring classified ads than look at the person in front of them. And making conversation was a hard no.

'Once, me and Trudy were coming home late and a drunk woman was masturbating on the Tube.'

'You're joking!'

'Nope. The carriage was half-full, but everyone pretended not to notice. Trudy thought it was hilarious!'

'That sounds like her,' I laughed.

'And loads of celebs have taken the Tube. If Rihanna, Jay-Z, Harry Styles and Benedict Cumberbatch can do it, so can you. You'll be fine!'

She was probably right. And like she said, it was only a couple of stops.

'We're getting the Tube.' I lowered the privacy screen to speak to Phil directly. 'Please just meet us at the theatre later.'

'Okay,' he confirmed.

'Ready?' I unbuckled my seat belt and looked out of the window to check it was safe to get out. We were stationary at the traffic lights, so the coast was clear.

'Yep.'

'Wait there.' I walked to Mia's side and opened the door.

'Thanks.' She stepped out.

A gust of wind hit us and Mia shivered. I was glad I had a jacket. London weather was so temperamental.

'Here.' I wrapped my jacket over her shoulders.

'What about you? It's my fault for leaving my jacket at the office.'

'It's been a while since I've been on a Tube, but I remember them being hotter than an oven. I'm not giving you my jacket to be a gentleman, it's just so I won't overheat when we get in the carriage,' I smirked.

'In that case, I'll accept.' She smiled and my chest expanded. 'Come on, we better cross.'

Mia took my hand and my heart raced. Travelling on the Tube during rush hour would rank high on the list of most people's least favourite things to do, but as she led the way to the station, adrenaline rushed through me.

'I'm guessing you don't have an Oyster card?' she asked as we walked towards the entrance.

'Correct.'

Mia slid her hand out of mine and I instantly missed the feel of her soft skin.

'Use my debit card.' She reached in her handbag and gave it to me.

'I can't let you—'

'I know I'm hard up, but I don't think a few pounds is going to make a big difference. Just tap it on the yellow reader.'

Mia went ahead, breezing through the ticket barriers, and I followed.

As we got onto the escalators, I nervously looked to my right and then my left, paranoid that someone might recognise me.

'Relax.' Mia turned around from where she stood on the step below. 'And if you don't want to draw attention to yourself, keep to the right of the escalator so people can walk down on the left.'

Unsurprisingly, when we got to the platform it was packed. We had to wait for two Tubes to pass before we eventually squeezed on, and luckily by that point we were at the front and were able to snag two seats.

Just like Mia predicted, everyone's eyes were fixated on their phone screens, books or newspapers and I felt like an egomaniac for even thinking that anyone would have the slightest interest in me.

The driver announced that the next stop was Charing Cross and as the people in front of us moved towards the exit, I had a clearer view of the passengers sitting directly opposite.

A woman in her twenties caught my gaze. Her eyes widened.

Uh-oh.

'Oh my God!' she shouted, reaching for her phone. 'Are you…? Can't be! Are you Liam *Stone*?' She held up her mobile.

'Smile,' Mia whispered in my ear.

I quickly engaged my brain in time before the woman snapped away.

'Yeah,' I answered.

'Oh my God, oh my God!' She fanned herself. 'I can't believe it's *you*!'

The other passengers turned to see what all the commotion was. And of course, the train chose that exact moment to stop in the tunnel.

There was nowhere we could go and nothing I could do, so I decided to roll with it. I was sure they were harmless.

I smiled and nodded in acknowledgement to the people staring.

'What you doing on the Tube, bruv?' a guy called out.

'Just trying to get from A to B, like you, mate.'

'Respect.' He extended his arm, greeting me with a fist bump. 'If I had your money, there's no way you'd catch me on this.'

'Can I have a selfie?' another woman across the carriage piped up.

I turned to face Mia. It felt wrong to take a picture without her.

'How about I take a photo for you,' Mia suggested.

'That'd be amazing!' She squeezed through and thrust her phone into Mia's hand as I stood beside her and smiled.

The train jerked forward and I caught the pole just in

time. Seconds later the doors opened. We'd arrived at Charing Cross.

'Nice to meet you.' I smiled at everyone. They were still bug-eyed like they'd seen a dinosaur rather than just me. It felt kinda nice.

'You survived!' Mia looked up and smiled at me as we walked from the platform to the escalators.

'Yep.' I smiled back.

Right now I wanted to kiss Mia. To thank her for coming tonight. For not laughing when I shared my career dreams with her. For suggesting we take the Tube. For paying for my ticket, even though she was struggling financially. For being so cool when people wanted to take photos. For making me feel so damn happy.

I was so glad she was back in my life.

Surviving the Tube was one thing.

But surviving without kissing or touching Mia again?

Something told me that was gonna be a lot harder than I thought.

35

MIA

Liam and I jumped to our feet, clapping enthusiastically.

'That was brilliant!' I cheered along with the audience as the cast took a bow on the stage.

'Now you understand why I've seen it so many times.'

'I already want to see it again!' I gushed. 'Maybe next time we…'

I caught myself just before I put my foot in it. I was about to say that next time we could go together, but I already knew that wasn't going to happen. We'd agreed in the car that we needed to put the brakes on whatever had been developing between us.

When Liam brought up the fact that we needed to cool things, seconds after that panty-melting kiss, of course I was gutted, but I tried to put on a brave face. Everything I said was true: I knew he didn't do relationships and that we lived in different parts of the world. But that was logic. Logic was totally different to feelings.

My heart wasn't feeling logical. Neither was my libido.

The things I wanted Liam to do to me in the back of that car were unthinkable. Ever since last night, my fantasies had been running wild. I had no idea how I was going to keep my hands off him tonight or ever.

'What time's Phil meeting us?' I changed the subject, hoping Liam hadn't worked out what I was about to say before.

'Should be there now.'

'Great.' I picked up his jacket.

'Here.' Liam plucked it from my hands. 'Let me. Some people have spotted us down there, so I need to look like the perfect boyfriend.'

Liam held his jacket up behind me and I slid my arms into the sleeves.

'Seeing as we're keeping up appearances,' I whispered in his ear, 'maybe we should show some kind of affection too.'

I wrapped my arms around his waist, looked into his eyes and pressed my lips onto his. A low groan escaped his mouth.

'Fuck,' he murmured, his hand running down my back.

I pulled away gently, wishing I could superglue our lips together, permanently.

'Thank you.' I smiled. 'For inviting me. And for the kiss…'

'The pleasure was all mine, trust me.' His eyes darkened.

'Shall we go?'

'I need a second,' he said. 'Like I said, the *pleasure* was all mine…'

'Ah, got it,' I said, my gaze subtly dropping between his legs.

After a few minutes we filed out of the private box and through the exit.

There were a few paps, but this time I just grinned, which probably wasn't the kind of photo they were after. They wanted scandal and gossip. To see us looking unhappy or arguing, but these days, whenever I was around Liam, I always had a smile on my face.

Wow. What a difference a bit of fake dating can make.

A few weeks ago, whenever I was within five feet of Liam, I had a perma-scowl. Now I wanted to be as close to him as possible, all the time.

Shit. This was bad. I was falling for him. I could feel it. I had to rein in my emotions.

After getting in the car and putting on our seat belts, I pulled out my phone. I needed a distraction. Staring into Liam's beautiful eyes wasn't going to help. There were several messages from Trudy.

'Oh my God!' I laughed.

'What's up?' Liam turned to face me.

'You've gone viral!' I showed Liam my screen. 'Look! The Tube passengers posted their photos online. They're calling you a *man of the people*!'

We skim read the various articles that Trudy had sent over, which had headlines like 'Hot Hollywood Superstar Liam Stone Spotted on the Tube' and 'Sexy Liam Stone Shocks Passengers on London Tube'. The story had even gone transatlantic with 'Heartthrob Liam Stone Rides the Subway' on an American website.

There were quotes from passengers saying how nice he was and snaps of the photos I'd taken of him with the woman.

'Don't you think this is amazing?' I said excitedly, like a child high on sugar.

'I guess.' He shrugged.

'But this is what you wanted! Positive publicity! They've even mentioned in some of the articles that you have a 'serious girlfriend' and how you seem to be abandoning your *playboy lifestyle*. It's working!'

'Obviously it's better that they're saying nice things, but *really*? Running a story just because I took the Tube for two minutes? Is that really *news*? Thousands of people do that every day.'

'Not famous people, though.'

'I get that, but… never mind.'

'Tell me.' I faced him. He sighed deeply.

'I guess, I just always hoped that I could use my fame to do something more… *useful*. Instead it's just always so… superficial. Who I'm sleeping with, how 'sexy' or 'hot' I look. God.' He dragged his hand down his face. 'I sound so fucking entitled and ungrateful. This is why I didn't want to tell you. I know it's a first world problem and that I brought that kind of press on myself by dating so many women. I know I'm lucky. And I know I shouldn't complain. Forget I said anything.'

'Liam.' I rested my hands on his. 'Your feelings are valid. Just because you're successful and others have it worse than you doesn't mean your emotions don't count. Like I said earlier, there's nothing wrong with having dreams or wanting to make a difference in the world. I started my agency because I wanted to help couples fall in love and be happy. Other people save lives or help the sick and injured. Is what I do as impressive as that? No, but I still believe what I do is important. So is your job. And what you did on the Tube tonight *was* meaningful.'

'Come on!' he scoffed.

'It was! You made their day! You spread joy and happiness. I bet afterwards they called everyone they knew to tell them they'd met you. They'll treasure those photos for the rest of their lives. Just those few minutes you spent giving them the time of day will stay with them forever. You have value. Never forget that.'

Liam was still. I could hear the cogs turning in his brain as he processed what I said.

'Thank you.'

'For what? Everything I said is true.'

'Maybe. I'm just not used to hearing it.'

He looked at me, his eyes filled with sadness. I was so used to loud, confident Liam, so seeing him like this just made me want to wrap my arms around him and hold him tight.

I wasn't sure who'd filled his head with these negative thoughts about his worth, whether it was all of the bad press taking its toll, an ex or a combination of both, but he had more to offer than he realised.

'We're here,' Phil's voice boomed. 'Roads were clear.'

'Thanks.'

Phil parked in front of the house, then jumped out to open my door. Liam appeared and held out his hand to help me out.

By now, we'd held hands multiple times, but the feeling never got old. The sensation of having my palm wrapped in his made me feel so protected, so safe, so happy.

Liam scanned our surroundings. There didn't seem to be anyone lurking. There hadn't been for a while.

A thought popped into my mind. If we were both looking for a way to pour cold water on our feelings, I'd just found the solution.

After opening the door and switching off the alarm, Liam kicked off his shoes, then headed towards the stairs.

I didn't move. I stood a few steps away from the front door.

'You coming?' Liam turned back to face me.

'The paps have stopped hanging around outside and it's much calmer. I think we're too boring for them now. So I was thinking, you know earlier we agreed it'd be better to put the brakes on... not let what happened last night happen again... maybe it'd be best if I went back home.'

Liam's face fell.

The house was so silent, never mind a pin, you could hear a feather drop. We stood at opposite ends of the hallway rooted to the spot.

'Is that what you really want?' Liam's voice cracked.

'No. You?' I held my breath, waiting for his response.

'No.' Liam started walking towards me. 'I want you to stay. I want to do so much...'

Now he was in front of me and his beautiful scent flooded my lungs. I swallowed hard. My heart raced. The urge to move my head forward a few centimetres so that we could kiss was strong.

'What do you want to do?' I bit my lip.

'You don't want to know.'

'Tell me.'

Liam stepped forward, his lips almost touching mine.

'I want to pin you against this door, lift up your dress, tear off your underwear and bury myself inside you again,' he growled. 'Then I want to bend you over that shitty sofa and fuck you again. I want to make you come so hard you won't even remember your own name. I just want you, Mia.'

'I…' My brain scrambled. Liam hadn't even touched me yet and I'd lost the power of speech and the ability to think clearly.

Heat and desire pulsated through my veins. What he said was so hot. I wanted all of the things he'd said and more.

His eyes darkened and his chest heaved.

Before either of us had time to register what we were doing, our mouths crashed together and our hands were everywhere.

I tugged at his belt buckle and zip, whilst he lifted up my dress. Within seconds he had me up against the door, with a condom in his hand.

As I yanked down his trousers and boxers and rolled the condom onto his rock-hard dick, he pushed my knickers to the side, then plunged into me.

I wrapped my leg around his waist. Jesus, this felt so good. Even more intense than last night.

Liam continued ploughing into me, then started rubbing my clit.

Oh. My. God.

I was already seeing stars. But when he trailed kisses along my neck, I knew I was close to the edge. His sexual skills were off the scale.

'I'm… I'm going to c-come!' I cried out.

'Not yet, baby.'

'I can't…'

'Okay, but after you come, I'm gonna carry you upstairs and make you come again.'

I nodded, squeezing my eyes shut as the wave ripped through me.

Liam emptied himself inside me, letting out a loud, slow groan before his body stilled.

We held each other, Liam resting his head on my shoulder, our chests still heaving, our hearts racing.

'So much for keeping our distance…' I said, my breath still ragged.

'Like I said, you're addictive.'

He pulled out, rolled off the condom, cleaned himself up, then scooped me up into his arms.

'Come on.' He carried me up the stairs. 'I'm taking you to bed.'

'Looks like I'm staying here tonight, then,' I said as he sat down on the bed and wrapped his arms tighter around me.

'Tonight and every night.' He kissed the top of my head.

'But what about when you go back to LA?'

Liam froze.

'I don't know. That's the truth. But what I do know is that I enjoy being with you. Not just the sex, although, *damn*…' He kissed my forehead and I rested my head on his chest. 'Maybe we shouldn't overthink. Just enjoy it. We can think and talk when the time comes. What d'you reckon?'

My head told me it was a terrible idea. That I should remove myself from his big, warm, delicious chest immediately, leave and never come back.

My head told me that I was on a fast track to Heartbreak City.

My head told me that I was already falling for him, and agreeing to *think and talk when the time comes* had disaster written all over it.

But like I'd said before, feelings weren't always logical. So I ignored my head and let my heart speak instead.

'Okay.' I lifted my head and his lips met mine. 'I'll stay. Tonight and every night, until the time comes.'

36

LIAM

I stepped out of the shower and wrapped my towel around my waist. I couldn't believe it was almost ten in the morning. I'd slept like a baby.

A lot of that was down to having sex with Mia. After I'd carried her to our bed, we'd gone another two rounds before collapsing into each other's arms. It wasn't just that physical exhaustion that made me sleep soundly, though. It was also because, for once, my mind felt calm.

I wasn't worrying about my career and what a fuck-up I was like I did most nights. I wasn't fretting about another story leaking in the press. And I wasn't concerned about my feelings towards Mia. She'd agreed to stay here every night, and knowing that somehow brought me some kind of peace.

When she'd said she was going back to her place, it was like a hole had been carved in my gut. A weird empty feeling took over, which shocked me. I'd got used to having her around. It was like how it used to be. Back when we were best friends. But a million times better.

Because this time, I wasn't a teenager who spent his nights wondering what it'd be like to kiss Mia. To touch her. To be inside her.

Now I'd experienced all of those things and it was even more amazing than I'd imagined.

I was kidding myself to think we'd be able to do it just that one time and cut all ties. And when she'd kissed me at the theatre, I knew it wasn't just for show. She felt the connection too.

Was I worried about what would happen when I had to go back to LA? The truth was, it was better not to think about it. I just wanted to enjoy this whilst it lasted.

It wouldn't be forever. All relationships ended. My parents' marriage was a shitshow and the so-called 'happy couples' I knew spent their days living a lie. They publicly presented themselves as the perfect partners, but at least one of them was fucking someone else on the side. Sometimes they both were.

I didn't want that kind of life. I did enough acting for my job. The last thing I wanted was to have to put on a performance at home.

That was why I wasn't concerned. I had zero expectations about where this would go, because I knew that everything, even an amazing connection like what I had with Mia, was temporary. And knowing that made things easier. We'd enjoy each other's company, whether that lasted another week or month, and then we'd move on. Get on with our lives.

I caught sight of my back in the full-length mirror. Red scratches were visible across my skin. No wonder I'd felt that sting in the shower. Mia liked to dig her nails into me when she came, and seeing as that had happened a few times last night, she'd left her mark. Knowing that I'd made her happy made me feel so damn good.

After getting dressed, I headed to the stairs, but stopped outside the office door.

There was nothing in my diary today, so technically, I could spend it doing whatever I wanted.

I pushed the door open, walked to the desk and switched on my laptop.

My heart thudded. It had been ages since I'd felt like doing this, but Mia's words yesterday had triggered something deep inside of me.

There's nothing wrong with having dreams or wanting to make a difference in the world.

You have value, Liam. Never forget that.

Mia sounded genuine. She believed in me. She saw me. Knew that there was more to me than just the money, fame and how I looked.

Everything she said was different to what people had told me all of my life. And that was why I'd started my secret project: writing a screenplay. But I'd never finished it.

Whenever I tried to sit down and write, all I could hear was other people's voices in my head.

Stay in your lane.

You're not good enough.

Those roles are for proper actors, not you.

The negative voices always won, so even if I got as far as opening my laptop, I usually ended up closing it soon afterwards. I'd tried to finish this damn screenplay for two years, but rarely managed to write more than a few pages before the self-doubt crept in.

But today felt different. I wanted to try again. I actually felt like maybe I could do this.

Mia's words jumped into my head again:

You're Liam fucking Stone. You can do anything.

Fuck it.

I pulled out the chair, sat my arse down and opened up the document.

Adrenaline and excitement raced through me as my ideas came flooding back.

After reading through the last few scenes I'd written to refresh my memory, I started typing.

And this time, I didn't stop.

37

MIA

'I'm home!' I said, shutting the door behind me.

Saying the word 'home' sounded strange, but that was how it felt. I was comfortable here. I liked coming home to Liam.

I was about to remind myself that this was temporary and I shouldn't get carried away when Liam appeared in the hallway and gave me one of his megawatt smiles.

It wasn't the smile he put on for the cameras. It was the one where his whole face lit up like a Christmas tree, his eyes sparkled and his laughter lines crinkled. The smile that made my heart flutter like a butterfly.

'Hey, you!' He wrapped his arms around me, lifted me off the floor, then spun me around. 'I missed you.' He pressed his lips onto mine and every nerve ending sprung to life.

'What a welcome!' I said when we both came up for air. 'Talk about knowing how to make a girl feel special.'

'I try.' He grinned. 'I'm in an extra-good mood!'

'Oh yeah?' I took off my jacket and shoes. 'Tell me more!'

I followed Liam into the kitchen. There was a chopping board with onions and peppers resting on the counter.

After sliding onto the stool, I leant forward, eager to hear about his day.

'Well, of course I'm happy because of an amazing woman…' He smirked.

'Should I be worried?' I smiled.

'You know I'm talking about you.' He grinned. 'But I'm also feeling good because I started working on my screenplay again!'

'You're writing a screenplay? Oh my God!' I jumped off the stool so fast I almost twisted my ankle, raced over to the opposite side of the counter and threw my arms around him. 'That's brilliant!'

'Thanks!' Relief washed over him. 'I started it a couple of years ago but kept stopping. I wasn't sure I could do it or if it was any good. But when I'm writing, it gives me such a buzz.'

'I'm so glad to hear that! And? How was it? I'm guessing it wasn't half as bad as you thought it was, right?'

'Yeah. It still needs work, but it's got potential. We'll see. But seriously, thank you.'

'For what?'

'For encouraging me. I was so in my head with it being bad and all the things people had told me over the years about staying in my lane were swimming around my brain for so long that I doubted myself. But the stuff you said on the way to the theatre helped blow those negative thoughts away just enough for me to open my laptop. And once I did that, everything flowed.'

'I'm so happy for you! And like I said before, I was just telling the truth. You're capable of *so* much.'

'I appreciate that. And I believe you, because let's face it, if you were lying, I'd know,' he laughed.

'Yep. Telling the truth is my superpower!'

'I know you said I don't have to thank you, but once we've eaten, I have a surprise for you.'

'Oooh!'

'Don't get too excited. I haven't bought you diamonds. It's just a kind of throwback gift.'

'I'm intrigued. Whatever it is, I'm sure I'll love it! Do you want some help with dinner? I'm no chef, but I can chop vegetables.'

'Nah, thanks, but I'm good.' Liam walked to the fridge, took out a bottle of wine, then plucked a glass from the cupboard. 'Here.' He handed it to me. 'All I need is for you to sit down, relax and talk. I've told you about my day, now I want to hear all about yours.'

For the next hour, whilst Liam cooked some meatballs with homemade baked sweet potato fries, we chatted easily.

I told him that I'd had multiple emails and calls at work today, which I attributed to being seen out with him on the Tube, but most of them weren't serious leads. Just people who wanted my services but weren't prepared to pay, or those wanting to know how they could meet someone famous.

I wasn't giving up hope, though. The awards finalists would be announced soon and that should help bring in some more serious interest.

After dinner, Liam led me to the living room.

'Okay, so I need you to close your eyes while I bring out your surprise.'

'Okay!'

I heard him leave the room and when a gorgeous waft of his woody scent hit me, I knew he'd returned. I caught the sound of something being put on the coffee table.

'Open your eyes.'

'Oh my God!' I looked down and laughed. 'Connect 4! And wait, Jenga too! They're my favourites!' Happy memories from our teenage years when we spent hours in the school holidays playing together came flooding back. 'Thank you!'

I jumped up, leant over the table and gave him a long, slow kiss.

'Mmm…' Liam groaned as he gently pulled away. 'If you keep kissing me like that, then it won't be Connect 4 that I'll want to play.'

'Oh yeah?' I teased.

'Yeah. My hands and mouth would love to play with your body.'

'What part?' I bit my lip.

'Well…' He trailed his hand across my shoulder, then moved it lower, skimming slowly over my breasts. 'First I'd play with your nipples and these perfect tits…' Goosebumps erupted over my skin. 'And then I'd trail my tongue down your stomach.' His hand moved south towards my waist. 'Then I'd play your clit like it's my favourite instrument.'

He swiped his finger between my legs and it was like the air had been sucked from my lungs.

'I-I'd like that… a *lot*.' I ran my hand across his chest.

'Me too. But not now.' He picked up a chair and put it

on the opposite side of the coffee table and my horny vagina wept. 'The night's young. We'll play in bed together later. Right now, I'm gonna whoop your arse.'

'Dream on,' I scoffed. I was happy to know playtime was only being adjourned and not cancelled tonight. 'It's been a few years since I played, but if you still play like you used to, I'll be whooping *your* arse.'

'We'll see.' He raised his eyebrow. 'Wanna start with Connect 4?'

'Go on, then.'

I picked up the boxes and took everything out of the packaging. As I tipped the colourful Connect 4 discs onto the table, I was filled with a different type of excitement.

Playing games like these had always been something Liam and I did. Back then, none of our family or friends were interested, so it was one of the things that bonded us.

The fact that he remembered and took the time to buy these so we could play them together again after all these years meant a lot.

I didn't need to ask what colour he wanted. Liam was always red and I was always yellow. It was how we'd always played. I pushed the discs over to his side of the table.

'Ladies first.' He gestured towards me.

The familiar click of our plastic discs being dropped into the grid made me smile. Each move sparked a fresh wave of memories.

It wasn't long before Liam secured the first line of four discs. He won the next couple of games too, but I soon caught up. It was crazy how easily we fell back into the rhythm of how we used to play. He always tried to start in the centre or close to it. As I watched him consider each move carefully, it was like no time had passed.

Speaking of time, what felt like minutes later but must have been at least an hour, we'd played six rounds.

'Three all!' I announced as I won the game.

'Whoever wins next is the champion,' he declared as he pulled the catch to empty the discs. 'So have you really not played this since we were kids?'

'Nope. Don't you remember? My family weren't interested in board games.'

'What about Boris?'

'The only games he liked were playing with our finances.'

'How d'you mean?'

I took a deep breath.

'He's the reason I'm in this mess. He used all our savings on different get-rich-quick schemes. He ran up so much debt that we had to sell the house. He used my credit card too and ended up screwing up my rating. That's why I can't get a loan, why I'm renting a shitty flat and why this competition prize money is so important.'

'Shit. I'm sorry, Mia. You know my views on Boris.'

'Oh, and he cheated too. Found that out when I went over the credit card statements he'd diverted to his email account. Apparently it was my fault because I was always busy working and "neglected him".'

Instead of understanding that getting my business off the ground was hard work and trying to support me, he went and fucked other women.

I still wasn't sure if he'd cheated through our whole relationship. I think it probably started when he realised I was serious about setting up my business. He didn't like the idea of me making a success of myself. Maybe he thought that if I did, I'd leave him behind.

Boris always craved money and success. He liked to 'win'. But he didn't want to put in the hard work that it took to make it. He wanted the easy way. That was why he got sucked into those stupid schemes. And when the funds in our joint accounts ran out, he decided to steal from me and use every penny I had instead.

'What a dick.' Liam shook his head. 'He didn't deserve you. I never understood why you dated him in the first place.'

'You want to know the truth?'

'Course.'

'It was because I couldn't have you.' I blew out a breath. Somehow getting that off my chest instantly made me feel better.

'What? I was crazy about you, Mia. *You* were the one that wasn't into *me*.'

'*Come on!*' I knew that after the interview, Liam said he'd liked me, but part of me thought he was just romanticising the past. 'You were always with a different girl. We'd talked about going to the school dance together and then next thing I heard you were going with Natalie Davies.'

'That was only because Boris told me you'd agreed to go with him!'

'No! I only agreed after Natalie told me *she* was going with *you*.'

'Well, shit. I think we both got played.'

I wouldn't have put it past Boris to have lied. He was always jealous of Liam, especially when he got picked for the football team and Boris didn't.

He hated that I was friends with Liam. I guessed Boris wanted a way to get Liam out of the picture, and it worked.

'Classic miscommunication.' I shook my head. 'We were young, but still. We should've talked about it.'

'I know why I didn't. You were too important to me. I didn't want to tell you how I felt and risk it ending our friendship. With all the shit going on with my parents, back then it felt like you were all I had.'

My stomach twisted. At one point, things were so bad with Liam's parents he was at our house every day just to escape what was going on.

His parents' relationship was always so up and down. They'd fight, then make up, then fight again. During the low points, I did everything I could to be there for him. That was why it felt like a giant kick in the gut when he took someone else to the school dance. I'd thought that we had something special. And the idea of him getting close to someone else crushed me.

'God, what a mess we made. I didn't raise it because I was worried about you rejecting me. You were the most popular boy in school and even though we spent time together and had a few *moments*, I just never truly believed you'd choose me. So when I heard you were going with Natalie, who was the prettiest girl in school, it confirmed that.'

'Is that why you were so cold to me?'

'Yeah. I was hurt. And everyone was talking about how you and her had sex and that killed me. That's why I avoided you.'

'And then you started dating Boris properly.'

'Yeah. Boris seemed nice. He wasn't you, but I couldn't have you, so I had to move on.'

'Fuck. I didn't realise. For the record, *you* were the prettiest girl in school, not Natalie. I never really got over you. I tried. The girls I went with never came close to what we had. It sounds shitty now, but I think I was trying to numb the pain. I was using sex to distract myself from the arguments at home and the fact that I was missing you. So many times I went to speak to you, then talked myself out of it. And when I finally did, after Mum dropped the bombshell about moving to Spain, you ignored me.'

'What?' I frowned. 'I couldn't believe it when I heard you'd left. Even though at that point we hadn't spoken properly for a while, I at least thought you'd come and say goodbye.'

'I did! It all happened so quickly. Mum decided on the Friday night and we were gone by the Saturday afternoon. I came to your house that morning. Alice said you'd gone out with Boris. I told her to pass on the message that I needed to talk to you urgently. She said she would. And when you didn't, I assumed you didn't care because you were so into him.'

My jaw crashed to the floor.

'Alice didn't tell me anything! And I wasn't out with Boris. I remember—I was food shopping with Dad!'

'You're kidding?'

'Do I look like I'm joking?'

'And what about the voicemail?'

'What voicemail? When did you send it?'

'After I left your house.'

'I didn't get that either! What the hell?'

'I told you I was leaving. That I missed you and our friendship. I said if you wanted to stay in touch to call me soon because I didn't know how long I'd have my number.

I kept that phone for weeks hoping you'd get in touch. And when you didn't, I just thought we were done for good.'

'Fuck.' My jaw hung open. 'I don't know what to say.'

I cast my mind back to that day. Dad had asked me to come with him to Brixton Market. Then we went to the supermarket. But if Liam had left a voicemail, why didn't I get it?

'Hold on. I didn't have my phone with me. I remember because Dad asked me to call Mum to check something and I couldn't. I ended up using his instead. If Alice didn't pass on the message, there's a chance she deleted the voicemail too. She knew my password.'

'But why would she do that?'

'She always liked you and I think she was jealous of our friendship. Shit. All that time wasted. All of those years. I should've been there for you. It must've been a nightmare being dragged through the divorce, then getting uprooted to another country and thinking I didn't care. I'm so sorry.'

'It's not your fault.' Liam took my hands in his. 'You didn't know. Can you believe their divorce was confirmed on the fourteenth of February?'

'Oh my God. So that's why when I first came here you called Valentine's Day a bullshit day?'

'Yep.'

'Oh, Liam.' I rubbed his shoulder. 'I didn't know.'

'There's no way you could've, so don't worry about it. We both should've communicated better. There's nothing we can do about it now. At least we're friends again. That's what's important.' He tucked a strand of hair behind my ear.

'I'm glad we've made up. Hating someone is exhausting. Especially someone you used to really like…' A warm smile touched my lips.

'Come here.' Liam pulled me in to him and we sat there, holding each other in silence for a few minutes. It was like all of the emotions we'd bottled up over the years were expelled with that one action and when we finally pulled away, we were starting anew.

'You good?' Liam asked.

'Yep. Want to play some more?'

'Definitely. But I hope you remember what you just said about the fact that hating someone is exhausting in a few minutes.'

'Why?'

'Because, Tutti-Frutti, I'm about to win the next game!'

'Tutti-Frutti?'

'Yeah. That's the name I have you saved under in my phone.'

My heart bloomed. I kind of liked it.

'Better than Mamma Mia.' Our eyes locked and we both smiled.

'Glad your new nickname meets your approval! So as I was saying, I'm about to be crowned Connect 4 Champion. And when I beat you at Jenga too, you're *really* going to hate me!'

'Enough of the fighting talk. Time to put your money where your mouth is, Stone.'

I went on to beat Liam at Connect 4, then when we moved over to playing Jenga and a bad move from me caused the tower to collapse into a heap of wooden blocks and Liam declared himself the winner, it wasn't hate that filled my chest. It was laughter and gratitude.

The fact that fate had brought us back together, we'd had a chance to clear the air and I'd got answers to the questions that had swum around my head for decades made my heart so happy.

Tonight Liam and I had really bonded. Not because of our sexual chemistry, but because of our shared history. The easy conversation and the time we'd spent playing together reminded me why we used to be such good friends.

Playing the games had been fun, and although we'd pretended to care, it didn't matter who'd won.

We'd reconnected emotionally and *that* was the most important thing.

38

LIAM

The doorbell rang. I put down my water and let Nate in.

I was glad to be training today. I wasn't used to having so much free time. Back in LA, my days were always filled with filming, rehearsals, press junkets or meetings. All I had in the diary over this week was a shoot for a shaving company.

'How's it going?' I asked as Nate stepped inside.

'I'm cool. You?'

'All good. Ready for this session.' I walked up to the gym and Nate followed.

'That's what I like to hear. Let's get you warmed up.'

About twenty minutes later, a sharp ringtone vibrated around the room.

'You wanna get that?' I asked.

'Sorry, man. Thought I had it on silent. Ignore it. I'll switch it off in a sec.' The ringing stopped, then a minute later it started again. Nate winced.

'It's okay, get it. Might be urgent.'

Nate went to his bag and pulled out his phone. 'Shit. It's Andrea. She never calls in the morning.'

Andrea was his fiancée's teenage daughter. After what he'd been through when he'd tried the whole relationship thing back in LA, I never thought I'd see the day that Nate settled down with one woman *and* took on the responsibility of her kid too.

'Answer. Don't worry about me.'

'What's up, Dre? Fuck. Calm down. Okay.' He nodded. 'Yeah. I'll get there as soon as I can.' Nate hung up.

'What's happened? Is she okay?'

'Andrea's got an important play tonight, but the lead and understudy got food poisoning, so there's no one to play his role and she's freaking out.'

'Oh shit.'

'Yeah. Now the cast are kicking off and she doesn't know how to get them under control. Mel's at a meeting in Paris until later this afternoon, so Andrea's asked me to come. I don't know what I can do, but she's been working on it for months to raise money to stop the community centre from closing and now she's worried they'll have to cancel, so I have to try and help.'

'What's the play?'

'*Beauty and the Beast*. She needs someone to play the Beast and can't find anyone to do it at such short notice.'

'So basically she needs someone who's butt ugly and knows how to act? I'd be perfect for that!' I smirked.

'Now's not the time for your jokes, man,' Nate warned.

'I'm serious! I'll do it. I played that role ages ago at drama club and I probably still remember the lines. Well, some of them anyway. But you said it's tonight, right? I could learn it by then.'

'For real?'

'Yeah. I'm not doing anything today and you're like family, bro. And Andrea's basically your kid, so course I'll help.'

'If you could, that'd be a big deal for her. And for me. I'd really appreciate it. But you know it's just at a community centre, right? The set's gonna be pretty basic. And you'll be acting with non-pros. It'll be a lot different to what you're used to.'

'I know. Don't worry. As long as there's someone there to pick out the yellow M&Ms from my diamond-encrusted bowl and a bottle of Dom Pérignon chilling in my dressing room, it'll be all good.' I grinned. Nate's face fell. 'I'm *joking*! Like I said, I'm happy to help. Are they doing the musical version?'

'Nah. There's no songs. Like I said, it's probably not the kind of production you're used to.'

'It's fine. Without the songs it'll be easier as I'll only have the lines to learn. Tell Andrea the show will go on! Give me ten minutes to shower and I'll come with you.'

Fifteen minutes later we were in the car on the way to the community centre. Nate had forwarded me the script Andrea sent and I'd already started reading it.

As I went over the pages, everything came flooding back. It was similar to what I'd learnt years ago. *Beauty and the Beast* was one of the first lead roles I'd got at drama club.

I remembered it clearly because it was one of the few performances Dad had bothered to come and watch. I was so happy he was finally taking an interest in something I was passionate about. Until I realised it was because he was banging my drama teacher behind Mum's back.

Didn't know why I was so surprised. Dad had a habit of fucking women that weren't his wife.

About a year later, Mum found out he'd been screwing our neighbour too. That was the last straw. She said she couldn't take any more of his shit and announced she was taking me to Spain for a fresh start. It all happened so quickly. I had to leave the home, everything and everyone I knew behind.

My chest tightened. Thinking about that wasn't helpful. I pushed the memories out of my head and focused on the page. I had a job to do. Nate and Andrea needed me. I wasn't gonna let them down.

It took about forty minutes to arrive. Nate was right. The community centre wasn't like the multimillion-dollar studios I was used to. The small one-storey building needed a fresh lick of paint and there were tiles missing from the roof, but it didn't matter.

We stepped inside. There was a group talking loudly on the stage. A girl with long brown hair waved a script around and begged everyone to calm down.

'There's no way someone will be able to learn Sam's lines in less than a day!' a young woman spat.

'I've already told you!' the girl with the script shouted back. 'He's a professional!'

'Bull! Why would a pro want to work on an amateur play at short notice, for free?'

'Because he wants to help,' I called out, striding towards the stage.

The hall fell silent and the young woman who was shouting at the girl I now guessed was Andrea froze. Everyone's mouths dropped open.

'That's...! You're...! *No way!* Can't be!' the mouthy woman said.

'I *told* you he was a professional!' Andrea said smugly before mouthing *thank you*. I smiled in acknowledgement.

'Come on, ladies and gents.' I stood in front of them. 'Let's get to work.'

∼

We rehearsed for three hours straight before breaking for lunch. Andrea was a good kid and once they'd got warmed up, the cast were cool too.

At first they were nervous (especially when Nate warned them not to take photos or tell anyone, especially the press, that I was here), but when they realised I didn't want any special treatment, they relaxed.

I was loving it. Nothing beat the feeling of being on stage. I couldn't wait for tonight.

I pulled out my phone. Mia had messaged to say hi.
Me
Hey gorgeous. How's your day going?

Seconds later, she came online.
Tutti-Frutti
Just had a new client sign up! She called weeks ago after a friend I'd matched recommended me, but when I followed up, she didn't want to go ahead. But now she's changed her mind! Must be the Liam Stone effect!
Me
Congrats! But I'm sure it's nothing to do with me and everything to do with you.

Tutti-Frutti
You're so sweet.
Me
I try…
Me
Mind if we rain check dinner tonight?
Tutti-Frutti
Everything okay?

I filled her in on what had happened and where I was.
Tutti-Frutti
OMG, that's brilliant! So happy you're back on the stage!
Me
Me too!
Tutti-Frutti
This is going to be so good for you. Do you know if they're still selling tickets?
Me
Think so.
Tutti-Frutti
Send me the link and I'll buy one. I'll ask Trudy if she's free to come too.

Warmth flooded my chest. Mia was struggling financially, but she still offered to buy a ticket because she wanted to support me.

And she understood why I wanted to help. If Geena or my LA friends heard I was doing this, they'd laugh. Yeah, it wasn't the National Theatre, but

it mattered. Not everything was about money or status.
Me
I'd love that. I know Andrea and the cast would too. Thanks.
Tutti-Frutti
No worries!
Me
Better get back to it. See you tonight!
Tutti-Frutti
Can't wait! And don't forget to send me the details.
Me
On it.

I fired off the link Nate had sent earlier, then I practically skipped back to the stage to join the cast.

And for the first time in ages, I felt something I hadn't for a long time when it came to acting: excitement.

39

MIA

The sound of the audience cheering as the play ended was deafening, but in the best possible way.

Liam and the cast joined hands, stepped towards the edge of the stage and took a bow.

I jumped to my feet and whooped at the top of my voice whilst Trudy stuck her fingers in her mouth and whistled loudly.

'Your boyfriend is bloody talented,' she gushed.

'He really is!' My heart expanded with pride.

It'd been years since I'd seen him in a play. When we were friends I'd go and see the performances at his drama club. Back then he was good, but now? Everything I'd said before was true. His talents were wasted doing the same films. He deserved to be on the stage or writing. He shouldn't have to choose. I'd love to see him do whatever he wanted.

Liam was wearing a mask and even when he removed it, thanks to the make-up and wig, I didn't think the audience realised he was playing the Beast. But judging from the comments from the people in the row behind me, they still thought he was great. I know they weren't experts or fancy theatre critics, but that didn't matter. What I loved was that he wasn't being judged on his looks or what people read online. Tonight the only thing that mattered was his performance.

As the cast left the stage, Trudy and I headed around the back to a tiny room where the cast had congregated. Everyone was hugging each other excitedly.

Liam patted the shoulder of the girl who played Belle, who was Nate's stepdaughter, Andrea. At one point she forgot her lines and looked mortified. But Liam quickly mouthed them to her and within seconds she was able to recover. So sweet of him.

Liam's gaze caught mine and his face broke into a smile. He excused himself from Andrea and came over.

'Hey, you.' He kissed me softly on the lips.

'You were amazing!' I wrapped my arm around him.

'She's right!' Trudy added. 'You were brilliant. Shame you've got an agent, otherwise I'd snap you up. I'd kill to have someone with your talent on my books!'

'Thanks. And never say never, Trudes.' Liam smiled. 'Back in a sec. Just need to say a few words.'

'Course! Go do your thing!' I stepped back to give him space.

'Ladies and gents.' Liam stood at the front of the room. 'You were all fantastic! I know it wasn't easy and you were worried about how it'd all turn out, but you knocked it out the park! It was a privilege to share the stage with you tonight.' He put his hands together in a gesture of thanks.

'Thanks for helping us!' Andrea said. The whole room clapped with appreciation.

Once Trudy and I had congratulated the cast and Liam had said his goodbyes to Nate and Melody, we left the community centre.

We walked Trudy to her car, then went to find Phil, who'd been waiting outside.

'So'—I put on my seat belt and turned to face Liam—'how do you feel?'

'Fucking amazing!' His smile was so big, it could light up the whole of London. 'It's like... I can't even put it into words. The nerves before you deliver the first line, the adrenaline that races through your veins, connecting with the audience right in the moment... nothing beats hearing their laughter or gasps and getting that live reaction. And I loved watching the others perform... it was just *everything*. I feel so... *alive!*'

'I'm really happy for you! And this is just the beginning!'

'I hope so.'

'I'm *telling* you, it's going to happen! What do you want to do now to celebrate your long-awaited return to the stage? Want to go out?'

'You know what?' Liam stroked my face. 'I'd just like to go home and chill with you. Maybe we can go crazy and order pizza.'

'Whoa. Really? What about your shoot?'

'A few slices of pizza won't kill me. And I've got training tomorrow, so I can work extra hard to make up for it.'

'Or we can start early and burn some calories together tonight...?' I grinned.

'Now, *that's* an idea I can get on board with.' He leant forward and kissed me, sending shivers down my spine.

A night of pizza and passion with Liam?

Count. Me. In.

40
MIA

The pizza arrived ten minutes after we got home, so luckily we didn't have to wait.

'Should we eat in the dining room tonight?' I grabbed two plates and glasses from the kitchen. 'Just for a change?'

'Sure.' Liam followed me, clutching the pizza box.

After offering me the first slice of Meat Feast, he dived in and took one for himself.

As I watched him turn the corners inwards, I laughed.

'What's funny?' He frowned.

'Nothing. It's just cute that you still eat pizza like that!'

'Like what?'

'You literally fold it in half like a sandwich! Just like you used to.'

'Never really thought about it. Just stops everything falling off.' He took another bite. 'This tastes so fucking good!'

'When was the last time you ate junk food?'

'So long ago I can't even remember. But damn have I

missed it.'

'That and ice cream, right?'

'Fuck, yes!' Liam's eyes widened like a light bulb had just gone off in his mind. He reached for his phone. 'Hi, yeah. Do you deliver? Great. Can I get a tub of cookies 'n' cream, and do you have tutti-frutti flavour? Excellent. One of those too, please.'

He'd ordered my favourite. God, this man was amazing. And I wanted to show him how much I appreciated him. I dropped my slice of pizza on the plate and got up.

'What's up? Aren't you hungry?'

'I am. I'm very hungry. But I don't feel like eating pizza right now.'

'I can get you something else if you want?'

'I'm hoping you can.' I marched to his side of the table and dropped to my knees.

'What are you…' Liam frowned. As I reached for his belt buckle, the realisation hit him.

'You were amazing tonight. Helping out those kids, impressing everyone with your talent. That was very hot.' I unzipped his jeans. 'And remembering my favourite ice cream flavour too. *Also hot.*' His dick strained against his boxer shorts. I didn't even need to feel him to tell that he was rock-hard. 'And I think all of this good behaviour should be rewarded.'

'What did you have in mind?' Liam said, his eyes fixed on mine.

'You can keep eating your pizza, but I'm in the mood for some cock.' I slid my hand inside the opening of his boxers and his hard length sprang free.

After wrapping my fingers around his shaft, I opened wide, then slid him in my mouth. Liam tensed, then groaned. I heard the sound of his pizza slice being dropped on the plate, then the rustle of a serviette.

'Fuck, Mia.' Liam gripped my hair, pushing himself deeper into my mouth. 'That feels amazing.'

I moved him slowly in and out. At one point he thrust so deep I almost choked, but I kept going.

Next I licked him from the base to tip. He was already leaking pre-cum and I circled his head, savouring the salty taste.

'Mmm.' My gaze flicked up to his. Liam's eyes rolled back in his head.

'Mia.' The sound of him calling my name in a strangled voice was such a turn-on. 'You don't know how many times I dreamt about you sucking my cock. I'm not gonna last. So if you don't want me to explode in your mouth'—he paused, trying to catch his breath—'you'd better stop now.'

'No way.' I shook my head. 'You know me. Once I start something, I like to see it through to the end.' I slid him back in my mouth.

Bobbing my head up and down, I increased the rhythm. It wasn't long before Liam tensed. A feral groan echoed around the room as he emptied himself in my mouth.

He thrust a few more times, then when I was sure he was done, I slid him out slowly, and wiped my hand across my damp lips.

Liam slumped back on the chair, his chest heaving. Seeing him there, with a satisfied grin across his face was everything. After all the pleasure he'd given me, I was glad I'd done something to make him happy.

'Wow,' he said finally. 'That was better than my

dreams. Thank you.'

'My pleasure.' I sat up. 'So... how much are you willing to break your healthy eating ban tonight? There's something else I want to do for you.'

'I don't think anything's gonna top that BJ'—he reached for another serviette to clean himself up—'but what were you thinking?'

'Nothing sexual. Just, I remembered you used to like chocolate chip cookies, right?'

'Yeah!' He smiled, tucking his dick back in his boxers and pulling up his jeans.

'As a treat, I bought some cookie dough. It's hiding in the fridge. All I have to do is cut them into pieces and put them in the oven. What do you think? Want some?'

'Yeah! Thanks! That's really sweet of you.'

'Okay!' I jumped up and headed to the kitchen. I had a glass of water, then prepared the cookies on a baking tray. Just as I'd finished putting them in the oven and setting the timer, the doorbell rang. 'I'll get it!' I called out.

It was the ice cream. Once I'd collected the bag from the delivery driver, I took it to the dining room. Liam was standing in the doorway, his eyes dark with desire.

'I'll just get some bowls and spoons,' I said.

'Forget the spoons. And we won't need bowls.' He grabbed my arm and pulled me over to the dining table. 'Take off your clothes.'

'What?' I frowned. 'Let me put the ice cream in the freezer first so it doesn't melt.'

'Melted is *exactly* how I want it,' Liam growled, then gently pushed me against the table. 'So I'll ask you again. Take off your clothes.'

We held eye contact as I stripped down to my underwear, then sat on the edge.

'Tutti-Frutti, I need you *completely* naked.'

I took off my bra and knickers.

'Good girl. Now it's my turn to thank you. Properly.' He trailed a kiss along my neck. 'For inspiring me to write again.' His mouth moved up to nibble my ear. 'For coming to support me tonight…' His tongue moved down to my collarbone. 'For that epic BJ'—he swiped over my erect nipple—'and for encouraging me to have some balance by eating whatever I want for a change.'

'You don't need to thank me.' I smiled, my body fizzing with anticipation. 'But if you insist…'

'Oh, I do. Having pizza for the first time in months tasted great. But you're the only dish I want to eat right now, so lay back and spread your legs. I'm about to devour you for dessert.'

Holy shit.

It took me less than a second to lay myself back on the cold marble. Liam reached in the bag and pulled out the tub of ice cream, then tipped it upside down and squeezed the carton so the melted liquid drizzled over my breasts.

As the cold cream hit my chest, I flinched and my nipples hardened.

Liam rolled down his jeans and boxer shorts, then straddled me, his dick rubbing against my clit.

He leant forward and licked the ice cream slowly off my nipple.

'Ohhhh,' I moaned.

The sensation of his warm tongue and the icy cream short-circuited my brain. With every lick and stroke I wanted more.

My hips bucked upwards. My body ached for him. I

wanted Liam to touch between my legs. I wanted to feel his tongue *there*.

He licked inside my thighs, across my stomach, everywhere except where I *needed* him. I knew he was doing it on purpose and it was driving me crazy.

'There.' I pushed his head between my legs, but still he resisted. 'Put some ice cream *there*…'

Liam lifted his head, ice cream covering his mouth.

'You want me to put some ice cream here and lick your greedy pussy?' He swiped his finger against my clit and I cried out.

'Yes,' I panted.

'Don't worry, sweetheart. I'm gonna eat it, but I won't be putting any ice cream there. Wanna know why?'

'Why?' I struggled for breath.

'Because I want to be able to taste *you*.'

He dragged his tongue down my stomach before trailing my inner thigh but deliberately ignoring my clit, again.

'Please.' I thrust my hips up. 'If you want me to beg, I will.'

'Tell me what you want, Tutti-Frutti.'

'I want you to lick my pussy. Please. I need you.'

Liam teased me again. At one point I needed him so badly it felt like if he didn't put his mouth on me I was going to die. And just as I was about to beg again, he climbed off, pulled my body to the edge of the table and dropped to his knees.

Then, he finally spread my legs and buried his tongue inside me.

'Oh God!' I screamed.

Seconds later, the oven timer sounded, like it was

alerting me that an orgasm was about to erupt.

Liam was sucking and circling my clit and my body felt like a bomb that was seconds away from detonation. 'The…' I struggled to speak—my brain had turned to mush. I realised that the alarm was still sounding. I didn't want anything to interrupt the surge of pleasure pulsing through me. But I didn't want to start a fire either. 'Th-the cookies… They're going to… ohhh… burn.'

Liam lifted his head and I instantly missed the heat from his mouth.

'Let them burn,' he growled. 'The whole damn world can burn down right now. Nothing else exists when I'm fucking you.'

He buried his head back between my legs and I knew that after hearing those words, there was no way I'd be able to hold back.

As Liam's tongue flicked against me, once more, then twice, then three times, that was all it took. The wave built inside me, ripping through me like a tsunami.

'Ohhhhh, Jesus!!!' I dug my nails into his back and lifted my hips off the table before collapsing back down. My chest heaved and my heart raced.

Every time I thought Liam had given me the best orgasm in my life, he went and smashed his own world record.

'Satisfied?' He sat up.

'*More* than satisfied,' I replied. 'If this was a survey, you'd be scoring a thousand out of ten.'

'Just a thousand?' He tilted his head to the side. 'Seems like I've still got some work to do. Mind if I put my cock inside you now? I'd like to do you right here.'

I'd never done it on a dining table before, but it was on

my secret fantasy list.

'Give it to me.' I laid myself open for him again.

After rolling a condom down his hard length, he thrust into me. I cried out. Partly from ecstasy and partly from the sheer size of him.

As he rocked on top of me, I wrapped my legs around his back.

'You good?' His face creased.

'Yeah, you feel amazing. Don't stop.'

Liam picked up the pace and as he pummelled into me the pizza box flew off the table, followed by the glasses, which smashed on the floor.

And the oven alarm was still going off, the scent of melted chocolate and cookie dough wafting into the room. But I didn't care. We had time before it became dangerous. Liam was inside me and like he said nothing was going to get in the way of him making me see stars again.

'I want to go on top,' I said.

Before I first had sex with Liam, I didn't feel confident in my bedroom skills. But now, seeing the way he looked at me, with desire, lust and affection made me feel like I was the sexiest woman in the world.

'Hell yeah.' He gripped my body, then flipped me over like I was as light as a feather. I straddled him and lowered myself back onto his dick.

As I rocked my hips back and forth, Liam fixed his gaze on me.

'That's it, baby. Ride my cock like a good girl. God, Mia. You're so fucking beautiful.'

He reached up and played with my breasts, pinching my nipples, then slipped his fingers between my folds and circled my clit.

Game over.

I rode him faster, my boobs bouncing as my nails dug into his solid chest.

My second orgasm ripped through me and I cried out again. Liam gripped my arse, lifting his body off the table, then a raw, loud rumble shot from the back of his throat as he came.

I collapsed on his chest, our bodies slick with sweat and sticky ice cream.

'That was incredible,' he said in a low, husky voice, his heart pounding against my chest.

'It was.'

We were just so connected, so in tune. Our bodies fitted together like the perfect pieces of a jigsaw puzzle.

After we'd recovered, we peeled ourselves off the dining table. Liam reached for some serviettes. He handed me a few to clean myself up, then rolled off the condom and wiped himself too.

'We made a real mess!' He laughed as he took in the sight around us. Broken pieces of glass, pizza slices, the empty box and what was left of the cookies 'n' cream ice cream were all strewn across the floor.

'Yeah!' I chuckled. 'The oven probably doesn't look that pretty either.' The smoke alarm sounded. Looked like that was our cue.

'*Now* we can turn the oven off. But let me carry you. With the glass on the floor, it's not safe for you to walk.'

'My hero!' I smiled.

'Damn right.'

Once he found a safe spot to step down, Liam lifted me into his arms and carried me to the kitchen. The cookies were burnt to a crisp, but no real damage was done.

After I'd opened the door and turned off the oven, he carried me upstairs and laid me down on the bed.

'Ahhh,' I sighed, taking in the feel of the soft duvet and mattress beneath me.

'Softer than the dining table, right?'

'A lot! But it was fun to try. Another fantasy sex location ticked off the list.'

'Now I know you can manage the hardness of the table, maybe next time we can try it on that shitty sofa.'

'I'm willing to try it anywhere with you.' I smiled.

Liam climbed up on the bed behind me, his hard dick pressing against my bum. He was like the Energizer Bunny. Always ready to go.

'Want another round?' I asked.

'We could. Being inside you is my new favourite hobby. But right now, I just wanna hold you. That okay?'

'Course.'

For any other guy, snuggling might not be a big deal, but for Liam this was huge. Holding each other wasn't something he'd do with just anyone.

His sweet breath tickled the back of my neck, sending shivers down my spine. He slid his arms around my waist, resting his hands on my belly.

I squeezed my eyes shut. The warmth from his palms felt so soothing.

Just being held like this felt so intimate. The only time my ex had wanted to cuddle was when he wanted sex. So to be held without any obligations or expectations that it'd lead to something physical meant more than Liam could ever know.

And that was why, with my heart full and Liam's arms caressing my stomach, I quickly drifted off to sleep.

41

LIAM

I was almost there. Since Mia and I had gone to the theatre last week, I'd been working on my screenplay every day. And I'd got up extra early this morning because I couldn't wait to get back to it. If I kept going at this pace, maybe I could have it finished by the time I went back to LA in a few weeks.

My chest tightened. I wished I didn't have to go back. The time I'd spent in London had been great. Being with Mia was incredible.

Seeing her face in the audience last night was like a shot of adrenaline. I was determined to do a great job not just for the cast and the cause, but because I wanted her to be proud of me. I was gonna miss the way she always encouraged me. The way she saw the *real* me.

And last night. Damn. I had no words. It wasn't just feasting, then fucking her on the dining table. Or because she gave me the best BJ I'd ever had. It was how she took care of me. Remembering my favourite cookies. Buying them for me but keeping them hidden until I was ready to add some balance to my diet and allow myself a treat. She was just a woman in a million. I didn't know how I was gonna let her go.

But I couldn't think about that right now. It was out of my control. All I could do was enjoy the time we had together whilst it lasted.

The doorbell rang. I'd been so caught up in writing that I'd forgotten Nate was coming over. We didn't get to train properly yesterday, so he'd booked me in for a session this afternoon.

Normally I'd be obsessing about burning off the pizza or ice cream. But I reckoned that with the exercise I'd done with Mia last night, I'd be fine.

I buzzed him in.

'Hey, come up, but give me a minute. I just need to finish something.'

'What you working on?' Nate appeared at the office door.

'Just a… screenplay.' My voice wavered. I paused, waiting for him to laugh. Apart from Mia, no one else knew, so it still felt weird saying it out loud.

'Nice one!' He slapped me on the back. 'What's it about?'

'Haven't quite got the elevator pitch worked out yet, but basically it's about a male escort who discovers he's got a four-year-old daughter and gives up his career to raise her after the mum dies unexpectedly.'

'Sounds cool, bro. What you gonna do with it once it's finished? Pitch it to the studios?'

'Not sure. I'm not exactly Mr Popular in Hollywood right now.'

Being seen with Mia had helped, but to get this off the

ground would need serious investment. I'd put my own money behind it and maybe some contacts and friends might help too, but even that wouldn't be enough.

'Fuck that. You don't need them. When you're ready, let me know. My brother-in-law, Nico, has his fingers in different pies and he's always looking for new business opportunities. Can't make any promises, but I reckon he'd back you.'

'Seriously?' My eyes bulged. His brother-in-law was a billionaire. I'd never met him, but I'd read a few articles and knew he was a big deal.

'Yeah. You and me go way back, so I'd vouch for you. And after you helped Andrea out last night, it's the least I can do.'

'Wow.' I swallowed hard. 'That would be… thanks. I'd really appreciate that.'

'No worries. I got you. I'll leave you to it. Let me know when you're ready.'

Yesterday I was buzzing with excitement after getting back on stage. And now today, I was filled with another emotion I hadn't felt for a while: hope.

Although nothing was guaranteed, after years of doubting myself, getting my dream off the ground finally felt like it could become a reality.

My chest felt like it'd just been inflated with a balloon pump.

I couldn't wait to tell Mia.

42

MIA

'You're welcome! Glad it went so well. Let me know how date number two goes! Great, you too. Take care.' I hung up.

'Another happy client?' Trudy asked.

'Yep! That was Winifred. She was single for three years and I matched her with a doctor called Neo. They had their first date last night and he just called her to arrange a second one!'

This was what I loved about my job: knowing I'd helped clients to make a great connection. Fingers crossed it'd blossom into a long-lasting relationship.

'Amazing! So…' Trudy came over to my desk. 'Aren't you going to open it?'

Before Winifred called, I'd received an email from the competition organisers.

Inside that message were the words that would seal my fate.

Their decision would decide whether my business would succeed or fail and confirm whether the fake-dating thing with Liam had been worth it.

Actually, that part wasn't true. The last week with Liam had been pretty magical.

When I got home from work, he'd greet me with a hug and a slow kiss. Sometimes that would lead to us getting naked, but most nights, he'd take my hand, lead me to the kitchen pour me a glass of wine and ask about my day.

Then we'd cook together (well, Liam would cook, whilst I passed him the ingredients or did basic things like chop the veg). We'd eat, play classic games (last week we added Operation and Guess Who? to our collection) or he'd read me what he'd written that day.

I was so proud of him for finding the courage to work on his screenplay. I didn't know much about the film and TV industry, but his idea sounded brilliant.

'Earth to Mia!' Trudy shouted, snapping me out of my thoughts.

'Sorry, I was just thinking about something.'

'Let me guess—you were dreaming about Liam?'

'Sort of… it's just I want you both to be here when I open the email.'

I glanced at my watch. It was only a few minutes past six. Liam was meeting me here so that we could go for dinner at my parents.

Yep. We were doing *that*. I'd put it off for as long as possible, but there was no escaping it. Although Liam and I were together now and I didn't have to worry about us being 'found out', I knew there would still be that expectation that we were going to have a happily-ever-after.

Now my parents would be expecting us to get married, have kids and settle down. But even though a husband and family were what I'd always wanted, I knew it wouldn't happen with Liam. And trying not to let my mum and dad get carried away was going to be difficult.

There was a knock at the door. As I looked up, my face flushed with excitement. It was Liam.

'Sorry I'm late.' He burst in. 'Traffic was a bitch.' He bent down to kiss me softly on the lips and my whole body lit up.

'Look at you two.' Trudy grinned. 'You're adorable! So now Loverman's here, you gonna open this email and put us out of our misery?'

'What email?' Liam asked.

'It's a message from the competition organisers. I'm pretty sure it's going to say whether or not I reached the finals.'

'What? Wow! And you haven't opened it yet?'

'No, I wanted you both to be here. If I don't make it through, I'll need all the moral support I can get.'

·I'd become addicted to Liam's hugs. If it was bad news and I was wrapped in his arms, I knew he'd instantly make me feel better. And Trudy would know the right thing to say to console me. Even if it was just 'Fuck 'em! It's their loss for not choosing you.'

'You won't need moral support, Mi.' Liam brushed his thumb gently across my cheek. 'You'll get through. I just know it.' My heart fluttered. It meant a lot that he believed in me.

'I've been trying to tell her that all blinking day!' Trudy huffed. 'Come on, babes, open it.'

My trembling hand hovered over the mouse.

Three.

Two.

One.

Here goes nothing…

I clicked into the email and held my breath as I scanned the text.

'Well?' Trudy asked.

My face broke into a smile and my heart soared.

'I got through!' I jumped out of my seat. 'I'm in the finals!'

Liam lifted me up in the air and spun me around as Trudy screamed.

'I knew you'd do it!' Liam put me down, then planted another kiss on my lips. 'You're fucking amazing!'

'Thanks!' I said.

'So proud of you, bestie!' Trudy gave me a big squeeze.

'I can't believe it! I'm so relieved.'

'This is just the beginning,' Liam added. 'You'll see.'

'I have to win the competition first!'

'Whatever happens, you're gonna fly, Mia.' He looped his arm around my waist. 'You're talented. People will see that. Success is coming.'

'He's right.' Trudy rubbed my shoulder.

'Thanks. I couldn't have got this far without you two.' My phone buzzed on the table. I looked down. It was a text from Mum. Probably checking we were on our way. 'We'd better go.'

After I'd replied to the email, thanking the organisers for my nomination, we headed down to the car and set off.

'Liam!' Mum beamed as she opened the front door.

'Mrs Bailey! Great to see you!' Liam kissed her on the cheek.

'Oooh.' She grinned. 'What a charming young man

you've grown into. And none of that Mrs Bailey foolishness. It's Carmen. Or call me Mum!' She winked.

I winced. We'd barely been here a minute and she was already hinting at wedding bells.

'Has our special guest arrived?' Dad came into the hallway and kissed Mum gently on her cheek before striding over to Liam. 'How are you, son? It's been a while!'

'It has!' Liam smiled. 'How have you been, Mr Bailey?'

'You're family!' He slapped him on the back. 'Call me Chris or Dad.'

They must've planned this whole *call me Mum/Dad* routine.

Whilst my parents disappeared into the kitchen holding hands, Liam and I stepped into the dining room, where Alice was seated. My chest tightened. I was still annoyed that she hadn't passed on that message from Liam.

'Hi, sis.' Alice got up and gave me a stilted hug.

'Hey.' I patted her back gently.

Before I'd arrived I'd felt okay about how I looked, but next to Alice, I felt four feet tall. Her make-up was immaculate, her long dark hair extensions reached the centre of her back and looked like they'd just been applied and I knew from the cut of her dress that it had to be designer. Being around her always made me feel inadequate.

'Wow! Liam Stone!' Alice's eyes sparkled as she planted her lips on his cheek. 'You look *amazing*! Mmm, and you smell great too!'

'Alice,' he said flatly. 'Long time.'

'I know! *Too* long!' She rubbed his bicep, and I wanted

to swat her hand away like a mosquito. Liam stepped back and her palm dropped.

'Where's Jack?' I asked.

'At the office. Had to work late.' She waved her hand dismissively. 'Are those the new Louboutins? And is that dress a vintage Roland Mouret?'

I frowned and was about to say she was crazy because I couldn't afford either when I remembered I was wearing the stuff Liam got me.

'Yeah, the shoes are Louboutins.' I was so shocked when I saw the red soles. 'Not sure if the dress is a Muret.'

'It's *Mouret*,' Alice corrected me. 'Celebs like Meghan Markle used to wear his designs all the time.'

'Oh.' I shrugged.

'Actually,' Liam jumped in, 'that's not the Roland Mouret. We destroyed that one… remember, babe, in the kitchen?' The corner of his mouth twitched mischievously.

My eyes widened and heat flooded my cheeks as I remembered him ripping it whilst I was spread across the marble island.

'Yeah.' A grin spread across my face. 'I remember…'

'The dress my gorgeous girlfriend is wearing is a Victoria Beckham.'

'Really?' Alice gasped.

'Only the best for my lady.' Liam pecked me on the cheek.

My heart fluttered. I hadn't paid much attention to the label, but Alice was into this stuff, and as silly as it sounded, it was nice to have something better than her for a change.

And it wasn't just my outfit she was jealous of. It was

Liam too. I hated when she always used to flirt with him. Actually, now was a good time to have that little chat.

'I've been meaning to ask you something, Alice. Liam mentioned that on the day he left for Spain, he asked you to pass on a message for me to come and see him urgently, but you didn't. Why?'

Her face fell.

'What? I don't remember that. Anyway, that was *years* ago.' She rolled her eyes. 'Did I show you the diamond necklace Jack got me for our anniversary?'

'No,' I muttered as we took our seats.

'Let me see if I have a photo.'

She'd deliberately avoided answering the question, which made me think that she *did* remember but was too chicken to admit it. Anger bubbled in my chest. As Alice scrolled through her phone, Liam reached under the table and squeezed my hand. I instantly felt better.

'You still like rice and peas?' Mum asked Liam as she returned to the dining room with Dad, clutching various dishes.

'Yes!' Liam's face lit up. Looked like he was giving himself a well-earned break from his strict eating regime. 'Have you made curried goat too?'

Mum nodded.

'She remembered how much you used to like it,' Dad added.

'Never understood why it's called rice and peas,' Alice tutted. 'Peas are green. Those are kidney *beans* with rice, not *peas*.'

'It's what we call it in the Caribbean, so that's just how it is,' Dad said.

Alice had never been a fan of the Jamaican food Mum

and Dad cooked, like curried goat, which as the name suggested was pieces of goat in a curry sauce. She didn't like eating carbs either. I couldn't imagine a world without rice, chips, pasta or pizza.

'Don't worry.' Mum walked towards the kitchen. 'I made you a salad.'

Once Mum returned to the table with Alice's salad, we all got stuck in.

'So,' Mum said as she finished a mouthful of rice. 'It's so nice that you two lovebirds finally made time to come and have dinner with us.'

'We've both been really busy,' I replied.

'Little Liam is such a big star now! Only feels like yesterday that he was helping me in the kitchen! I always thought he was sweet on you, Mia.'

'She did.' Dad nodded.

'And what good timing too! We were so worried about Mia. She's been single for so long! Thank goodness for Liam! Now you can be happy, like Alice.'

As if I needed reminding that my sister was the gold standard. Alice beamed and Liam squeezed my hand again.

'Speaking of being happy, I have *big* news!' Alice shouted dramatically. 'I made partner!'

'That's brilliant!' Mum rushed over to give her a hug.

'We're so proud of you.' Dad joined Mum, planting a congratulatory kiss on Alice's cheek.

'Congratulations!' I said with as much enthusiasm as I could. Even though I couldn't forgive her for not passing on that message, I was happy she was doing well.

I wished that for once I could do something that would

make my parents proud of me too. All I ever did was make them worry.

As a grown woman, I shouldn't need validation from them, but as stupid as it was, I still did.

'Congrats,' Liam said. I felt his eyes burning into me as my parents fawned all over Alice like a newborn kitten.

'How about you, Mia?' Mum's face creased as she and Dad returned to their seats. 'How's everything with the agency? Has business picked up yet? I do worry. Your job at the bank was so stable and... maybe they'll have you back if you ask.'

'It wasn't as stable as you think. They're closing high street branches and taking most banking online,' I said, avoiding the main question.

'True.' Dad nodded. 'Now I have to travel into the city to find one. Your mum's right. Running a business is risky. I can ask if anyone knows of any jobs going. Alice, do you have anything at your firm for Mia?'

'Dad!' I jumped in. The last thing I needed was to work with my sister. 'I don't need another job. Running my agency is what I want to do.'

'But if it's not working—'

'Actually,' Liam jumped in, 'Mia had some fantastic news today too!'

My head shot round to face Liam.

'Really?' Mum straightened in her seat.

'Yeah, she... actually, I should let Mia tell you.'

I glared at Liam, trying to communicate that I didn't want to.

I was happy that I'd reached the finals, but I had no intention of telling my family. They'd get their hopes up. And if I didn't win, they'd be disappointed. Again.

The table's gaze was pinned on me. Even Alice's eyes were wide with anticipation. Dammit. There was no going back now.

'I-I got through to the finals of the Happily Ever After Awards,' I mumbled.

'What?' Mum gasped. 'That's great, Mia!'

'Excellent!' Dad smiled.

Butterflies erupted in my stomach. They actually looked thrilled. So this was how it felt to make them happy. It was like I was standing under the sun.

'It really is.' Liam grinned. 'I'm so proud of her. The competition is tough, so it's a massive achievement. The judges know how talented she is.'

My heart inflated like a hot air balloon.

'That's… *nice*,' Alice said. 'When are the finals?'

'In three weeks,' I replied, sitting up straighter.

'Can we come?' Mum said.

My jaw dropped.

'You—you want to come?'

'Of course!'

'Well, I…'

'Amazing!' Liam added.

'But I might not win,' I blurted out, self-doubt flooding my thoughts.

'You deserve to.'

'Awards ceremonies are *so* awkward,' Alice sighed. 'Ninety per cent of the finalists will be disappointed and then they have to pretend to be happy for the winners.'

She was right. If I lost, Mum and Dad would feel sorry for me again.

'We'd love to come!' Dad ignored Alice's comment.

'Great!' Liam said. 'Shall I book a table?'

I nodded, my mind whirring.

Thankfully the rest of the evening went quickly. As well as my parents filling us in on their anniversary plans, they bombarded Liam with questions about life as a Hollywood star. Alice was also keen to know which celebs he was friends with.

'We'd better head off.' I stood up from the table.

'That's a shame,' Mum said.

After we'd said our goodbyes, we headed out to the car, then set off.

'Thank God that's over,' I exhaled.

'Sorry if I did the wrong thing by mentioning the awards. I could see Alice was getting to you, so…'

'It's okay. Thanks for having my back.'

'Why didn't you want to tell them?'

'Because like Alice said, if I don't win, it'll be embarrassing. I don't want to let my parents down. They're already going to be disappointed when… we don't end up settling down. And they already think my business is a failure and unless I lift that trophy, I'm going to prove them right.'

'Why do you want this award so badly? You know you're good at what you do and your clients believe in you. If it's the money, I can help.'

'Thanks, but it's more than just the money. The credibility and exposure winning will bring is priceless. They'll run a double-page spread in their magazine, which has a big circulation. Being able to say I was featured in *Happily Ever After* magazine on my website and marketing materials alone is huge. Plus, the closer we get to Christmas, the more people will be thinking about finding a partner.

The New Year and Valentine's Day are also important seasons. Winning will help me capitalise on that.'

'But why do you need to rent an office to matchmake? If the rent's so high, aren't you better off working from home and meeting clients at a decent coffee shop when you need to? That'd cut your overheads massively and take some of the pressure off.'

'No. When you're asking people to pay for a service like this, they expect you to operate from a nice place. It puts them more at ease.'

'You're the expert.' Liam held his hand up in surrender. 'I don't know anything about matchmaking, but I just thought people cared about whether you can find their dream partner or not. The rest is just… not important.'

If only that was true.

Right now, I could only think of one thing: winning.

With my business on the line, it was important before, but now my parents knew, it was more critical.

I couldn't disappoint them.

I needed to win.

It was the only option.

43

MIA

'Ready?' Liam peeked his head around the bedroom door.

'As I'll ever be.' I smoothed down the front of my bright yellow backless dress, then turned to face him.

'Mamma Mia!'

'I thought we were done with that nickname!' I rolled my eyes.

'It was never supposed to be something bad. When I called you that, I meant it as a compliment. Just like I do now. You look... wow! That dress is fire! So like I said before: *Mamma Mia.*'

'Oh.' I swallowed. 'I didn't realise. You should've told me sooner that it was a compliment. Thanks!'

'And spoil the fun of getting you all worked up?' He stepped forward and brushed his thumb across my cheek.

'If the car wasn't coming to take us to the awards ceremony, I'd suggest you find another way to get me *all worked up.*' I smiled.

'Don't tempt me,' Liam growled, then pushed his lips

onto mine. He was going to ruin my lipstick, but I didn't care.

His phone buzzed. Liam pulled it out of his pocket.

'Car's outside. How you feeling?'

'Nervous.'

That was an understatement. My stomach was in knots. So much was riding on this award, and as much as I wanted to be excited, the consequences of not winning were getting to me.

I wasn't just anxious about the ceremony. I was also sad about Liam leaving. In twelve hours he'd be gone.

As we'd originally agreed, he was flying back to LA first thing in the morning. And I had no idea when and if I'd ever see him again.

Every time I'd tried to bring up the future, he'd reminded me of what we'd said: that we'd just enjoy the time we had together.

I couldn't complain. I'd gone into this with my eyes wide open, knowing that Liam lived on the other side of the world. I knew Liam didn't do long-term relationships. This was only temporary.

And I should be grateful. This had started out as a mutually beneficial business transaction. It was never supposed to be anything more. So the fact that I'd got to enjoy companionship, endless laughs and amazing sex too was a bonus. Wanting more was being greedy.

'Nerves are normal.' He squeezed my hand. 'But I've got you.'

'Thanks.' My eyes flicked to his and my stomach fluttered.

God, I was going to miss him.

I'd miss his smile. The way his eyes lit up when he

saw me. The way he made me laugh. His supportive words. His hugs.

Everything.

We headed to the car. It didn't take long to get to the fancy five-star hotel on London's Park Lane where the awards were being held.

As we pulled up, there were swarms of photographers outside.

I checked my teeth in the mirror to make sure I didn't have lipstick smeared all over them. Liam got out, then reached for my hand.

He led me down the glamorous red carpet, and as soon as the paps spotted us, they called out our names.

'Let's give them something to talk about,' Liam whispered in my ear, then lifted my chin before planting a soft kiss on my lips.

The sound of dozens of cameras clicking surrounded us.

Liam led me through the revolving doors and my shoulders relaxed. Although I was more comfortable in front of the cameras than in the beginning, it still made me anxious. I was worried about doing something embarrassing that'd end up being seen all over the world. I definitely wasn't going to miss the paps when Liam went back.

My stomach churned. I really didn't want to think about him leaving. I needed to keep my mind in the present. Enjoy the time we had left.

'I'm just gonna take a leak.'

'Okay,' I said. 'I'll wait here.'

'Wow, wow, wow!' Trudy walked towards me. 'Someone call the fire brigade! You look H-O-T!'

'Thanks.' I smiled. 'It's not too much?' Normally I would've opted for a safer colour like black, but the yellow was so striking I couldn't resist.

'No way! The colour suits you and the cut-out at the back is sexy as hell. You'll look great on the front page tomorrow! The paps took a photo of me too. I hope it doesn't end up online. I only noticed when I went to the loo that I had broccoli in my teeth!'

'Oh no! You look great, though!' I said, admiring her scarlet minidress.

'Cheers. I put on my best frock, just for you.' Trudy did a little twirl and then bowed, which made me chuckle. 'How you feeling?'

'Very nervous.' The knots in my stomach grew tighter.

'Understandable. But they'd be nuts not to give the award to you! By the way, your folks are already here. I caught them snogging earlier!'

'Doesn't surprise me! I'm just going to the toilet. Liam's in the gents. Back in a sec.'

I pulled out my phone to text my parents, then entered the toilets. Gillian was standing at the mirror, reapplying her hot pink lipstick.

'Mia.' She plastered on a fake smile and stretched out her palm. I put my phone down beside the sink and shook her hand. 'So *interesting* to see you reached the finals this year.' She continued shaking it before dropping it abruptly and flicking her platinum-blonde hair over her shoulder.

'I'm very excited to be here,' I said diplomatically.

'I suppose it was only a matter of time before they had to put someone like *you* through. These days everyone's trying to be *woke*.' She rolled her eyes.

'Excuse me?' My nostrils flared. 'I'm here because of

my abilities. Not because of a diversity quota. That was what you were implying, right?'

'Gosh, so sensitive!' She clutched her chest dramatically. 'I didn't mean to offend.'

'And why would having more diversity in the competition be a bad thing?' I put my hands on my hips. 'Everyone with a proven track record who's demonstrated a strong ability in their field should have an equal chance of winning, whatever their background.'

'Of course you have *some* ability.' She waved her hand dismissively. 'And nice touch with the movie star boyfriend thing.'

I knew I didn't like Gillian, but now I hated her even more. Whether Liam had stepped in to help or not, if I didn't have a solid matchmaking track record, they wouldn't have even considered putting me through. I wanted to win to wipe that ignorant smile off her face.

'Speaking of boyfriends, how's your personal assistant doing?' I raised my eyebrow. 'You know, the one I saw you coming out of the toilets with at the conference.'

Her face fell. Busted.

'Anyway'—she pushed out her chest—'I'd wish you good luck, but it's pointless because I'm going to win. Even having a famous boyfriend who's *so in tune to your needs* won't help you tonight. I've got this in the bag.'

How did she know that I'd said that Liam was so in tune to my needs in the interview?

'We'll see about that.' I stormed into the cubicle.

She might be confident about winning, but I had a good chance too.

Once I came out of the toilets, I spotted my parents standing arm in arm next to Liam and Trudy. I'd reluctantly invited Alice and Jack, who hadn't arrived yet, and Liam had asked Nate and his fiancée, Melody, too.

I hoped that the ceremony would start straight away so that I could get it over and done with. But first there was a three-course meal. I supposed they had to justify the extortionate ticket price. Liam had generously paid for everyone, which was sweet of him.

As I walked into the grand hall, I gasped. Love heart decorations and displays of red roses were strategically placed around the perimeter.

The sea of tables were covered with thick white linen, polished cutlery and wine glasses and sprinkled with heart-shaped confetti.

The stage had a backdrop with the Happily Ever After and the various sponsors' logos, and a huge flying Cupid, complete with a gold sparkly arrow was suspended from the ceiling. It was all very glamorous.

Food was served relatively quickly and everything looked so fancy. I reached into my bag to get my phone to take a photo of the dessert, but it wasn't there.

'Shit,' I said, retracing my steps. I'd had it earlier. In the toilets. When I was about to text my parents. Then I'd seen Gillian. I jumped up.

'You okay?' Liam touched my arm.

'I left my phone in the toilets.'

I raced back into the hallway and spotted Gillian walking towards me.

'Not now,' I huffed.

'Looking for *this*?' she called out, dangling my phone in the air.

'Yes!' Relief washed over me. 'Thank you.'

'Or more specifically…' She opened the phone flap

and pulled out a piece of paper. My eyes widened in horror. 'Are you looking for *this*?'

No. No. No.

Please, God, no.

'Wait... I...'

Gillian opened the piece of paper.

'"Four dates, to include first date, interview, one other date and the ceremony"... so cute! And so sad! I thought you just said you were here because of your abilities?' She smirked.

My stomach plummeted and bile rose in my throat.

'What are you going to do? What do you want?'

'Want?' she laughed. 'There's nothing *you* can offer *me*. I told you, I'm going to win. Anyway, telling tales isn't nice. Us girls need to stick together, *right*?'

She flashed an evil grin, tucked the piece of paper back into my case and handed the phone back to me.

'Th-thanks?' My eyes narrowed. She'd seen the contract between me and Liam and knew we'd faked our relationship but she wasn't going to do anything? Sounded fishy to me.

'But if you ever feel the need to disagree with us *sticking together*, I've taken a photo of your sad little contract, in case I need it in the future. Enjoy your night, and try not to look too sad when they call out my name!'

She breezed past me, leaving my jaw on the floor.

I returned to my seat in a trance.

'What's up?' Liam asked. I took his hand and led him out of the hall into a corner.

'Gillian knows,' I whispered.

'Knows what?'

'She found this...' I showed him the notepaper.

'Shit. And what did she say?'

'Basically she said she'd keep quiet, but I think the understanding is that I keep my mouth shut about what I saw her doing at a conference.'

'Bitch.'

'I know.'

'Forget her. We'll think about it later. Let's focus on you taking home the award. The ceremony's about to start.'

Just as we returned to the hall, the compère came to the stage.

'Ladies and gentlemen. Welcome to the fifth annual Happily Ever After Awards.'

'It's him off the telly!' Melody pointed, her armful of bangles jangling loudly. I hadn't even noticed it was the presenter of a popular game show. I was too distracted.

'Looks much fitter in person.' Trudy licked her lips. 'This is it! Good luck!' She rubbed my shoulder.

I looked to the back of the room. Alice and Jack still weren't here. Maybe that was a good thing. Less pressure.

'You okay?' Liam kissed my cheek.

'Trying to be.'

'Just remember, you're a winner, no matter what. Okay?'

I nodded and looked at the stage, my mind still whirring about Gillian finding out. But I couldn't focus on her now. I just had to keep my fingers crossed she was wrong and the award would go to me.

The compère ran through the different categories, and our table applauded the finalists and winners politely.

When the nominees for Sex Toy of the Year appeared on the screen, Dad's eyes popped.

'Oh my!' Mum fanned herself with the awards programme.

'Looks impressive!' Melody cackled as the bright pink vibrator appeared on the screen. 'If I didn't have this stallion'—she stroked Nate's beard—'I'd be ordering one of those for myself!'

Nate shook his head and laughed.

'Sweetheart, that only has ten different settings and you know I have more ways to get you off than that...'

'He's not wrong!' Melody grinned and the whole table burst out laughing. Sounded like Melody and Nate had explosive chemistry in the bedroom just like me and Liam.

Liam. I couldn't believe tonight would be the last time we'd be intimate together. Maybe I should be ordering the vibrator. And the Felati-*ohhh*—the oral-mimicking vibrator that'd just appeared on the screen.

As the compère tried to keep a straight face whilst talking about the product's authentic licking and sucking capabilities, Mum whispered something in Dad's ear. I definitely didn't want to know what she'd said.

Even if I had the money to order every toy on the shortlist, nothing would compare to feeling Liam inside me or the sensation of his mouth all over my body.

I pushed the thought out of my mind and as the Sex Toy of the Year winner was announced and the company representative walked to the stage, I clapped, hoping that soon I'd be going up to collect an award too.

After several more categories were announced, the moment finally came.

'Now we're moving on to the Matchmaker of the Year award. Here are the nominees.'

As the compère read out the names of each of the five

finalists, our photos flashed on the screen, then a video clip of our clients giving testimonials followed.

When mine appeared, my parents cheered and Liam, Trudy, Nate and Melody whooped, whistled and banged on the table enthusiastically.

My face broke into a smile. Knowing they were rooting for me made my heart flutter. Then the nerves returned.

I swiped a napkin from the table, then dabbed it across my forehead to mop up the beads of sweat.

Come on.

I willed the compère to put me out of my misery. If this was a TV talent show, right now he'd say they were going to a commercial break to build the suspense.

'And the winner is…'

I held my breath and Liam gripped my hand tightly.

This was it.

Please, please, please let it be me.

Please.

I really need this.

'Gillian Madeley! Congratulations!'

So that was it.

I'd lost.

Gillian was right. She'd won.

As the realisation hit me, the air was knocked out of my lungs. My stomach felt like it'd been carved out with a chainsaw. But I couldn't show it. I had to put on a brave face.

Using every ounce of strength, I plastered on a big smile, then reluctantly pulled my palm from Liam's hand to give her a round of applause.

'So sorry,' Liam whispered in my ear.

'Outrageous!' Trudy snarled. 'You were robbed!'

My parents looked at me like I was a sick puppy that'd been abandoned on a street corner. The pity and sadness in their eyes almost made me burst into tears.

This was what I'd dreaded: letting them down.

All of this was for nothing.

I was going to lose my business. The only job I'd ever had that I really enjoyed.

And as well as that, I was hours away from losing the only man I truly loved.

Yep.

Somehow, in that moment I realised—I loved Liam.

I'd always loved him. Long before the world knew his name.

I'd loved spending time with him ever since we were kids. That was why I was so upset when I thought he'd left without saying goodbye. Turning that love into hate was my coping mechanism.

But these past two months hadn't just rekindled my original feelings. They'd amplified them.

The truth was, I loved Liam so much it hurt.

Now the question was whether I was brave enough to tell him before he left for good.

44

LIAM

Gutted.

I didn't know shit about the matchmaking industry, but Trudy was right. Mia was robbed. It should've been her collecting that award. Not that scheming woman.

Her threatening Mia wasn't right. And I wanted to tell her that to her face. Whatever the consequences were, I'd deal with them. But right now, the most important thing was taking care of Mia.

Once the awards ended, we left via the back exit, where Phil was waiting.

'You're gonna be okay.' I faced Mia as she put on her seat belt. 'You don't need them to be successful. If you want, I can—'

'I know you're about to offer me money again, and I'm grateful, but I can't take it. I need to make it on my own. That's important to me.'

'Okay. Come here.' I opened my arms and wrapped them around her.

For the whole journey, Mia rested her head on my shoulder and sobbed. I rubbed her back, stroked her hair and tried to reassure her. I wished there was more that I could do. That I could wave a magic wand to make her happy so that we could enjoy the little time we had left together.

My chest tightened. I couldn't believe that in just a few hours, I'd be heading back to LA.

I desperately wanted to stay with Mia, but I'd committed to this dumb role. I wished that things were different, but we'd agreed that I'd leave the morning after the awards. And we'd both said that things between us would only last as long as I was in London, so we had to stick to that.

Phil pulled over.

'Mi, we're here. You ready to go inside?'

She peeled herself from my shoulder and sat up.

Mascara tears stained her cheeks. Seeing her cry and knowing how upset she was made my heart break.

Once we were safely inside, I led her to the sofa. Her eyes were bloodshot and still watering. Shit.

'Want some tea?'

I hadn't had much practice at consoling girlfriends. I'd never stuck around long enough to deal with these kinds of emotions, but whenever people cheered someone up on British soaps, they always offered to make a cuppa. I hated the stuff, but if it'd help Mia, I was willing to try.

'Please,' she replied, avoiding my gaze.

After boiling the kettle and pouring the water over the teabag, I bought the mug along with some milk and sugar to the living room.

'I don't know how you take it, so…'

'Have you ever made tea?' The corner of her mouth turned up a little, like she wanted to smile. That was a good sign.

'Don't think so. My parents were coffee people. And this kind of tea isn't that popular in LA.'

Mia's face fell and a fat tear rolled down her cheek. So much for making her smile.

'Hey.' I sat beside her and wrapped my arm around her back. 'I know you're gutted about not winning, but you can still use the nomination to promote yourself. In Hollywood, they always mention when someone was an Academy Award nominee. Being shortlisted is still a big achievement.'

'It's not just the awards,' Mia said quickly.

'You're worried about the rent increase?'

'No! It's…' She paused. 'You're leaving in a few hours and I… I'm going to miss you.'

'Oh, sweetheart.' I pulled her into me and inhaled her sweet scent. 'I'm gonna miss you too, Tutti-Frutti. So much.'

I really was. But there was nothing I could do.

'Isn't there… never mind.' Her body stiffened.

'What?' I pulled away and lifted her chin. 'Tell me.'

'Isn't there any way we could make this work?'

My gaze dropped to the floor.

This was such bad timing. Mia was already devastated about the awards and now I was about to crush her heart even more by telling her that we couldn't continue. If I'd known things would get this messy, I'd never have agreed to this arrangement.

Who was I kidding? These two months with Mia had

been incredible, so as hard as leaving would be, I wouldn't have changed that for the world.

'Mi.' I looked her in the eyes, which made things worse. I hated seeing her upset. 'It's what we agreed... we both knew this could only be temporary. Remember our conversations?' Mia nodded. 'I'm in LA and you're here. And I'm... I'm not good at relationships when I'm in the same city as a woman, so the long-distance thing would be even worse. We've had a great run and I'll remember our time together, forever. I don't want us to end up hating each other again, so it's better we part on good terms. This way, we can go out on a high.'

I placed my hand on hers and she pulled away.

'I'm going to the bathroom.' Mia stormed out of the room.

Fuck.

I understood why she was pissed. I wasn't happy about the situation either, but it was for the best. Better that I upset her now before we got in any deeper and I screwed up. Which would only be a matter of time.

Like I'd always said, relationships always ended, so what was the point in trying? And Mia thought I looked hot now, but what would happen when I stopped working out and my looks faded, or if my career ended? There was no guarantee I'd get an investor for my screenplay. And everyone knew my days as an action hero were numbered.

Of course I'd love for us to be happy together. But this wasn't a movie. This was real life and I had to face facts.

Just like Dad, I wasn't capable of maintaining a relationship. He'd broken Mum's heart and the last thing I wanted was to do the same to Mia.

She didn't realise it now, but I was doing her a favour.

Setting Mia free to find someone who could give her the happy ending she wanted. She'd get over me.

I didn't know how I'd get over her, though. Mia was the most incredible woman I'd ever met and the thought of her with another man made me physically sick. But I had to put my feelings aside and do what was best for Mia. And that was to let her go.

Forever.

45

MIA

So stupid.

I glared in the bathroom mirror, chastising myself.

Liam was right. We'd agreed that this couldn't go any further than tonight. So why had I asked for more when I knew that he wasn't in a position to give it to me?

And to think I was going to tell him that I was in love with him.

Like I said: *so stupid.*

And crying in front of him like a baby was pathetic.

I couldn't weep over losing at the awards or losing a man that I'd never really had. I needed to be strong.

After wiping away the mascara streaks from my cheeks, I cleaned the rest of my face before getting in the shower.

Once I'd finished, I walked to the bedroom. Liam was sitting on the bed.

I grabbed my nightclothes and pulled the air mattress

out from the wardrobe. Sleeping in the same bed as Liam tonight wasn't wise. I had to get used to being alone. Again.

'You okay?' he asked.

Yeah, everything's peachy. My business and my love life are down the drain, but whatever.

'I'm *fine*.' I straightened my shoulders. 'Ignore what I said earlier. You were right. This was just a business agreement.'

'I didn't say that…'

'I knew what I was getting into and you were very clear about what you could offer, so no harm done. Thanks for your help. You played the boyfriend role really well. Even though I didn't get the result I was hoping for, I still appreciate everything you did. I'm sleeping in the spare room.'

Sleeping in there after my encounter with that scary spider frightened the shit out of me, but I couldn't stay in the same bed as Liam.

'Come on, Mi.' Liam's face crumpled. 'You don't have to do that. It's our last night. Let's spend it together.'

'Actually'—my eyes flicked to the floor. I couldn't look at him. It was too hard—'I should go home now. I'll have to leave for good in a few hours anyway, so I might as well do it now.'

I pulled out my suitcase, then started dragging my own clothes off the hangers and shoving them inside.

'Mia!' Liam jumped off the bed and gripped my hand. 'Stop! I know you're hurting and I'm sorry, but it's better this way. I can't give you what you deserve. But that doesn't mean you have to go now. Stay. Let me hold you.'

'No!' I shrugged his hand off.

The last thing I needed was for him to wrap those strong arms around me. Remind me of what I'd had. And what I'd be missing. I needed to draw a line under things ASAP. Like a plaster, it was best to rip it off quickly.

Once I'd gathered my clothes, I got dressed in the bathroom, then swiped all of my products from the shelves and into my toiletries bag.

I'd left all the expensive dresses and shoes Liam had bought me. He'd already given me enough. I didn't want him to think I was taking advantage now that our agreement was over.

After getting my phone downstairs, I ordered a taxi. When I returned to the room, Liam had his head in his hands.

'The Uber's three minutes away.' I zipped up my suitcase, then moved towards the door. 'And don't worry, I'll check there are no paps lurking so you won't get any negative press about me leaving.'

'I don't care about the fucking paps!' Liam jumped up and grabbed my hands. 'All I care about is *you*.'

'Like I said'—I moved my hands—'I'll be fine. *Please*. I have to go.'

This time, my gaze met his. Seeing his eyes watering floored me. I didn't think he'd be bothered about me going, but he actually seemed upset.

Not enough to try, though. Not enough to fight for me.

'Bye, Liam. And thank you, genuinely. For everything.'

I walked to the stairs. I desperately wanted to hug him one last time. To press my lips onto his. To inhale his intoxicating scent. To turn and have a final glance at the man I loved so much.

But I kept on walking. Down to the hallway, where I put on my coat and shoes, then out the door and into the taxi.

Leaving Liam far behind me.

46

MIA

It'd been a difficult four weeks.

Reluctantly, I'd handed in my notice at the office. I had no choice. I couldn't get myself into more debt.

I knew if I asked, my parents would try and lend me some money, but that wasn't the solution. What would happen the next time the rent increased or some other unexpected costs popped up? I had to prove that I could run a business, by myself.

So that was that. I had to work from home. I wasn't looking forward to it, but I'd come too far to give up now.

Trudy was understanding. She said she was happy to work from home and had mainly agreed to share the office space and rent to help me out, which made me feel worse. And that was saying something, because since Liam went back to LA, I'd been feeling pretty low.

That night after I'd left Liam's place, I'd gone back to my flat.

It felt weird to be home. It was eerily quiet and so cold. I'd tried to put the heating on, but it wasn't working, so I'd spent the night wrapped under the duvet in several layers of clothes. But it didn't matter how many blankets I piled on, nothing warmed me up. I just felt hollow.

As I lay there, I told myself that although I was missing Liam, the pain was temporary. It was the first time I'd slept in a bed alone since we'd got together, so it was normal that it'd felt weird. In a few days, I'd be fine.

Except, it'd been a month, the heating had been fixed and the bed still felt as cold as it had back then.

The stories in the press hadn't helped. 'Liam Breaks Off Romance to Return to LA' headlines dominated the tabloids, gossip magazines and websites for more than a week.

After that, they must've got bored and started focusing on the new film he had coming up with Hollywood goddess Nina Rose and how she was helping to *console him*. Thank God there hadn't been any photos of them snuggled up together. I hoped it wasn't true, but I knew if I saw any images of his tongue down her throat it'd kill me.

So yeah, there'd been that. And the pitying looks from strangers who recognised me in the street. I didn't know what was worse—the sad looks from relatives when I was single or the 'poor thing got dumped by a movie star' stares I got now.

Anyway, like the saying went, there was no point crying over spilt milk. I just had to try and save my business, forget about Liam and move on.

I packed up the last of my things, took a final glance around the office, then locked the door for the last time. I'd miss this place.

After handing in the keys, I trudged outside. A gust of

frigid wind hit my face. I tightened my scarf around my neck.

Just as I was about to cross the road, I saw a woman standing on the corner with a bright red sandwich board. What she had written on the front stopped me in my tracks.

Looking for True Love
Interested? Call me!

Underneath, her number was listed.

A few passers-by pointed and laughed before snapping photos.

As I got closer, I saw that she was shaking and had tears in her eyes. I wasn't surprised she was upset. I knew how it felt to be looking for love. Things must be really bad for her to resort to such extreme measures.

'Hi,' I said softly. 'You okay?'

'You mean, apart from feeling cold and humiliated?' Her face broke into an awkward smile.

She had a lovely smile. She had dark hair and was dressed in a long grey coat.

'How long have you been out here? It's freezing.'

'About an hour, but it feels like ten.'

'What's your name?'

'Kelly.'

'Nice to meet you, Kelly. I'm Mia. Why don't I buy you a coffee? We can have a chat and get you warmed up.'

'That's really kind, but I have to do this. It's my last resort.' She exhaled an icy puff of air.

'What have you tried so far?'

'Dating apps, speed dating, blind dates… and everything ends in disaster.'

'What about a matchmaking service?'

'My friends try to set me up and Mum and Dad are

always suggesting men. But I haven't tried a professional service. They're expensive, aren't they?'

That was one of the good things about when I'd started the agency. To build up that pool, I hadn't charged, so I was able to help people from all backgrounds find love.

But I couldn't do that forever. A lot of work went into what I did, so obviously I had to charge for my time. I had bills to pay, but I also hated that my services would only ever be accessible to people with money.

Now that I was working from home and my overheads were much lower, maybe I could take on a new pro bono client.

I hadn't found my own Mr Right, but I knew how to find the right match for others. As well as benefiting Kelly, it'd distract me from worrying about my own love life.

'I'm a professional matchmaker and I'm looking for a pro bono client. Should we go and grab that coffee? I believe I can help you.'

47

LIAM

I slid off my shoes and collapsed on the sofa.

It'd been a long day. And the fact that I had to do it all again tomorrow and the next day and the next for another seven weeks filled me with dread.

We'd started shooting the new movie and as I'd predicted, I hated it.

When the car took me to the set that first morning, after yet another sleepless night, I'd convinced myself that getting back to work properly would be a good thing. It'd take my mind off Mia, who had dominated my thoughts every second, minute and hour since I'd returned from London.

The nights were the hardest. Everything felt empty without her. This house. My bed. And I wasn't talking about the sex.

Yeah, of course I missed it, but it was more than that.

I missed waking up in the middle of the night and feeling the heat from her body beside me or her warm breath tickling my skin. I missed her laugh. I even missed her whooping my arse at Connect 4.

Usually, I didn't get attached to women. As bad as it sounded, by the next day I'd forgotten about them. But not Mia. She'd lived rent-free in my head for years before we got together.

Now she wasn't renting space in my head. She'd taken out a lifetime mortgage.

I was kidding myself to believe I could forget about her. It'd been a month and instead of thinking about her less, every day that passed I loved her more.

Yeah.

Newsflash.

I loved Mia.

So damn much.

I rubbed my jaw and blew out a breath. If I was being honest with myself, I'd fallen in love with her all those years ago and never stopped.

But back then it was puppy love. This right now was the real deal.

It was weird. Whenever I'd heard that stuff about finding a person so special that they were the first thing you thought about when you woke up and the last person you thought about when you went to sleep, I'd thought it was bullshit.

And I'd never understood how you could spend all day with someone, go to sleep and still be excited all over again to spend time with them the next day. But that was how I felt.

I wanted to spend today with Mia. And tomorrow. And every day after that.

I wanted to play games together, go to shows together…

I just wanted us to be together.

All the time.

But how could we have anything long-lasting when we lived on different sides of the world?

And how could I give her a relationship when I'd never been in a serious one before?

I guess I had to learn that sometimes in life, we didn't always get what we want.

48

MIA

Funny how one chance meeting could transform your fortunes.

As I sat at the desk in the corner of my living room and scrolled through the dozens of sign-up forms that had flooded my inbox in the last seventy-two hours, I couldn't believe my luck.

There were emails from people across the UK, from different ages and backgrounds, who were willing to pay for my services. Not because they wanted a rich boyfriend or because I was a finalist for the awards. They'd got in touch because they related to Kelly.

We'd sat in the coffee shop for hours. After a string of dating disasters, her friend had suggested she tried yet another new dating app.

At that point Kelly had said she'd rather stand on a street corner with a sign asking for a boyfriend than subject herself to cold swiping again. Her friend thought she was joking, but Kelly was deadly serious. She bought a separate phone (in case any weirdos contacted her) and a sandwich board, then went for it.

I'd told her I'd help her without charge, gave her the link to the sign-up form and said that once I received it, I'd be in touch. I didn't think much more about it until I woke up yesterday to a phone full of notifications.

At first I thought it was another story about me and Liam, but thankfully it wasn't. Kelly's story had been featured in the press. They wanted to know what had happened since she'd stood on the street corner, and Kelly had mentioned she was now working with me and was confident I'd help her find the one.

And since then, my emails had blown up. The media wanted to follow the progress of her story, and a respectable website called OnTheDaily.co.uk had asked if I'd like to get involved too, by doing an interview now to show the beginning of the process and then a follow-up once I'd successfully paired Kelly up.

That website was huge and the publicity would be priceless. It'd already brought in a wave of new clients.

I leant back on my chair and smiled. It was happening. I could *feel* it. This was the big break I'd been waiting for.

Liam was right. I didn't need awards or a fancy office to make it. My career was back on track.

But even with the distraction of the excitement of this opportunity with Kelly and the possibility of new clients, there was still a hole in my heart.

Like Kelly, I'd been looking for love. The difference was, I'd found it. Then lost it again. And now I felt like something was missing.

I knew there was one thing that would make me happy.

Well, it wasn't a thing. It was a person. A very special person.

I was missing Liam.

If only there was some way we could work things out.

If only there was a way we could be together.

If only there was a way to get him back.

49

LIAM

'I'm gonna head off.' Nate picked up his bag.

'What time's your flight?'

'In a few hours. But you know what LA traffic's like.'

'Yeah. Shame you can't stay longer.'

'I know, man. But I gotta get back to my lady.'

Hearing Nate saying he had to get back to Melody stirred something inside my chest.

The realisation hit me that I'd never have someone to come home to. My stomach twisted. There'd never be someone at home missing me and counting down the hours until I came through the door.

I'd almost had that. With Mia.

Almost.

But *almost* didn't count.

'You thinking about her?' Nate's voice jolted me out of my thoughts.

'What?'

'I said, are you thinking about *your* lady?'

'I don't have one,' I said quickly.

'So you *weren't* thinking about Mia?'

'Maybe. Doesn't matter.'

'I know you're scared to admit how you feel. I was too. Me and Melody used to hate each other. I fancied her, but didn't want a relationship. I'd planned to stay single forever. Remember, apart from that one slip-up, I was always a one-night stand kinda guy. I was only supposed to hook up with Mel once at my sister's wedding, but then… we just had a connection. After that it was game over. There was no way I was gonna be without her.'

It was like Nate was inside my head. I thought I'd be a bachelor for life too. And my connection with Mia was off the charts. Nate's life was more straightforward, though.

'Your situation was different. At least you lived in the same country. I want to be with Mia. The truth is, I love her, but…' My chest tightened.

'But what?'

'I'm worried I'll fuck things up. That things won't work out.'

'That's normal. I was worried about getting hurt again, but you love her. You've been back in LA for weeks and she's still stuck in your head and your heart, right?'

'I think about her all the time.'

'That's what love does to you, bro. I know you're scared, but take the leap. Sometimes you gotta choose love over fear.'

Hearing those words sent a jolt of electricity straight to my heart.

Sometimes you gotta choose love over fear.

For so long I'd held back my heart. I'd told myself it was because of what had happened with my parents. Their relationship hadn't lasted, so mine wouldn't either.

I'd kept everyone I'd dated at a distance because I didn't want to get hurt or go through the trauma of a break-up. Or worse, divorce.

Now that I thought about it, I think I'd put a cage around my heart because I wasn't just trying to protect it. I was *preserving* it. Waiting to give it to the right person. To the one person that I knew deserved it. The person I already loved.

Mia.

I'd always loved her. And I knew that my heart belonged to her, so I'd fucked around because I wasn't willing to give it to anyone else.

I hoped that one day we'd find each other again. And we did. But then I stupidly let her go. Because I was feeling things I'd never felt. Emotions that were deeper than I'd thought was possible.

I loved Mia so much I was afraid that if we continued with our relationship and it ended, it'd destroy me.

But not being with her was already eating me up inside.

Why waste this time hurting by being apart from her, when I could be with her and be happy. Every day?

Me and Mia weren't my parents. We weren't my LA friends.

We were the real deal.

I didn't want to be afraid.

I didn't want to be alone anymore.

I wanted to live. To be happy.

I wanted to be with the woman I loved.

I wanted to be with Mia.

I wanted her in my life.

Permanently.

I wanted to choose love over fear.

'When did you say your flight to London was?'

'In a few hours. Why?' Nate frowned.

'Wait for me.' I raced out the room. 'I'm coming with you!'

'Huh?' Nate shouted.

'Don't you have filming on Monday?' Nate followed me.

'Yep. Don't care. They can fire me if they want.'

It wasn't just my love life I wanted to change. I was done with the action movies. Now that my screenplay was finished, I wanted to pursue my own dreams. Turn it into a TV series. Write more of my own screenplays. Act on the stage. Do whatever the hell I wanted.

'Fighting talk. I like it!'

'Damn straight. You're not the only one who needs to go to London to see their lady. I'm gonna see Mia. And tell her I love her.'

50

MIA

I took a deep breath, straightened my shoulders, then put my key in the door.

My parents were throwing a party at home to celebrate their fortieth anniversary. Of course I was happy for them, but after my sister's party, I wasn't looking forward to another family gathering.

I hadn't spoken to my parents properly since the awards. Although the business was starting to take off, I knew they'd think it was too early to get excited, so I'd avoided their calls and just sent texts to say that I was super busy. Dealing with their disappointment at me not winning and breaking up with Liam was too difficult.

But I couldn't let my parents down. I wanted to be here for their big celebration.

The sound of reggae music boomed through the air and the scent of my mum's fried chicken wafted from the kitchen.

My stomach rumbled, which was an improvement from the constant churning it'd done for most of the day.

'Mia! You're here!' Mum rushed over to me. She looked lovely in her sparkly ruby-coloured dress.

'Hi, Mum. Happy anniversary!' I handed her a gift bag and a silver helium balloon.

'Thanks, darling! Your father's in the living room. Go and say hello. He's missed you. We both have.' My heart fluttered. I wasn't expecting a warm welcome.

I walked through the crowd, praying no one would want to stop and talk. Dad spotted me and came over.

'Sweetheart! You made it!' He pulled me into him. I wished I could rest my head on his shoulder and let him stroke my hair like he did when I was little.

I wanted to tell him how much I was missing Liam and hear him say that everything would be okay. Silly, really. I wasn't a little girl anymore and Liam was gone. I needed to accept that and move on.

'Of course I came!' I said, holding back the tears. 'I couldn't miss your big celebration!'

'Since the awards, you've been avoiding us,' Dad shouted in my ear. It was difficult to hear over the music.

'I-I…'

'Come.' He led me out of the room. 'Let's find your mother.'

Mum was in the kitchen, stirring a big silver pot.

'Hello, you two!' She smiled.

'We need to have a chat with our daughter.' He opened up the back door and I followed him into the garden.

Mum put the lid on the pot and a couple of minutes later she joined us, clutching a pile of coats.

'Put these on!' she demanded. 'You'll catch a cold.' Right on cue a gust of wind hit me and I shivered. In hindsight, coming outside in just a knee-length dress and tights in November wasn't a good idea.

We sat on the green plastic garden chairs on the paved area of the small garden. Mum and Dad kept them out all year round because sometimes, even when it was cold, they liked to sit outside and drink tea.

'So about—' Dad started.

'I'm sorry I disappointed you,' I jumped in. 'At the awards.'

'You didn't disappoint us!' Mum placed her hand on mine.

'No,' Dad added. 'We were so proud.'

'Proud? How can you be proud? I didn't win!'

'But, Mia'—my mum shook her head—'look what you've done! You were brave enough to follow your dreams. Even when people around you, like us, told you to stay at the bank, you believed in yourself. You believed in your *talent*. You didn't know anything about running a business, but you didn't let that stop you. You went for it. And you help people find love and get paid for it. How amazing is that?'

'Your mother's right. When we saw that video on screen and heard all the lovely things your customers said about you, I was so proud.'

'Me too,' Mum added.

Dad leant over and gave me a kiss on the cheek. I went to open my mouth and then closed it again.

I didn't know what to say.

'Th-thanks.'

'I know we don't say it often enough, but we love you. And we're sorry if we haven't been as supportive as we should've been. We were just afraid. As parents, we just want the best for our children, and we're old-school. We're not high-flying entrepreneurs like you. We've always played it safe. We've never been brave enough to do something like what you're doing. And we projected our fears onto you. We're sorry.'

Wow.

My gaze darted from Mum to Dad and back again. The look in their eyes said they were genuine.

I couldn't believe it. They really were proud of me.

I'd waited so long to hear those words from them. It felt good.

'And if you need help with money, we can lend a hand,' Dad added. 'That's one of the reasons you entered, right? To pay the bills? We don't have much, but we'll give you what we have.'

'Thanks, but it's okay. I've moved out of the office and I'm working from home, so it's taken some of the pressure off.'

'What about your clients?' Mum asked. 'Will they visit you at home?'

'No, I'll meet them in a coffee shop or hire a meeting room.'

'Maybe you could ask your sister if she has some space in her office. It's very big there. Me and your father went to visit it last week.'

It was going so well...

'I'm sure it was very impressive,' I snapped. 'Just like *everything* she does. That's one of the reasons I kept my distance. Because as happy as I am for her, I know that Alice will always be the golden child. She's your favourite and I'll never compare to her.'

'That's not true! We love you both equally,' Dad jumped in.

'Your sister is... vulnerable.' Mum lowered her voice. 'She's not as confident as she pretends to be. She needs a lot of reassurance. That's why we always praise her. You've always been the confident one, so we never thought you needed our encouragement.'

'What?' I frowned. 'No. *She's* the confident one. Alice has all her shit together. The perfect job, the perfect husband, the perfect marriage, the perfect life. I may have been "brave" to start a business, but I lied to win a competition.'

Shit. The words flew out of my mouth before I could stop them.

'What?' Dad frowned.

The cat was already out of the bag, so I might as well tell them the truth. I took a deep breath.

'Liam.' My gaze dropped to the ground. 'I thought I needed a partner for them to take me seriously. So I asked Liam to pretend to be my boyfriend to help me win.' I blew out a breath. 'That's not brave. That's pathetic.'

It felt good to get that off my chest. When I looked up, I expected to see more disappointment in their eyes, but instead Dad wrapped his arm around me.

'Liam might've started out as your fake boyfriend, but there was nothing fake about what we saw when you two came round for dinner. Or how you were together at the awards.' Mum raised her eyebrow. 'It was pretty obvious to us that you two genuinely love each other.'

If only that was true.

'Liam *cares* for me, but he doesn't *love* me. Otherwise he would've fought for us.'

'It's not always that easy,' Dad said. 'That poor boy went through a lot with his parents. Give him time. He'll do the right thing.'

It'd been over a month. If he wanted me I would've known by now.

'Yes. Little Liam was always a good boy.' Mum nodded.

She always spoke about him like he was still a kid. I knew they meant well, but I'd already spent too much time hoping Liam would find his way back to me.

And when I wasn't playing memories of us together in my head on repeat, I was dreaming up ways to initiate something myself. Like wondering whether I should call or jump on a plane to see him.

But then I saw sense. I'd already stepped out of my comfort zone when I'd asked if we could find a way to make it work, and he'd turned me down. So why would I risk being humiliated again?

He'd said no once, so I had to accept and respect his decision. And as for going over to see him, I didn't even have his address. Plus, I was supposed to be sensible and save money to invest in the business.

No. It was over.

Maybe in another life, under different circumstances, it would've worked out. But not this time.

The sound of something being knocked over snapped me out of my thoughts. I looked up to see Aunty Doreen by the back door. I wondered how long she'd been there. Knowing her, she'd heard everything I'd said about Liam.

And knowing how much she liked to gossip, it'd only take a few minutes for her to broadcast it to the whole world. Great.

'There you are!' she said.

'Did you need something, Doreen?' Dad asked.

'I came to tell you that Alice is here and I think the rice is burning.'

Alice appeared behind her. Her hair was in a messy ponytail and she was wearing jeans and a jumper. Alice never missed a chance to dress up.

'You okay, Alice?' I asked. 'Where's Jack?'

'He—he had to… work.' She avoided my gaze. Something was wrong.

'On a Saturday?' Mum frowned.

'Mum, maybe you should check on the rice, and, Dad, I think the music's going to stop soon.'

Luckily they both got the hint. I needed to find out what was wrong. Once Mum, Dad and Aunty Doreen had left, I patted the chair beside me.

'What's going on?'

Alice dragged her feet over to the seat, then sat down.

'It's over with Jack. We're getting divorced.'

51

LIAM

We'd landed in London. I didn't have long before I had to get back to the airport and fly to LA again, but hopefully I'd have enough time to tell Mia how I felt. I hoped I wasn't too late.

Once Nate collected his luggage, we headed out through the arrivals gate. I lowered my cap and scanned the sea of people waiting to be reunited with their loved ones.

But just as I was about to walk to the exit, I stopped in my tracks.

'Motherfucker!'

Nate's head whipped round to face me.

'What's up?'

'Look over there. To the left. Recognise them?'

Nate squinted, then his jaw dropped.

'Hold up. Isn't that the woman who won the competition Mia entered?'

'Yeah.'

'So, she's kissing her husband. What's wrong with that?'

'Because that's not her husband. That's the senior dickhead judge of the awards. The *married* judge who didn't have time to ask us any more questions at the interview because he had to get back home to his wife and kids.'

'Oh shit.'

'The same dickhead who upset Mia and made her feel like she wasn't good enough'—I ground my jaw—'when all the time, he was cosying up with one of the candidates, who coincidentally happened to win.'

Rage blazed within me. All I saw was red. I wanted them to pay for making the woman I loved cry. I clenched my fist, ready to storm over.

But then I remembered why I was here. To see Mia. To tell her I loved her. Every second counted. And I wasn't gonna waste time on those cheaters.

'He's lucky I'm in a hurry.' I took a quick photo. I needed Mia to see this, so she'd know that her losing had nothing to do with her ability. And to think that bitch Gillian had tried to blackmail Mia too. 'Let's go.' I turned and headed to the exit.

Nate and I got separate taxis. I needed to get to Mia's place ASAP. It was only when the driver parked outside her building that I realised I didn't know which number she lived at.

I called her. The phone rang out.

I tried again. Still no answer.

'Can you wait here?' I handed the driver some cash.

'Okay.'

If I had to knock on every damn door to find her, that was what I'd do.

There was no one in the first flat. The person in the second one I tried cracked the door, then slammed it shut when she realised she didn't know me. An old lady opened up on my third attempt.

'Sorry to bother you, but I'm looking for Mia. Do you know what flat she's in?'

'Who wants to know?' She folded her arms.

'Erm, I'm Liam, Liam Stone, and we kind of dated and…'

She narrowed her eyes, looked me up and down and then her eyeballs popped out of her sockets.

'You're that actor! The one in the papers! I didn't recognise you! But you broke up, didn't you?'

'Sort of. Long-distance stuff, y'know. But I'm trying to find her, so if you can just tell me what number she lives at, I'll—'

'D'you want to come in and have a cup of tea?'

'Mrs…'

'It's Mrs Reynolds, but you can call me Crystal.' She grinned.

'I'd love to, Crystal, but I have to catch a flight in a few hours, so I really need to find Mia.'

'Oooh, you're going after your girl! Just like in the movies! Flat seven, first floor.'

'Thank you!'

I raced up the stairs, then along the hallway. Once I found Mia's flat, I knocked on the door. Once. Twice. Then a third time.

Shit.

I tried calling her again. No luck.

She must be out.

But I'd travelled over five thousand miles to see her, so there was no way I was giving up that easily.

And just like that, an idea hit me.

I knew exactly how to find her.

52

MIA

'You're what?' I gasped. I couldn't believe what I'd just heard. 'But you two are the perfect couple. You just celebrated your tenth anniversary!'

'It was... all a lie,' Alice mumbled. 'We've been unhappy for years, but I just didn't want to admit it. Mum and Dad are so happy and Granny and Granddad were married for ages too. I didn't want to be the one to break the family's perfect marriage track record.'

'Shit. I'm so sorry.'

'In a way I'm relieved.' Her eyes watered. 'Pretending that I had all my shit together was exhausting.'

'What happened? Why are you breaking up?'

'We wanted different things. He wants to have kids now and live in a little village in the countryside. But I've only just made partner and I want to travel and see the world before I have kids. He wanted to just order a takeaway for our tenth anniversary. I wanted to celebrate properly. We had our issues before, but I think the extravagance of the party was probably the last straw for him.'

'Oh, Alice.' I rubbed her shoulder.

'We had a massive argument on the night of your awards. I wanted him to come, but he said he didn't want to lie anymore. And I was too embarrassed to come on my own. I knew if I said he was working again, you'd get suspicious. Everything's a mess.'

'Come here.' I pulled her into a hug and she sobbed on my shoulder.

All this time I'd had Alice on a pedestal. I thought I was the failure because I hadn't found *the one*. I thought Alice had it all, when really she was feeling the pressure to follow in our parents' and grandparents' footsteps as much as I was. Just showed that things weren't always what they seemed.

'I'm sorry about you and Liam.' She sat up. 'I was always jealous of your friendship and the way he looked at you. That's why I didn't pass on his message. I'd just broken up with Wade and I was angry. And when I listened to that voicemail Liam sent you, I just... I... I knew he liked you and thought it wasn't fair. You already had Boris. You didn't need Liam too. You had two guys interested in you and I had no one and I... I deleted it.' Her gaze dropped to the floor. 'It was a shitty thing to do. I know that. I felt guilty the next day when Mum told you he'd left and I wanted to tell you, but I knew how bad it'd look. And the more time went on, the worse it was. So I kept quiet. I wouldn't blame you if you never wanted to speak to me again.'

'You can be a pain in the arse sometimes, but you'll always be my little sis.'

Her head jerked up in surprise.

'Thanks. You've always been a good person. I wish I

could be more like you. You're so smart and brave. I'd never have the guts to start my own business like you did.'

I pinched myself. I was still trying to get my head around my parents saying they were proud of me. But hearing Alice apologise and call me brave blew my mind.

Right now I should feel triumphant. But I'd never wanted to be in competition with her. I was genuinely sorry that her marriage hadn't worked out. She was my little sister, and although we'd had our ups and downs, I wanted her to be happy.

'You think I'm brave, but I think you are too. For admitting that you're not happy and doing something about it. Lots of people are too afraid to end their marriage and waste the rest of their lives.'

I remembered Liam saying something similar when we'd first met to discuss the terms of our fake-dating agreement. God. Would there ever be a time that I'd stop thinking about him?

'I don't feel brave right now.'

'You're strong. You'll get through this. And when you're ready to find love again, I'll hook you up!' I knew she wouldn't be thinking about that yet, but I wanted her to know that divorce wasn't the end.

'Thanks. Even though Jack and I have been leading separate lives for a while, I still think it'll be a long time until I get back on the horse.'

'Take all the time you need.'

'And what about you and Liam?'

'Don't know.' I shrugged. 'I love him, but…'

'If you love him, you should fight for him, sis.'

I paused. This was the part where I was supposed to say I'd tried and he wasn't interested and it was over. But somehow, my conversation with Alice had triggered something within me. The desire not to give up.

I was sad without Liam, so I had nothing to lose by trying again. I'd call him and see if we could talk. Properly.

'You're right.'

'Well, don't sit around here! Call him now!'

'I need to make sure you're okay first.'

'Go!'

I squeezed her hand and raced into the house. I'd left my bag in the living room when I went to hug Dad. I'd barely taken two steps out of the kitchen into the hallway when Aunty Doreen cornered me.

'Mia.' She gave me a pitying look, like I was a child whose friends hadn't turned up at their birthday party. 'I couldn't help but overhear your conversation earlier. *So* sad. When I first heard you were finally dating again, I was happy for you, but I didn't know it was all a lie! You should call yourself a match *faker*, not a match*maker*!' She laughed and my eyes narrowed. 'Poor thing.' She rubbed my shoulder. 'I knew you weren't happy being single, but you must've been *really* desperate to lie. If you like, I can ask my son if he has any friends. You might be too old for them now, but—'

'Let me stop you right there.' I stepped forward and put my hands on my hips. 'Thanks, but I don't need your help. Being single isn't a disease. Single people don't need your pity. Finding love is *hard*. Even when it's what you do for a career. Yes, I'm a professional match*maker* and, yes, I'm single. So what? Life doesn't always turn out like we hoped.'

'That's true, but—'

'And another thing!' I was on a roll and wasn't going to stop until I'd said my piece. 'Not everyone *wants* to be coupled up and you need to understand that's okay! Yes, I was desperate to pretend to have a boyfriend to win a competition and, yes, I also want to find real love. And I did. Even though things with Liam didn't work out, I'm still glad it happened.'

'Well, that's—'

'Still haven't finished! Whatever did or didn't happen is none of your business. So in future, don't ask about my relationship status or comment on my ovaries. I don't ask you about your marriage or how often you and Uncle Clayton have sex, so butt out of my love life!'

Aunty Doreen's jaw plummeted.

Good. Hopefully now she'd think twice about asking inappropriate questions.

I marched off, holding my head high. But as I glanced at the door I froze.

It wasn't just Aunty Doreen's jaw that was on the floor. Mine hit the ground too when I saw who was stood there.

It was Trudy, but she wasn't alone.

When his delicious woody scent hit me, I realised I wasn't dreaming.

Liam was here.

53

LIAM

As I caught sight of Mia, my heart jolted.

Damn.

I knew I'd missed her, but seeing her just metres away made my whole body light up.

She looked beautiful. Mia was dressed in a long-sleeved silver dress that stopped just above her knees. The neckline only showed a hint of cleavage, but somehow it was the sexiest thing I'd ever seen.

Then again, Mia could wear a potato sack and still look amazing.

I swallowed hard. I'd barely slept during the flight because I was thinking about what to say to her. I didn't do this emotional stuff. I hadn't had any practice, so I wasn't good at it.

Sometimes my movies had some 'moments' where my character would ask his love interest for forgiveness, but I'd always have a script to follow. But right now, this was all me.

'Hey…' I said, meeting her eyes. God, I'd forgotten how much I loved her eyes.

'H-hi,' she stuttered.

And then we just stood there, staring at each other. I didn't know how much time had passed. I was just glad I'd made it here.

When she didn't answer her door or phone, I'd decided to call Trudy. She'd told me it was Mia's parents' anniversary. Trudy was on her way over and said if I wanted, she'd wait so we could go together.

So here I was. Finally reunited with Mia. Without a clue what I was going to actually say to her.

'Maybe you two should, um, go somewhere a little more… private?' Trudy broke the silence.

I'd been so caught up in looking at Mia and in my own thoughts that I'd forgotten I was in the middle of her parents' hallway.

I was sure there was loud music playing when I'd arrived, but the volume had been turned right down. As I broke my gaze, I saw that a crowd had gathered, their eyes fixed on us.

'Yeah,' I said. 'Some privacy would be good.'

'Come upstairs,' Mia suggested.

The crowd parted and I followed her, feeling the heat of a dozen eyes on my back.

Mia opened the door to her childhood bedroom, switched on the light, then stepped inside.

It was just as I'd remembered it. Pink duvet. Old photos pinned to the walls and a pile of board games on the shelf in the corner.

'You've still got our old games!'

'Yeah. Mum kept our rooms like a shrine. They keep threatening to turn mine into a gym, but they never touch it. I think it makes them feel like we're still living here.'

Mia sat on the bed and looked up at me with her gorgeous deep brown eyes. My heart raced. I was so nervous.

'So… you came back…' Her words hung in the air.

That was my cue to tell her why I was here. To tell her everything. I went to speak, but it was like someone had cut out my tongue.

I opened my mouth.

Come on. You can do this. Just tell her how you feel.
Love over fear.

'I… I miss you.'

'I missed you too.' She looked up.

I sat next to her and took her hands in mine.

'I've never done this before, so bear with me. I didn't want to end things. But I was afraid. Y'know, about the stuff we spoke about before. So it was easier for me to just leave. I hoped I'd forget about you. Not because I wanted to, but because then it'd be easier. If I forgot about you, I wouldn't get hurt. But I tried. *So hard.* And I just couldn't get you out of my head. I love you, Mia. I've *always* loved you. That's why I'm here. I want to be with you. If you'll have me. I really wanna make this work.'

Mia's eyes widened and she froze.

The silence stretched for what felt like hours.

I needed to know what she was thinking. Whether she felt the same.

Even if she didn't, I was proud of myself. At least I'd tried. If I had to go back to LA knowing she'd moved on or didn't feel the same way, I'd know that I'd done what I could, but had just left it too late.

I'd blown it. Shit.

'Okay. Got it.' I leant forward, kissed her on the cheek, released her hands and went to get up.

'Wait!' She grabbed my arm. 'Do you really mean it?'

'Every damn word.' I looked her straight in the eyes, pulled her into me, then pressed my mouth on hers.

As our lips moved together, it felt like my body came back to life. Before I got here, I was broken, but now, Mia's kiss had healed me. Being close to her instantly repaired the hole in my heart.

Nate had said the power of a good woman was magical and he was right.

I ran my hand along the back of her neck. I loved the feel of her soft skin. I'd missed it. And her scent. God. I wished I could bathe in it so that wherever I went she'd feel close to me.

Eventually we pulled away.

'You don't know how long I've wanted you to say those words,' Mia said, her breath ragged.

'You don't know how long I've wanted to say them to you.' I brushed my thumb over her cheek.

'So how can we make it work? What about the film you're doing?'

'I don't care about that. I'll quit, if it means being with you.'

'But don't you have a contract?'

'Yeah,' I exhaled. 'Geena would kill me if she knew I was here.'

'She doesn't know? When are you due back on set?'

'In about twenty-two hours...'

'Oh my God!' she gasped. 'You flew nine hours just to see me for one night?'

'The flight was about ten and a half hours, but, hey, who's counting?'

'You're crazy!'

'Damn right. I'm crazy for you. But I didn't think this was a conversation we could have on the phone. I wasn't even sure if you'd take my call...'

'I was actually about to call you!'

'Yeah?'

'Yeah.' She smiled. 'How did you know I'd be here?'

'Trudy. When I went to your place and you weren't there and didn't answer your phone, I called her.'

'Oh, my phone's in my bag. Well, I'm glad you came. It's a long trip to make for... how long do we have together now?'

'About half an hour...' I winced. 'It would've been a bit longer if your neighbour downstairs hadn't kept me chatting...'

'Mrs Reynolds, right?'

'That's the one. Although she said I could call her *Crystal*.' I smiled.

'Such a charmer! My boyfriend even gets the old ladies going!'

'*Boyfriend*.' I smiled. 'I like the sound of that a lot more than *fake* boyfriend.'

'Yeah. You know I've still got you listed in my phone as My Hot Boyfriend, though...'

'I thought you'd changed that as soon as I handed back your phone!'

'I wanted to. But somehow, I just didn't get around to

it. Maybe because I wanted it to be true. But not just because you are obviously gorgeous. You're more than pretty packaging to me, Liam. You always have been. It's your heart that I love the most. I love all of you.'

My heart swelled.

Well, fuck.

Mia loved me.

Right now, I felt like the luckiest man alive.

'You make me so damn happy, you know that?'

'I do now.'

'And I don't know how we'll make this work, because you're right. I need to finish this film. Not just because they'd sue my arse off, more because it'd be irresponsible to let everyone down. There's only six more weeks, so if you can wait for me, I promise that after that, I'm done with the action films. I want to get my own stuff off the ground. So we can talk about how we can both pursue our dreams and be together.'

'I like the sound of that. And of course I'll wait! We've already been apart for a month. What's a few more weeks?'

'And maybe you can come over and visit, if it won't interfere with your work?'

'I'd love that!'

'How's everything going with the agency? You'll never guess who I saw at the airport!'

'Who?'

'Mr Grumpy Dickhead Morgan. Cosying up with Gillian Madeley.'

'No way! Gillian doesn't surprise me. I knew she was a cheater. But Mr Morgan's got a wife and kids too.'

'Yep. What they do behind their partners' backs is their

business, but to me it shows the whole competition was a fix. You didn't win not because you weren't good enough, but because of his relationship with Gillian. Look at this.' I showed her the photo with their tongues down each other's throats.

'Now it makes sense! That's how she was able to quote what I'd said about you being *in tune with my needs* back to me. Clearly Mr Morgan had discussed my interview with her. They probably laughed about it whilst they were in bed together.'

If Mia wanted to, she could use that photo. I didn't care if Gillian outed our fake relationship agreement. What she'd done was much worse. They were both arseholes. They deserved each other.

'Doesn't matter.' She shrugged. 'I'm not going to do anything about their sordid affair. Karma will catch up with them. It's their families I feel sorry for. Anyway, I'm doing just fine without the award. Work's going great!'

She filled me in on Kelly and the influx of clients she'd had since then.

'I knew you'd succeed. You're so talented.'

'Thanks for believing in me. And I believe in you too.'

'I finished my screenplay.'

'That's brilliant!' She threw her arms around me. 'You're going to do amazing things. And whether it's bringing your show to TV screens around the world, or acting on stage, I'll be there, cheering the loudest!'

'How did I survive so long without you?' I kissed her softly on the lips.

'No idea!' She laughed and the sound made my whole body come alive. 'But now you've got me forever.'

'Promise?' I said.

'Promise. Now come on. We better get you to the airport. The quicker you go to LA and finish this film, the quicker we can start our new life together.'

'I like the sound of that. I love you, Tutti-Frutti.'

'I love you too, My Very Talented Boyfriend.'

EPILOGUE
MIA

Three months later

As I looked down at the huge, hairy tarantula sitting in my palm, my heart raced.

'Smile,' the instructor said as I posed for a photo.

If someone had told me I'd be able to hold a spider, never mind a bloody tarantula, in my hand, I would've laughed in their face. But yet, here I was at the spider course Liam had booked me on, conquering one of my biggest fears.

I couldn't wait to show him the photo when he came to meet me.

Once I'd done the last few fear-busting exercises and collected the certificate showing that I'd successfully completed the one-day course, I headed outside.

Liam was already there waiting, flashing my favourite smile.

'Hey, you.' He kissed me softly on the lips, looping his arms around my back.

'Mmm, hello to you too,' I said into his mouth. There was no way I was ready to pull away from him yet.

'How'd it go?'

'Good! I even held a tarantula!'

'No way!'

'Yep!'

'I'm so proud of you!'

'Thanks! What time do you need to be at the community centre?'

'Not for a few hours. So I was thinking we could go home first and have an early dinner. I cooked chicken cacciatore.'

'My favourite! I think the first time you made that, you must've put something in it to make me fall in love with you,' I laughed as I remembered the first night I stayed at Liam's place and was bowled over with his cooking.

'Damn. The secret's out,' he chuckled as we made our way to the Tube station.

Yep. Liam didn't mind taking the Tube if we had a quick journey to make. Sometimes it was easier. And if he was recognised, he happily posed for a selfie.

It didn't take long for us to get home. Right now we were renting a house in Notting Hill. When Liam decided to move back to London after filming wrapped in LA, I thought he'd just find somewhere to stay on his own. But the first night I came round to visit, he handed me a key and asked if I'd like to move in.

I didn't even need a second to think about it. After all the time we'd spent apart, the idea of waking up in Liam's arms every morning and snuggling up with him every night sounded like heaven.

Living with Liam was even better than I could've hoped. Unlimited hugs, lazy Sunday afternoons together, game nights, chatting about our days over a glass of wine and dinner. And I didn't know how it was possible, but the sex just got better and better.

'Want some garlic bread?' Liam opened the fridge.

'You having some?'

'Yep.' Liam grinned. 'And now I don't have any more underwear shoots, I can have ice cream for dessert too.'

'Ice cream is always a good idea.'

'Damn right! I got tutti-frutti and cookies 'n' cream for us to share.'

'Perfect!'

Liam had decided he wouldn't be taking off his clothes anymore. Well, unless it was to get naked with me, of course. There'd be no more underwear shoots or gratuitous nudity on screen. He wanted to be known for more than his body.

Looked like he was going to get his wish too. When his agent announced she had to stop work to go and care for her sick grandmother who lived in the country, Liam remembered Trudy's offer to represent him and asked if the offer still stood.

Of course, Trudy bit his hand off and had already secured him a leading role in a top theatre production in London. Rehearsals started next month and he was so excited.

Speaking of plays, Liam had also started mentoring some of the cast from the drama club at the community centre. Although doing the performance of *Beauty and the*

Beast had raised a good amount of money, that alone wouldn't have been enough to save the place, so Liam had donated his own money to cover the cost of keeping it open and doing some renovations. Tonight we were going along to watch their latest production and see how the new, updated centre looked in the flesh.

That wasn't the only development in Liam's career. Next week we'd be going to Paris to meet Nate's brother-in-law, Nico, to discuss him backing Liam's TV series. If Liam got the go-ahead, he'd be able to work with Nico's people to find the right team to bring his screenplay to life. I was so excited and had my fingers and toes firmly crossed for him.

My career and the agency were going from strength to strength too. I'd set up a beautiful office space at home in a room that overlooked the garden. It might not have views of Tower Bridge, but the lush trees and pretty plants were all the gorgeous scenery I needed.

Thanks to my lower overheads and the influx of new clients, I was close to clearing all of my debts, without any financial assistance from Liam, family or friends. Plus, next week I'd be interviewing some candidates to become my assistant.

Kelly was still a client. After the article came out on the website OnTheDaily.co.uk, it attracted a lot of attention and she felt overwhelmed, so asked to put the search on hold.

She'd given me the green light to start the search again now, though. I'd met someone recently that I thought could be a good match. On paper he wasn't what she had in mind. But my gut told me it could work, so hopefully she'd be open-minded enough to at least try dating him.

Sometimes the people we least expected were perfect for us.

I could say that was true for me and Liam. But then, something within me always knew he was the one. I was just too afraid to see it.

Not anymore, though. Liam and I had a long and happy future ahead of us. Thank God Trudy helped us get together.

Alice was going through the divorce proceedings with Jack, but she was doing okay considering, and we were getting on better. I told her that breaking up with Jack would leave them free to both eventually find the person they were meant to be with.

I really believed that. If I hadn't broken up with Boris, I wouldn't have ended up with Liam. And I'd found that what I went through with my ex and experiencing how hard it can be to be single in your thirties and beyond had made me more relatable to my clients. So many had experienced the lows of dating and relationships, so they felt like I understood what they were going through.

So in a strange way, although I'd felt like a failure when I was going through it, I was grateful for those hard times. They'd made me stronger and helped me appreciate what I had with Liam even more.

'Oh, sweet memories.' I smiled.

'Yep.' Liam wrapped his arms around my waist. 'We have a lot of those. But I'm excited to see what new ones we'll make here.'

'I love this house so much.' It was a shame we were only renting. But the owners weren't interested in selling.

'I know. That's why I just bought it.'

'What? No way! I thought they said it wasn't for sale?'

'It's funny how people can change their minds when you make them a ridiculous offer they can't refuse.'

'I don't know what to say!' I squeezed him tight. 'Thank you!'

'You're welcome! I love it here too. It'll be a great place to raise kids one day.' He brushed my cheek. '*Our* kids.'

'Yeah?' Things were going well with Liam and I'd always hoped he wanted us to have a real future together, but given his past, I didn't want to push him.

'Yeah. I want it all with you. Marriage, kids, the whole nine yards.'

'Oh my God!' I pressed my lips onto his and gave him a long, slow kiss. 'How did I get so lucky?'

'*I'm* the lucky one. I don't know whether it was fate, luck or a combination of both, but it's like you were made for me.'

'I feel the same. This may have started out as pretend, but like my granny always said whenever I was worried about meeting my Mr Right, "true love will always find you".'

I realised now that when she'd also said 'the right man will come back to you', she was talking about Liam. She'd known he was the one for me all along.

'That's true, baby.' Liam kissed me again. 'You can't fake what we have. Me and you are the perfect match. Always were, always will be.'

Want more?

Want to find out what happens when Liam and Mia travel to Paris to meet billionaire Nico and discuss Liam's screenplay? Join the Olivia Spring VIP Club and **receive *The Match Faker* Bonus Chapters for FREE**! Visit https://bookhip.com/BHLAZNX to find out more!

If you enjoyed the *The Match Faker*, you'll love my **new steamy enemies-to-lovers novel, *The Romance Library*. Order your copy from Amazon now!**

Read Nate and Melody's love story!
Find out how these two enemies became lovers in the steamy romcom *My French Wedding Date*
Order the ebook or paperback from Amazon or read it for FREE in Kindle Unlimited.

ENJOYED THIS BOOK? YOU CAN MAKE A BIG DIFFERENCE.

If you've enjoyed *The Match Faker*, **I'd be so very grateful if you could spare two minutes to leave a review on Amazon, Goodreads and BookBub**. It doesn't have to be long (unless you'd like it to be!). Every review – even if it's just a sentence – would make a *huge* difference.

By leaving an honest review, you'll be helping to bring my books to the attention of other readers and hearing your thoughts will make them more likely to give my novels a try. As a result, it will help me to build my career, which means I'll get to write more books!

Thank you so much. As well as making a huge difference, you've also just made my day!

Olivia x

ALL BOOKS BY OLIVIA SPRING

The Middle-Aged Virgin Series
The Middle-Aged Virgin
The Middle-Aged Virgin in Italy

Only When it's Love Series
Only When It's Love
When's the Wedding?

My Ten-Year Crush Series
My Ten-Year Crush
My Lucky Night
My Paris Romance
My Spanish Romance
My French Wedding Date
My Perfect Happy Ending

Other Books
The Romance Library

The Match Faker
Losing My Inhibitions
Love Offline

Box Set
Ready To Mingle Collection

ALSO BY OLIVIA SPRING

Only When It's Love: Holding Out For Mr Right

Have you read my second novel ***Only When It's Love?*** Here's what it's about:

Alex's love life is a disaster. Will accepting a crazy seven-step dating challenge lead to more heartbreak or help her find Mr Right?

Alex is tired of being single. After years of disastrous hook-ups and relationships that lead to the bedroom but nowhere else, Alex is convinced she'll never find her Mr Right. Then her newly married friend Stacey recommends what worked for her: a self-help book that guarantees Alex will find true love in just seven steps. Sounds simple, right?

Except Alex soon discovers that each step is more difficult than the last, and one of the rules involves dating, but not sleeping with a guy for six months. Absolutely no intimate contact whatsoever. *Zero. Nada. Rien.* A big challenge for Alex, who has never been one to hold back from jumping straight into the sack, hoping it will help a man fall for her.

Will any guys be willing to wait? Will Alex find her Mr Right? And if she does, will she be strong enough to resist temptation and hold out for true love?

Join Alex on her roller coaster romantic journey as she tries to cope with the emotional and physical ups and downs of dating whilst following a lengthy list of rigid rules.

Only When It's Love **is a standalone, fun, feel-good, romantic comedy about self-acceptance, determination, love and the challenge of finding** *the one.*

Praise For *Only When It's Love*

'**Totally unique and wonderful.** Olivia's book has a brilliant message about self-worth and brings to life an important modern take on the rom-com. Most definitely a five-star read.' - **Love Books Group**

'I guarantee **you will HOOT with laughter** at Alex's escapades whilst fully cheering her on. If you like romance, humour and a generally fun-filled read then look no further than this **gorgeous, well-written dating adventure**. Five stars.' - **Bookaholic Confessions**

'Such a uniquely told, **laugh-out-loud, dirty and flirty, addictive novel.**' - **The Writing Garnet**

Buy *Only When It's Love* from Amazon today!

AN EXTRACT FROM ONLY WHEN IT'S LOVE

Chapter One

Never again.

Why, why, *why* did I keep on doing this?

I felt great for a few minutes, or if I was lucky, hours, but then, when it was all over, I ended up feeling like shit for days. Sometimes weeks.

I must stop torturing myself.

Repeat after me:

I, Alexandra Adams, will *not* answer Connor Matthew's WhatsApp messages, texts or phone calls for the rest of my life.

I firmly declare that even if Connor says his whole world is falling apart, that he's sorry, he's realised I'm *the one* and he's changed, I will positively, absolutely, unequivocally *not* reply.

Nor will I end up going to his flat because I caved in after he sent me five million messages saying he misses me and inviting me round just 'to talk'.

And I *definitely* do solemnly swear that I will *not* end up on my back with my legs wrapped around his neck within minutes of arriving, because I took one look at his body and couldn't resist.

No.

That's it.

No more.

I will be *strong*. I will be like iron. Titanium. Steel. All three welded into one.

I will block Connor once and for all and I will move on with my life.

Yes!

I exhaled.

Finally I'd found my inner strength.

This was the start of a new life for me. A new beginning. Where I wouldn't get screwed over by yet another fuckboy. Where I wouldn't get ghosted or dumped. Where I took control of my life and stuck my middle finger up at the men who treated me like shit. *Here's to the new me.*

My phone chimed.

It was Connor.

I bolted upright in bed and clicked on his message.

He couldn't stop thinking about me. He wanted to see me again.

Tonight.

To talk. About our future.

Together.

This could be it!

Things *had* felt kind of different last time. Like there was a deeper connection.

Maybe he was right. Maybe he *had* changed…

I excitedly typed out a reply.

My fingers hovered over the blue button, ready to send.

Hello?

What the hell was I doing?

It was like the entire contents of my pep talk two seconds ago had just evaporated from my brain.

Remember *being strong like iron, titanium and steel* and resisting the temptations of Connor?

Shit.

This was going to be much harder than I'd thought.

Want to find out what happens next? Buy *Only When It's Love* from Amazon today!

ACKNOWLEDGEMENTS

I'm so grateful to the following people for helping me to bring *The Match Faker* to life:

- **My amazing husband**: Thanks for the unlimited hugs, love and support.
- **My fantastic beta readers: Mum, Emma and Loz** for your invaluable feedback.
- **Rachel:** for the beautiful illustration and cover design. I love how hot Liam and Mia look!
- **Eliza:** for your eagle-eyed, excellent editing skills.
- **Helen:** for your great proofreading.
- **Dawn:** for keeping my website looking pretty.
- **Aunty Blossom:** for giving me an insight into the film and theatre industry.
- **The brilliant bloggers, Bookstagrammers, ARC readers** and **BookTokers** who read and wrote wonderful reviews for this book.
- And **to YOU, lovely reader**. Thank you for

continuing to buy and read my books. Because of you I'm able to do my dream job every day. I appreciate you SO much!

Lots of love,
Olivia x

ABOUT THE AUTHOR

Olivia Spring was born and raised in London, England. When she's not making regular trips to Spain and Italy to indulge in paella, pasta, pizza and gelato, she can be found at her desk, writing new sexy romantic comedies.

If you'd like to say hi, email olivia@oliviaspring.com or connect on social media.

TikTok: www.tiktok.com/@oliviaspringauthor

- facebook.com/ospringauthor
- twitter.com/ospringauthor
- instagram.com/ospringauthor

Printed in Great Britain
by Amazon